THE FOOL

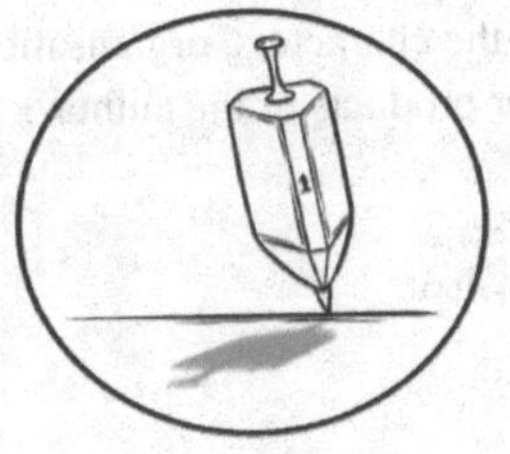

Laura J Fitzwilson

This is a work of fiction. All of the characters, organisations, settings and events portrayed in this novel are either products of the author's imagination or are used fictitiously.

Copyright © 2025 Laura J Fitzwilson

All rights reserved.

Cover by Matthew Revert

A catalogue record for this book is available from the National Library of Australia

ISBN-13: 978-0-9756202-3-6

First edition: July 2025

Visit the author's website at laurajfitzwilson.com

This book contains depictions of grief and trauma. While suggestive at times, all romantic scenes fade to black before they become explicit. A full content advisory can be found at https://laurajfitzwilson.com/content-advisory-for-the-fool/.

For my family

Acknowledgement of Country

The Fool was predominately written and revised (and revised, and revised) on Wadawurrung Country in regional Victoria, Australia. I'd like to take this opportunity to pay my respect to the Traditional Custodians of this land and their Elders—past, present and emerging. I acknowledge that sovereignty was never ceded and that it always was, always will be, Aboriginal land. First Nations people in Australia have been custodians of storytelling here for tens of thousands of years and I am honoured to contribute to a tradition so important.

The Fool is set in a world that shares some similarities with our own, on a continent that resembles Australia. I couldn't have written a fantasy!Australia story without acknowledging the way our culture's European influence has impacted the First Nations people who have lived in our Australia for 70,000 years. There's structural racism that is embedded in the culture of both our Australia and the fictional world in this story. We, like these characters, are often not aware of it. As the author, I've tried to be very aware of how I have portrayed these complex issues. Please don't think I condone the racism in this story.

In saying that, it's important to acknowledge that I'm a white, first-generation immigrant to Australia, and while my intentions are sincere, I know that I'm not able to judge the cultural safety of this work. To help me, I had a wonderful chat with the Chief of Culture, Public Relations and Engagement at the Ballarat and District Aboriginal Co-operative. Thanks Shu, for helping me make this book something I can be proud of.

<u>*Glossary*</u>

Canticalica. The smallest country in the Trinitas Empire. Ruled by the Dietrich family and mostly known for being cold and having quite good goat's cheese.

continent, the. The land mass that the Empress was guided to by the Trinity, home of the Trinitas Empire. It exists to the far south of the old world, further than any had dared travel before. Prior to the Empress landing, there was very little of value outside of its truly spectacular coastline. The Trinitas Empire consists of twelve countries that don't span the entire breadth of the continent, with much of the western portion left to the prevenient.

Empress, the. The immortal woman who was kissed three times upon the lips by the Trinity, and blessed so that when she spoke, her words reshaped the world. Her magic passes down to her children and to their descendants in turn.

fool. Compulsory entertainers at court, fools are not technically considered citizens while in service. They are not entitled to names, gendered signifiers or personal characteristics that might indicate humanity. Records of their births and deaths are erased. They are not beholden to any law of the land, but answer only to the Consortium of Fools. Their role is to humble monarchs and comment on their rule—and to entertain, of course.

hebestag. A coming-of-age celebration for descendants of the Empress, taking place on or near their twelfth birthday, which originally was the age that a person could be considered an adult.

The centrepiece of the evening is a performance of magic that the young mage has worked on for many months. This performance (if not the whole celebration) is open to the public.

iridium. A very hard, very heavy and very brittle metal which nullifies magic.

old world, the. The place and people who rejected the Empress, and who she rejected right back. The Empress closed a barrier around the Continent to keep the heretics of the old world from discovering her people.

magic. The force through which the Empress and her legitimate descendants can shape the world, out of the goodness of the Trinity. There are many rules, but at its core magic works by conjuring the idea of a thing by using words that inspire reverence in the individual user.

pedispass. A game played in the southern parts of the Trinitas Empire. A ball is conveyed into goals through the application of feet and general athleticism.

Praecentor. The capital city of Canticalica. It is bordered by the Fluvius River.

prevenient. Those who came before; those who anticipated the Empire. The prevenient people welcomed the Empress to the continent and were welcomed into the Trinitas Empire in return. When they had proven their devotion sufficiently, the Empress graciously elevated them to a status equal with the true citizens of the Empire. They can be most easily identified by their dark skin, unless their ancestry is diluted by repeated unions with the paler true citizens of the Empire.

revenant. An image of a dead person, conjured with powerful, dark magic. In stories, mages capture the spirit of someone who has passed on like a butterfly in a net, but some scholars theorise that they're pulled from the memories and imagination of those who look upon the magic instead of from the person themself. The Empress has so far neglected to confirm this one way or another.

Sommertide. A celebration that takes place on the longest day of the year, where all citizens are free from work and status.

Sword and Shield. The law enforcers and armed forces of Canticalica. Made up of Swords (predominately offensive), Shields (predominately defensive) and Helms (leadership). Members give up their right to marriage and inheritance, but children are not explicitly forbidden.

Trinitas Era (TE). The current era, which began the day that the Trinity blessed the Empress. Each year consists of twelve months, three in each of the four seasons. The year begins with spring and proceeds as follows: Erstus, Duo, Trei, Vierus, Funque, Sechs, Siebten, Achto, Nonem, Tecem, Eltus, Zuolf. This story takes place in 906 TE.

Trinity, the. The god with three faces, who casts a hidden shadow.

vertling. A fortune telling game played with a three-sided spinning top. Each side represents a face of the Trinity. Players ask a question and the side it lands on indicates the answer, with the Beginning representing yes, the End representing no, and the Middle representing maybe. As with everything, the hidden god's shadow casts doubt and exceptions to any fortune.

Prologue

LEOPOLD DIETRICH CONSIDERED HIMSELF A REALIST, as many pessimists do. His particular brand of pessimism was narcissistic, in that it was mostly concerned with his flaws, which he could recite alphabetically if called on to do so. This was not a highly desired party trick and did not lend itself particularly well to career counselling.

'These goals are a teensy bit generic,' Leo's shaper said, in the chipper tone she reserved for her deepest criticisms. 'They're also very similar to the ones you created at your third-year review.'

They were, in fact, identical to the ones Leo had used at his third-year review. He didn't create them then, either. His dorm-mate, Dion, had a habit of impatiently providing Leo with no-nonsense solutions to things he was working himself up about when he got sick of Leo pacing around their room. He gave these solutions a C+ level of effort, which Leo sometimes expanded on. Other times, as with the goals, he ended up deciding that C+ was actually a fine thing to aim for every now and then.

'Some say that consistency of character is a virtue,' Leo said, hoping that his expression was somewhere in the realms of innocent or earnest.

'Maybe,' Sasha said doubtfully. 'But next year is the year that we expect you to specialise. Your goals should guide you.'

Leo nodded, at a bit of a loss for what to say. He didn't know what he wanted to specialise in. He didn't know what he wanted to do after he left the Trinitas Academy. Coming here in the first place was supposed to have let him put off deciding that. He'd expected to figure something out along the way, but he was starting to suspect that in three years time he would be just as aimless as he was when he was sixteen and had joined the Academy, pretending a greater interest in studying magic than he actually felt so that he'd be allowed to be anywhere that wasn't home. His dream—everyone's dream, or so it seemed—was to belong somewhere. This did not provide any direction what-soever.

'Let's talk about what you like,' Sasha said.

'I'm guessing you mean beyond cheesy ghost stories,' Leo said.

'No, no, let's start there!' Sasha said. 'That's an avenue for creativity, don't you think?'

Leo grimaced. That had been meant as a joke.

'I'm not very good at conjuring scries,' Leo said. 'I'm more of a reader than a storyteller.'

In honesty, he was pretty good at making up stories on the spot. His scries didn't always come out exactly as he intended, but he could usually roll with what he'd created. It just wasn't exactly a princely occupation, and he'd never be *the best* at it. His father could forgive one of those criteria not being met, but not both of them. And besides, the thought of anyone looking at a scry he had created as something more than a whim filled him with dread. Sketches were supposed to be messy. If he was caught actually trying at something, he might catch fire.

'But do you *like* it?' Sasha asked. 'Because passion will always allow for greater advances than natural skill alone. Passion fills us and consumes us. Passion is always the answer in these meetings.'

'Right,' Leo said.

Sasha waited for Leo to announce his most heartfelt desire with shining eyes. She was probably very passionate about her job, or at least about the word "passion", which was nice. Not everyone had that. Leo hated feeling like he was leaving her hanging, but he also didn't have anything to say.

'What else do you like?' Sasha asked. 'We can build up to passion.'

Leo wondered what she would come up with if he said card games or something truly unoccupational like midyim berry and peach pie or the noise the library cat made when he woke her up.

He could come up with something better. It was just that thinking about the future felt worse than being caught out caring about something. He was the third-born prince to a tiny kingdom, which may have given him some respect at the Academy if people weren't always walking in on him singing to his socks as he folded them or if the student body wasn't made up of magic users and therefore descendants of the Empress. All it really meant was that his life options were intimidatingly expansive and unavoidably public.

'Leo?' Sasha asked.

'I'm pretty good at healing,' Leo said, because he was, but mostly because he didn't think anyone could think badly of a healer.

Sasha straightened the notepad on her desk, then two pens and a ruler, which made up the entirety of her non-decorative desk items. Leo watched in the same way he would watch the first drops of rain from heavy clouds if he was an hour's walk from shelter.

'You're a blessed student,' Sasha finally said. 'I want to help you reach your potential, because you have so *much* potential, and I would hate to see that potential go to waste.'

Leo attempted to smile as though he was grateful for her investment in his future, but from Sasha's expression he wasn't pulling it off, so he stopped. People didn't use the word "potential" for things that were already good. Leo comforted himself with the thought of impersonating Sasha to his friends later. Maybe today he would be able to beat her record for the most repeated word in a sentence.

'Let's meet again in a week,' Sasha said. 'You can have a bit more of a think about what you would like to specialise in and we'll be able to sort that limitless future of yours out!'

'Awesome,' Leo said, giving her a thumbs up. Sure, the only thing he had ever wanted to be was *whatever the opposite of my dad is*, but one more week should be plenty of time for him to figure out the rest.

Sasha beamed.

THE FIVE MINUTES PRIOR to a universally loathed class had a certain magic to them—they contained in them a million possible scenarios that could prevent students from attending. This magic inspired Leo and Dion to stay in the first-floor common room for as long as possible before they had to leave for numerology, a subject so pointless that Leo didn't think even their teacher believed in it. On this day in late Nonem, on the cusp of a winter that promised to be almost as cold at the Trinitas Academy as it would be back at Leo's home, the worst possible outcome occurred: something happened to prevent Leo from going to class.

'Have you decided what you're going to be when you grow up?' Dion asked.

'Your mum,' Leo said, without looking up from the homework he was copying.

'Mhm,' Dion said. 'And which subjects will you specialise in to achieve this goal?'

'I can't answer that without being too mean or really crass,' Leo said. 'Shut up, would you? I can't hand in nothing again and I can't copy this and insult your mother at the same time.'

'It's three,' Dion said. 'I can't believe they make us do numerology in sixth year. The answer is always three.'

'Except when it's four,' Leo muttered, feeling a very undevout exasperation for a religion that put an asterisk of "ah, but there is always the *hidden* god" at the end of its obsession with triangles and trinities and everything else related to threes. He could never say it to anyone, but sometimes he thought that the allowance for fours was so that they could have twelve months in a year and have buildings with four walls. 'Shut up.'

There was a creak outside and Leo and Dion both looked up to see the door open with the courtesy of someone unfamiliar to the room. A grave woman of about sixty stood at the entrance, not coming in any further. Dion slowly slid his papers into his bag in a way that aimed to be surreptitious, though the woman clearly wasn't part of the teaching staff. She was wearing clothes Leo vaguely associated with his kingdom's army, but he'd always avoided looking at them.

'Pardon the interruption, Your Majesty,' she said to Leo. 'I've come from Praecentor with news.'

Leo's eyebrows lifted in bewilderment.

'Your accent's not bad, but you're missing some nuances.'

'The word you're looking for is "hello", Dietrich,' Dion muttered.

Leo ignored him and continued. 'Kings and queens are addressed as majesty, princes as highness. Or you can just call me Leo.'

'Forgive me, Your Majesty,' she said. 'Perhaps we should speak alone.'

The silence in the room that followed that statement was almost physical. It had a weight. It buzzed along Leo's skin and rang in his ears as though his head was a bell the messenger had struck with a sledgehammer, and though the sound was gone, his hearing was mutilated.

Dion stood up, shouldering his bag.

'I'll tell them you won't be in class today,' he murmured. 'Sorry about your folks.'

S THE CARRIAGE SLOWED, the cadence of its wheels on the gravel road became clearer, crunching over rocks in a song that sounded like home. Of course, Leo had been in many carriages to many different places and most of them ended with this slow, earthy chorus, but it always made him feel like he was coming home after going somewhere far away. Tonight, it happened to be true.

Leo ignored the offered hand and stepped stiffly out of the carriage under his own power. Maforc Castle, with all its sharp angles and cold stone, welcomed him in. It was worlds apart from the enormous castle that housed Trinitas Academy, the Empire's only formal institute for magical learning, where Leo had spent the last six years almost without interruption. Maforc didn't need to be that large—Canticalica was a small kingdom with just two cities, and calling them cities was very generous. The capital, Praecentor, had a population that fluctuated with the seasons, but never quite exceeded thirteen thousand, and it was rural enough that Leo had twice heard of kangaroos blundering their way into market streets, by what logic no one could guess at.

Leo approached the heavy, oak doors with legs that felt exactly like he'd been riding in a carriage for the past several days, and two Shields opened them for him. He nodded in acknowledgement as he passed them and tried to ignore the sound of six pairs of footsteps shadowing him as he crossed the threshold.

He managed to tolerate his entourage of Swords, Shields and Helm across the courtyard and through the entrance hall of the Round Tower. Ingrained politeness kept him from asking why they hadn't buggered off yet as he made his way up the first flight of stairs and past room after anonymous room, but eventually he reached his limit. He turned.

'Thank you for your service,' he said pointedly.

'Your Majesty,' the Helm said, the same one who had told him that his parents and brother were dead with about as much sensitivity as could be expected of a soldier. 'I would feel more comfortable if you were escorted at least until the royal apartments.'

'Thank you for your service,' Leo repeated.

The Helm hesitated for a moment longer, then bowed. She turned, and her five other companions followed her back down the corridor. Leo sighed with relief and exhaustion. He didn't think he could stand having a parade of babysitters following him around on top of everything else. He was twenty-two, for Trinity's sake. He had a sword and training in combative magic; he wasn't helpless. Outside the castle, he could understand. But his father had never had guards dogging his steps inside, and Leo wouldn't either.

He turned the corner then stopped in surprise. Across the entrance hall to the living quarters, a young man of about Leo's age was sitting on the stairs, which seemed like it probably wasn't allowed and like it must be uncomfortable, and also like he was completely in Leo's way. The stairs were vast, but it felt rude somehow to walk around him. The man stood up when Leo approached—not with the deference that Leo had received in the last few days, too unhurried for that, but not disrespectfully. Leo didn't recognise him, but he hadn't recognised a single one of his guards, either. The man was shorter than Leo, like most people, with tanned enough skin and a broadish nose that indicated he probably had prevenient blood, and dark hair forming chin-length, tight curls. He was attractive, but not distractingly so; he was really only noteworthy in that there was no one else to look at.

'Your family is in the Oak Library,' the man said. 'Would you like company?'

Not particularly, Leo thought. Then, *Who are you?* But neither of those thoughts felt polite and he'd used up all his assertiveness on his guards, so instead he tilted his head in what was almost a nod.

'Thank you,' he said.

The man turned so he was facing the same direction as Leo and they walked up the stairs together in a silence that didn't match up with Leo's idea of company, especially not from people who wanted something from him. And that meant everyone right now, with the possible exception of the people waiting for him in the library.

'Sorry,' Leo said, 'but do I know you?'

'No,' the man said easily. 'And I wouldn't presume to know you either, though of course you are known. I'm sorry for your loss.'

What loss? Leo wondered, then he nearly laughed at himself for forgetting. *Get a grip*, he told himself firmly.

'Thank you,' he said, his voice sounding stiff, but thankfully not amused.

They walked in silence some more. It might have been peaceful, but Leo mostly felt on edge. He hoped that it was just his grief and uncertainty. He didn't want to feel this paranoid every time he walked with someone he didn't know while here. But then, he didn't want to be here at all.

Leo couldn't think of anything to say, so the silence continued. It was late enough that the hallways were empty and the sound of their boots echoed eerily off the stone walls. Like maybe they were the dead ones, trapped in a mirror realm where no living person existed. Or maybe like it was nighttime. It was probably the fact that it was late that was making Leo slightly hysterical. It had been a long few days.

'I'll leave you here,' the man said, coming to a stop at the large door that separated the royal apartments from the guest ones. He bowed his head slightly and turned without being dismissed.

'Who are you?' Leo called after him.

'Someone very important and handsome,' the man called back, walking backwards for a few steps so Leo could see his smile. Leo forgot to smile back until it was too late and he'd turned away again.

Behind the door, the stone floor ended and timber began, reaffirming a barrier that was already more than implied. The difference in temperature was immediately recognisable and welcome. Stone took a lot more magical energy to keep warm, but it held defensive magic better, and the carpets and rugs required to make it habitable gave the impression of wealth. Those reasons explained why much of the castle was stone, but not why Leo was walking across intricately patterned floor-boards. When he was a child, he had learnt exactly where to step so as to not make the nightingale floors sing in the creaking voices that announced the presence of unfamiliar steps. It wasn't magic, just simple construction. It was with a childish kind of whimsy that he picked his way lightly through the quiet path instead of using a dignified stride that would have the floors complaining. There was no one to see him choose a small amount of joy in the midst of a shitty time. He had the feeling he would need every ounce of love he had for his home in the coming days.

He made his way to the library, which he supposed he was allowed in as much as he liked now that he was an adult, now that his parents weren't going to tell him to leave them in peace. If they did, they would have bigger problems. Revenant and blood magic problems, the kind that only featured in badly told ghost stories. *Pull yourself together*, he told himself for about the millionth time that day. He didn't have the luxury of falling to pieces. He was already sick of shoring up his mental walls, which currently felt like they were made of damp sand.

He didn't slow as he walked through the open door of the library or as his steps became muffled by a thick rug, but he paused when his remaining family came into view, gathered around the fire in silence as if sitting for a portrait. The floor shifted and sang under the toe of his boot and he moved his weight off it self-consciously. It made no difference; his siblings were already looking at him.

'Lee,' Con said, smiling and walking over to him. Their embrace was a brief one where each patted the other on the back, bringing just enough violence into the hug to satisfy their masculinity quotient. Con was stronger than Leo remembered, and he remembered him pretty strong. He remembered him taller, too. It was disturbing to look down to meet his older brother's eyes. He'd outgrown Con years ago and he knew this, but he seemed to forget when their only communication was through letters.

'Don't hoard all that love to yourself,' Ada said dryly. She offered her hand to Leo, who brought it to his lips with as much ironic formality as it had been offered with. Con snorted. Ada trying to make him feel off-balance made Leo feel more at home than anything else could have.

Max stayed by the fire. Leo went to him and crouched with his arms out. Max huffed a little sigh and hugged Leo around the neck, letting go immediately. It was the kind of hug Leo used to give to people his parents insisted he was related to, who he would only ever meet once and for whose benefit he was forced into uncomfortable clothes and boring meals. Ouch. He stood. He met Con's eyes and Con made a subtle grimace.

The absence of Dicky, even if he would have been at least as stiff as Max, was almost tangible. Leo hadn't seen his twin in over a year. It felt like Dicky was just standing them up, like he was too busy sucking up to their dad to welcome Leo home. Except this time he wouldn't wake Leo up before sunrise in a misguided attempt at making up for it. He'd never do that again. Leo couldn't wrap his head around it. He wished he was back at the Academy.

'How was the trip?' Con asked.

'No, I refuse to do small talk,' Ada said. 'We're too large for it. Tell us gossip instead, Leo.'

And she'd done it. He felt off-balance. He rarely had gossip on good days, but today …

'Oh, stop that,' Ada snapped. 'It's not inappropriate. We're going to be talking about nothing else for months, we can at least practice a little healthy denial when it's just the four of us.'

'Ada, come on,' Con said. 'He's been on the road for three and a half days.'

'So he should have heard plenty from his drivers and guards,' Ada said. 'I don't need to know all the parties involved. I thrive on all information, not just relevance.'

'I want to go to bed,' Max said, before Con could respond. 'You said I had to stay up until Leo got here. Now I want to go to bed.'

'You don't want to hear gossip?' Leo asked, even though he had none. He would make something up, which was always an option Ada allowed so long as it was funny or interesting.

'No,' Max said.

Leo wanted to say something, to insist they stay in one room for just a bit longer, to hold on to this feeling of family that wasn't quite familiar for as long as possible. It wasn't like he knew what to do with Max, who had only been—Holy Trinity, had he really been only two when Leo had gone to the Academy? —but that wasn't important. Everyone waited, as if they could tell Leo wanted to speak and didn't want to interrupt him. Leo let out a breath and the moment slunk away to die under the garden shed.

'I'll take you to bed, kiddo,' Con said. He held his hand out and Max examined it for a moment before deciding that he'd allow Con the honour of holding it, and then they were gone. Ada and Leo waited until their footsteps faded on the floorboards, which didn't protest the presence of familiar feet.

'He doesn't like me either, Your Majesty,' Ada said.

'Please don't,' Leo said.

'Try not to pull that face when you hear your new title from other people,' Ada advised.

She joined Leo next to the fireplace and wrapped her free arm around herself. Leo had brought the cold in. He tried not to stare at her sling. Danya could have healed that in a heartbeat, Leo was sure. He could heal it now. He knew not to offer. Ada glanced up at Leo before looking away to the mantle instead.

'Tell Con I said this and I will pluck every one of your leg hairs from you one by one,' she said, 'but you'll be okay. We'll be right there with you the whole way. You won't look out of place when you're surrounded by family.'

'I will if I try and get crowned in the kitchen because I've misplaced the King's Hall.'

'Yes, well. Don't do that.'

Leo laughed sadly.

'Are you okay?' he asked. He touched the shoulder of her slinged arm gently to clarify. He wasn't going to ask if she was okay with their parents and Dicky being dead. What if she said no? What if she said *yes*?

'I'm fine,' she said stiffly. 'Don't ask Con that or he'll actually decapitate you with his very pretty sword. We're not particularly comfortable being the focus of concern, not when we're still …'

'Burdened with breath?'

'Exactly.'

Leo pulled the tie from his hair and shook it out from the simple braid he'd kept it in for the trip. It was down to his shoulders now, which he had liked earlier that week, when he didn't have to worry about what was fashionable for a king. Ada leaned slightly out of the range of his elbows, but didn't step away. Her own hair was also loose, an identical blonde hue to Leo's, though a few inches longer. If the hair didn't obviously signal that they were related, their matching caramel eyes that seemed to always fall into a resting bitch face definitely did.

Leo and Ada stood in silence until Con returned. Ada heard him first, human guard dog that she was, and her sharp turn of the head signalled it a good two seconds before Leo could hear anything. Con dropped into one of the armchairs melodramatically.

'He's too old to be read a bedtime story,' he reported mournfully. 'And too cool to be told one against his will. He covered his ears so he didn't have to hear me anymore and glared at me like Ada used to when I tried to manhandle his hands away.'

'Congratulations on not being turned to stone,' Leo said.

'He was a shit *before* they died,' Ada said. 'I don't know what we're going to do with him now.'

'You know, that nurturing goodness is definitely what Danya sees in you,' Con said.

'How is Danya?' Leo asked. 'Why isn't she here?'

'Because about fifty arseholes think they're higher on the priority list to see you than Danya and keeping it a family-only affair was the only way to spare you them.'

Leo patted Ada consolingly on the uninjured shoulder in

meagre recompense for suffering an evening without her girl-friend. She jabbed him in the ribs and he stopped.

'Ada, come on, what did we say about not being dicks to Leo?'

'He'd like it too much,' Ada said, nodding wisely. 'And that would make things awkward.'

Leo choked out another laugh, which made for two more than he'd expected today. He impulsively pulled Ada into a hug that was both given and received with the spirit of a headlock. She spiked up like a cat and tried to wriggle free. He held her firm. Her fault for being cheeky.

'Fine!' she said. 'I'll be nice! Unhand me, scoundrel!'

Leo relaxed his hold enough for Ada to escape. She collapsed onto the divan in a way that made it very clear that either she or Con had picked up the drama from the other. Leo considered sitting on top of her, but he wasn't fourteen anymore, not even if being back home made him feel that way. And there was still a lot to talk about while they had a small window of privacy.

'So,' Leo said. 'What actually happened?'

Ada and Con sat up straight in jarring synchronicity. They shared a look, and when Ada turned and lay back down, Con looked at Leo reluctantly, as if he'd lost some kind of telepathic coin toss.

'We don't actually know,' Con said. Leo frowned at him, conveying that that was *not* a good enough answer. 'Okay, we know a bit. We know that eight were killed. We know our parents were right at the centre, like, so in the centre that there would be no disguising it was for them even if it weren't for the fact that they're, you know, them. There's a crater in King's Hall from the explosion and it threw off some kind of shock wave. Ada was pretty close, hence the,' he made a gesture with his arm as if he was a country boy making a very enthusiastic thumbs up, which Leo thought was supposed to be a mime of her sling. 'I was in the atrium. Got a bucketful of glass on me, but I don't even have the couple cuts I had anymore thanks to Danya's miracle cream. Dicky was right next to them. Obviously.'

'And we don't know who it was,' Leo checked.

'You want to see my chalkboard of crazy?' Con asked.

'Yes.'

'Of course you do. Look, it's impossible to narrow it down right now. I know we pretty much liked them, but politically? Apart from being rulers, which is enough, Dad made some … choices.'

Leo nodded distractedly.

'Speaking of said choices,' Ada said. 'Undoing them is going to require an amount of grace. You can't appear to be systematically unravelling all his legislation, even though I sincerely hope you'll be systematically unravelling all his legislation.'

Leo winced. Con looked at the stitching on a cushion as if it was very interesting.

'I haven't even been crowned yet.'

'I doubt I'm the first to get in your ear about policy,' Ada said dismissively. She swept her leg in a dramatic arc so that she could swap the way her ankles were crossed. Leo watched her production of comfort with trepidation.

'Actually, I think you were. You were probably whispering about self-determination while you were still in a crib.'

'And Dad was probably whispering about the importance of respecting authority into Mum's belly while you were in utero, so he had three years on me. We need a plan.'

Ada climbed to her feet and stepped towards Leo in what was transparently the beginning of a very inspirational speech. Con stood and grabbed her uninjured wrist.

'We need to sleep,' Con said. 'Cabinet has a month off; you'll have plenty of time to puppet Leo before they resume. If you start machinating now, you'll make yourselves all manic and you'll look like zombies for the funeral.'

'We couldn't have that,' Ada muttered.

'No, we couldn't,' Con agreed, as if Ada hadn't been oozing sarcasm. He let go of her. The three of them formed a near-perfect triangle of misery, though none of them were ready to look at their feelings yet. 'I know you're clever, Ada, we all know you're clever. But there's more to being a ruler. You can't get people to listen to you just because you're clever. You have to do the right things, look the right way, smile at the right people.'

'I'm doomed,' Leo said, matter-of-factly. A morbid laugh escaped him before he could rein it in. 'I'm actually doomed. Fuck you for joining Sword and Shield, Con, seriously, fuck you. It should have been you.'

'And you have to be stone cold and decisive,' Con said. 'So I would've been dead within two days, and you'll just have to manage, won't you.'

The energy left Leo. He felt every centimetre of his journey on his body and the accumulative age of his parents and twin on his soul. He sighed and lifted his hand to place it on Con's shoulder. He looked wearily between his two siblings.

'We're not going to be our parents,' he said. 'We're going to be able to have conversations that aren't about politics, we're not ever going to scream at each other—we're not going to forget that we love each other.'

'They loved us,' Con said softly.

'We'll always show it,' Leo conceded. Con didn't argue that one.

Behind Leo, the fire danced and popped to its staccato beat. It outshone the muted lamps and fell just short of illuminating the titles of the many shelved books. It exposed the way the past few days dragged the soft skin under three sets of eyes down. And it provided the ambience that all good fires provide, like Leo had felt back at the Academy when he visited the small pub close there with friends, and a lifetime ago in these rooms as well. It usually warmed Leo in a way that extended past the physical, but tonight it couldn't quite touch him. Comfort was a bit much to ask for, given the circumstances.

TRADITION, THOUGHT LEO, was a bitch.

He was in stiff clothes he hadn't worn since his grandmother died three years ago, and he had suffered the powder the attendant had puffed onto his face, but the thing that was really making him uncomfortable was the fact that he had to do this next bit alone.

Ada crouched quietly across the room and the movement caught Leo's attention. When he looked over, she and Max pulled ridiculous faces at him, her screwing up her face and waving her hands and Max jutting his jaw out and pulling the skin under his eyes down. Leo laughed in surprise, and suddenly his siblings were completely composed again and stepping sedately into the cathedral, hand in hand.

'She is such a bad influence,' Con sighed, but he was smiling too. He punched Leo gently in the shoulder and took his place. When Ada and Max were halfway down the aisle, Con started walking. And Leo was alone.

'Trinity, don't let me trip,' he breathed, throat tensing with the melody he didn't dare release. It was impossible to sing in a whisper, but he was so used to pretending he could that it brought the same comfort a proper prayer would. Some king he was. Embarrassed to be caught praying here, of all places.

The angles of the cathedral had never felt inviting to Leo. He had grown up in a round tower, in a bedroom that curved with the wall and which he associated with comfort and safety. The cathedral and the chapel were both made of triangles that were supposed to enhance magic, and their edges felt so sharp they could cut. The cathedral entrance was on a point and it stabbed towards Leo. He couldn't remember ever entering it alone—for all their differences, Dicky could always be counted on to stand next to him. But it was his turn, so he did.

The assembled guests were already standing, as they would have risen for the first of the family who entered—some cousins who Leo had barely recognised at breakfast. All eyes were on him, leaving him feeling excruciatingly conscious of his expression. He wasn't sure exactly what the king should look like at his parents' and brother's funeral, but he was sure he wasn't looking however that was. The aisle went on forever and he thought that maybe his first act as king would be to demand that the cathedral that was erected over six hundred years ago be halved in length.

He took his seat in the chair (almost a throne, really) reserved for him, ahead of the foremost pew that might have been in any other church not frequented by royalty. He took some comfort in the familiarity of the seat that had been his for years, and even more from the shared nervousness that was evident on Con's face. Ada leaned across Con to whisper.

'You look very handsome. Like you're plotting to kill anyone who speaks to you.'

Leo raised an eyebrow at Ada's apparent death-wish and attempted to relax the severity of his scowl. Ada's nonsense actually made him feel a little more comfortable in his skin; there were worse impressions to give off than murderous. Ada relaxed back into her chair and affected devoutness in the direction of the bishop. She was the least devout magician Leo knew, or at least she was in organised settings. She liked making her own rules. The fact that she gloried in doing this was presumably why the Trinity let her continue.

Leo glanced at the three empty chairs to his right. He didn't know if one of them was going to be his once they had finished with leaving spaces symbolically reserved for ghosts. Someone would tell him. Or worse, much worse, maybe he'd have to decide himself.

He remembered sitting in the seat Con was in now, too small to even reach the footstool and too young to care about that. His dad passing smuggled-in lollies down the aisle. His mum exasperated but indulgent, taking the package and passing it to Con, who took one and passed it to Dicky, then Leo, who took two and pretended they were stuck together, passing it to Ada, who was too young to subtly get into the packaging. Leo had given her one of his, then the process reversed until the lollies were back inside Richard's pocket. They were in the front row and the bishop could obviously see them, but it was still a shared secret. It had made Leo flush and jitter with excitement. It had made him love his family.

For a horrifying moment, Leo thought he might cry. The fact that he absolutely did not want to do so while he was effectively in front of his kingdom and wearing makeup made the tears press against the back of his eyes with even more urgency. He managed to take a deep breath and find that numbness again. He'd be able to cry later.

The funeral was long and stilted by formality, which effectively removed the threat of any displays of emotion. The Trinity's benevolence and virtues were sermonised exhaustively. The Empress's blessings were delivered as though the Empress would have any idea who the deceased were. Max started fidgeting half an hour in, which was an impressive amount of time to keep still for an eight-year-old in Leo's book. When he had been that age he had been forced to sit through the wedding of one of those unfamiliar cousins who had preceded them into the cathedral. This had to be worse. While Leo's impatience back then had been magnified by his complete apathy towards the event (not knowing the cousin or her groom at all), Max must now be exhausted from the last week of grief. Leo would have to find a way to reach out to him, but after last night's reception, he wasn't feeling optimistic. Con was probably already doing more than Leo ever could—he'd always had a way with kids—but it was Leo's responsibility too. He couldn't delegate when it came to being there for his family.

When the bishop stopped speaking, Max managed not to audibly sigh, but his body melted with relief into his chair. Leo didn't let himself grimace, but he knew that despite the ceremony being nearly over, they weren't even a quarter through the day. The bishop stepped back from the podium and he, Con and Ada stood to take their places behind the three coffins that were raised up on matching marble platforms as old as the cathedral. Leo thought he recognised Danya's touch in the intricate woodwork, but he might have been imagining it. There was something vaguely messed up about going through with this tradition given the circumstances of their deaths, but Con and Ada had had no idea how to articulate this to the priests who organised this, nor had they had any alternative suggestions. So, here they were.

They linked their hands in gentle solidarity. At the altar, the bishop lifted his arms and the congregation began to sing. No words, just a gentle *'Ah'* that would continue through the ceremony, the pitch guided by the bishop's conducting.

Leo didn't need to look at his siblings on either side of him to know when to start the incantation. In magic and with these two, he didn't think he'd ever feel out of synchronisation, even on a day like this, even with the sporadic nature of their visits to each other over the last six years.

'We stand faithfully in rapture / Prisms to fracture the light / Calling on inferno to capture / To kindle, to spark, to ignite.'

At the sound of their voices, pale rainbow flames erupted in spiralling patterns from the base of each platform, consuming the coffins while leaving the marble they rested on intact. The flames tornadoed far above their heads into the cavernous roof.

'One of three, first steps, first words, they're blessed / Two of three, they live, its highs, its lows / Three of three, in end, they have their rest / In the close, as we know, all things slow.'

Ada shifted slightly, steadying her stance. Leo thought she was the strongest magician out of the three of them, but he also hadn't been home in a while. And it was a tough day. He squeezed her hand and strove to pour more of his own magic into the spell to allow her a small reprieve. It disconcerted him when she gripped his hand in return, but he didn't allow it to interrupt the song.

'Three devotees to conjure a course / Three watchers to welcome the chill / Three flames to consume the source / Three stanzas to bid them be still.'

When they came to the end of their song, the flames faded from the air like smoke dissipating and there was no trace of the coffins. Leo had sung the song under his breath for most of his ride home in preparation (keeping his magic carefully dampened so as not to set the carriage alight), determined to get it perfect. Only very powerful spells required the reverence that came with singing, and Leo was relieved that it had worked despite their never practising it together before. And it was over so fast.

They dropped each other's hands, magic over. Ada touched Leo gently on his arm and led him and Con into a hug, her frame stiff with the discomfort of displaying affection so publicly (and probably with hugging in general). Even so, her arms were steady around each brother's back. Leo thought he understood. It was an assertion of their solidarity. His father would have been proud to see his values living on, maybe especially at Ada's hand. He'd believed in presenting a familial front. Leo felt Max's smaller arm reach to join the hug and he and Ada made room for him. He squeezed Max's shoulder in appreciation. It helped to remind him that not everything was done with an agenda. Sometimes a hug was for comfort and love. This one … was both.

T HE NEXT FEW HOURS WERE TORTUROUS. *Give me death before you give me small talk,* Leo thought, which was probably in bad taste, what with the funeral and all. The carriage ride back to the King's Hall gave them a brief respite before they each endured the company of countless nobles offering their condolences then engaging in conversations that ranged from banal to unabashedly self-serving. Leo couldn't even lean on his siblings, because to do anything else but separate would deprive too many important people from contact with at least one of them. Max got away with clinging to each of them in turn, but he wouldn't for much longer. Leo felt out of practice. The last six years had featured the kind of manipulation that came with young adults posturing about to impress each other, not this.

'Your mother was a saint,' said his aunt Sofia, who he hadn't seen in over a decade. 'An absolute saint.'

'She was,' Leo agreed awkwardly and not quite sincerely. He'd had to memorise the deeds of saints when he was younger and his mum was just a mum. Okay, a queen. But also just a mum.

'And your father,' Sofia said. 'My brother was extraordinarily clever.'

'Nobody could disagree with that,' Leo said. It had sounded more flattering in his head.

Within the next ten seconds, Leo knew he was going to be told how much he resembled Dicky for the millionth time, except for some observation of "not-quite" that made the observer feel clever for saying it. *How like your brother you are. But you are taller, of course.* Leo was pretty confident that if he and Dicky were to swap clothes like they used to as children, and if somehow Dicky could manage to remove the enormous stick from his arse for just five minutes, none of these people would be able to tell the difference. He looked past Sofia's head, desperate for a diversion, and saw his cousin Elias hovering. As much as he didn't really want to talk to him, it would at least be less awkward than this.

'Elias, hi,' he called.

'I must be going, your grandmother possibly needs me,' Sofia said, as Leo had hoped. Their family was full of more fractures than the hastily repaired floor they stood on. Elias waited until she escaped before approaching Leo properly and gripping his forearm in a greeting more common in his kingdom than Leo's.

'Well, this is shit,' Elias said, extraordinarily accurately.

'A bit, yeah,' Leo said. 'I mean, no, completely shit.'

'I was talking to a girl before for half an hour before her dad came up and I realised she was our cousin. This family is something else.'

Okay, shit as in a shit party, not as in *Leo, it must be pretty awful that you're an orphan.* Leo was unsurprised that Elias was trying to pick up at a funeral and barely surprised that he wasn't particularly sympathetic. It wasn't as though their respective immediate families had gotten along. Actually, they apparently had for a couple of years while Leo had been at the Academy, but it was short-lived. This was probably why Elias knew the family well enough to not care that three of them were dead. Leo's father had been far from the only one to burn familial bridges—barely any of the Dietrich family were cursed with an inconvenient level of empathy—but he had definitely been responsible for this particular gap. Thankfully, Elias didn't seem to be holding it against Leo. Leo didn't consider himself an exception to the coldness that seemed to come with the territory, but he at least resolved to never fall out with his siblings with the same ease the rest of the clan did.

'Are you staying long?' Leo asked.

'Empress's *truth*, no,' Elias said. 'It's freezing here and I saw the amount of luggage Grandma came with. Unless I find a girl worth staying for I'll be gone by the weekend, as soon as I can get a blessing on the carriage.'

Well, that was at least something to be grateful for. Leo was no longer sure that he had been right to swap Sofia for this. He'd remembered Elias being less slimy. Leo looked around the room with careful carelessness.

'She's not related to us,' he said, pointing subtly to the first courtier who was attractive enough to prove a distraction and who had been far enough back in the cathedral to definitely not be a relative. Elias looked and his eyebrows went up as he considered.

Elias shrugged and said, 'Nothing else to do.' He clapped Leo on the shoulder and headed off in the woman's direction.

Leo felt like sagging in relief until he was sitting on the floor, but he hadn't repressed his emotions his whole life for nothing. He was able to snag a canapé from a passing waiter before someone else demanded his attention. He shoved the fancy bundle of meat and pastry into his mouth and nodded with his mouth full as the man introduced himself and then promptly started crying. Leo felt like he should probably cry too, or maybe touch the man sympathetically. He didn't do either.

It was both incredibly boring and incredibly stressful. It was also relentless. At one point, Leo found himself talking to two of his dad's brothers and his mum's sister at the same time. His aunt had never met his uncles before and the kingdoms his uncles belonged to had been in cold war for the last two years. Each of the uncles was pretending the other didn't exist yet managing to have a conversation with Leo despite this. One uncle said something about violins to Leo. The other uncle said something that was also about violins to Leo, without indicating that the other uncle was involved. Then his aunt asked the two uncles collectively if they played and one of them just walked away while the other one answered that he did. Leo thought the one who left probably didn't. He excused himself to the bathroom and ate half a plate of fruit-on-cheese-on-cracker things while sitting in front of the sink until he felt guilty enough to return.

'You will be wanting an expert in classic architecture to oversee the repairs,' a countess of somewhere or other said to Leo a bit later. 'The ones who work on modern buildings would be completely clueless.'

'We want to do it properly,' Leo nodded. He didn't even know if that was a decision he would be involved in, but he assumed whoever was did, in fact, want to do it properly. He didn't know how much longer he could stand any of this.

'I am glad to hear that,' she said seriously, as if the afternoon of a fairly significant funeral was an excellent time to be discussing renovation. She didn't even have the excuse of being related to him, but Leo had suspected for some time that if you got old enough you simply stopped giving a damn about basically anything. 'I am sure you are just as appalled as we are by the recent surge in modern buildings,' she continued, without any indication of who "we" might be. 'They are downright disrespectful. As though godliness is not *fashionable* these days.'

'Excuse my ignorance in architecture,' Leo said. 'It was barely touched on in my studies.'

'Oh,' the countess said, looking taken aback. Perhaps she was expecting him to have inherited his parents' allergy to admitting shortcomings. 'I see.'

Leo kept eye contact with her until she curtsied and left. He'd been told he didn't have an inviting face, which was something everyone wanted to hear while on a date. He would have attempted to smile like a proper king, but he didn't think he would be expected to for some time and he was taking advantage of that. He adjusted his black cuff, suddenly conscious of his duties to mourning. It wasn't like it had been in the past—he was allowed to work and be in society, but he was going to be expected to make his grief public. He met Con's eyes across the room and Con nodded sombrely and made a gesture that looked like a wave but had been code for *kill me now* since they were children. Leo searched the room for Ada and found her near the massive doorway, walking back into the room. A moment later he saw why she'd dared to leave, and it took everything he had not to groan.

He *hated* the fool.

The fool cartwheeled into the room, over and over until it twisted in the air and landed on both feet, arms up in the air with celebration. Of all the Empress's institutions, Leo found the Consortium of Fools the most pointless and frustrating. He hated the fact that a castle had to have a fool as much as his father had, but he knew why Ada had fetched it. The whole court was now turning into the centre to watch and, apart from a few, conversations had ceased. As Leo looked, he thought the fool looked different than he remembered, though it was hard to tell through all the paint and costume, and he'd never really liked looking at it. It would have been nice, Leo reflected, for his home to feel a bit more familiar.

The fool bowed once, twice, then on the third it tumbled over until it was rolling, holding its ankles. When its momentum took it to standing again, its mouth was wide with astonishment and it stumbled violently to the side. A few muffled laughs simmered through the crowd as it lurched into a lady and took her down with it, rolling her over and up to standing before she could protest. She clutched at the neckline of her dress and made a strange *'Oohhooarrh'* noise, but the fool had already moved back into the centre of the space it had created, arms wide. Leo's heart sank when their eyes met. He almost wanted to insist on an extended family dinner in a very small room to escape.

'Your Majesty,' the fool said, bowing so low its nose touched its knees. While its head was down, it made a loud farting noise before leaping forward as though wanting to separate itself from the scandal of it all. Leo had been right; its voice was higher and younger than the old fool's. He doubted this one was an imp-rovement.

'Your Majesty,' the fool said again, once the guilty laughter had properly ceased. The crowd didn't seem to know if they were allowed to find anything funny on the same day as the funeral, especially not a fart joke. 'Will you do me the honour of accepting my riddle?'

There was no right answer. Leo did what his father had always done and gave a terse smile and a nod.

'If you're fit, you may evade me, if you've a sword you may employ me, I come for rich, I come for poor, and I've just landed at your door. Who am I?'

Yeah, this was not the fool Leo grew up with. He had never guessed the old one's riddles. Or maybe he had improved his skill at deciphering riddles, but he doubted that.

'Death,' he answered quietly.

'I'm sorry, Majesty, my ears are in my hat! I'll have to ask you to please repeat that!'

'Death,' Leo said, louder.

The fool clapped and laughed gleefully and cartwheeled towards Leo, landing closer than comfortable. Leo refused to flinch. Up close, the fool's face was smooth and free of wrinkles, its eyes dark abysses almost blending with its pupils in the middle of thick eyelashes and garish paint. Leo wondered if he was supposed to be unnerved. He stared impassively.

'One more, please and thank you!' the fool shouted. Leo again managed not to flinch, but it was a close thing. Every muscle in his body felt tense.

'One more,' he agreed.

'I cannot vote, I cannot drive, I've spent so little time alive. In everything I need some aid and for my services I am not paid. Who am I?'

It was too easy, but so was the last one. The fool was grinning as widely as a cracked egg. Maybe it didn't mean to make Leo look stupid. Maybe this one was kinder than the last.

'A child.'

'No, Your Majesty,' the fool said, covering the painted smile on its cheeks so it could make its face a pantomime of sorrow. Its voice rang clearly through the room. 'A king.'

Leo wanted to palm his face in exasperation. He wanted to punch the fool. He made himself laugh instead. Ha ha. Polite, but unconvincing. The best he could do.

'Thank you for your riddles, Fool,' he said.

The fool reeled back and Leo realised it was about to bow again. This time he did jolt backwards, because he was no longer certain he wasn't going to be headbutted for the sake of a joke. The fool bowed and held its hand to its mouth to make the farting sound again. When it straightened, it pulled four balls from its sleeves and started juggling them.

Leo watched it prance away, the balls rising and falling so smoothly through the air that it was hard to believe that they were being thrown at all. He looked over at Ada and made the same *kill me now* gesture Con had earlier. She smiled like a damned cat.

'**T**HIS IS NOT ACTUALLY GOOD FOR ME,' Leo said.

'Fresh air!' Danya declared. 'Freedom!' She cast her eyes around. She did things in sets of threes.

'Hats!' she cried, and Leo could have sworn her black, fluffy curls expanded with excitement.

Leo gave Ada a look that was supposed to communicate how little he was enjoying this as well as to interrogate her choice in girlfriend. Ada smiled peacefully back. Leo thought that Ada enjoyed the way that Danya always caused such a commotion that Ada was free to plot in the shadows. But then, Leo thought all of Ada's actions came back to her plotting in the shadows.

If Danya saw this sibling communication, she didn't pay it any mind. In truth, Leo *was* sick of being cooped up inside with too many people assessing his every gesture and grading it against whatever standards they held for kings. Sure, the people at the market were judging him as well, but none of them were looking at him like they would eat him if he didn't pass muster. The consequences for looking like a fool out here just weren't as high as they were in the castle, so Leo didn't resist as Danya pulled him over to a market stall and perched possibly the most ridiculous hat Leo had ever seen on his head.

'Um,' the stallholder said. Leo turned to her, blank-faced. 'Looks good, Majesty,' she said, every syllable awkward. She held up a mirror and averted her eyes. He wished people would just look at him.

'You've a face for hats,' Danya said. 'You always have. Or maybe it's your head? Hair? What do you think, Ada?'

'Well, it certainly draws attention away from his freckles,' Ada said.

Leo turned his head to the side. The hat's colouring and texture reminded him of the tortoiseshell cat that hung around the library at the Academy, which wasn't necessarily a negative. But it was an unflattering, gnomish cone and it had strange wires protruding with fuzzy bits at the end, giving the impression that there were flies circling him.

He felt kind of dickish when he thought about leaving without buying anything, seeing as he very clearly had the means to. He also felt dickish about expressing any kind of opinion when the salesperson was likely the milliner responsible for this monstrosity.

'Whittle,' he said, luxuriating in the shape of the word between his lips. It was a word that could be said with emphasis, which his magic liked.

The hat transformed, losing its attachments and shaping itself cosily to Leo's head. He smiled at his reflection. It was still recognisable, but it was also something that he could wear. And it was *warm*. Praecentor was colder in Autumn than the Academy got most winters, and only a few deciduous trees still clung to scant leaves. It was a miracle it wasn't raining. He turned his smile to the woman holding the mirror, but her expression quickly levelled his.

'I didn't mean to offend,' he said hurriedly, reaching for his coin purse.

'No no,' she said, voice cold. 'The Trinity blessed you with magic so that you can have whatever kind of hat you like. I'm just grateful the Empress doesn't have more legitimate descendants, or I'd be out of a job.'

'I could never replace you,' Leo said as he pressed a couple of coins into the woman's hand, sincerely meaning it. Even if he wasn't already skipping out on a much more important job, he couldn't do hers. He didn't really care about hats, and he would be risking his passion for his magic if he used it on things he didn't care about. If he didn't appreciate his power, the Trinity wouldn't see the point in him having it anymore.

'Well, thank you for your patronage,' she said, with a graceless curtsey.

Danya wove her arm through Leo's and patted him on the hand, guiding him away.

'Perhaps don't rub your magic in their faces,' she suggested quietly.

'I thought people *liked* seeing magic,' Leo said.

'Some do!' Danya said.

'And others wonder what the world would be like if we used it to feed and clothe them, instead of entertaining ourselves in our fancy castles while we count the money we have taxed them,' Ada said dryly.

'Magical food doesn't have nutrition,' Leo protested.

'Did you learn that at the Academy?' Ada asked, raising an eyebrow at him. 'I think the peasants missed class that day.'

'Never mind that,' Danya said, squeezing Leo's arm. 'Look, candles!'

Leo glanced over his shoulder but let himself be dragged onwards. They stopped at other stalls and bought some truly useless things in order to fulfil the prescription of retail therapy that Danya had given them in service of diluting their grief, which she said was making their auras murky. Leo couldn't see auras (if they were even a thing) and thought that was a rude judgement to make besides, especially as it had only been a week since the funeral. He wasn't going to complain about leaving the castle, though. When their arms were full of things no one could possibly need, Ada called the intentionally inconspicuous Shields over so that they could carry them instead, which seemed a bit undignified to Leo.

'You blend in more now,' Danya told them cheerfully, balancing a vibrant bouquet of flowers on a shoe box. A stray shoot of gum leaves seemed determined to stay in the Shield's face until Danya tugged it free of the bouquet and wove it into her hair.

Around lunch time, the market began to disperse, or at least die down. Leo found a stall selling a savoury pastry wrapped around meat and gravy that was a speciality of Praecentor he hadn't had in years, and almost said he could therefore die happy, but then he remembered that he'd buried half his family pretty recently and it was probably in bad taste.

And just like that he was thinking of his parents.

It wasn't a wise decision among his siblings. Ada had once commented wryly that having daddy issues was a side effect of having a daddy. Con had begged her to never say the word "daddy" in his presence again. Leo wasn't convinced that everyone was victim to the issues they shared, or if the term really covered it—it was kind of flippant and now that he was gone it was harder for Leo to see their dad as an okay guy, if he ever really had. Not that he had ever hit them or anything. He didn't need such crude methods to keep them in line. Ada had said she used to hate Leo, just a little bit, for what she perceived as him running away to the Academy and escaping their parents. At his lowest, Leo wasn't sure she was wrong. He wasn't sure the hate was all in the past or all that little, either.

Ada kicked Leo's foot lightly and interrupted a line of thinking that wasn't going anywhere productive. Thinking of his parents was bad enough when they were alive; now it made him think of the fact that he'd never get to say such-and-such or do another thing again, or worse, that he had a new and crushing responsibility that he wasn't doing justice. When he was born, he'd been third in line. He shouldn't be dealing with this.

'Illuminate us,' Ada instructed. 'We love to hear your thoughts and laugh at them.'

Leo knew his face could not have looked like he was having happy thoughts, but he also knew he was expected to lie.

'I was wondering about boats,' he said. When had he last seen a boat? Where did that come from? He hadn't been to the Fluvius in a year and a half, which was ridiculous given that it flowed on all sides of the city. His carriage had driven right over the river without him seeing it on his way in.

'Oh?'

'What kind of person lives on a boat? Do they get seasick when they walk on dry land? Do they name the barnacles?'

'Did you know that the barnacle's penis is the longest in proportion to its body size out of any animal?' Danya asked.

'I did not,' Leo said.

'Mmm. It's so they can reach the other barnacles. You know, because they're stuck in place?'

Ada leaned slightly into Danya then sat up straight again. This was a big display of love from her. Leo feigned looking shocked.

'Shut it, Polly,' Ada said.

Leo threw the container that had held his lunch at her. He had hoped he'd outgrown Ada's nicknames.

THEY WENT BACK HOME soon after that, all piled into a polycarrier full of people who looked guilty for having chosen to take public transport at the same time as royalty. Leo looked at the sign advertising ticket prices that insisted fare evaders would be prosecuted. He did not have a ticket. Ada and Danya didn't seem perturbed. He supposed it was unlikely that an inspector would stop them.

Leo's chancellor, a thin man in his 50s with permanent

shadows under his eyes belying never-ceasing alertness, accosted them before the gates of the castle had even closed behind them. Leo's shoulders went up defensively.

'You always make that face when you don't know a name,' Ada murmured. 'It's Walsh.'

'Your Majesty,' Walsh said, inclining his head. 'Highness. Enchantress.'

'Walsh,' Leo said.

'It's Forster, Majesty,' Forster said. Leo held in a sigh and didn't look at Ada. He had no idea if that was on purpose or not. 'Your heads of avenues are waiting for you; you were scheduled to meet with them an hour ago.'

'Forster. You've all been doing this a long time. You don't need me to tell them how to polish plates or whatever.'

'No, but we do need someone to review the budgets,' Forster said.

Leo *did* look at Ada this time. She smiled and took his hand. In the same second, the air around them erupted in floral-scented smoke. Ada was of the opinion that she shouldn't suffer a bad smell just because she wanted to escape an enemy. Or, you know, a member of staff who was just doing his job. Leo let himself be pulled away under the cover of smoke, which was exactly how he had gotten out of the castle that morning (though he knew his escape had been *allowed*, given how quickly Ada had spotted the Shields tailing them). They made it to the stables and climbed up onto the roof. Danya leapt to the nearby window first, unlocked it with a brisk 'Disengage' and lifted herself in. She held out her hands considerately to catch whoever jumped next, so Leo took them as he had when he was much younger and much more likely to fall out of a window. Ada landed beside him while he was still batting dust from the stable off his knees.

'Where—' Leo started, but he was tackled to the ground in a calamity of jingling bells before he could finish the thought.

The women laughed, which told him almost as much as the bells.

He pushed the fool off him and stood. The fool grabbed him around his ankles and Leo wobbled dangerously. He couldn't imagine the fool of his childhood doing this to his dad.

'I'm a mage,' Leo warned, then, 'also your fucking king. Could you not?'

'Answer me these questions three, then maybe I will let you be!'

Leo looked to Ada.

'Sorry,' she said, 'all out.'

Leo didn't believe that she could ever run out of the various potions and powders she kept stashed in her clothes, but he also didn't think she was in any way merciful, so he turned to Danya plaintively.

'I've been trying to get a plant to bark,' Danya told Ada, seeming unconcerned with Leo's predicament.

'Trees have bark,' Ada said, as they both turned away and started to walk leisurely down the hallway.

'No! Like a dog!' Danya said.

Leo watched them turn a corner and decided that was enough. He got halfway through a word that would fling the fool away when it chopped its hand against the backs of Leo's knees as if it was felling a tree and Leo collapsed, worse than he had when he was tackled. The air whooshed out of his lungs and his traitorous body was confounded by the sensation. It didn't matter how often a person was winded—it was always inconveniently disruptive. Leo glared at the fool as he tried to gasp for breath, the motion feeling like he was doing it backwards.

'Answer me these ques—'

'Fine,' Leo wheezed.

'Where is your brother?' the fool asked.

Leo frowned in confusion. That wasn't especially foolish. It was *asked* foolishly, with that infuriating voice and off-putting face paint freezing and concealing its expression into something approximating joy but landing closer to mania. But it was pretty straight-forward. Leo couldn't think of any other implications and knew the fool was well aware of all their schedules, so he decided to answer directly.

'Training? Or, no, it's the afternoon. He'll be on guard somewhere, I don't know where.'

'And why is he not with you?' the fool asked.

'Sword and Shield isn't actually that interested in giving personal days,' Leo said, still kind of baffled and a little defensive. 'It's not inappropriate; there's precedence. He's doing his duty.'

'And where should you be right now?'

Ah, there was the other shoe. Leo had completely caught his breath back and was now lying on the floor with the fool as if they were at a sleepover. He didn't need this. He rolled away but the fool launched itself like a frenzied whale to flop perpendicular across his back.

'I am highly trained for combat,' Leo said, voice strained from the pressure to his lungs.

'I am highly trained for foolishness!'

Leo would have liked to express his disbelief that foolishness was a trainable activity, but he'd seen the acrobatics involved and the body laid on top of his was too heavy for him to be getting into a debate. Besides, the Consortium of Fools was presumably in place for a reason beyond enforcing castles' participation in their order. Leo wasn't so heretical as to question the Empress's judgement, no matter how personally inconvenient.

'Where should you be right now?' the fool sing-songed.

'The damned—' Leo groaned and tried to wriggle free. Yes, he was highly trained for combat. He was highly trained with a sword in his hand and magic wrapped around him. He almost couldn't be touched when it came to a formal fight. Apparently this had led to some blind spots. He was struck with the possibility that the Academy had cared who he was and had gone easy on him because of it, but it wasn't the time to be thinking of that. 'Heads of avenues meeting,' he grunted. 'Could you let me up?'

'Of course, of horse, of sauce!' the fool said.

It rolled off Leo and flipped itself upright like a pancake on narcotics. Leo climbed up, feeling as grumpy as a cat who had fallen in bath water and only had himself to blame.

'Shall I escort His Majesty?' the fool asked, bowing in half as it had a week ago at the funeral.

'No need.'

Leo stalked down the hallway and was horrified to hear the jingle of bells following him. They had a strange rhythm about them, as if the fool was prancing along in a pattern, but Leo didn't turn to look. He greatly hoped that the fool was only going in the same direction as him and would turn away soon.

He turned a corner and the bells followed. He quickened his stride and the bells' tempo increased. Finally, he decided he'd had enough. He turned and felt his cape turn after him, collecting itself around his thigh then falling back in place.

'What do you want,' he asked, voice flat and carefully neutral. For now.

'A fool serves as a cat does, and both want only cream.'

Leo imagined himself stomping his feet over and over. He imagined flinging the fool out the window and watching it land in horse shit. He imagined turning into a bird and never bothering with the human race ever again.

He nodded calmly and turned, breathing deeply as he did. Much as his dad had hated the old fool, he had trusted (as all kings probably do) that fools as a whole were obligated to be on the side of their kingdoms. This meant that royal secrets were safe, gossip was not passed on from staff to employers and no one could send a fool anywhere it didn't want to be sent. Perhaps especially when the place one wanted to send a fool was *away*. So long as the Empress liked having them around, there was nothing for it. Leo kept walking at a more sedate pace and used the time it took to get to the concourse rooms to brainstorm his excuse. The jingling was distracting, but he'd rather say something halfway eloquent on his arrival than appear like a sullen child that a clown had dragged out of bed.

It wasn't a part of the castle that he frequented. He remembered walking down this corridor when he was maybe eleven and hearing his parents arguing. Richard's face had been vicious. Gisela's face had been heartbroken and vulnerable, but Richard wasn't stopping. He had whispered with more venom than Leo had thought possible to express. There was no doubt in his mind that his dad had hated his mum then, and he didn't doubt it now. He had been standing in the hallway, but quietly, so neither of them had noticed him. Richard's expression had cleared, then he had stepped back into the room where people had been waiting for him, staff of some kind. Gisela had wiped tears off her face and bounced on the balls of her feet, blowing air out of her lungs as she gathered herself. Leo had heard Richard's voice call her in, and she had gone. Had it been obvious that she'd been crying? Did Richard care? When Leo had peeked in the room, Richard's arm had been around Gisela, as if she had been upset about something else and he was the good guy comforting his wife.

Leo was filled with fury all over again at the memory. What a useless way to feel. It hurt just as much as missing him did.

The other rooms were empty, so Leo opened the primary concourse room door with confidence. The table fell silent as they looked at his entrance then all rose with a cacophony of chairs scraping against stone. His heart was pounding a solid beat in his throat and he did his best to breathe evenly enough to calm it without exposing the fact that he was nervous.

'Apologies,' Leo said. 'I hope Forster excused my terrible behaviour on my behalf. I was spending time with my sister.'

He felt the fool behind him, inappropriately close in a transparent attempt to unnerve, a guard against outright lying. He knew that if he bent the truth at all, it would be delighted to expose him and watch him flounder.

'Welcome, Your Majesty,' Forster said.

He gestured to an empty seat, the one that belonged to Richard. Not anymore, obviously. Leo took it and tried very much not to feel like an understudy who had left his script at home. *I was not supposed to be here*, he thought resentfully. The fool folded itself placidly into a corner on the floor and stared right at Leo, who did his best to ignore it.

'We were discussing the budget,' someone across the table said. Leo nodded at her to continue, trying not to be distracted by Forster's pen racing across paper next to him. 'All avenues of staff have overspent their budgets in service of the funeral and the associated guests. Sir Conrad advised us to do the essential work of contracting additional staff to cater to the meals and rooms but not to use it as an excuse to go out and purchase new dinnerware.'

Leo nodded again. That was wiser than anything he could say on the spot. He hoped Con was standing in the sun without cream to protect him; it'd serve him right for being better at the job that he had weaselled his way out of.

'However, even doing that incurred significant costs, which I used my authority to push through or halt according to my judgement.'

Forster pushed a piece of paper towards Leo, making Leo suppress an annoyed huff. He couldn't be expected to catch up with a meeting he hadn't prepared for with people he didn't know, where he didn't even know the *topic*, and read at the same time. He glanced at the paper. It held a rough drawing of the table, names and titles next to each chair. Leo hoped he looked like he was reading an important and official document as he memorised it, then lightly folded it over to conceal it. He didn't want to look down before addressing someone, and his Academy-honed memory was good enough to hold the information. His affection for Forster skyrocketed.

'And you're wondering where to get the funds, Treasurer?'

'Yes, in short,' Hanna said. 'At the moment we're unavoidably spending from our future budget, which is made more problematic by the fact that we will have to spend a significant amount on an unplanned coronation in a few months.'

'Which we will be delighted to do,' Galland, the head of catering, said.

'Which we will be delighted to do,' Hanna repeated, not looking particularly delighted. 'At this point, it's not a question of *if* we should borrow money, it's who from.'

Leo felt his heart, which hadn't really settled to normalcy, beat heavier and louder. He wasn't prepared for this and he definitely shouldn't have tried to skip out on it. He couldn't remember the names of the surrounding kingdoms all of a sudden. He wasn't sure he could be trusted to remember the names of his siblings.

'I don't understand,' Leo said. He pinched the bridge of his nose as he condemned himself for admitting that. Then he recognised it as a habit he had picked up from his dad and stopped immediately. 'Are we really that little in,' a microscopic and yet eternal pause occurred while Leo dragged the right word from his mind, 'surplus?'

'We're in *debt*,' Hanna said, frowning. The air was suddenly not as oxygen rich as it had been. She looked at Leo as if he had asked something insane and possibly dangerous. 'We've been in debt for decades.'

'But my father was an economist,' Leo objected. 'That was his whole … thing.'

Hanna's wary disapproval melted into something like pity. Leo's dread increased. That was worse.

'No, never mind,' Leo said, sounding as calm as he could in the hopes that his obvious ignorance would somehow be forgotten about if he pretended he had it together well enough. 'I'll get the … particulars off you later, we don't want to drag this meeting out unnecessarily. What do we need to do to close for the day?'

'Direct, like his father,' Leo heard the bishop whisper to his neighbour. He ignored it, even though he wanted to defend himself. It probably wasn't actually an insult.

'I propose cuts to all avenues in the interim period so that we are still able to make our current repayments without taking out another loan immediately,' Hanna said. 'I have the figures here. We can last out another month on the remaining budget for the year if we're frugal.'

'It's not a question of frugality!' Galland said. 'There are still visitors lingering after the funeral and many of them won't go home until after the coronation, if then! Ask the king to throw them all out on their backsides before you ask me to feed a castle this full on inits!'

'The same applies to housekeeping,' Abigail said. 'We have no choice but to keep our contracted maids on—there are only so many beds a person can make up before you need another set of hands. We're scraping by on essential cleaning as it is; long-term maintenance will suffer if we continue to prioritise the obvious and neglect the insidious.'

'King Richard left instructions for grounds and recreation to be always catered to,' Coral said. 'He cut Princess Adelaide's classes when he wanted to restock the grounds with deer, if that indicates the priority level.'

It did, but not for the deer. As if Ada needed another reason to be resentful of Richard.

'This is where we were before your entrance, with a bit more detail on all parts,' Niklaus said warmly, speaking over the next protest before it had time to begin. His obvious amusement could be put down to the fact that as High Justiciar he wasn't really affected by budgets. 'None of the avenues would like their budgets to be cut.'

Leo felt absolutely speechless. He had half expected the meeting to be dispersed by the time he had arrived, but he didn't doubt that they'd been arguing for over an hour and that if he didn't say something they would continue for hours more. But what could he say? What would Con say? What would his dad have said?

'Oh, there once was a queen with a taste for cuisine!' the fool belted out suddenly. Leo's hands jumped to cover his ears. 'While she ate and she ate, all her people were lean!'

'The point is—' Abigail tried to say, but Leo could barely hear her at all over the song. The rest of the room wasn't paying attention to Abigail either, order completely abandoned in favour of half a dozen conversations, undoubtedly all about how little control Leo had over, well, anything.

'The taxman came down like a hideous rat!' the fool continued.

'Can someone make it leave?' Hanna shouted.

'On her people as she grew more and more fat!'

Leo used the cover of the song to cast a spell that filled the fool's mouth with cake. A prank spell, but he couldn't use anything nastier in front of his heads of avenues.

'Let's adjourn for the day. Please take some time to review your budgets and attempt to cut costs wherever you can. If there's any way to share resources or—'

'But the thing about rats is that though they are mean—'

Leo gave up and left the room before he could hear the gruesome end to that particular song. Forster followed on his heels, arms full of papers.

'I will organise a time,' Forster said. 'We should have been meeting with Sword and Shield fifteen minutes ago, so this is a convenient inconvenience.'

'Oh,' Leo said. He'd been hoping to go and hide in his bed for an hour or so, or maybe a week if he could have it.

'And then you have been invited to afternoon tea with Sir Desmond and his family, whose vassal we owe money to, so you cannot cancel on them. I warn you, they are zealously in favour of the Empress. As is correct, but perhaps be on your guard.'

'Oh.'

'And then your tailor, because you only have two black outfits and will be wearing nothing else for three months.'

'Oh.'

'Which will take us to dinner, and I have taken mercy on you and made it a family-only affair.'

Leo stopped in the middle of the hallway, took Forster by his upper arms and said sincerely, 'Thank you.'

'Yes,' Forster said uncomfortably.

Leo released him and they resumed their quick pace.

'Should I send Lady Hanna to your library after dinner?' Forster asked.

'What?'

'To discuss the treasury.'

Leo was silent as he considered how little he knew about what state his kingdom was in. He thought about how much of an idiot he had looked when he assumed that they were in surplus. Richard had cut Ada's classes, Coral had said. Leo definitely needed Hanna to give him a thorough education. But he didn't *want* one. And his instincts weren't entirely wrong. He couldn't afford to look like he didn't know what he was doing.

'Can you send me some summaries?' Leo asked. He ran his hand over his hair and found it frizzing out of his braids. Wow, because he was tackled. Before the meeting. He was tackled before the meeting and his hair had done something weird and then he'd sat through the whole meeting. He loved being the king. He forced his thoughts back to the lesser issue of his kingdom's dying economy. 'I need …'

He looked at Forster and thought about the map of the table he'd drawn for him. He hadn't realised how certain he'd been that he would have to figure all of this out alone until Forster had thrown him that small lifeline. Leo wondered how much he could trust him.

'How much can I trust you?' he asked, putting a hand to Forster's elbow to bring them both to a stop again.

'I won't impose a limit on it,' Forster said.

'I'm … young,' Leo said. Forster looked at him politely, not commenting on this very obvious statement. 'I was supposed to have three more years at the Academy, then learn how to be a *prince*, not a king. I was going to learn all this—finances, politics, whatever—in some nebulous future time that wasn't now, and I was only going to learn it to be helpful to Dicky.'

'Yes,' Forster said slowly.

'But I'm— I— I need people to take me seriously. Don't you think?'

'It is generally valuable for a kingdom to respect its king,' Forster said.

'Right. So. I'm behind, and you know that, and I think they probably all know it too.' He pointed back to the room they'd left to indicate the heads of avenues. 'But I need, especially if we're in the state that Hanna says we are, for them to know that they can't just say a lot of technical jargon and get me to nod along.' Leo sighed in resignation. 'I need people to take me seriously,' he repeated.

Forster looked Leo up and down. Leo was conscious of his posture, which had been drilled into him so much that he sometimes felt it was too straight and sometimes thought it would never be as good as Con's. He took a breath and pushed all the irrelevant thoughts out of his head so that he could just do his damn job for two minutes.

'I am taking you seriously, Your Majesty.'

'Thank you,' Leo said gravely. 'I'll meet with Hanna tomorrow, whenever you think is the best time. For tonight, I need some notes. I can't go into that kind of meeting completely blind.' He took a moment to organise his thoughts, and Forster allowed him it without a hint of impatience. 'How much money we have, what we owe, who to, how much money is devoted to each avenue's budget for the rest of the year that is apparently now for a month, how much money they usually get, what the expenses have been for the past week and what they are on a normal week, plus whatever she thinks I should know that I've forgotten.'

Forster nodded as he wrote down this list on the top sheet of paper on his pile. He didn't seem bothered by Leo not pausing after each item, thank the Trinity and the Empress both, because he didn't know if he could remember it all if he had the space to forget between each word.

'Are you my adviser?' Leo asked, as they began to walk again.

'No, I'm your chancellor,' Forster said. 'Secretary. My title on the books is Royal Chancellor, but either is a fine descriptor of my services. There hasn't been an adviser at court in decades.'

"In decades" seemed to be shorthand for "during your dad's rule, in which things sucked but people dealt with it because he sure thought he knew best". Ada had told Leo that he should be dismantling just about everything. He hated when she was right.

'Would it be an imposition if I asked for advice sometimes?' Leo asked, trying to sound polite and feeling like a child.

'I would be honoured,' Forster said. He didn't say anything until they reached the entrance hall. 'Humility was not one of your father's many virtues, and your brother took after him,' he said carefully. 'It is … encouraging, that you have the grace to listen.'

Leo didn't let his step falter and gave Forster a close-lipped smile of acknowledgement. He decided to ignore that the words had even been spoken. It was the only way he'd be able to get through the day.

THE INVESTIGATION INTO LEO'S FAMILY'S DEATHS wasn't going anywhere.

Sword and Shield's reports were frustratingly vague and no one could give Leo a straight answer about who they thought had done it or why. Leo got the impression that there was a lot of talking and not much *looking*. Con and Ada shared this belief and it was difficult to say who it frustrated and angered most.

Con took it as a personal failing, as if he was responsible for every action of the organisation he was an almost-trained member of. Ada also took it as a personal failing as she considered herself capable of achieving anything and knowing everything, and it baffled her that she hadn't been able to conjure the plotters' heads at her slightest whim. Leo mostly felt guilty that he didn't have the time to devote to it and, worse, reassured by the fact that if his siblings couldn't turn up anything he was unlikely to have any more success, effectively letting him off the hook. He had made time for it tonight to stave off some of that guilt.

'Leutesland wouldn't have used a bomb,' Con said, his stride not breaking as he paced back and forth in front of his chalkboard of crazy.

'Acting out of character is a perfect cover,' Ada said, as she'd said several times already to stop Con from dismissing a suspect.

'I can't leave everyone up here, Ada!' Con said.

'Memesis!' Danya said brightly, and a copy of the board squeezed out of the first one. Show-off. She didn't even think about it. Leo reflected that Canticalica's apprentice enchantress should be a lot better at magic than a half-trained magician, even if *he* was that half-trained magician. It still made him want to pout, just a little bit. 'Now you can take whoever you want off it.'

'Thanks, Danya,' Con said, smiling gratefully. Ada just scoffed without moving from where she was lying upside down on the couch, calves dangling over the back and hair brushing the floor. 'I don't see anything wrong with looking at the most obvious suspects first. Which means Rinderplatz.'

'Rinderplatz is an ally,' Danya said.

'We owe them money,' Leo sighed. 'I assume you've taken that into account?'

'Yes,' Con said, pointing at Leo. 'Which is just a whole 'nother pickle.' Ada scoffed again at his phrasing. No one paid attention to her. 'Because, look, it's not that I don't understand the logic.'

'Dad sucked, that's the logic,' Ada said.

Danya patted Ada on the forearm and looked at Leo with tragic eyes. Leo was not the one best equipped to reassure Ada, nor to get her out of a mood. That was Danya's domain, or maybe Con's if Ada was in the mood to acknowledge how much she cared about him under her spiky exterior or if Con was in the mood to argue with her in the fun way. Still, Leo sat on the floor next to Ada's head in a show of solidarity.

'Yeah,' Leo agreed.

'Come on, Lee,' Con said. 'It's not that simple and you both know it. Looking like we were in debt let us …'

'Commit tax evasion?' Ada supplied. 'Heaven forbid we contribute to the wellbeing of the Empire.'

'It wasn't just *looking* like we're in debt,' Leo said. 'Which is really fun and cool to be trying to sort out. Cheers, Dad. Thank you for technically just *avoiding* taxes instead of committing actual crime.'

Con set his jaw in hard lines that reminded Leo so uncomfortably of Richard that he started to feel nervous. Leo hadn't been scared of him while he lived, not consciously, but he couldn't deny that now … things were different. He'd had to excuse himself to hyperventilate in private last week when Galland had marched across the lower dining hall and his boots against the floorboards had sounded too much like the way his dad used to express his dissatisfaction. Leo had never hyper-ventilated at Richard's boots when he was alive, only cringed at the promise of tension, the threat of hatred delivered from someone who was supposed to love, but in the end he had always coped with it. Now he couldn't think about it or he'd end up with mundane nightmares where his parents turned their backs on him and he woke up in sweat and shaky breath.

'Con,' Leo said, his discomfort making him sound colder. 'Let's move on.'

Thankfully, Con knew that Leo sounded like a dickhead when he was stressed, and his face softened into normalcy. He gave Leo a small smile.

'Sorry,' Con said. 'Yeah. The pickle is that we have no way of fixing that quickly. We can stop spending on the, well, the ridic-ulous things that he spent on, which would free up some money if it wasn't for …'

'Funerals and coronations,' Leo said.

'Yup. Besides, we owe money to Leutesland too. And, uh, everyone.'

'I'm working on it,' Leo said. 'Hanna treats me like I'm four, but I *am* working on it. Let's just focus on the cheery matter of who did our parents in.'

'And Dicky,' Con said.

'Right,' Leo said.

He seemed to be in denial about Dicky's death. It wasn't *literal* denial, because he was very aware that it shouldn't be him on the throne, but it wouldn't stick in his mind. Dicky had been his twin. No matter the fact that they weren't what anyone would recognise as close, Leo took his existence for granted, even now. Some tiny inner child that somehow still believed that people were old when they died insisted that Dicky's time shouldn't be up until a few minutes before Leo's.

Con turned back to the boards, tapping his stick of chalk against his hand. Ada slipped down the couch until she was right way up on the floor next to Leo. Leo put his hand on her knee and pushed it back and forth a bit. Ada looked at him as though this was a funny trick an infant had done, which was not to say in an *un*affectionate way. Leo watched her for a couple of seconds after she turned away. Sometimes he forgot that she was the young one, seeing as she was always the one looking after him. He shook that train of thought off, only to look at Con and think about how he was always looking after him too. Con had always fit the archetype of protective older brother to a tee. Leo could vaguely remember Ada being too young to walk and Con looking after both of them and Dicky. Con hadn't always liked his responsibility, but Leo knew he'd have died or killed for any of them at any point. He knew it like he knew that when he took a step, his foot would fall on the ground.

'I just don't know,' Con said. 'I've been basically obsessing over it, but I can't figure it out. The magic was neither common nor uncommon and no one particularly benefited from his death, or any of the other victims'. I know you're not exactly experienced, Lee, but you're not so much an idiot that your taking over makes us more vulnerable.'

'Thanks, Con,' Leo said. 'It's compliments like that that get me through the day.'

'You're very competent,' Danya said. 'Also hard-working. And tall.'

Leo smiled at Danya. There wasn't a lot of flattery about Leo's ruling going around.

'Teeth!' she reminded him.

Leo tried to pull his lips back from his teeth in a way that retained some of his smile. Danya waved her hand back and forth so-so. Leo sighed. He was trying to get better at that whole "public face" thing. He felt like every aspect of his life involved trying at the moment.

'There's no new information, so this is useless,' Ada said. 'Someone blew them and several others close to them up. The magic used was easy enough for Danya and me to recreate without even working together, while not being anything known enough for it to be associated with a particular region or type of spellcaster. No one has stepped forward to claim it, no one has loomed over the funeral or danced merrily on their graves, no one has attacked the baby king'—'Thanks,' Leo said. 'I live to serve, Your Majesty,' Ada said—'in short, unless they come forward or otherwise distinguish themselves, there's a greater chance of Con winning a game of wordstacks than of us finding the killer.'

'Hey,' Con complained. 'And I think you're missing some of the nuance.'

'Is solving this really so much of a priority? You losing sleep over it isn't ideal,' Leo said.

'This isn't just closure, Leo!' Con said. 'It isn't revenge! *Trinity*, who do you think I am? We are living in a world where someone wanted our dad and his heir gone so bad that they were willing to die for it and I really don't think that the brains of the operation were blown up that day. And we don't know why! If the why happens to be our cousins wanting to take over the line of succession, or someone who wants whoever in power more than us for whatever reason, then they'll be back. They'll be back to kill you and Ada and Max and they've already proven that they can get right past all our defences. Which I honestly thought were overkill until recently, but now I don't hate the Helms' suggestion of putting spikes in the river.'

'That wouldn't stop someone from infiltrating a party,' Leo said.

'No, but …' Con sighed and hit his board with the side of his hand twice in quiet rhythm.

'I'd rather know too, but it's not happening tonight,' Ada said.

Con looked dejectedly at his boards. Flags sat next to motives sat next to precedents sat next to reports from Sword and Shield. Leo wished he could have used this supposed family bonding time for sleep instead. All it was doing was making him stressed about yet another thing that he didn't have control over.

'Shall we change the subject?' Danya asked.

'To what?' Ada asked.

'Books? Friends? Food?'

'Who Con's crushing on?' Leo suggested.

Ada and Danya laughed as Con turned red at a rate that would have made an ordinary bystander wonder if he was fatally choking. Con looked around anxiously, shushing them.

'What, the discussion of assassination was allowed to be public knowledge but your love of the week isn't?' Ada asked.

'That's not fair,' Danya laughed. 'He's been in love for at least three weeks before.'

'I have a sword,' Con said weakly, stepping behind one of his boards.

'That's what we need,' Leo scoffed. 'More regicide.'

It was at that moment that the doors of the library exploded inwards with the force of the fool's kick. Leo watched, mouth open, as the fool presented itself, limbs outstretched dramatically. It took him several strikes of the mental matchbox before he remembered what they'd been discussing and he rushed to help Con cover up his boards.

'What are you doing here?' Leo asked, trying to unbutton the cloak from his neck, a task made more difficult by the fact that he'd already thrown it over a board.

'I never have managed to quite decide on my favourite homicide!' the fool declared.

Leo bonked his head on the board. He hated the fool's songs.

'There's democide and senicide, patricide and androcide. I thought it might be famicide, but now I find me set beside, a gentleman so glorified, though totally unqualified, I think I am quite justified, in wisely choosing regicide!'

Leo dug the toe of his boot into the heel of the other to kick it off and into his hand with a dexterity that was shamelessly augmented by magic every morning. He then threw the boot at the fool's head.

The fool grinned at Leo as it hit, giving off the strong impression that it could have ducked if it'd wanted to. It waited a half second after it was appropriate then flung itself backwards as if from the impact, flipping over and back onto its feet.

'It is my very favourite of all of the words,' the fool said, still grinning widely.

'It could be worse, Polly,' Ada said. 'Its favourite word could be regiphilia.'

Leo threw his other shoe at her, but Danya caught it with a hasty 'Halt!' while it still touched the tips of his fingers. With a dramatic gesture and the simplicity of 'Vengeance', she used it to kick him in the head then set it on fire. With *one* word.

Magic demanded complete understanding and reverence; almost everyone Leo knew had to rely on whole sentences or even prayers to enact spells with multiple components. No one at the Academy had been such a show-off. Quite possibly, no one there had been on Danya's level. In a very real way, she was born to be Canticalica's Enchantress. Leo looked forward to the day she took over; Erwina, the current Enchantress, had been avoiding him for some reason. He didn't have time to worry about it.

'Danya!' Leo protested.

'Now you have to go to bed bare-footed,' she said. She stroked Ada's hair back soothingly, as if a) Leo's boot had actually got her, and b) Ada needed soothing, ever.

'There once was a king too poor to own shoes!' the fool sang. 'Everywhere he went, his feet would cut and bruise. And though this was quite a sight to amuse, it left the poor king in a state of the blues!'

'Retrieve,' Leo groaned, holding his hand out to catch his boot.

He was somewhat gratified when the fool watched it warily. Leo might not be able to cast complex ideas with such brevity, but he could find magic in most words. It had been a pretty significant edge over his classmates. Admittedly, he had the advantage of being royalty. Though every magician by definition was descended from the Empress, his bloodline could be traced back to her through multiple branches of firstborns and noble marriages. Of course, Ada liked to remind him that the idea that royal lineage resulted in stronger magic was the kind of thing that those in power liked to hear, regardless of its truth.

'That's probably conspiracy,' Leo said, in a matter-of-fact tone. 'I'm pretty sure you're not supposed to gleefully sing about the death of the king like a demented parrot with a rhyming dictionary. Con, you should arrest it.'

'I'm not going to arrest it,' Con said. 'I mean, I can't, for one thing. In eight months I could! But also I wouldn't, because I'm not an idiot.'

'You could try and get along better, you two,' Danya said.

'I am not the one singing about its death!' Leo said.

'You would be most welcome to, Your Majesty,' the fool said solemnly, bowing.

Leo genuinely considered it for a moment, but his spontaneous songs never rhymed and were kind of embarrassing. His dorm-mate back at the Academy had teased him constantly and good-naturedly about his habit of singing to his books as he ordered them or to the kettle as it boiled, or to just about anything when he couldn't stand the quiet. Sometimes even peaceful silence put him on edge.

'Could you just piss off, please?'

'Let it stay, Leo,' Danya said. 'No one else can beat me at wordstacks.'

Leo sat next to Ada on the floor again, hugging his remaining boot to his chest and trying to think of a word for what he was doing that wasn't "sulking". Ada raised an eyebrow at him, evidently not inspired to sympathise.

The fool sat in the chair next to Danya's and she dragged the end table between them. Leo, feeling like everyone thought he was being a bad sport and unwilling to do anything more sig-nificant about it, got onto his knees to reach the other end table and grabbed the velvet pouch of tiles to pass to Danya.

'Thanks, Leo,' she said, smiling.

Leo attempted to smile back. Danya gave him an encouraging thumbs up. Leo slumped back next to Ada, feeling like a monkey they were all training to be human.

He'd smiled when he was little; he knew that and Con had said so when confronted with the task of improving Leo's smile now, a task that Leo hadn't charged any of them with but which they all were devoted to. He smiled now, too. It was just when he tried to do it on purpose that it didn't work, and not being able to fake happiness was a pretty terrible quality in a king.

Leo hadn't really had friends when he was a child. He was a twin; what need was there to make friends when you'd shared a womb with one? Dicky had been fun until Con joined Sword and Shield and given up his place in the royal succession, though he'd always had a dorky standoffishness with other people and an interest in topics most people would consider deeply uninteresting. And there was Con, six years older and impossibly cool; then there was Ada when Leo turned three, their birthdays only a few weeks apart so that she almost seemed like a birthday present. There was an endless parade of courtiers' children, none of whom wanted much to do with Leo. Danya had been around and was just a year younger than Leo, but she was shut up in Lyric Tower until she was nine, so none of them encountered her until she had more freedom of movement.

Con made friends easily. Ada didn't, but she didn't seem to care—the only person whose friendship she'd actively sought out was Danya, and that had worked out for her. Leo didn't make friends easily, and he wished he did. By the time he was ten, his wish to be like Con had paid off in as much as he could do a passable imitation of coolness, so he had friends from then, but it was never *easy*. Well, he had people he could sit in the same room as and talk with. Real friends probably felt comfortable asking each other to hang out. He was lucky that teenagers tended to find "liking things" pretty passé because he could look bored or aloof with the best of them.

He thought (he feared) that he was just too anxious for smiling, that he had been for most of his life and that something was broken because of it.

There had been one child who stood outside the category of courtiers' children, but he was long gone. He hadn't been Leo's friend; he'd actually kind of scared him. Leo's comfort zone was in reading, following Con around and pretending to have magic before he did with Dicky and Ada. Raven had tackled him and stuffed frogs down his collar. Leo had hated it when Raven was even in the same room as him, because he was louder and messier than anything Leo had ever encountered. It had reminded Leo of leaving the castle boundaries and entering Praecentor's busy business district for the first time, when he couldn't cover his eyes and ears at the same time to drown out even a little of the cacophony and couldn't trust that he would be safe even if he *did* manage to dampen one of his senses.

Leo had breathed a sigh of relief when Richard had discouraged his fool's son from hanging around the family, despite knowing that it was a shitty, elitist move even then. Maybe it had done him some amount of good to be around a normal kid, one who didn't care if he was the king's third son, even if he didn't appreciate it back then. But he was still glad he was gone, even if the fool currently in the room with him was just as bad and didn't have the excuse of being a child.

'Tell me what you're thinking about,' Ada demanded, in a convincingly casual way.

Leo looked at her blankly, mind still ruminating on his assorted failures instead of being present in the room. She pushed his knee back and forth a bit and he got the message: she was at least somewhat in his corner. He was good at improvising, probably in no small part because of the threat of this question that was posed semi-frequently when one hung out with Ada for any measure of time.

She always seemed to time it when Leo was thinking unhelpful thoughts. Her demonstrations of love needed to be filtered and translated through several permutations before she would allow them to be seen, but they were there, if you knew where to look.

'I was wondering if someone could put magic in tattoos,' he said.

'Elaborate,' Ada said, tone haughty as though judging his performance.

'If you blessed the ink, or maybe sang while you were …' Leo pointed his finger at his arm and jabbed it a few times to represent the physical act of giving someone a tattoo, 'I can't see why it wouldn't work.'

'Tattooing is a fairly long process. You couldn't sing the whole time,' Ada said. 'Unless it was for something small. And you couldn't take it off; it wouldn't be like how you put on whatever charms you do of a morning.'

'What would be wrong with having extra agility or whatever permanently?' Leo asked. 'My gloves are charmed. I mean, I have to freshen them all the time, but—wait, what if you sang while you were making clothes?'

'You are making it incredibly obvious that you have never made an item of clothing right now,' Danya said, turning in her chair. Leo felt petty victory at having called her attention away from the fool. 'Look at the fibres in your tunic! Would you sing while you were knitting them together? Or while you were stitching it all up? What about while you're shearing the sheep or treating the wool? While you were raising the lamb?'

'That would be a seriously enchanted tunic,' Leo said.

'And don't get me started on armour,' Danya said. 'Would—'

'I'm gonna go ahead and not get you started on armour,' Leo said. 'I'll have a less contentious thought.'

'And a more interesting one,' Ada said.

Danya turned back around and started accusing the fool of stealing some of the tiles from the board, which had definitely happened. Leo looked around the library for inspiration.

'Okay,' he said, grinning at Ada and then fixing his eyes on the back of Danya's head, ready for her reaction. 'What if you could eat a magic cake …'

Danya enchanted every tile she had to fly at Leo's head, who only just managed to bat them away, laughing.

'Not one in the kingdom would believe me, if I told them I had heard the king in glee,' the fool sing-songed.

Leo's self-consciousness returned like the inevitable stumble of a wave back to the shore and he coughed. Danya threw a tile half-heartedly at the fool's forehead.

'Does anyone want a drink?' Con asked cheerily. 'I thought I might get us all drinks.'

'You have to be up at sunrise,' Leo sighed. 'And I should be too; I've got to meet Coral tomorrow and they have the whole,' he gestured vaguely, 'nature. Thing. They're a morning person. If I catch them early, they might not bite my entire head off.'

'Coral's nice,' Con protested.

'Not to me. I've been brutal on their budget,' Leo said darkly. 'If I'm blown up tomorrow, I mean, check to see if it was the previous guys first, but second suspect is Coral.'

'Too dark, Leo,' Danya said.

'Not dark enough, Polly,' Ada said.

Leo climbed to his feet and pushed Ada's head affectionately into the couch.

'Okay, no drinks,' Con said. 'Doesn't mean you have to go, we can …'

'I know you love me, but this display of desperation is honestly embarrassing,' Leo joked. 'Don't stay up too late. Or do, I'm not …' *your dad*, he nearly said. Yikes. 'Any kind of authority where you ragamuffins are concerned.'

'Let him go, Connie, he just used the word "ragamuffins". The poor idiot is clearly out of his mind with exhaustion,' Ada said.

Leo bowed ironically to his family and his nemesis and left the library for his rooms. The floorboards only squeaked twice and he wasn't even consciously thinking about where he stepped. Sure, he hated most aspects of his life, but at least he wouldn't feel like an outsider whenever he went to take a piss soon.

LEO STUMBLED, which meant that when Con shoved his shoulder with his own, he went down with the grace of a toddler. Con's sword hovered just above his chin and Leo smacked it away irritably.

'I see what you mean,' Con said. 'They *did* go easy on you. Or maybe they're all too cultured for real combat in the capital.'

'You're six years older than me,' Leo said breathlessly. It was cold on the ground, though Con had been right when he'd said that Leo would warm up once they got started. '*And* you've been training in Sword and Shield for eight years. And you're not even *trying* to use magic.'

'Magic's overrated in combat,' Con shrugged. He held his hand out for Leo to take. Leo glared at it for a second before he accepted the help up. 'And you're too old to be making excuses like that, Lee.'

'How do I get better?' Leo groaned.

'Well, there's this crazy thing that they've been teaching me called "you just train, dummy". It's pretty simple. What you do is you *just train, dummy.*'

Leo rolled his shoulders and held his sword in a ready position. Then he had the awful thought that he might have learnt everything wrong and needed to start from scratch.

'Am I doing this right?' he asked.

Con straightened from his stance and walked over. He compared his own grip to Leo's and shrugged.

'I don't think there's anything wrong with your technique,' he said. 'And you're not actually that bad. But I'm telling you right now that Ada would have a shot at beating you in a fight.'

'Yeah,' Leo sighed. Ada had been sneaking out to practice with Con since she was a kid, so that wasn't really the insult it might have sounded like to unfamiliar ears. But he would have liked to think that his own training could beat her "training" of sparring with Con when they were both free, which surely couldn't be that often. *At least he didn't say Dicky*, Leo thought. He didn't think his pride could take that hit.

'C'mon. Don't even try to think about magic; it's messing with your concentration. I'll slow down.'

Leo rested his weight on his back foot and held his sword with his relaxed right hand. His left hand provided balance in a position that was ready to cast, even though he was going to take Con's advice. It was habit and he wasn't going to try to retrain everything all at once. Con raised his eyebrow at Leo and Leo took that to mean that he should be the one to advance. He took one last steadying breath and sprang forward.

Con was moving slower, but it barely made a difference. He anticipated Leo's every move. He knocked the sword away harmlessly as it came towards him, following through with a strike of his own. Leo found himself relying on dodging the blows more than parrying them. Leo saw exactly how Con redirected his final thrust before he stabbed the point of his sword to Leo's belly, but he could do nothing about it.

'Aaaand you're dead,' Con said, lowering the sword's point. He tapped his finger against his hilt contemplatively. 'Maybe I should teach you forms. I don't know if that's allowed. Sword and Shield is protective of that kind of thing.'

'I'm the *king*,' Leo said. 'Why does that get me zero special treatment?'

'Aw, it gets you some,' Con said. 'You're allowed to see

secret documents.'

'Woo,' Leo said.

Con snorted with amusement at the complete lack of enthusiasm in Leo's voice.

'Do you really not see anything good about being king?' he asked.

'Oh, is the ban on me bitching about it over?' Leo asked, raising his eyebrows

'Absolutely not,' Con grinned. 'This is just a temporary ceasefire that we will not be telling Ada about.'

Leo stretched out his neck, rolling his head through the tight muscles as he tried to think.

'I'm third-born. My princely training was stand up straight and don't slouch when you're sitting, and when someone talks to you pretend like you really like them and don't embarrass yourself.' Leo met Con's eyes and pointed his sword at him. 'And then you joined Sword and Shield when Dicky and I were fourteen and Dad had to train up Dicky to be mini-him instead. And he had *no* time for me unless something I'd been doing for months without it being a problem was suddenly the worst thing anyone had ever done in the world and worth shouting at me about until I cried or shouted some secret back at him just to make him stop. Or both. And you seem to have forgotten, but pubescent boys feel a lot of shame and anger when they've expressed emotion, and I think he liked that. I think he liked that he could make me hate myself.'

Leo dropped his sword and took a deep breath. Con waited, not taking this opportunity to defend Richard like Leo had kind of been afraid he might. Leo took another breath, but it was less steadying. Every time he tried to say what was constantly bubbling in his mind, Con and Ada calmed him down, told him it was all alright and kept him standing. And maybe that was good. It was easier to prevent a breakdown than talk someone out of it once it had started. But he had no one to talk to. The thought of putting this in a letter to Dion when he now wasn't sure if their friendship had been more than forced proximity was mortifying.

'So I left for the Trinitas Academy, because he was starting to ask what the hell I was going to do with my life, because obviously I was supposed to have that figured out at sixteen. And he could be nice about it. He said that whatever I chose, he was sure I would be the best at it. One time he said that he'd still be proud if I chose to be a hairdresser because he knew I'd be the best hairdresser in the whole continent, and he would gladly tell the world that was a role worthy of a prince. And I think that was him being kind. It felt kind at the time. Like he believed in me. But I'm not sure, maybe it was a threat.

'But that's the thing, I was supposed to do something worthy of a prince, I was never supposed to be king. I don't know what I'm doing! And sometimes I actually get through a day and I think yeah, I managed that pretty well actually, and then that *fucking* fool comes along and does a stupid dance and performs a limerick about how pathetic I am and I have to *laugh* because if I shove it in a cannon and shoot it into the bottom of the Fluvius, the Consortium will send a new one and put Ada in charge in the Empress's name or something. I should probably look into how that works. But even reading the *word* fool makes me want to punch something.'

Con smiled at Leo sadly.

'I get it, Lee. I wanted to come to Dad's rescue when it criticised him too.'

'It's not about that,' Leo insisted, but Con's words were like a bucket of cold water thrown over his anger. 'I feel like if it didn't exist then … everything would be okay.'

His voice got quieter and quieter as he spoke. He suddenly felt very childish, more than the fool had ever made him feel.

'Everything?' Con asked, not even trying to hide his amusement.

'Yes,' Leo said, straightening himself to put his mask back on. 'I'm quite close to achieving Empire-wide peace, actually. I got a letter yesterday and the Empress wants to marry me and have all my babies. Every one of them. She said it wasn't even about my really great ruling that for some reason no one gets here, probably because it's above their comprehension, it's because someone showed her a scry of me and she thought woah, that guy is seriously hot.'

'That's why there's always flowers being delivered here!' Con said, smacking his forehead like it all made sense now. 'Please may I kiss your shoes?'

'How about you show me how to fight instead, like a useful soldier-brother,' Leo said. His grin felt a bit clenched. He wondered if it gave away how much he wanted to hit something with his sword.

'Okay, hot stuff,' Con said. 'Let's see what you've got.'

Half an hour later, Con insisted that Leo was improving. Leo was fairly sure that he was just being encouraging, but he also really wanted to accept the praise. Con left to shower before his curfew restricted him to his barracks, so there was no one to see Leo give up on standing and sit on the ground against a stone wall.

Or so he thought. A figure stepped out of the darkness and leaned against the wall too, though standing up. Leo recognised him as the man who had greeted him on his first night back in the castle.

'Wonderful work, Majesty,' the man said.

'Thanks,' Leo said dryly. He considered standing up, but it wasn't like the man hadn't already seen his indignity. He would stand up when he was more confident that his legs wouldn't shake. He dragged his sleeve across his forehead, hoping that he was one of those people who made sweating look good. He suspected he was not.

'I would have thought a king was above the need for advanced martial skills,' the man said. 'You're quite good.'

Leo gave the man a disbelieving look. He had won two points against Con and he thought he could attribute them to chance more than anything else.

'You are,' the man said. 'Sir Conrad is an exceptional fighter. You would be able to beat other Sword and Shield members, I'm sure.'

'Because they'd let me,' Leo sighed. He pulled the ties from his hair and shoved them in his pocket. His braids felt sweaty and constrictive, so he slowly pulled them loose.

'I doubt you need my reassurances,' the man said. 'You didn't answer my question.'

'You didn't ask a question,' Leo pointed out. He relented. 'I think any king should be able to defend himself, but it's probably more urgent to those whose predecessors were assassinated.'

'I doubt sword fighting would have been much of a defence against an explosion,' the man said, voice gentle.

Leo shook his hands through his hair, airing it out, then piled it into a bun on top of his head. The cool air against his damp neck was bliss. He probably didn't look very regal, but he probably hadn't while Con was kicking his arse either.

'It might not be an explosion next time,' Leo said. 'And the fool has tackled me four times in the last three weeks. I'd like to be able to defend myself against someone whose primary weapon is a pie to the face.'

'Has it done that to you?'

'No,' Leo said. 'I really hope it's not listening. It seems to come out of nowhere. Last thing I need is to give it the idea.'

'I promise I won't tell it,' the man said solemnly.

Leo huffed out a breath in tired amusement.

'What's your name?' he asked.

'You don't remember?' the man said, adopting an expression

of betrayal. 'Your Majesty, I know you're a big deal, but that's just not cool.'

'You didn't tell me,' Leo said.

'Mmm,' the man agreed. He examined the ground for a moment then sat down next to Leo, one leg extended, the outer one bent so that he could rest his elbow on his knee. 'Have you exercised so severely that you can no longer walk?' he asked. 'Because I won't carry you. I suppose I could fetch someone.'

'You're not very patriotic,' Leo said. 'But no, I'm fine.'

'Yet here we sit.'

'You don't have to.'

'I'm providing His Majesty with company. Improving my patriotism. How am I doing?'

In all honesty, Leo didn't know how he felt about being kept company. He hadn't been completely isolated at the Academy, but he was the kind of guy who had a few close friends, not the kind of guy who got along with everyone. Friends who didn't come to the funeral, but did write nice letters about it, so maybe not as close as he'd thought. Being back home, being king, he was getting used to people expecting him to treat them like they were friends and he thought he was doing an okay job at faking it. This was different somehow. Maybe because most of the people trying to get cosy with him were much older than his twenty-two years and this man was a peer, in age at least.

'I'm fine with sitting here alone,' he said. 'Consider your patriotic duties fulfilled. Unless you're actually here because you want some kind of favour, in which case I'm still fine with sitting here alone.'

'Majesty, you're very impressive,' the man said, with some condescension, 'but there isn't anything you could promise me that would inspire me to do anything for you if I didn't feel like it.'

Leo frowned at the man in confusion. The man smiled mildly

back. Leo had no idea if he was serious or not. *Everyone* wanted something from him. Leo didn't think that arguing this would make the man tell him anything, so he might as well pretend that he was the one person in the world who wanted to be around him without an ulterior motive. He looked forward again. There were flowers in a garden bed dividing a couple of walkways in front of him worth looking at and they'd closed their petals for the night. There was a lot of plant-life around, which was something Leo missed when he was away from home. He didn't want to think about how much it cost to maintain.

The man brushed his fingers along the back of Leo's hand to get his attention. He had it immediately.

'Are you planning to stay here all night?' he asked softly.

'What would you do if I said I was?' Leo said. His tone was dry, as if it was a joke. He didn't know if it was a joke.

The man shrugged. 'I don't have anywhere to be.'

The man straightened both his legs and directed his gaze to the flowerbed that Leo had been looking at. His clothes were good quality and fit well, but they weren't lavish. They were practically anonymous, the blue of them barely registering in the moonlight. Who was he? Staff wouldn't talk to Leo like this.

'I'm not. Going to stay out here all night, that is.' Leo stopped staring at the man and looked forward again. Why was he staring? *Don't be a fool, Dietrich*, he told himself. 'It's just a lot, you know?'

'Going to bed?' the man asked.

'Well, yeah,' Leo said. The air was starting to feel cold rather than refreshing, so he undid his bun and let his hair act as a kind of scarf. 'I've got to walk all the way there, which is just *so many* stairs, and then I've either got to bother the staff about a bath or clean up with the basin or just go to bed fully clothed, which is seeming like the most likely scenario right now. And I have to wake up early because I have a breakfast thing with a duke who is convinced *I* was responsible for the attack in order to take the throne. And then tomorrow is going to be another day of—'

Leo cut himself off. The man looked like he was actually listening, which was something of a change of pace, but that wasn't necessarily a good thing.

'I don't know why I said all that,' Leo said. 'I don't suppose you could forget it?'

'Probably not,' the man said. 'I can promise that I won't gossip about the fact that you may not have bathed after exercising, or whatever it is you said that has you looking like I've caught you stealing particularly important biscuits from the kitchen.'

'Thanks,' Leo said. 'I don't want to give you the impression that I … find it all a chore.'

'Honesty is an overrated trait,' the man said, nodding with an ironic half-smile.

Leo's lips twitched up a bit.

'I don't usually talk like that. It's probably just because I haven't been spending time with anyone my age, not since the Academy, when I could talk about anything and the worst that could happen was being called a dork or something.'

'*Are* you a dork?' the man asked.

'No, I'm actually very cool,' Leo said solemnly. 'I won a prize for how popular I was. They chanted my name at the ceremony. In all honesty, it was a bit much.'

The man laughed. Leo found that some of his energy had returned. He'd felt defeated before and hadn't even realised it. Talking, even a little, helped. Made him feel more normal. He climbed to his feet, bracing a hand against the wall to steady himself. The man got up with considerably more grace, but he hadn't gone from exercising to sitting on a hard, stone floor, so Leo tried not to let it bother him.

'It has been a pleasure, Your Majesty,' the man said, with a polite and unnecessary bow that seemed out of place after how they'd been talking. 'Good luck with the stairs.'

'Thanks,' Leo said dryly.

Leo watched as the man walked away in the direction of Lyric Tower. What was in Lyric Tower for anyone to go there at night? The library was its most notable feature, much vaster than the one in Leo's family's quarters. Well, that was its most trafficked area; the greenhouse at its peak was more striking if you were a fan of rare and magical plants. Leo only really went in there to visit Danya. None of those things explained why the man would be going there at night. Unless the man was part of the clergy, but surely he would have been less … cool.

Leo felt like an idiot. Why hadn't he insisted on knowing who the man was? He didn't know how he'd even go about asking anyone without giving the impression that he cared, which felt mortifying. He dragged his hands down his face and forced himself to set off towards his bedroom. The man was probably a courtier playing with making himself memorable to the king. Leo probably wouldn't even see him again.

6

LEO AND DICKY WERE at their most identical when they were a little older than Max. They were Dicky-and-Leo, all one word. The tailor fitted Leo in red and Dicky in blue in an attempt to distinguish them from each other, but when they got in the habit of stealing each other's clothes as a method of disguise, they each got the same new name of "boy".

Leo remembered Con sitting both of them down and recruiting Ada to find some distinction, any point of difference at all. Ada made constellations out of the faint freckles scattered across their noses. The next day, Leo and Dicky stayed in the sun for hours until new freckles over burnt red skin ruined her work.

They liked being identical. It was fun to confuse people, especially people who should know better. They liked to swap what few classes and activities they didn't have together so that they always had the ones they liked. Con had the best success rate at identifying them, though he couldn't describe how it was that they moved differently that clued him in.

One day, while using wooden swords to knock the heads off thistles in a gorge outside the city, Dicky suggested that they swap for good.

'Why?' Leo asked.

'If Dad and Con died, I think you'd be a better king than me,' Dicky said.

'You were born before me,' Leo said. 'The Trinity did that for a reason. I'll still help you, though.'

'Maybe the Trinity made us identical because they *wanted* us to swap,' Dicky said. 'Maybe it was the fourth god.'

'That's dumb,' Leo said. 'The unspoken god doesn't even count, people only ever talk about it when they want to justify why the vertling got something wrong.'

'That's heresy!' Dicky said.

'Your *bum's* heresy,' Leo said, and Dicky hit him with his sword until he took it back.

'I don't think you even *will* get to be king after Con,' Leo said later. 'Con's going to have a million babies and they'll all be ahead of us in line. You can do whatever you want.'

'But what *if*,' Dicky said.

'You could always make Ada be queen,' Leo said. 'And then none of us would have to worry about anything because the kingdom would have all burnt down.'

ADA ENTERED LEO'S ROOM without knocking, interrupting one of his few free hours. She plucked the novel from his hands and flicked to the title page. Leo's annoyance was slightly allayed by the fact that her finger kept his place between the pages.

'The Farmer's Haunting,' she read. 'That sounds terrible.'

'It is,' Leo said. 'I'm pretty sure he's being haunted by a snake. Not even a ghost snake, I think there's just literally a red belly in the wood pile.'

'Don't spoil it, I'll read it when you're finished,' Ada said. 'You do know that there are *good* books out there, don't you?'

'They're not as fun,' Leo said.

He handed Ada a bookmark and she examined the uneven stitches for a moment before slotting it into the book and taking a seat without commenting. Ada had made that bookmark when she was five or six, learning how to cross-stitch on small projects that didn't matter. Leo liked the reminder of an Ada who was unguarded in her feelings. If asked, he would say that he liked the reminder that Ada had once been bad at something. Something more tangible than the way being around people she didn't know and like was difficult bordering on intolerable for her.

'So, Your Majesty,' she said, making Leo's lips harden despite the fact that he should probably be used to the title now. It was different coming from family. 'You have begun your rule in quite a timid way.'

'I'm getting my bearings,' Leo said. 'I know you want me to revolutionise the country and then get started on revolutionising the Empire for dessert, but I have to defer to experts sometimes.'

'I couldn't agree more,' she said. 'Consider my expertise at your service.'

Leo had been expecting this. In truth, he'd been expecting it a lot sooner—it had been almost two months since the funeral. But the timing made sense. If she'd approached him earlier, he wouldn't have had space in his head to listen to her.

'Okay,' he said. 'Let me put on the table the fact that I have a cabinet made up of Hanna, Niklaus and Forster, as well as three lords and a lady you don't care about. I can't just lay down laws without getting a majority to agree with me.'

'Of course you can,' Ada said, waving her hand carelessly.

'Let me rephrase,' Leo said. 'I *won't* do that. Everyone in Cabinet has been doing this a lot longer than me and they know a lot more about the kingdom than I do. I'm not saying I won't listen to your advice, I'm just saying that I'm glad I have other people to vet my ideas.'

Ada narrowed her eyes at Leo for a moment, then nodded in reluctant acceptance.

'Besides,' Leo said. 'I can't imagine the fool's reports of me are in any way flattering *now*. The last thing I need to do is have it reporting back to the Consortium that I'm a dictator.'

'You say this as if its judgement of you is set in stone,' Ada said. 'If it knew you were acting on my advice, it would probably become your greatest champion.'

Leo looked at Ada flatly. She didn't take it back. Leo had trouble believing that the person who had recently capered around very distractingly in the background while he was attempting to thank the castle Shields for their work was capable of generosity. Ada liked to twist the fool's actions into being in Leo's best interest, possibly because it made Leo throw things at her.

'Go on, then,' Leo said, nudging Ada's foot with his own. 'Hit me with what I should be doing.'

'Make a seat in your beloved cabinet for a prevenient elder,' she said immediately. 'Our father's inability to consider them as a distinct group that deserves to make decisions on its own welfare was frankly bullshit.'

Leo's eyebrows went up. Ada's passion for prevenient issues wasn't the surprise; that was well established. It was the fact that she was placing this criticism at Richard's door when Leo hadn't heard of *any* country doing what she was advocating for.

'Glad we're starting with something small,' Leo said. 'Just changing the structure of my government, that's all.'

'It's step one,' Ada said.

'It's step … something,' Leo said. 'Hang on, back up, let's go back to this distinct group thing. The Empress landed here almost a thousand years ago. Everyone has *some* prevenient blood.'

'Do we?' Ada asked, with a look on her face like Leo had played the exact wrong card.

Leo hesitated for a moment, wondering if one of the classes Ada had missed out on for want of deer in the forest was genealogy. But even if it had been, it would have felt weird to claim prevenient ancestry when it wasn't there.

'No,' Leo said.

'And why is that?' Ada asked. 'After all, if things are *so equal*, then why would our family have gone out of its way to avoid mixing the races?'

'I don't think it's avoiding,' Leo said. At Ada's raised eyebrow, he sighed. 'No, look. Come on, who do you think I am, Dicky?'

'You bear a certain resemblance,' Ada said.

'I'm not saying it wasn't a choice, but I think our ancestors were ranking their marital choices based on magic, not race. It's only been legal to marry prevenient people for what, four hundred years?'

'Less,' Ada said.

'And magic is only passed down to legitimate children, so even though I'm *sure* descendants of the Empress were getting friendly with prevenient people way before they could get married, there's been a limited number of generations where there could be magical outcomes there. So yeah, a lot of magicians look a lot like us, but that's not out of racism.'

'Because we fixed racism, didn't we?' Ada asked. Her tone was saccharine, and it reminded Leo of any number of perfectly nice family gatherings that had ended with raised voices.

'Ada, did I not *just* say I'm not Dicky?' Leo groaned, letting his head fall back.

Ada didn't say anything in reply, so Leo lifted his head up, throat tight with the fear that he'd said something wrong. She was watching her hands, dragging her thumb nail along her opposite pointer's nail as if feeling for imperfections.

'Sorry,' Leo said.

'For what?' Ada asked. Her voice was steady, but she didn't look up. 'I'd take you over him any day. If it had been you in the blast, I might actually be sad.'

Leo frowned and he took a breath without knowing what he was going to say. There was nothing *to* say to that.

'I haven't even been crowned yet,' he said, instead of having a genuine conversation about their feelings. 'Can you suggest something a little less controversial?'

'I dislike the fact that it is controversial,' she said.

'That doesn't stop it from being controversial,' he said.

Ada looked up again, a dangerously intelligent look in her eyes.

'Subsidise the cost of disability aids, even partially. Offer incentives for professionals like doctors and teachers to work in smaller towns so that those people can access healthcare and education. Remove the tax break landlords get from owning multiple properties.'

Leo pointed at her, sitting up straighter.

'That last one sounded like it might actually generate money,' he said.

'So would the other two, eventually. More people would be able to work for higher incomes, which we tax.'

'I can't do "eventually" solutions yet,' Leo said. 'I'm listening, Ada. I just have negative money. I have to play by Dad's rules for a little bit longer.'

Ada assessed Leo for a long moment, then nodded.

'I will come up with some things that won't cost anything,' she said, rising from her chair.

It sounded like a threat.

Leo waited until the door was fully closed, plus a few extra seconds, before singing a quiet prayer for mercy. He didn't think the Trinity particularly cared about his fate, but it didn't hurt to keep them updated. Maybe it would give them a laugh.

LEO WAS FAIRLY CERTAIN that Galland and Abigail thought he was an idiot, and he didn't really have a way to prove them wrong. Not only had he not shadowed Richard around for more than a couple of days at a time since he was sixteen and left for the Academy, he also wouldn't have benefited from that in this instance. Catering and household management had been left up to Gisela. Leo had seen her at it, but he hadn't paid attention. He had always had full faith that she'd take care of it and (horribly) Richard had set an example that didn't rank it as important. He'd dearly love to ask one of his siblings to do it, but Con was busy with Sword and Shield and Ada would throw him off one of the towers. At eight, Max was probably a bit young.

'But King Leopold is not in the habit of throwing impromptu feasts, or even dinners,' Forster said slowly. 'Far be it for me to predict royal behaviour, but I doubt this will change.'

'It won't,' Leo said.

'It *should*,' Galland said severely. 'You put too much stock in schedules, Forster.'

This was such a true statement that Leo couldn't think of a response. It wasn't that Forster didn't allow for an amount of spontaneity in Leo's schedule—Leo was able to find hours here and there to recharge alone or catch up with his family and, despite his fears during his first week or two as king, Forster had never stood outside a bathroom with a watch in his hand. It was just that Forster unfailingly accounted for every minute that Leo was both on and off the clock. Leo was rarely late to things, and when he was he'd find that Forster had allowed just the right amount of time for whatever it was to go over. If it wasn't for the fact that most of Leo's appointments seemed to concern how little money they had available, Leo would have given Forster about three raises already. And he wasn't even crowned yet.

'I am the Royal Chancellor,' Forster said. 'That is the job.'

'"The job",' Galland said, making air quotes with his fingers and scrunching up his nose, 'is to make the king look good. King Richard was popular because he was endlessly generous with his time and his food.'

'Didn't that drive you mad?' Leo asked. 'It drove Mum mad. I would have thought …'

'Galland liked being a favourite,' Abigail said. 'It drove *me* mad.' After a moment, she added, 'Respectfully.'

Galland glared at Abigail. Abigail ignored him, instead looking at Leo as though they had a shared connection over this. Leo wasn't sure which reaction he liked less.

'I was capable of rising to the challenge,' Galland corrected haughtily. 'My staff are highly skilled.'

'Well, that's good,' Leo said in an attempt to get the conversation back on track without encouraging or insulting either of them. 'Because we've got the coronation coming up and it'll probably be as big a deal as the funeral, right?'

He chastised himself inwardly. That shouldn't have been a question. He wasn't ever going to be Richard's second coming—he wasn't Dicky—but he did need to be at least a little assertive.

'It will,' Forster agreed.

'We need more staff,' Galland and Abigail said in almost perfect unison.

Leo wanted to shake them until they absorbed the fact that there wasn't any money. He wanted to tell them that out of all the things on his plate—the finances, the pile of policies on Leo's desk so tall it was in danger of toppling whenever he sighed too heavily, the fact that his family's killers were still at large, for Trinity's sake—what order the courses came out was just *bafflingly* unimportant. He doubted that would do any good, but it might make him feel better. Instead he directed his gaze to the ceiling and considered the problem. Forster had warned him that despite the fact that he was ostensibly in the kitchens to discuss the coronation feast's menu and agenda, they'd both be taking the opportunity to bring their budgets up again. He hadn't told Leo what to say, because he never actually did that. Even when Leo asked for his advice, Forster mostly asked Leo open-ended questions and guided him into finding his own way. It was a good thing. It was also wildly inconvenient.

'How much time do we have?' Leo asked Forster.

'As much as you need, Your Majesty.'

Leo nodded and turned back to Galland and Abigail. 'Do you have a proposed run sheet and menu prepared?'

'You might not have anything to do, Your Majesty, but the staff will need the kitchen for dinner,' Galland said.

Of course, *of course* they'd hear that Leo was making time for them and take it to mean that he wasn't valuing *their* time. Leo met Galland's eyes and held them.

'Do you have a run sheet and menu prepared,' he repeated.

'Yes,' Abigail said, standing up and going to a drawer at the end of the kitchen immediately.

Leo didn't drop eye contact. It wasn't that he wanted to punish Galland for not taking him seriously, but … no, that was pretty much it.

He didn't like that neither of them had thought to bring the folder with them. It meant that they didn't think he would know to ask for it and that they hadn't intended to walk him through it if he didn't. But maybe that was paranoid or uncharitable. Just because he personally felt like he wasn't measuring up didn't mean that everyone around him felt the same. He wasn't really in the mood to take it in good faith though.

Leo slowly read over the paper in front of him. He could guess at most of the shorthand and knew the basic structure of the day thanks to Forster, but there were gaps. And the run sheet only covered the day itself, without any of the extra things that Galland and Abigail were asking for. He reminded himself not to treat his staff like the enemy.

'Okay, slow roasted wallaby,' he said, pointing at one of the menus. 'I take it that would be prepared earlier and free up someone on the day.'

'But then there are the sides,' Galland said, leaning forwards.

'Would there not be sides if we chose something else?'

'Well, different ones.'

Forster cleared his throat and leaned forward as well.

'Perhaps you could outline how many staff are required for each task, at which point,' Forster said. 'If you'll forgive my interest in scheduling.'

It was excruciating to do this, and yet undeniably necessary. It became clear very quickly that they *did* need extra staff, but with a number of adjustments, each of which seemed to cause Galland severe physical pain, they were able to at least reduce the impact. And after battling over food preparation and delivery with Galland came the decorations, cleaning and attending to various important people that Abigail was responsible for. Leo realised he was spoilt as he interrogated the two staff about the process of polishing silverware and whether tablecloths were better than bare tables. He didn't know how long it took to sweep Queen's Hall (and in fact hadn't realised that was even necessary with it out in the open). He had no idea what went into cleaning clothes. The most complex thing he could cook on his own was an omelette, and he'd never put any thought into what ingredients went into any of the meals he was provided with. On some level, he was aware that there probably weren't many kings who would know what to do with this kind of thing, but he still was frustrated. Galland and Abigail could very easily have been taking advantage of the gaps in his knowledge, but more than that, Leo felt whatever notions he had about his own self-sufficiency were deeply misplaced.

In the midst of their planning, the kitchen staff were forced to fill the room, as Galland had predicted. To their credit, they didn't make a fuss over the fact that Leo was there. A few times Leo heard a joke being cut off as if its teller reconsidered whether they wanted it heard, and Galland threw more than a few dirty looks in the two chefs' direction as they swore at the people moving around them, but this was easy enough to ignore. And Leo didn't hate the sense of something like normalcy. At least until the fool loped in like an emu with too many legs.

Leo flinched at the clamour of several heavy pans and their lids clattering to the floor, hand dropping to the hip where his sword rested. He didn't especially like wearing one all the time (it reminded him of his teenage years, when it had been fashionable to appear ready to duel at a moment's notice and when he and his friends would bare their blunted blades over just about anything, and he'd outgrown that), but being able to defend himself was the reason he could, at least within the confines of the castle, walk around and have his meetings uninhibited by guards dogging his every step.

The fool burst out from between a couple of servers who were trying to clean its mess up and took two great running strides before it leapt into a cartwheel over the table. Papers took flight as its palms caught on them and pushed them into the air. Leo stood, fumbled to grab them and didn't catch a single one before they fell to the floor. The fool grabbed Leo by his waist and flung him to the side so that it could pick up the papers itself.

Leo narrowly avoided crashing into a cook with a very sharp knife and drew in breath to scold the fool for pulling this kind of stunt in the kitchen of all places, when he turned and saw that the fool was very quickly and efficiently folding the papers into darts. The fool threw one and Leo watched impotently as the menu he had invested considerable time and effort into danced a lazy loop-de-loop before it fell neatly into the pot of soup the other cook was stirring.

'THAT'S IT!' Galland roared. 'OUT OF MY KITCHEN!'

'I SERVE THE KING AS WELL AS YOU!' the fool thundered back, its usually sing-song voice replaced with something deep and authoritative that more than matched Galland despite its motley. It did that sometimes, choosing from a catalogue of impersonations whatever would cause the most disruption.

'If you serve me, then do as I say,' Leo said as evenly as he could, 'and leave.'

'Your Grace, I could sooner peel off my face than leave this place!' the fool cried, sing-song again. It flung itself at Leo's feet, prompting a frustrated noise from the kitchen hand who found her path suddenly blocked.

'Perhaps we had better continue this another time,' Forster said calmly.

'Fine,' Leo said through his teeth. 'Fine.'

He wanted very badly to stomp on the fool's fingers, but he resisted the urge. He hated how he always had to choose the higher road. He had asked Forster, trying not to sound like a petulant child, whether they could perhaps get rid of the fool. Exchange it for another if it was absolutely impossible to do away with the institution altogether. Forster had been sympathetic (perhaps because Leo had been dripping wet at the time), but firm. Fools had absolute immunity. *Absolute*. There needed to be someone who could criticise the leadership of a country without consequence. They were the Empress's eyes and acted with her judgement. Apparently. Leo didn't think the Empress would push him into a fountain five minutes before a meeting that Leo was admittedly not looking forward to, but who was he to say? Leo privately thought that the Empress had been alive for too long and thought it was funny to make her descendants deal with mild to moderate humiliation to balance their Trinity-given right to rule.

'Well?' Leo demanded of the fool. 'Are you coming with me?'

It was the last thing he wanted, except for them both to remain here, disrupting people who were only trying to do what Leo assumed was a high-pressure job. Galland had spent a not-insignificant amount of time during their meeting appealing to Leo's emotions, telling him how food was the best way that people expressed their regard for one another, the *ultimate* way that a household was judged. Abigail had agreed that food was the obvious gesture of welcome but insisted that while a person whose environment was catered to would never notice what a maid did, one who was left with dirty towels and a foul-smelling room would feel more insulted than a person whose soup wasn't quite piping hot. Leo thought they both had good points even if he didn't like the energy they said them with and found himself more inspired than ever to avoid being a nuisance to the household staff if at all possible.

The fool lifted its head and smiled at Leo beatifically, then leapt to its feet. It bowed gravely, putting itself further in the way of yet more staff.

'Your Majesty, I would follow you to the bottom of the Fluvius River,' it said, eyes wide.

'Fine,' Leo said, turning on his heel and leaving. Forster remained, unfolding darts and arranging a time for a follow-up meeting. Unfortunately, the fool kept its word and followed.

'I would follow you to the tippy top of Mount Wroth,' the fool continued, affecting an exaggeratedly subservient posture at

Leo's side as they climbed the steps, the bells on its shoes jangling ceaselessly.

'That won't be necessary,' Leo said. 'I don't really like the cold.'

The fool erupted into hoots of laughter that the feeble joke, if it could even be called a joke, did not deserve. Leo winced. The headache he had been trying not to think about for the last two hours of pouring over cramped writing and listening to Galland's complete lack of inside voice was starting to become unignorable.

'I would follow you to one of Enchantress Danya's poetry readings,' the fool said.

'Ah, so you are in love with me,' Leo said. 'I'd wondered.'

At this, the fool started laughing again. If the previous not-joke had prompted it to the kind of laughter that would make someone three corridors away look around in alarm, the fool now howled in a way that could genuinely be mistaken for a noise of pain. When the fool took this production to the next level by falling over, clutching its sides as it trumpeted its completely fabricated mirth, Leo kept walking. If he was lucky, the fool would fall all the way down the stairs and someone would throw it in a laundry basket.

ON AN OMINOUSLY GREY MORNING, almost three months into his rule, etiquette stated that Leo and his family were well on their way towards being okay with the loss of their loved ones and Leo found himself, quite literally, in his father's shoes. They were too small. This seemed much worse than their being too big. They had always sounded big.

'You could always just wear your own, no one looks at shoes,' Con said, which was exactly the kind of thing Leo might have said if their positions were reversed and it was him wearing the shoes that fit perfectly.

'Hmm,' the tailor said.

The budget had been cut. Obviously. So, both Con and Leo were having some of King Richard's clothes tailored to them for the coronation, clothes that were older than Leo was and had been preserved carefully since Richard had started to make the buttons work a bit too hard. Despite not having magic to aid her, the tailor had been mostly successful, but while one could wear thicker socks if their shoes were roomy, shoes could not be extended if their wearer couldn't even get their heel all the way in. Leo didn't have the knowledge of how shoes were constructed to attempt intervening himself with magic, assuming that the tailor would trust anyone but herself with something of that nature.

'My own shoes are fine,' Leo said, feigning optimism in the face of the tailor, who should not have been as scary as she was.

Truthfully, part of him was relieved. He didn't want to hear Richard's footsteps everywhere he went. He had been plagued with frequent nightmares since he'd come home, and they often had the backdrop of heavy footsteps stomping carelessly over the creaking floorboards of the family's wing of the castle. It was a sound that indicated that Richard was home. It unnerved Leo when Richard was still alive and it *terrified* him now, even when there was absolutely no threat anymore.

'Hmm,' the tailor said.

'C'mon, Guin,' Con wheedled.

'*Hmm,*' Guin insisted.

Leo looked up at the ceiling and resented the fact that he still didn't know most of the staff's names by sight. Con couldn't know them all, but it often seemed like he did. Leo didn't think he'd know as many even if he had been living here the last six years. Con was just more social, more kind. More able to literally fit into their dad's shoes. Very little of this life came easily to Leo.

'Just make Leo's arse look so good that no one even thinks about his shoes,' Con said, struggling to keep a smile contained.

'The royal arse will look perfect,' Guin said. 'So will the legs, arms, neck. Guin does not want this spoiled by his shoes.'

'C'mon, Guin!' Con said.

'No! Guin will not come on! Look at this!'

She dragged a stool close to where Leo was standing with an awful screech of wooden leg against floorboards and hauled his leg up so that one foot was on it. Con smiled at him encouragingly, though Leo couldn't have said whether that was to inspire patience for the spectacle their tailor was making or if it was to congratulate him on his increased balance since they had begun training together. Leo wondered whether being able to not fall over backwards in front of a diminutive and bossy woman was worth the dignity he lost every time Con wrestled him into submission. He decided to take the win.

'This leg!' Guin said, gesturing emphatically, 'is a toothbrush! It is up and down and has some maybe useful roundness on top, that is what it is!'

'Thanks?' Leo said.

'But see!' Guin said. She put her hand under Leo's raised knee and lifted so he was forced onto tiptoe. 'I spy one single curve, do not tell me that you are missing the curve, Conrad.'

'I'm not missing the curve, Guin,' Con said. 'He doesn't wear heels because he towers over everyone as it is. Please don't put him in heels.'

'A king *should* be tall!' Guin announced. 'He should also have,' she backhanded Leo across the chest without looking, 'tits!'

'*Should* he?' Leo asked.

'Look upon this Conrad,' Guin commanded, striding over to Con. There was only one Conrad to look at, so Leo didn't struggle with obeying. 'This is a man for whom one must tailor. This is a man with legs!'

Con covered his mouth, which was absolutely ineffectual in obfuscating his badly repressed laughter.

'Leo has legs,' Con said, almost stammering around his laugh.

'He has toothbrushes!' Guin said.

'I'm not … I have *some* shape,' Leo said.

'You will have shape once Guin is done with you,' Guin said.

She strode over to Leo and he took his leg belatedly down from the stool. She took his hand in hers and pressed it earnestly.

'You will eat more before I have to dress you for your wedding,' she told him.

Leo nodded helplessly, choosing to procrastinate his horror about an inevitable wedding. The thing about being the spare twin all his life was that he'd always taken for granted that he could find love with someone who liked him as a person at some vague future point. But a king must have heirs, a thought that *also* horrified him. He was worse with kids than he was at dating, and that was saying something.

In the end, he was allowed to wear his own shoes.

TWO WEEKS LATER, Richard's clothes fit better than any other clothes Leo had worn ever had, but he couldn't shake the knowledge that he was wearing his dad's clothes.

'A smile for Guin?' Guin asked.

Leo gave her a reluctant smile. It wasn't even that he couldn't smile when he had to anymore, he just rarely thought to unprompted and it wasn't particularly convincing when he did.

'You and that Conrad share your smiles,' she said. 'And he uses them all up. Such is the way it goes with big brothers. You may take a couple just for yourself. He will not miss them.'

Leo attempted a wry smile, but his heart wasn't in it. That was a depressing idea, that his smiles would deplete his brother's and vice versa. Guin made a face like a displeased frog and he stopped trying.

She pulled Leo's shirt down so that it fit better beneath his jerkin. Her hands were cold on his sides and the fabric shifted in such a way that made him conscious of the fact that it hadn't been sitting right and now it was. She tucked him in and fussed with his cloak. One clasp sat on his shoulder in the shape of a thylacine and the other was a plainer gold button under his other arm, more on his chest than his side.

'You must learn smiling,' Guin said. 'For you are not so much in mourning now and you cannot perambulate the grounds looking like a fish. You have gold in your clothes, Leopold!'

They're not my clothes, Leo wanted to say. *That's not my name*, maybe. *I don't look like a fucking fish* was probably his most likely complaint. But unfortunately, none of his protests would be true, so he kept them to himself.

'They'll call me Leopold the Grim,' he said. 'Dad didn't get a "the". He was just King Richard.'

'Richard the Smug,' Guin suggested. She hopped off the step stool she needed to reach Leo's shoulders and pushed it away. 'No, you will not be getting cross. The ex-king was very smug and you know this.'

It hadn't occurred to Leo to get cross. That was one of the more timid adjectives someone could put next to his dad's name. He'd once heard a woman say that King Richard was the much more obvious reason that "dick" was an insult. He wasn't going to get cross with the woman who sometimes used pins on his inseam for calling his dad *smug*.

'Besides of which'—Guin knelt down to fuss with Leo's shoes, but this didn't disrupt her talking—'we are not discussing that man, we are discussing this one.'

Aren't we always discussing him, just a little bit? Leo thought.

'Why do you not use my fool?' Guin asked, though why she would want to claim ownership of the worst person in the universe, Leo could not begin to comprehend. 'My fool comes to me and says that you find it aggravating, why do you do this?'

'Because it aggravates me,' Leo said.

'No,' Guin said. 'This is not true. It is a very good fool. Now it! It has some tits on it!'

'No.'

'Yes it does, I have provided it with many clothings.'

'No, I wasn't—' Leo groaned. Leo might have more muscles too if he was constantly flipping all over the place. 'Yes, it has a more impressive chest than me, no I will not discuss its tits.'

'They are bountiful, Leopold.'

'*Guin.*'

Guin straightened. She dusted off Leo's shoulders, then his arms, then his back. She reached up and pinched Leo's cheeks, probably trying to get some pink into them.

'Ow,' he said dryly.

'My fool also sees the sun,' she said.

Leo resisted the retort. How on the blessed Trinity's name anyone could tell the colour of the fool's skin under all its clothes and paint was beyond him. Well, by seeing it down to its underwear to make new clothes for it, he supposed. Besides, his attendant was waiting with makeup as soon as Leo was finished with this, so he'd look … probably even more pale, actually.

He'd love to see more sun. There was a beer garden close to the Academy that he used to go to, sometimes with an optimistic bundle of papers that he didn't study. The owners had two dogs who meandered around and got fed way too much. Maybe Leo could arrange to have some of his meetings in the Queen's Hall, which wasn't so much a hall as it was a garden big enough to host extravagant events while still having intimate alcoves. He could at least have lunch there sometimes, surely.

Guin stepped back from her fine-tuning of Leo's appearance and clapped her hands together in satisfaction.

'You look like a violin. A very sexy violin. You are welcome.'

'Thanks,' Leo said, with about seventy per cent sincerity and thirty per cent bafflement.

'Do for me a face that is thankful and happy that you are being given a crown,' Guin commanded.

Leo's face, if anything, became blanker at this request. But okay, it wasn't like he could practice with anyone else. He tried.

'Okay, and less like you are about to cry now.'

Leo gave up and decided to think about something he actually would be thankful and happy about. He imagined the bishop, instead of giving him the crown, telling him that he wasn't allowed to be the king anymore and he'd have to go back to the Academy instead. Not only that he was being given a reprieve but that he was being forced into it.

He felt terrible for the imagining, but it still made him smile.

He was happy to be king—or at peace with it if not happy. He wanted this coronation. He was the best person for the job—the *only* person, because if Ada was queen and managed to avoid burning Canticalica to the ground on her first day, she would hate the bureaucracy even more than he did. And if the prospect of not being able to choose his own spouse depressed him, he didn't want to think about Ada not being allowed to choose Danya. Besides, while all his vague princely training of how to make small talk with important people hadn't prepared him for the state of the kingdom, he was handling it. He was *close* to handling it. He was just tired, and it felt hopeless sometimes. He knew from his studies that any class that he felt like he was bad at was a difficult one to endure.

'Okay yes, this is at least something,' Guin said. 'It is still not a good face, but it is better than this.'

Guin stood still and drew all the expression from her face. Even her eyes looked vacant. It was supremely creepy, and Leo was glad when she stopped.

'Do I really look like that?' he asked.

'No,' Guin said. 'Guin has better legs than you.'

Guin left soon after and Leo waited in the empty room for Sebastian to come make up his face. When no one appeared after a couple of minutes, he flapped his arms against his side like a penguin and turned to snoop through the drawers in the room. The furniture, like all the furniture in the castle, was the kind of old that made Leo nervous about breaking a hinge or something. He loved the castle, even loved the furnishing, which made it all the more heartbreaking that so much of it wanted replacing or repairing. There were linens in the cupboard, which wasn't very interesting, but as standing in an empty room wasn't either, Leo kept looking anyway.

'Gonna be late to my coronation because my face is naked,' he sang quietly. *'That's okay, I'll make the after party.'*

'Very dignified,' someone laughed.

Leo felt his entire body grow hot with embarrassment and froze. He tapped his fingers on the wood of the drawer he had just closed and tried not to sweat through his shirt. He didn't actually know how to control his sweating. It hadn't been covered at the Academy, which seemed a pretty huge oversight right now. He turned, not even sure who would talk to him so casually outside of his family.

At the door was the man Leo had met on his first night in the castle, then after his first training session with Con. He was dressed up for the coronation and he looked a lot less forgettable, though, clearly, Leo hadn't forgotten him in the first place. He'd looked out for him but had never seen him around.

'What are you doing here?' Leo asked.

'Your brother is convincing your attendant that it would be better for everyone if he took his break with him right now,' the man said, smiling wryly. 'But I'm actually pretty good at make-up, so …' He held out a wooden box illustratively. 'May I come in?'

'Uh,' Leo said, trying not to get distracted by plotting Con's gruesome murder. *Today* of all days, he had to make things awkward with the man who laid out Leo's underwear. There were thousands of people in this city. 'Yes.'

The man came into the room and gestured at a couch that had once been red and was slowly metamorphosing to pink in splotchy areas. They sat down, box between their hips but knees almost touching. Then the man scooted closer and they absolutely were touching.

'So,' Leo said, feeling awkward in a very specific, thrilling kind of way that he did *not* have time for. 'You're good at makeup?'

'Yes,' the man said.

He failed to elaborate. Instead he tucked tissue into Leo's

collar to protect his clothes. Leo waited. The man took the lid off a shallow wooden cup to reveal pale powder inside and chose a brush.

'How?' Leo asked.

'Practice,' the man said, grinning. He clearly knew exactly how annoying his reticence was. What was more, he *liked* that he was annoying Leo. Which felt kind of illicit, especially on the day of his coronation.

The man dipped his brush in the powder and lightly tapped it to shake the excess off. Leo kept his head still as the man dragged the brush in slow circles over his forehead, then his cheeks. The brush was impossibly soft and left his skin tingling. The man's dark eyes were focused, which let Leo look at him as much as he liked. He wanted to close his eyes to remove the temptation, but he couldn't seem to make himself.

'What's your name?' Leo asked.

'Still not telling,' he said.

'Why not?'

'Come on,' the man said as he put aside the pale powder and picked up a bowl of pink blush instead. 'Isn't the mystery sexier?'

It was lucky that the man was still dipping his brush in the powder, because Leo jerked and made a strangled noise and the alternative universe where it resulted in pink streaked across his face was not a flattering one. The man smiled.

'Sorry, was that a bit much?' he asked. 'Do you shoot conventionally?'

'No!' Leo said. 'I mean, no, it wasn't too much, but also yes, no, I'm not exactly aiming towards a particular kind of person; it's—'

'Hold still, Majesty,' the man said, rescuing Leo from his own words.

He was more careful with the blush than he had been with the foundation, caressing the brush slowly over Leo's cheekbones. Leo felt as though his body was blushing plenty without needing any extra help, but he hoped he wouldn't be during the actual event. Staying quiet and still seemed like the infinitely easier option when compared to trying to rescue his awkwardness with more words. He didn't speak even as the man put the brush away and replaced the lids carefully.

'Put this between your lips,' the man said, handing Leo a small square of dark pink paper. Leo obeyed. 'Wet them first,' the man said, slightly exasperated.

'This isn't my daily routine,' Leo said.

'No, you don't really need it. I don't trust you to keep still if I line your eyes, so you're done.'

'I can keep still.'

'I think you'd look like a fool, anyway. And we can't have anyone else knowing that you are one.'

'Hey,' Leo said. It didn't sound remotely scolding.

'Oh, he can smile!' the man said. Leo immediately closed his lips. 'I'm sorry, is that an illegal thing for a king to do?'

'No, I just,' Leo started. 'I'm shit at it.'

'I didn't realise it was a skill that one could be good or bad at.'

Leo frowned, because no, not for most people. He decided to demonstrate and smiled on purpose. He didn't like being conscious of the air against his teeth. He stopped pretty quickly.

'I take your point,' the man said. 'But that wasn't how you smiled when you were thinking about how incredibly funny I am.'

Leo felt his lips move slightly upward, but he was thinking about it too much to do anything more than that.

'I thought you had a jester or something,' the man said. 'Why not have it tell you knock-knock jokes until you're used to it.'

That was an awful thought. Leo could only imagine what kind of jokes they would be. He didn't actually like getting his feelings hurt as a matter of daily business, funnily enough. He also didn't like that he couldn't just say "hey, stop hurting my feelings" to someone who was specifically paid to do it. By him, no less.

'I think I'll manage.'

The man finished assembling all the makeup back in its box and pulled the tissues from Leo's shirt. Leo watched his hands as they curved into a resting position on the box.

The man met Leo's eyes. He cocked his head to the side like a bird and his lips parted as though he was going to speak but then he closed them again. A breath later, he said, 'Don't trip, Majesty.'

'Thanks,' Leo said wryly. And, because he wanted to be able to find him and because he really did want to know, mystery be damned, 'What's your name?'

'I *have* told you before,' the man said. 'I just wasn't as pretty then.'

Leo frowned, uncertain. He'd been away for six years. Almost all his old friends had moved on to try and find some other rich person to marry, or at least were telling their parents that that was why they were out socialising in cities as far away from home as possible. The ones who remained he hadn't known since he was sixteen and he had been terrible at keeping in touch with. He'd sought out a couple, but after an awkward lunch he realised the only thing they'd had in common back then was proximity, which depressed him. But he wasn't so bad at friendship that he could have forgotten someone like this if he'd known them well enough that he should remember their name.

'I'm sorry,' Leo said.

'You're late,' the man corrected, with an amused smile.

Leo yanked back his sleeve urgently to look at his watch, which he had also inherited from Richard. He wasn't late, but yeah, he should go. That had nearly made him panic. He stood and hesitated, looking at the man, who had relaxed into the couch, arm thrown along the back.

'Don't worry about me, Majesty. I have a seat reserved. I suppose you do as well, but yours is slightly more pressing.'

Leo didn't know what to say, so he settled for nodding.

'Oh,' the man called out, just as Leo was stepping out of the room. Leo turned back. 'Happy birthday, Majesty.'

Leo attempted a smile that definitely didn't feel like one. It hadn't been his idea to combine the two events, but it was easier on the budget and his comfort to have one instead of two. He left the room, wondering exactly how it was that the man managed to make his title sound like a condescending pet name.

TWO WEEKS AFTER his mercifully uneventful coronation, Leo backed out of the King's Hall silently when he saw that the fool was in there, performing a song he probably didn't want to hear the lyrics of. The melody was catchy and the courtiers clapping a beat around the fool seemed to be enjoying it, but Leo didn't trust the fool to be singing something innocent or to not adjust its lyrics to torture Leo if it caught sight of him. So, instead of heading in for a snack he would only be eating out of boredom anyway, he set off in a random direction. He had the rest of the day off and didn't quite know what to do with himself. He made his way out of the castle and into the brisk, sunny afternoon. He loved Erstus in Praecentor. After the last few months, the spring warmth was more than welcome. He swung around to the stables with the vague idea that he might say hello to his horse, even if he wasn't really dressed for riding. He hadn't ridden often at the Academy and hadn't taken Korbinian with him to do so, which meant that he wasn't in the habit anymore. Not that he really had time, but he could at least brush Korbinian sometimes, if only so the silly, old thing got some individual affection.

The stables smelt like they always did and awoke a vivid memory of hiding in Con's first mare's stall when they were kids. Leo would have been about five and awed by Con's eleven-year-old coolness, and Dicky and Ada had been left behind with a nurse. It was freezing, probably the middle of Eltus, so there hadn't been the distant chatter of staff that surrounded Leo now. There had only been the gentle sound of the horses breathing and the faint smell of manure that lingered even in the clean stalls, layered over with the stronger smells of hay and leather and horsehair. It was peaceful. Leo and Con had sat on the brick of hay in the stall and hadn't spoken. Not until Leo had asked if Richard was going to throw Gisela out of the castle.

'That'd almost be funny,' Con had said darkly. 'It's her castle, technically.' There had been a pause while Leo tried to figure that one out. It hadn't made sense until years later, when he learnt that his dad had married into his rule. Then Con said, 'Nothing's going to happen, Lee. It never does.'

'But what if it did?' Leo had pressed.

'I don't know. Maybe we'd go with Mum. Stay with her, I mean. Maybe we'd run away.'

Leo hadn't understood this, either. Their dad was the fun one. He hadn't seen the conflict enough yet to realise that the games and treats weren't worth how he treated them when he wasn't in those infectious good moods. It hadn't made sense that staying or leaving with their dad wasn't an option.

Then Con had lifted Leo up onto his hip so that Leo could touch the mare's soft nose. She had nibbled at Leo's hair and Con had said that was what he got for having hair that looked so much like hay. Con's hair was brown, unlike the rest of his siblings. Not even quite like their mother's.

Leo walked slowly down the stable's aisle, wondering just when he'd stop reliving memories that didn't matter anymore. When he'd move on. He was done with childhood; it seemed unjust that it continued to follow him.

When he saw a small, blond head crouching in one of the stalls, for a second he thought he was still in his memory. But it was just Max, sorting a collection of rocks into three piles.

'Hey,' Leo said.

Max jumped despite Leo's friendly tone. His hands were tight around two rocks and he looked at Leo with wary defensiveness.

'Hello,' Max said.

'What're you doing?' Leo asked, leaning his elbows on the top of the stall door. There wasn't a horse inside, which left plenty of room for all the other random things that Max had accrued. Besides the rocks, there were old horseshoes lined against the wall, wilted flowers, three boots with dirt and sticks in them, some brassy jugs and vases of various sizes and a collection of sticks that were either smooth and even or gnarled and twisted. There was also a small cart that Leo remembered from his own childhood, perfect for transporting similar odds and ends.

'Nothing,' Max said. Then, 'Sorting,' he relented.

'Do you want help?' Leo asked.

Max stared at his rocks for a few long seconds.

'Okay,' he said. 'But you can't mess anything up.'

Leo opened the stall and only hesitated for a second before sitting down cross-legged next to where Max crouched. The straw would brush off.

Max pointed to one of the piles. 'Those are quartz,' he said. 'They might have gold in them.' He pointed to the next pile. 'These are pretty, and sometimes pretty ones are worth something. And these ones are ones that I thought were good but actually suck.'

'Okay,' Leo said. He picked up a smooth, green stone. 'Pretty?'

Max examined it with haughty authority.

'Yes,' he said. 'But you can't just decide it like that. You have to be careful.'

Leo nodded and picked up another rock. He took his time looking at it, not daring to peek at Max except out of the corner of his eye. He'd learnt over the last few months that Max was independent and resented being talked down to. Asking how he was feeling only resulted in a dirty look. He only rarely accepted help, and when he did it was usually with the air of someone who was doing his helper a favour by letting them feel useful. He reminded Leo a lot of Ada, which made sense. Con looked after Max more (even with his Sword and Shield duties), but Max looked at Ada like she held the answers to the universe. Leo privately thought Ada was a little scared of him.

'I like this one,' Leo said, showing Max a dark one with a few brown speckles. Max looked it over carefully.

'You can have it,' he said. 'For one init.'

Leo struggled not to laugh. 'I don't have any money on me. Can I pay you later? Most places seem to accept my word.'

Max nodded.

'Are you saving up for something?' Leo asked. 'Do you need more pocket money?'

'I don't want pocket money. I have rocks.'

'Well, sure, but—'

'All I want is dumb stuff like lollies. And you don't have money, so I'm finding my own. There could be a hundred term worth of gold in my quartz. Maybe two, I don't know.'

Leo looked at the jagged white rocks. He doubted any of them would have gold in them, but he remembered Richard saying something similar to him when he was younger. Richard had liked to point out all the things that made the kingdom of Canticalica so prosperous, things that Leo was sifting the truth out of as subtly as he could so that Hanna wouldn't look at him like he was an eight-year-old sorting quartz in a stable.

Max shouldn't have known about their money difficulties. When Richard was in charge, it seemed like only the heads of avenues knew. Con and Ada hadn't, which said a lot. But now that Leo was king, now that whatever consequences there were to telling seemed less significant than they had under Richard's rule, whispers were spreading that maybe Canticalica wasn't as wealthy as it claimed. It scared Leo. If their debtors thought they couldn't make payments, they might panic and ask Leo to pay back the full amount immediately.

'We have money for you to have lollies,' Leo said gently.

'I don't think there's all that gold in *these*,' Max said, shaking his head dismissively. 'I have lots. Coral is going to crack them open for me and I'm going to let them have five per cent of the profits.'

'That's smart,' Leo said. 'But we have enough to—'

Max looked at Leo, challenge in his eyes. Leo fell silent.

'I'm not giving you a percentage just for sorting,' Max said. 'I gave you a discount on your rock.'

'Thanks,' Leo said.

He felt like he should be fixing this, but he didn't know how. What was this relationship even supposed to look like? He knew he wasn't Max's parent, but Max didn't *have* parents anymore and it couldn't all fall to Con. Con couldn't be around most of the time anyway. Leo was too young to have guardianship over an eight-year-old. He thought he was too young to have custody of a country too, but that was another matter.

'How are you feeling?' Leo asked, even though he didn't expect an answer.

'I miss Mum,' Max said, voice defensive.

Leo paused in the motion of picking up a quartz rock, then made himself move naturally again.

'Me too,' he said.

'Not as much as me,' Max said. He dropped back from his toes onto the floor of the stall and hugged his knees to his chest. 'No one does. They all just think about Dad and Dicky all the time.'

'Yeah,' Leo said, unable to argue with that. 'She gets forgotten a lot, doesn't she.'

'Yes,' Max said.

Leo put the quartz down and put his hand on Max's shoulder.

'Do you want a hug?' he asked. Max shook his head. 'Do you want to talk about her a bit?'

Max took a big breath and nodded. He didn't speak. Alright, Leo could say some things.

'She had a really nice laugh. And she laughed a lot. It felt good to tell her jokes because she was always ...' he trailed off, kicking himself for nearly saying "laughing" as if he wasn't a good speaker. Why did he care about that with Max? He shook himself and continued, 'And she listened, like you were worth all of her attention. Mostly.' If Richard wasn't in the room.

'You don't tell jokes,' Max said.

'I mean, I guess I'm more for wry comments than actual jokes, but I know some,' Leo said.

He looked up at the empty hooks on the back of the stall door and thought. When his mind spun like a carriage wheel overhanging a cliff without any traction, Leo thought, *Oh Trinity, I don't know any jokes*. Was he really that miserable? No, okay. He took a breath and let his mind slide along associations in the calm manner he did when he was in an exam or on the spot trying to make a political call. It was a relief when something snagged.

'Okay,' he said. 'It's long, but it's worth it:

'There were these triplets who had lived their lives saying all the right things and dressing the right way—completely devout to the Trinity. They were like if Danya had never been corrupted by Ada, but even more. So, on their twenty-seventh birthday, the Trinity comes before them and says they'll grant them each three wishes. The first triplet says, "I wish I had my own kingdom," and the Trinity makes her a queen. The second says, "I wish I had the most beautiful wife in the world," and a really hot woman pops out of nowhere and clings to him. The third says, "I wish my right arm always spun around," and that happens.

'Then, the first wishes for a library full of every book ever written, the second wishes for a huge house on a beach, and the third says, "I wish my left arm always flapped up and down". The first and the second triplets are looking a bit weirded out, but whatever. So, the first uses her final wish for a dog who will live as long as she will, the second wishes for, uh, the ability to always think of good jokes on the spot, and the third wishes that she was always jumping up and down.'

Leo paused for a moment to build suspense. Max had a small, anticipatory smile.

'Okay?' Max said.

'So, the first and second triplets are pretty happy with their wishes but they can't go enjoy them until they figure out what was going on with the third triplet's. She turns to them and says, "Guys, I think I messed up."'

Max did not laugh. He regarded Leo for a long moment, as if this joke required critical reassessment of Leo's entire character. Leo attempted to prompt Max into laughing with an unconvincing smile.

'Don't tell that joke again,' Max said. 'It's okay that you're not funny.'

Leo opened his mouth to protest, then gave up. He couldn't defend himself when he thought the height of comedy was a pun and his mortal enemy was someone who, by all reports, knew every joke in the book and plenty of its own as well.

'Don't you have to go tell the kingdom what to do?' Max asked.

'Are you trying to get rid of me?' Leo asked, a bit hurt. Okay, so his joke was bad. He didn't think it was *that* bad.

'You're usually too busy to hang out with me.'

Ouch. Leo didn't know how to respond to that. He didn't even know how to change the subject and keep spending time with Max now that that had been put out there. He felt like if he protested too much, Max would think he was insincere and just here because he felt bad. Leo probably would have thought that at Max's age.

'I guess I'm usually pretty busy,' he said, shrugging a shoulder in an almost casual manner. 'But I have the afternoon off and I want to hang out with you, if you're okay with that.'

'You don't have to,' Max said.

'I want to,' Leo repeated. Mostly. He felt pretty awkward. He grasped for his number-one way of diverting attention from himself: putting it on someone else instead. 'Want to go bother Ada?'

'I don't know,' Max said.

'We could get lollies first?'

'Ice cream,' Max said.

It was a nice day, but in a spring, wear-a-scarf kind of way.

'I don't even know if anywhere would sell ice cream this early in the year,' Leo hedged.

'I know a place,' Max said.

Leo gave Max two thumbs up instead of answering. His teeth felt like they were chattering already.

THE ICE CREAM WAS PRETTY GOOD, even if Leo had to suck his cheeks in in an effort to warm them in between licks. Max bit into his unconcernedly. Leo was pretty sure he used to be able to do that too, but it felt like a long time ago now. He also felt like Max climbed the stairs leading to the castle easier than him. Twenty-three felt like too early to be feeling old. He didn't usually, but Max's youth and the unfamiliar exercise of walking around in search of ice cream had tired him.

At the foot of the internal stairs, Max looked up at Leo.

'I require a piggy-back ride,' he said solemnly.

'No way,' Leo said. 'You don't seem tired at all. I am a million years old and my calves are killing me.'

'You never give me piggy-back rides,' Max complained. 'Con does.'

Leo stared at Max. 'You're manipulating me,' he said suspiciously.

'What does "man … manplation" mean?' Max said, eyes too wide for actual innocence. The kid had an advanced vocabulary. Leo had heard him call a flock of magpies "rambunctious" a couple of weeks ago. 'Pleeeeaaaase,' Max said.

'Fine,' Leo sighed, dropping to a knee.

Max grinned, a full, kid-grin that contained the sun itself, and Leo felt okay about his decision. Then Leo stood up with his new burden and felt less okay about it. Climbing the stairs did not improve his perspective, but Max provided cheeky encouragement the whole way. Leo was about ready to crawl on his hands and knees by the time they reached Ada's favourite sitting room and he could put Max down.

'I feel so refreshed and happy,' Max said, with another infectious grin.

Leo wiped the sweat from his forehead with his sleeve and laughed breathlessly.

Max opened the door and they found Ada lounging, a book held loosely in her hand and her head tilted suspiciously in their direction. Their arrival had been loud enough to break through her focus, which truly said something—when Ada was reading a book, the world could crumble around her and she'd insist on it waiting until she finished the chapter before she was asked to react.

'What do you want?' she asked.

'Leo doesn't know how to be around me on his own,' Max said.

'Max, that's—' true, unfortunately. Leo wiped his forehead free of sweat again. 'That's just not what you say after someone carries you up a million stairs.'

'What makes you think that the addition of my company will make this any easier?' Ada asked.

'I was actually thinking, because Max said he's missing Mum, that maybe we could just ... talk about her a bit. Con's obviously busy, but I thought it could use another sibling.'

'Oh,' Max said.

'Oh,' Ada agreed.

Leo crossed the room shaking his limbs out and then sank into an armchair that had seen better days. Max took the one next to him, crossing his legs in it. His expression was wary, like he wasn't sure how this would go. In all honesty, neither was Leo.

'Don't tell your joke though,' Max said.

'I wasn't going to,' Leo said. *Last* time he'd told that joke, people had laughed. 'Maybe we could share a memory of Mum.' Both Ada and Max looked at him expectantly and Leo realised he would have to go first. 'Like how she really loved swimming. I remember floating in the Fluvius when I was really young with her hand under my back. And she was talking to me, but I couldn't hear half of her sentences because the water kept getting in my ears. I don't think she was saying anything important, because I just let that happen and listened to the way her voice distorted around the water.'

Max smiled sadly. Ada looked like she was thinking very hard about what her own story would be. Her success was visible when she found one. She put down her book and sat a little straighter, legs still draped along the divan.

'She used to sing like you do,' she said, nodding to Leo. 'Just about what she was doing, and they never rhymed. Except for the ones she borrowed from musicals. She sang that one about boiled eggs and toast every time we had that for breakfast.'

'I forgot about that,' Leo said. He frowned. 'How did I forget about that?'

'Probably because you weren't here,' Max said impatiently.

'Probably,' Leo said faintly. 'It was just my habit at the Academy. I got introduced as "the guy who sings when he's nervous" once. And it's not even a nervous habit, I don't think. It's just when it's too quiet. Mum wasn't nervous when she was opening our eggs for us or whatever, was she?'

'I don't know,' Ada said. 'She put forward a very cheery front, but I think we all know that it wasn't …'

Leo looked at Max. Surely he didn't know. Ada caught his confusion.

'He was getting worse,' she said, and just like that they were doing what Max had said and talking about their dad instead of their mum again. 'Less careful. I got the impression that he thought he was justified in his tempers. More so than he used to be.' She looked away at the wall, staring at it like she was calculating something based on a formula she had long since memorised. 'I never really thought he liked her, but I was starting to think he hated her. I'm not even sure he liked *owning* her anymore.'

If Con had been there, he might have said something to moderate Ada. Leo was never sure how much to believe Ada about, well, anything, but he really wasn't sure when it came to emotional things. She was dramatic in a way that didn't necessarily cohabitate with truth. Leo didn't think she lied—it was just that she saw things in a high contrast world of vivid colours that didn't always correspond with subtleties. She was a glass fortress. She was nineteen.

'He didn't …?' Leo started to ask, but then he found it difficult to articulate exactly what it was he wanted to know.

'No,' Ada said, interpreting his aborted question easily. 'I think he wanted to, sometimes. But by holding back from physically hurting her, or us for that matter, he was "a good guy". I feel …'

Suddenly, Ada's sharp detachment seemed very brittle. Her

expression cracked; her lip trembled briefly before she sucked it into stillness. She took a breath, staring forlornly at the wall.

'I feel very petty complaining about him, considering other people's lives. I keep expecting Danya to tell me that I'm spoilt.'

'Yeah,' Leo agreed hoarsely. 'I couldn't. Before.'

Whenever he had thought about talking to a friend at the Academy, whenever someone had shared their own baggage about their family and he'd had an opening, the words had stuck in his throat. When he thought about putting it into words, he had no idea how to articulate what the experience had been. *My dad ignored me when he was disappointed in me, and it hurt my feelings.* It sounded pathetic in his head, and he couldn't bear for someone else to agree that it was. *It was proper ignoring, like he didn't like me anymore, and something that had been fine one day would trigger it the next.* And it had felt like a betrayal to complain about his family. Like giving up a secret, and for what? Talking about it wouldn't have made any difference at all. *Do you still like me? Please like me. I promise I'll be good.*

They were quiet for a few moments, then Max said, 'We were supposed to be talking about Mum.' His face scrunched up and his shoulders moved with quick breaths. 'You aren't even sad they're dead. You're just glad you don't have to deal with Dad anymore.'

'Max,' Leo said, horrified. He got up from his chair and crouched in front of Max's. 'I would give anything for them to still be here. Both of them. Dicky too. I have a lot of complicated feelings about Dad, but—' Nope, he needed to stop talking about Richard. He didn't know what to read into the fact that Max didn't seem interested in their dead brother at all, but that was a problem for another day. 'I miss her so much. She knew the names of all the birds, did you know that?'

Max nodded, still looking distressed. Ada sank to her knees next to Leo.

'Do you remember how she used to fix the flowers?' she asked. Max nodded again. 'And sometimes she'd go out and pick new ones, because she didn't agree with what the staff had put out.'

'She used to choose my clothes too, because she did it better,' Max said. His voice wobbled, but he was being drawn into their memories. 'And my food, and my classes, and my friends. She was always there.'

'Your friends?' Leo asked, reading something into that that he wasn't sure was there.

'I was her best friend,' Max said.

There were tears in Max's eyes, so Leo held out his arms and caught him when he slumped into a hug. He looked at Ada over Max's shoulder as he held him. Ada looked lost.

'She needed a reason to …' Ada said in a whisper, 'live, I guess.'

There had been times in Leo's childhood where he had felt forgotten. He would walk around the castle pretending to be a revenant looking at what it would be like if he wasn't there, imagining that it was exactly the same as it was when he *was* there. During the brief times he'd seen his family while he'd been a student at the Academy, he'd gotten the impression that Max was Gisela's pet and he'd been embarrassingly jealous. He couldn't imagine the grief Max must be feeling, but he was suspecting for the first time that maybe being a pet wasn't all that much better than being a revenant.

10

LEO MISSED MANY THINGS about the Trinitas Academy. He missed the heated, running water in every room. He missed that his only responsibility had been to complete homework, and that he could always talk his way out of punishment if he neglected to do it. He missed that *people knocked on his door before entering.*

'One day, you're going to walk in on something you don't want to see,' Leo told Ada sternly. The fact that he was playing a card game against himself while fully clothed and cross-legged on his bed was irrelevant.

'By all means, I can wait outside while you eject your hidden lover from beneath your bed,' Ada said. 'I might have knocked, but I heard you singing, which I felt was safe to interrupt.'

'You could *pretend* I have the option not to let you in,' Leo said. 'You're a princess, are manners too much to expect?'

'Oh, Empress *wept*,' Ada sighed.

She walked out of the room and closed the door. She opened it again, knocking as she did.

'Happy?' she asked.

'You do realise that was just coming into my room uninvited with a bit of extra noise, right?' Leo said.

Ada ignored this and came to perch on Leo's bed. She swapped two of the cards on his blanket around. Leo threw the cards in his hand at her, imagining wistfully that one might give her a paper cut. None of them even hit her.

'What were you singing about?' Ada asked, picking the cards up as if Leo had been dealing her in. 'Were you praying like a good little boy?'

'Yes, praying that you would respect the sanctity of my personal space,' Leo said.

Ada scoffed, eyes on the cards.

'I don't really *pray*,' Leo said. 'I just like to keep them updated.'

'The Trinity?' Ada asked. 'Oh Leo, the Trinity couldn't care less about you. You're very boring.'

'It's more for me than them,' Leo said, leaning back into his headboard. 'I figure out what's worth telling someone by telling them. You keep a diary, you know what I'm talking about.'

'A diary is a much better way of doing it,' she said. 'My eventual biographer will be very grateful that I wrote so many hilarious and insightful things down.'

'If they can translate it,' Leo said.

'Which they will need to do in order to be worthy of writing my legacy,' Ada said, unashamed to be a fully grown adult who still wrote her diary in code.

She made as though to draw another round of cards from the draw pile but stopped with her nails an inch above the bed.

'No, we don't have time for games,' she said, dropping her hand with no regard for where the cards landed. 'We're going out.'

Leo grumbled as he laced his boots, if only so Ada wouldn't get any ideas about making this a habit. He didn't think she was fooled, because he *was* going along with it after all. Leo recalled that his old dormmate Dion had a sister. Dion used to write long letters to her when he needed advice. Leo couldn't even imagine admitting to Ada that he appreciated her giving him an escape from the castle, let alone anything deeper.

PRAECENTOR OCCUPIED THE ENTIRETY of a decent-sized river island on the Fluvius. Very few people living remembered that it had previously been called Hump Island, and most of those who did had probably been cheerfully informed of this by Danya, who had read every book related to the city. Maforc Castle was placed almost in the centre, at the top of the hill that gave it its name, and the city staggered downwards around it. It was Canticalica's capital because Maforc was where the monarch ruled from, but their one other town that could generously be called a city had overtaken its population about a century ago. There just wasn't room to expand further on the island, and the small town that had cropped up on the bank of the Fluvius didn't benefit enough from being close to the city to make it popular.

Ada and Leo walked out of the castle and into the busy streets. Leo glanced around but couldn't see any Shields tailing them. He hadn't brought a hood with him, and while he also hadn't brought his crown, he wasn't exactly inconspicuous.

'I'm kind of shit at glamours,' Leo said.

'Of course you are,' Ada said, stride not slowing. 'You don't like to look at your face, so how could you know it well enough to disguise it? I find your modesty absurd, by the way. We would have been raised to royalty for our cheekbones alone even if we didn't have a drop of the Empress's blood in our veins.'

'I just mean that I will probably be recognised out here, and we didn't tell anyone we were leaving.'

Ada arched an eyebrow at him. If his expressions looked half as judgemental, no wonder people were constantly asking him to smile.

'Polly, the entire *point* of this excursion is for you to be noticed,' Ada said.

'Forster is going to kill me,' Leo muttered. 'If my adoring

citizens don't first.'

'Forster is the kind of idiot who would put his own head in your chamberpot to save you the exertion of shoving it in there yourself,' Ada said. 'Disregard everything he has ever told you.'

'*Adelaide*,' Leo scolded.

'*Leopold*,' Ada retorted.

If there was a way to make Ada feel shame … well, there was, but Leo would rather rub coal into his eyes than have her look at him the way she'd looked at their dad. Ada walked like she was as beautiful and fierce as a cassowary. As exasperating as he found her cocksure swagger, Leo never wanted to see her shrink in fear and remorse ever again.

'You're *safe*, Your Majesty,' Ada said. Leo barely cringed at the title now, which was something like progress. 'Do you know how many murders there were in Praecentor last year?'

'I simultaneously want to ask why I would possibly know that and also think that I probably should,' Leo said. 'I hate talking to you.'

'Five,' Ada said. 'And four of them were done by immediate family members of the victims, so you're actually at greatest danger from me, and I could kill you any time I liked.'

'Ada, we both know of *eight* people who were killed last year, *three* of whom were related to us, and unless you'd like to confess to something, they absolutely weren't killed by an immediate family member,' Leo said.

'Terrorist attacks don't count towards homicide statistics,' Ada said dismissively.

They arrived at a pedispass field before Leo could tell her that the precise number of murders hadn't actually been his issue. It would do no good to point out that the rarity of murders didn't guarantee someone as high profile as himself safety, because she already knew that. She loved to make him agonise over how to best articulate things that they both knew were obvious. She said it was training, because plenty of outsiders would love to do the same thing, and that he had better know when to cut his losses and how to dismiss them when they tried.

In truth, she wasn't wrong. It was a useful skill to have, especially when paired with the improvisation she had also drilled into him. *So, make something up,* she used to say, before he knew the game well enough to give up protesting. *Just don't be boring.*

'What are we doing here?' Leo asked.

'We're watching a pedispass game,' Ada said. 'Next time, we might even play. If you remember how.'

'Of course I remember,' Leo said. 'I've seen you perform every foul in the book. It was the only way you were ever going to get the umpire to whistle, seeing as I've never once seen you score a goal.'

Ada narrowed her eyes at him, clearly weighing up whether she should insist that she had indeed scored a modest handful of goals in her time playing defence or if she should punch him in the throat.

'Can random royalty really just join in games?' Leo asked, before she made up her mind.

'One of the few perks that comes with my station is that I may miss as many training sessions as I choose,' Ada said. 'I try not to take advantage of that,' she admitted, looking at the oval of shorn grass instead of Leo. 'I feel confident they'll have a spare bib for you if you offer your talents. Especially if you play for the Nightjars—they're hopeless.'

Leo resolved immediately to support the hopeless Nightjars. He probably shouldn't play favourites, but on the other hand … *He* would certainly respect a leader who admitted to liking things instead of aiming for bland, political neutrality every day.

'Do you think I'm allowed to barrack for a particular team?' he asked Ada quietly, just to check.

She peered at him through the corner of her eyes, as though unwilling to turn her face and admit that she was taking his question seriously.

'Yes,' she said. 'You should also make it known that you would burn the kingdom down if you weren't allowed to have goat cheese and apple-berry on fresh bread at Sommertide.'

'That's so mean,' Leo groaned, immediately wanting his favourite food. 'Ada, they won't be in season for *ages.*'

Ada laughed and leaned briefly into Leo's arm. He begrudgingly forgave her, because it was more hassle than it was worth to be annoyed with Ada. It was like that with all his siblings. He just didn't see the benefit in falling out with any of them when he knew he'd get over it at some point anyway.

It struck him that if Dicky hadn't been so near their parents that night, Leo would probably be playing the part that Ada was, advising the king. He would have been doing it more directly, without making Dicky earn his perspective and without opting out of matters that didn't interest him in the way Ada did. That reality felt immeasurably foreign.

The seats around the oval filled as much as it seemed they were going to and the game finally began. The obvious observation of him from the crowd wasn't as bad as Leo had feared. It probably wasn't even any worse than it was in the castle. He took a breath and distracted himself from his self-consciousness by asking Ada if she'd dismissed her latest maid yet.

'I am *wounded,*' Ada said. 'Your dearest sister—whom you love and adore and without whom you would perish—is cursed, and you make a mockery of it. If the people only knew what a cruel leader you are they would depose you with pitchforks and I would be helpless to stop them.'

'I'll take that as a yes,' Leo said.

'As a matter of fact, I have not,' Ada said. After a moment, she added, 'Because, by definition, my latest maid is the one I currently have, and the one I have had for the last week has not yet fallen prey to the curse.'

Leo laughed. Ada's lips lifted a couple of degrees in that playfully smug way they did when her drama had entertained someone. Most of her smile was in her eyes, and it was easy to miss.

'The last one was not only wicked, but I found out that I had already dismissed her before, a few years ago,' Ada said. 'That wretch, Abigail, she thought she could sneak her back in. But it was just the same as last time, of course it was!'

'Well, we all knew we would run out of people in the Empire eventually,' Leo said. 'Is Abigail really a wretch? I can't tell if she's taking advantage of me knowing shit-all about running a castle.'

Ada paused, but it was to leap to her feet and shout encouragement for the Wallabies' attack player who was moving in towards the goal, not to consider Leo's pretty significant concern. The opposing defence kicked it wildly out of play and Ada sat down with a dissatisfied noise. Before she could answer Leo, they were interrupted by an old woman dragging a child unevenly towards them.

The woman bowed gravely and steered the child in front of her, prompting him to bow with a hand on the back of the head. Leo turned in his seat and inclined his head.

'Good morning,' he said.

'Good morning, Your Majesty,' the woman said, in a gravelly voice that made Leo wonder if she'd inhaled smoke every day of her life or if she'd worn it out shouting. 'Sorry to disturb.'

'Not at all,' Leo said. He narrowly stopped himself from asking if he could help with anything. She would get to the point if she had one. He didn't need to offer something if it turned out he couldn't give it.

'My grandson has a bung leg,' she said, proving that yes, she could indeed get to the point. 'His doctor gives him all these exercises and he doesn't do them. He limps all over the place and can barely go a block without needing to sit on the side of the road.'

'I'm sorry to hear that,' Leo said. 'That sounds really hard for both of you.'

'You have magic,' the woman said, ignoring Leo's words.

'Oh,' Leo said, genuinely surprised. He'd barely interacted with common citizens since he'd made the misstep of transforming his hat into something more palatable and had assumed his magic wasn't welcome at this level. He was actually good at healing magic. This felt like a very fragile opportunity.

'Okay, sure,' he said. 'No guarantees—magic isn't perfect—but I can try. What is his actual diagnosis?'

The woman's eyes were carved from cement.

'Bung leg,' she insisted.

'You said he'd been to a doctor—'

'I don't take him to the doctor; his mother takes him to the doctor. His mother's more useless than his leg.'

Leo met the boy's eyes and gave him a small, sympathetic smile, more for enduring his grandmother than for the leg. The boy grimaced.

'What's your name?' Leo asked.

'Conrad,' the boy said.

'Oh, like my brother,' Leo said. 'Were you named after him?'

The boy nodded.

'Would you sit on this chair for me?'

The boy lowered himself into the seat next to Leo like an exhausted man relieving himself of a priceless weight.

'Would it be okay if I touched your leg, Conrad?' Leo asked, disregarding how strange it felt to use Con's name for someone else.

Conrad nodded and Leo crouched in front of him. As Leo

examined the leg, he asked questions about when the injury began (since breaking the leg three years ago), when it felt best (when he used it just a little bit) and worst (when he had to hurry), and so on. Around them, the crowd was mostly consumed with watching the game, but Leo was aware of those closest to them staring openly. He found that he minded much more on the boy's behalf than on his own.

'Do you know much about magic?' Leo asked finally, glancing up to extend the question to Conrad's grandmother as well.

''S magic,' the woman said gruffly, like it was impossible to say anything more on the subject. The boy just looked at Leo expectantly.

'I can make impossible things happen, so long as I understand exactly what I want to happen and I can feel ...' Leo tapped his chest, 'that it must be so, with my whole body. And I put all that knowledge and fervour into a word, or a phrase or song, and the words have to be good enough to earn the magic.

'Healing can be tricky, because sometimes healing a symptom can make a person feel worse—like if you take away a fever without doing anything about the underlying infection that the body is trying to burn out. It's also tricky because magic doesn't last. Magic basically works by making an idea real, and ideas don't stand on their own. But that's the case with most mundane medical interventions as well. You don't expect a bandage to replace your skin, you use it while your skin repairs itself.

'Conrad, I don't know what your diagnosis is and I don't have enough training in medicine to know for sure what we're dealing with here, but I think I have enough to do some good. I'm going to use magic on your leg, but you have to do something for me, too, okay?'

The boy nodded urgently. Leo could feel that the number of eyes on them had increased by a *lot* in the last minute and could hear snatches of whispers from people very interested in seeing what the king looked like when he was performing magic. He ignored them as best as he could.

'I need you to eat good meals, with meat, and drink lots of water. And I need you to do all of the exercises your doctor has given you, even though I hope this helps. I'm going to …' Leo searched for the simplest way to say it, which was very different from the way of saying it that he would need to actually perform the magic. 'I'm going to grow your bone and your muscles, and I need you to grow them as well so that when the magic fades, your body has built up around it and it doesn't need it anymore. Do you understand?'

'I understand,' the boy said.

Leo took a deep breath and placed his hand on the boy's thigh, over the bone that had been broken and had stopped growing while the other leg had been going through a spurt.

'Insensate,' he murmured, making it into a prayer. *Please, merciful Trinity, don't let him feel this*. 'Elongate. Maturate. Replicate.' He leaned heavily on that last word. Conrad's body knew itself, knew the length of his other femur that Leo needed this one to match. Leo had to let his magic be guided by that internal knowledge more than his external survey.

The boy's leg expanded under Leo's hand, barely perceptible. It felt like he had simply shifted his weight in his chair. To Leo's relief, he didn't so much as wince.

'Weird,' Conrad said quietly.

'Yeah,' Leo agreed.

'Could you fix everyone's legs? Or their arms or whatever? Or make them not sick?'

'I was seriously considering becoming a healer,' Leo said. 'But then I became king instead. I think I would have done a lot of good for some people as a healer, but I hope that I can make things better for more people as a king.'

'It really is a question of utilitarianism,' Ada said, in a tone of voice that promised she had much, much more to say on the topic.

'Ada, he's like ten,' Leo warned.

'Your grandmother healed people,' the old woman said. 'Your mother was foolish to dilute the royal line with a mundane man. When I was a child, the royal family blessed Praecentor with the Empress's magic every day. Anyone would think you don't have magic at all. None of you even had a Hebestag.'

'My friends threw me one at the Academy,' Leo smiled. 'About seven years too late, but it was nice. Dion—' Leo broke off. This woman didn't care about the ways that the Academy had felt like home. His heart panged as he felt the distance. No one had written to him since the stilted sympathy cards. They were too busy with their studies and he was too busy with his reign, and if they felt half as awkward about their peer suddenly becoming a king as he did, he couldn't blame them. 'Maybe Max will have one,' he said.

Leo met Ada's eyes, but he couldn't tell what the tightness in them meant. Had she wanted one? He didn't doubt that she would have enjoyed the opportunity to show off her magic in front of the kingdom, and he knew he had personally felt a bit deprived when it became clear his twelfth birthday wasn't going to be special. He'd shrugged it off to his friends, but the celebration at which a child of the Empress (as all legitimate descendants are entitled to be called) is declared an adult was an important tradition to miss out on. Of course, it was a symbolic adulthood. No one had considered twelve-year-olds adults for centuries.

He would have thought his father would have wanted to show off the legitimacy and power of his children, but Leo had never really gotten the hang of understanding Richard's motivations.

'Anyway,' he said, patting the boy's leg. 'Exercise. Eat well. It will feel weird for a bit, and your back muscles will need to get used to the new way of moving, so you'll still have some pain for a little while. I'd try to fix that, but backs are tricky. It'll be better if you can just build the muscles up yourself.'

'Thank you,' the boy said quietly.

Leo stood up and smiled at Conrad's grandmother with a polite incline of his head, then turned back towards the game. It was apparently half-time.

Behind him, Leo could hear conversation resuming. He realised that it had been so quiet because people wanted to hear what he had been saying. He felt his face grow hot, reacting too late to how observed he had been.

'Alright for some, isn't it?' someone said.

'Come on, that's what they should *be using it for,'* someone else replied.

'I could fix all the problems in this city in two weeks if I could do that,' the first person said.

Leo rolled his eyes to Ada, who smiled wryly in response. People had been trying to figure out a way to transfer magic to mundane people forever. Leo dreaded to think of what would happen if they figured it out. Revolution, presumably.

It wasn't the only feedback Leo was hearing against his will. He got the impression people didn't care if he heard them. The game resumed, and Leo tried to focus solely on it.

After ten minutes, he turned to Ada and spoke in High Trinitese.

'Is my attendance here optional?'

'Of course,' she replied in the same language. Her accent was better, despite Leo having been the one to live in Trinitas for six years. She had a way with languages.

'Then I'd like to opt out. I get enough criticism to not need it on my days off as well.'

Ada shrugged and reverted back to their native tongue.

'The game might as well be over, and I have things to do,' she said. 'Walk me back to the castle.'

'If you insist,' Leo said gratefully.

Leo knew that his dad wouldn't have needed to retreat, not from anything. But he also knew his dad wouldn't have been able to heal someone's leg. On balance, he'd rather help a boy have a better life than have a thicker skin.

As they walked up to the castle, Ada said, 'He was wrong.'

'Who?' Leo asked.

'The person who can't whisper for shit,' she said. 'I keep hearing people saying that the world would be better if everyone had magic, but with our current system there's almost a guarantee that every person with magic will have the means to be educated in how to use it. The mechanics of magic mean that understanding what you're doing is essential to using it. I wouldn't have been able to heal that boy's leg, as I don't particularly care about anatomy.'

'If Dicky could hear you saying that you don't want "The People" to have power ...' Leo teased.

Ada looked at Leo with a disdainful expression that any cat would be proud to wear.

'I also don't want every citizen to have a sword,' she said flatly. 'I want society to be decent enough that they don't *need* swords. I want doctors who can put into practice what we have needed to learn to make the magic work or to inspire potioneers who can facilitate magical remedies in the hands of mundanes. I want to improve education and opportunities.'

'You want *me* to do these things,' Leo sighed.

'If you wouldn't mind,' she smiled.

The excursion made sense now. It was going to be a lot harder to dismiss Ada's urgings about investing in schools now that he had met young Conrad.

11

THE WATER WAS SO HOT it turned Leo's hands red. His gloves, tucked in the pocket of his cloak, were charmed to keep water from seeping in, but he didn't need them. The kitchen staff certainly didn't have that option. The water would cool soon.

He didn't have time for this and he knew it. But if he didn't take half an hour to himself, he'd end up finding out how sharp his sword was and whether Forster could bleed or if he truly was made of stone. Maybe clockwork. Leo took a deep breath in and released it in a shuddery sigh. He needed to not think about Forster or any of the rest for five minutes. He needed to concentrate on the feeling of smooth ceramic in one hand, the softness of the cloth in the other, the hot water and even the detritus that circled lazily and slimily through the water as he cleaned the plate of the remnants of someone or other's lunch.

'Not only are you royalty—you're also magic,' said a voice from the entrance of the kitchen. 'Making this doubly as ridiculous, and each half of that ridiculousness is quite hefty.'

Had it been almost anyone else, Leo would have told them to piss off. But he couldn't choose to see the mystery man no matter how hard he looked, and he had looked as hard as he could without raising Ada's suspicions unduly. It was made more difficult by the fact that he didn't know his name. He still shot him a sardonic look instead of the attempt at a smile he might have on another day.

'You're obviously not magic,' Leo said. 'I don't think anyone holds washing dishes in enough reverence to be able to use magic on it without burning away their connection.'

'A joke, Majesty,' the man said with a tiny, self-effacing bow.

'I sent everyone away,' Leo said.

'Are you sending me away?' the man asked.

'No,' Leo said, directing it to the full sink.

'Good,' the man said, crossing the kitchen to lean against the bench next to the sink where it was much harder to avoid looking at him. 'I revel in special treatment, Majesty.'

Leo let a second more than was acceptable for banter pass, so he abandoned the thought of telling the man that he was special, or that he wasn't, or maybe that he was only allowed to stay because his presence was ignorable, or because it made Leo forget all his responsibilities for a while. It was easier to stack a clean plate in the sturdy dish rack and move to washing a bowl. This was why Leo was here. He needed something to do with his hands.

'You can't wash all these by yourself,' the man said.

'I know,' Leo said. 'I just need half an hour, I told them that.'

'You're inconveniencing the staff.'

'Yeah, well.' Leo dropped a handful of cutlery in the rack. 'I *am* inconvenient to them.' He looked fixedly at his hands, wishing he didn't have to think about his words right now. 'I'm not ...' Leo sighed. 'I'm not being melodramatic, it's just that they do have to run around after me, so I'll, I don't know. Make myself toast for dinner and even it out. And I need this, so I'm just not going to add feeling bad about it to the list of shit emotions I'm trying to get out right now.'

The man looked at Leo speculatively. Since Leo had returned home, he had been constantly experiencing a low-to-moderate level of self-conscious discomfort from his constant visibility that was something like stage fright. This man managed to provoke a pressure to perform that was completely other to that. It was like being at the Academy, trying to be cool with a peer.

'May I dry?' the man asked.

'You don't have to.'

'I'll feel like an absolute arse if I don't. Consider it the worst date of all time.'

Leo laughed, dropping his chin to his chest.

'There are so many things wrong with that,' he said.

'Name one,' the man said, a smile in his voice. Leo glanced at him and saw that he had a dimple in his cheek.

'Well, for starters, I don't even know your name.'

'An overrated and unnecessary piece of information,' the man said. He picked up a tea-towel and started to dry.

'Okay, well then there's the fact that Con was once on a date with a guy who literally shat his pants out of nerves, and then both of them pretended it hadn't happened for another half hour, even though the guy was sitting in his own shit and they both really knew that he was. So this can't be worse than that.'

The man had to put a plate down so that he could laugh properly.

'Wow,' he said. 'A better date than that. I'm incredibly flattered.'

'And it's you, so,' Leo started, aiming for teasing then flushing when he realised what he had just said. The man turned around so he was against the bench and leaned backwards so he could see Leo's face.

'Sooo ...' he prompted.

'So it wouldn't be the worst,' Leo mumbled.

'Even if I shat my pants?'

'Maybe don't test it.'

Leo placed a bowl in the dish rack and started on the next one, face still hot but more thrilled than embarrassed. The biggest problem was left unsaid, in that Leo didn't know if he was allowed to date full stop and he most definitely didn't know if he was allowed to date *this* man, whose station was as unknown as his name. Leo had visited most of the courtiers staying in the castle by now and hadn't found the man anywhere. He was pretty sure that despite his nice clothes, he was actually part of the staff. Maybe a merchant at best—someone with a friend or relative who could tailor clothes well rather than someone with the status to have access to one he didn't know. He'd suspected he wasn't someone his dad would approve of from the moment he hadn't provided his name, but the suspicion grew with every subsequent meeting. Leo wanted to believe that it didn't matter, but of course it did.

'What's wrong?' the man asked.

'Throw a dart blindly, you'll hit something,' Leo said. He winced at his candour. He was a security risk. He couldn't just go saying things to pretty boys. The fact that the man was very pretty was something that Leo had noticed more with every subsequent meeting as well.

'That sucks,' the man said, with genuine sympathy in his voice. 'That truly sucks. I almost can't believe that. I would have thought there were some perks. King Richard certainly seemed to enjoy the job.'

'We should give the kitchen back,' Leo said, looking over his shoulder.

'We should, but you seem to be on the verge of some kind of nervous breakdown, which would possibly be more disruptive to Canticalica than dinner being half an hour late.'

The man put his hand on Leo's shoulder and turned him away from the sink. He picked up one of Leo's hands, then the other, and carefully dried them. The towel was soft and the man's hands were firm, but gentle. Leo watched his dark brown eyes as they focused on the task. There were two gold freckles in one iris. He didn't want to be the kind of king who slept with staff on the side, like they were a shameful secret to tide him over until he found the real thing. But he really wanted to see if the man's lips were just as attentive, to find out if he could be the one to lead or if the man would disregard any authority Leo tried to have there as well.

'What's wrong?' the man asked again, meeting Leo's eyes.

'I can't remember,' Leo said.

The man smiled and his eyes dropped to Leo's lips. Leo's heart jumped, but he couldn't follow up on that implication. Anyone could walk in, and he really didn't want to be that kind of king, he reminded himself again. Leo pulled his hands out of the man's. The man didn't seem offended, but the mood softened.

'Sorry,' he said. 'I'm … I have a lot on my mind. The big one is Max—my brother—'

'I'm familiar with the prince, yes,' the man said, smiling gently.

Leo smiled back. Max was both the smallest and biggest issue plaguing him, but it was also the only one he could talk about. He still *shouldn't* talk about it, he was aware of that, but it was better than complaining about Sword and Shield's infuriatingly vague and unsettling reports that the attackers behind his family's deaths were still out there.

'He's struggling, I think. We're leaving him to the staff too much. His parents died, obviously. Con looked after us more than our parents did when we were kids but he's tits deep in training, and I want to help but I'm *neck* deep in stupid shit that doesn't even matter, and Ada is trying but she doesn't know what she's doing and she has other, mysterious, Ada stuff going on …'

'And Danya?'

'Has unofficially taken the title of High Enchantress now that Erwina's walked, so she's out too. In any other month I think that would have been headline news, but Danya just gets on with things so … I mean, none of us are *out*. We're just giving him these tiny portions of attention when we can instead of making everything else fit around him. It's just, it's so *unfair*.'

Leo stared behind the man's shoulder and remembered what it was like to be Max's age. As he'd said, Con was more present than either of his parents and had been for ages. He hadn't minded being alone either. He didn't want Max to not mind being alone. Belatedly, it occurred to him that the man had used Danya's given name. He wasn't sure if that was common practice.

'Hey,' the man said, touching Leo's shoulder again. Leo refocused on him. His expression was one of soft concern. 'Do you want a hug?'

Leo thought he might want a hug more than he had ever wanted anything. The promise of strong arms around him, holding him close because they wanted him there, offering comfort in a way that he would feel right down to his bones … he wanted that so badly. But he might cry if he was given it. And he didn't know the man's name. And he was the fucking king.

'I'm fine,' he said. He scrubbed his hands over his face and let out a big sigh. 'I'm fine,' he repeated.

'Do you want to sing about it?' the man said, with a small, teasing smile. Leo smiled back and punched the man lightly on the shoulder. 'I think I've just been exposed to the violence inherent in the system,' the man said, smiling wider.

'Oh, fuck off,' Leo laughed. Then, sincerely, 'Thank you.'

'For what?' the man said. 'Oh, this? No, I was craving a midday session of drying cutlery. You just happened to be here.'

Leo thought about kissing the man again. He thought about lifting the man's shorter frame up onto the bench and getting those legs wrapped around his hips until he forgot everything that was on his mind. He punched him softly again instead.

'I like that I can make you smile,' the man murmured. 'It really does suit you. But I think I'm okay with it being our secret too.' Leo looked down and smiled at the floor. That was easily the nicest way anyone had ever referred to his expressions, or lack thereof. The man put two fingers to Leo's chin and tilted his head back up. 'Your Majesty,' he said, with a shallow, performative bow, eyes never leaving Leo's. 'Until next time.'

'Next time,' Leo repeated.

He watched the man leave. It wasn't until he was fully out of sight that Leo remembered that he was in the kitchen and he should let the staff back in … just as soon as he could conjure up an expression that didn't look like he'd been trampled by a mob of kangaroos.

12

'COME IN,' Danya called, and Leo obeyed.

He had not expected to find her with company. He definitely had not expected to find her with the fool.

'Sorry,' he said awkwardly. 'You're busy.'

'No, I'm not!' she said. 'I am—'

'A *cruuuueeel* enchantress, abandoning me to the trenches of solitude,' the fool cried.

'You don't have to leave,' Danya said.

'One of us does,' Leo said.

Danya looked appalled. Leo felt an amount of guilt that was not *nearly* sufficient to make him take it back. He'd rather walk around with sand in his underwear for a week than drink tea with the fool.

'All the girls and boys are grieving, all because the fool is leaving,' the fool sang as it jangled in great lurches towards the door. Leo recoiled against one of Danya's shelves as if whimsy was catching.

Danya glared at Leo as they both listened to the retreating sounds of singing, jingling and stomping. Neither of them moved when they heard what sounded like someone covered in bells falling down the stairs. They both knew it was faking it.

'That was rude, Leo,' Danya said.

'I'm a rude guy,' he said, shrugging.

To demonstrate, he took a seat in one of her armchairs without invitation. He fidgeted with a hole in the upholstery. He met

Danya's eyes again and this time his guilt was probably enough to make him take back just about anything he'd ever said.

'It's *everywhere*,' Leo complained.

'Yes, that is its job,' Danya said coldly. 'Heaven forbid it take half an hour off from bothering you to come and see a friend!'

'You're its friend?'

Danya gave him a dirty look.

'It's fairly normal to make friends with your fellow servants,' she said.

Leo wondered if he could shelter within his tunic for the rest of his life. Danya wasn't a *servant*, she was High Enchantress. She was one of his heads of avenues; she had direct input into the running of the castle and the kingdom. But, as hard as it was to admit it, she *was* employed by the castle. She hadn't brought it up as bluntly before. It was strange to see a cross expression on Danya's face, but not unprecedented. It made Leo shift in his seat, not only because he didn't want to make her cross as a matter of principle, but also because he was in her space, with her tinctures and powders and books lining the sharp room. Despite the abundance of natural light and the cheery colours, the angles always felt cold to Leo, and besides, Danya was im-measurably powerful even when not in a place so supposedly tailor-made to enhance her power.

'Why are you here, Poldilocks,' Danya said pissily.

Leo considered drawing his sword. It could be funny. Instead, he scooted a bit closer to the edge of his seat and leaned forward.

'Do you know who Con is crushing on?' he asked.

Danya laughed, anger disappearing immediately. Leo breathed a little easier, because Danya wasn't the kind to conceal or fake her feelings.

'You had me thinking it was something serious!' she said. 'Why do you care?'

'Finding him means I can put off answering my letters. He

didn't turn up for his afternoon shift guarding some courtier, forgot her name. His Helm asked me where he might've got waylaid, but you know Con; he could be hiding with literally anyone in the castle.'

The laughter drained from Danya's face and she stood up. Leo's heart jolted without knowing why. It was enough that Danya was distressed.

'Fool!' she cried.

The door opened immediately. Leo stood, hand going to his sword on reflex.

'Find Con,' she said.

The fool didn't speak, not even to insult Leo; it just turned and sprinted down the stairs. Leo watched it go, deeply confused, then turned back to where Danya had crossed the room. She was pouring the pot of tea into a shallow but wide bowl, murmuring a scrying spell under her breath at top speed.

'Danya?' Leo asked warily.

Her head whipped up.

'Blocked,' she said. 'He is devoted to Sword and Shield more than anything else and someone's blocking me; he's not playing hooky. Leo, help.'

Leo staggered to her and took her hands. Not enough to just say the words, they sang together, Leo taking a steady melody and Danya harmonising from his lead. They stared at the tea, but it remained scarlet and useless in the bowl.

'He was at morning training,' Leo said. 'He must be still in the castle.'

H E WASN'T.
The fool found a woman in Shield uniform with her throat cut in her room, the arc of blood forming a gory circle. The fool's paint had two smudged rivers down it but refused to let it stop smiling in bright, false colours over its real grimace. Leo felt

something complex and anguished when he looked at it, but his anxiety for Con was demanding too much for him to feel sympathy for the person he hated or sorrow for a woman he didn't know.

'What a waste,' Danya said numbly. 'They won't even have gotten out of the city. Teleportation is uneconom—'

She broke off once her mouth caught up with the mood of the room. Leo stared at the woman, whose dark-blonde hair had been stained bright red from the neck down. She was handsome more than she was beautiful, with a strong nose and chin and piercing blue eyes. Leo wished the fool had closed them or perhaps the Helm who had arrived on the scene just before Leo and Danya.

'The city is too large an area for us to search,' Leo said. 'What are we going to do?'

'Fight blood with blood,' Danya said.

IT FELT WRONG to do this in the room where Leo had learnt how to write, where there were colourful paintings on the walls to encourage learning and where Max was still looking at the door his teacher had just left through.

'It's going to be okay, Maxi,' Danya said kindly, bending over slightly to be on his level.

Ada and Leo looked at each other over her back. Neither of them knew how to reassure him. They needed Con. They couldn't manage without Con. They may as well let the crown fall into the river if they didn't have Con, because who else would keep them together?

'We're just going to take a little blood,' Danya explained in gentle tones to Max. 'It'll hurt, but only a little bit, and then we'll be able to find Con. I know this is a lot to ask, sweetheart, but I need you to be brave for me so that I can find Con. You'll be helping save him, do you understand?'

'Danya,' Leo said, because he was pretty sure she was going to terrify Max speaking like that.

But Max squared his shoulders like Con did before he sparred and raised his little chin. Leo felt proud underneath his anxiety.

'How?' he asked.

'I'm going to take it from your upper arm,' Danya said. 'It'll hurt the least. Well, thigh would hurt less, but this is easier, okay? I'm going to cut with a special knife,' and from within her sleeves, Danya's dagger emerged in her hand, 'and then use magic to take it. Leo and Ada, too. Would you like me to cut you first or would you like to see one of them do it?'

Max looked at Leo immediately.

'Leo first,' he said.

Leo pulled his jerkin off and bunched up his shirt sleeve to his shoulder. He smiled grimly at Max then nodded to Danya.

Danya's dagger sped past him, past the wards he'd forgotten to remove and through the skin of his arm as if he was made of nothing more substantial than cream. It took a second for his body to realise it should be bleeding, more than enough time for Danya to hold up a hand to keep it still. Leo raised his own hand to take over the spell with a murmur so Danya could have the freedom to cut the others.

'Didn't hurt,' he told Max. Then he thought he probably shouldn't leave Max feeling bad if the sting alarmed him. 'Well, a bit. I know you can do it though.'

'Thanks, Lee,' Max whispered.

'You next or Ada?' Danya asked, her sweet smile somewhat marred by the dagger she was holding.

'Ada,' Max said.

Ada had taken her stocking down and held her calf out now.

'Thought it'd be easier than getting to my arm,' she said. Leo looked at her fitted dress; she was probably right. 'I'll hold it in place.'

'Thanks, love,' Danya said.

The knife flashed again.

'Okay, Max,' Danya said. 'Your turn.'

Max hesitated. Leo dropped to his knees in front of him, one hand still up and keeping his blood from spilling everywhere.

'I hate that we have to ask you to do this,' he said. 'I know this is probably scary. It *is* scary. I'm scared too, okay? Just a little cut and I'll heal you straight away. I'm a good healer, Max. Do you believe me?'

Max nodded. He closed his eyes and held out his arm without looking at it. Danya cut.

Ada and Leo dropped their magic at this signal and Danya caught and pulled blood from all three siblings into the air, into her mouth. Leo watched the blood flow from Max's wound and the second the blood stopped flying up and instead obeyed gravity once more, Leo held his hand over the cut and healed it with a murmured, *'Alleviate.'*

Max was trembling. Leo caught his hand and gently kissed the spot on his arm where he'd been cut, like his nurse had done for him when he was little.

'All better,' he said.

Max opened his eyes and looked at Leo. He wasn't crying, but his eyes shone and every point of his face was pulled down in misery.

'Thank you,' Leo said. 'You were really brave.'

'It'll help Con?' Max asked.

Leo nodded. Max nodded too, jaw too serious for such a young boy.

'Danya is being scary,' he whispered.

Leo turned. Danya's usually brown eyes had brightened to red, and veins stood out on her dark skin. She stared forward at nothing and wasn't responding to Ada's quiet words.

'Just girl stuff,' Leo told Max, smiling a little to show he was joking. Max gave him a sardonic look that came right from Ada. 'Sorry. It's fine, though. This is what we wanted.'

Danya gained alertness with a deep breath and smiled like her usual self, if her usual self came with a bloody dagger and demon eyes. There was a cost to blood magic. It corrupted, and it insisted that the corruption be obvious to everyone around the magician who messed with it.

'Leo,' she said, holding her hands out. Leo took them unhesitatingly. 'Pursue,' she crooned, eyes closing as though her magic was ambrosial on her tongue.

The room snapped into pitch blackness and Leo lost all proprioception for a heart-stopping second before his body and Danya's and the world lurched back into being. They were in the city, on a narrow and derelict street Leo had never been down. Broken glass crunched under Leo's feet as he stepped back to brace his weight on a run-down building. He had never teleported before and he didn't ever want to repeat the experience. His vision slowly cartwheeled and he could feel bile in the back of his throat. Somehow, he kept from throwing up.

'Where are we?' he asked Danya quietly, when his ears had stopped ringing.

'They're in there,' she said, pointing to a church.

It was barely recognisable as a place of worship; graffiti arced over the walls and the entrance was made unappealing by a murky puddle of water barring the way. One of the double doors listed drunkenly on its last hinge and the other was missing entirely.

'Beacon,' Danya murmured, crouching to press her hands to the grubby street.

A golden path an inch wide snaked its way away from them, presumably towards the castle to guide Sword and Shield to their position. Leo watched it go for a couple of seconds, then re-focused on the church. He jumped when he felt Danya's hand slip into his.

'Covert,' she whispered, holding a finger up to her grinning lips. She seemed *high* on blood magic, but Leo wasn't about to stop her.

They slipped carefully around the broken door and crept into the church. Danya led the way behind a pew that was missing a plank of wood from its back, where they could see without being seen. Her spell would deflect attention, but even with blood magic nothing could make them entirely unnoticeable if they didn't keep quiet and out of sight. It was in their favour that the attackers were all looking at their captive.

In the centre of the church, Con was hanging limply in dark chains that shimmered subtly when he moved. Iridium. Leo had only seen it once, when a teacher had passed around a thin bracelet to show them what it could do. It could only be worked into shape with very skilled magic due to its enormous density and its brittle nature, which was somewhat ironic considering its purpose. It was a noble metal, meaning that it didn't corrode or react with much of anything, and it was the only known way to dampen magic. When Leo had tried on the bracelet, he knew without saying a word that his magic was lacking. He'd never been aware of what his magic felt like before that moment, but the absence of sensation was jarring. It was like losing his sense of smell to a cold or wearing protective earmuffs that muffled sound. And that had been a small bracelet. Chains seemed like overkill.

'Is Sword and Shield worth this much to you?' a woman asked, drawing Leo's attention to the rest of the room.

There were nine people, all wearing cloaks. The woman was the only one with her hood down. Her skin was pale and her eyes were so vibrantly blue Leo could see them across the room.

'I *can't*,' Con groaned.

He sounded as weak as he looked. There were dark slashes

across his chest, staining his tattered shirt. His knee looked wrong, bent out of shape, and he wasn't putting any weight on it. The fingers on his left hand were purple with bruises.

'You can,' the woman said. 'As you have seen, we have magicians in our ranks. We've tested this before. With your lineage, your magic could empower half a dozen of us in our crusade. But we need you to surrender it. Believe me when I say that, one way or another, you will not have magic by the end of this interview. It is up to you whether you give it up or are put down for your refusal. We will not mourn the loss of yet another so-called royal who has done nothing to earn his position or remove the boot from the necks of the people who would never have chosen him to rule over them.'

'I *did* give it up,' Con protested.

'No,' she growled, stalking closer and raising a long dagger from where it was concealed by her cloak. She pressed the tip to Con's cheek and blood dribbled down his pale skin immediately. Her face was twisted in fury. 'You merely exchanged your foot for another's. The boot remains, and you benefit from it. Surrender to your destiny.'

She twisted the knife and Con cried out in pain. Danya gripped Leo's hand before he could move. Some quiet part of Leo warned him that there were *nine* attackers in there, any or all of whom could be trained magicians and fighters. He shouldn't pick a fight alone when Swords would be here at any moment.

'Surrender!' the woman demanded, voice scaling a wild octave of aggressive frustration.

Con cried out again and Leo jerked to his feet, dragging Danya with him. He unsheathed his sword and saw in Danya's expression grim determination mirroring his own. She held her palms together and looked to the sky.

'Aggressing in concert,' she sang, voice echoing in the cavernous room. Leo placed his hand on her back to share his magic, unable to lend his voice to unfamiliar words. 'Achieving symmachy / Here we assert / Vicious in symmetry.'

She spread her hands wide, and from her palms bloomed a brilliant, blood-red sword, shorter and thinner than Leo's, glinting sharply in Danya's tight grip. Leo had never seen Danya fight, but surely any partner of Ada's would know how to use a sword. Surely. It was too late to doubt now, because Danya's song had drawn the eye of everyone in the room. Everyone but Con. He wasn't moving.

'Your Majesty,' the woman said, with a mocking bow. Her expression was calm again, almost pleasant. 'If you and the Enchantress would be so kind to hand over your magic, we will gladly release Sir Conrad. I don't think I have to point out that you are outnumbered.'

'Are we?' Leo asked. 'Are there more of you skulking in the shadows? I'm only counting nine.'

'The arrogance of royalty,' the woman said, sounding amused. Four attackers moved carefully to flank her protectively and she smiled indulgently. 'Shall we find out if it's earned?'

'One moment,' Danya said cheerily, holding up a finger. 'Leo, would you like them dead or captured?'

'Let's say fifty-fifty,' Leo said. 'Round up on the side of dead.'

Leo leaned his weight on his back foot in ready position as a chorus of susurrations announced swords being unsheathed. He didn't get a chance to put Con's training into practice.

Danya swung her gleaming sword in a neat arc and cried *'Calamity!'* as she clasped both hands on the hilt and drove the point into the floor. Magic rippled in a savage, inexorable wave towards the attackers, knocking every one of them off their feet. Welts bubbled on their exposed skin and shocked cries of pain echoed through the room.

One of the attackers closest to the leader snatched her dagger from the ground next to her and, instead of getting to his feet, dragged the blade across one of his companion's pale throat. He snatched a clumsy hand through the gore and brought it to his lips. Leo watched in horror as it spilt down his chin. His eyes, already red from blood magic, burnt.

'Asylum!' he cried.

'No!' Danya exclaimed, stepping forwards with a hand outstretched. But she was too late. Every attacker save the one who had been sacrificed vanished from the church.

'Con,' Leo breathed.

He sprinted for where Con was strung up. He slipped on the attacker's blood and scrambled for his feet again. His panicked breath was all but choking him as he swung his sword with all his strength against the chains that bound Con to the obelisk. The iridium shattered. He dropped the sword and caught Con's limp body in one movement. He held the back of Con's head like he was an infant and put his face in front of Con's. He felt re-assuring breath against his cheek and heard himself make a helpless sound.

'He's alive,' he rasped, then he fell to the floor, holding Con tightly against his chest and letting healing magic seep through his embrace. 'Alive, he's okay, you're okay, I've got you, you're okay.'

The words tasted like magic even in their simplicity. All magic took was belief, ardent belief that you needed what you were asking for. Beautiful words had more success because magicians couldn't help but place more value in them, and that went double for singing. Leo found that reaching for his magic had never been easier than it was in that moment, holding Con with desperation in every taut muscle.

Leo remembered being eight, when Con was the coolest thirteen-year-old in the world, and feeling the smooth wood of a practice sword in his hands. They'd seen a play the night before and Con had said he knew how to recreate the sword fight between the hero and the villain. He guided Leo through it, and Leo had been almost dazed that Con would choose to play something so special with him when Con had a million friends. He always made Leo feel like he was worth spending time on. He had to be okay. He just had to.

Con's hand lifted and came to rest on Leo's shoulder.

'Hey,' Con said. 'Hey … Lee, hey. Don't cry.'

'You're okay,' Leo insisted, eyes squeezed shut so that he couldn't see any evidence to the contrary. 'You're okay.'

He kept clutching Con for a long time, until he felt the well of his magic drained almost dry, words turned scalding in his throat so that he couldn't deplete it entirely. And Con was okay.

IF ANYTHING, Leo had overdone it on healing Con. He almost regretted it when Con was still energetically pacing Leo's rooms after three days of no sleep, explaining his idea for a musical that would absolutely be a hit, Con just knew it. Almost, but not quite. Because Con was okay. It didn't matter if Leo was all but sleepwalking himself. Magic wasn't free.

For a block around the broken church they'd found him in, residents were walking without limps and seeing through once-blind eyes. One woman had grown an entire arm back. She was disappointed that it lacked the prominent muscles of her other arm.

Ironically, the attackers had inadvertently strengthened Leo's position. Magic wasn't exclusive to royalty, but it had been once. It was passed down through families, either in the same way that eye colour and illnesses were, or through the holy intervention of the Trinity, depending on who you asked. Magic reinforced the divine right of monarchs to rule and Leo's display of healing had sent a very clear message that he was legitimate. It was Forster's idea for Leo to go about business as usual instead of sleeping for a week as he would have liked. It gave the impression that Leo might have even more power than what he'd shown. Theoretically. If he didn't spoil it by passing out in the middle of the throne room.

Leo joined Con for breakfast on the fourth day after the attack and found that Con had settled from the heights of mania enough that he'd managed a five-hour block of sleep last night. He was still much too perky for this hour of the morning.

'What's on the agenda for today?' Con asked once he'd reported his success at sleeping, pushing aside the puzzle box he had been putting together. Leo wondered how long Con had been killing time in the family's private dining room waiting for Leo to get up.

'Um,' Leo said, more interested in the pastry on his plate than the question.

'I know you've got a meeting with Niklaus about graffiti, and another with Hanna about income tax,' Con said. 'But is that it?'

'They're both today?' Leo said. 'I told Forster that Hanna days shouldn't have anything else on them. She runs circles around me as is.'

'That's what Forster said yesterday,' Con shrugged. 'I thought we could go for a run before we get started. Or maybe in between the meetings. It'll freshen you up.'

Leo looked at Con with the energy of a five-day-old salad. If he'd had any magic to spare, he might have dredged up a word to communicate through some childish spell how little he wanted to do that.

'I would rather not,' he said cadaverously.

'Can't Danya do anything about …' Con gestured at Leo vaguely.

About the fact that everything Leo did was in half-speed. About the fact that his focus was shot and his memory was worse. About the fact that his skin was pale and sunken and his hair hung lank around his face despite being washed last night.

It was a good thing the attendant who dressed Leo and braided his hair in the morning was doing a pretty amazing job of making him look like a healthy and well-rested person with powders and creams, and it seemed like he wasn't gossiping about how much work that took. Leo hadn't and would never ask whether Con had indeed gotten up to mischief with him on the day of his coronation, but either way his professionalism hadn't wavered since. Leo would call for him after breakfast, after the threat of smearing makeup around his face with a napkin was past. Leo had gone without an attendant at the Academy and had been young enough to only have help for very formal occasions before he left. He'd been finding having one awkward and unnecessary up until the last week. He liked Sebastian a lot better now that there was no longer a war between them over who would tie Leo's boots. The answer to that was no longer Leo at the moment.

'More magic isn't the solution here,' Leo said, as he had said already several times. Con's focus seemed to be like a cannon at the moment—very powerful, but only when it was facing the right way. 'I'm fine. It's just a hangover.'

'Has this happened before?' Con asked.

'Sure,' Leo said. 'After almost every exam I ever sat at the Academy, and a handful of other times as well.' Then, realising that maybe honesty was better than making Con think that Leo did this to himself on a regular basis, he amended, 'Not this bad. I usually bounce back quicker.'

L EO WORKED THROUGH HIS MAGIC HANGOVER, leaning on Con's energy to get him through the days that were admittedly less taxing than they had been when Leo had first taken the crown. Con had been given time off to recover that he didn't think he needed (though Leo privately thought a manic Sword was not exactly an asset to the team), so he was happy to help Leo. No one minded. Leo suspected people would be okay with it if it became a permanent arrangement, given that Con was patient, sincere and quick to smile. Even the fool was gentler with Con around, telling barbless jokes instead of taunting and even leaving with a song that was barely insulting when Leo told it wearily to go away after a day of meetings.

A week into Con's time off, a princess of Rinderplatz who was eternally bored by her family's insistence on her forming a friendship with Leo idly said, 'I'm sure there was a pair of brothers who ruled my kingdom together at one point.'

'It's not unheard of for a monarch to promote someone to their equal outside of marriage,' Leo said neutrally.

'Hypothetically,' Princess Ursula said, 'were you to promote Princess Adelaide, for example,' she looked pointedly in Con's direction, making sure that Leo couldn't possibly mistake the fact that she wasn't talking about Ada, 'would you still be expected to take a wife?'

'Yes,' Leo said stiffly. He didn't like the reminder that that expectation existed and he wasn't thrilled about the princess so blatantly showing how little she wanted to marry him either. Not that he wanted to marry *her*, but it still wasn't flattering. 'I'd still need heirs.'

'Surely you could adopt a ward,' she pressed.

'I wouldn't do that without a spouse,' Leo said, surprising himself with how easily the words came. He hadn't really given it thought, except to hope that children were a thing to contend with *far* in the future.

'Hmm,' she said. 'You don't happen to be—'

'Is this tea from Rinderplatz?' Con interrupted. 'It's quite earthy. Is earthy the right word? It doesn't taste like dirt.'

'I don't know,' Ursula said. 'I just asked them to make tea.'

'It's tea-riffic,' Con said, smiling charmingly. Leo snorted inelegantly and covered his face to hide his smile.

'Are you quite alright, Your Majesty?' Ursula asked, an eyebrow raised in restrained amusement.

'Superb,' Leo said. He could do worse than expose that he found puns funny. What magician didn't?

Walking out of the rooms once they'd all made a sufficient amount of awkward conversation to appease Ursula's parents, Leo nudged Con's arm with his elbow.

'I think she'd like it if you were king,' he said.

'You're imagining it,' Con laughed. 'She would never want you to compete with anyone. She clearly loves you very much.'

'I'm very lovable,' Leo said. A few steps later, he ventured, 'It wouldn't be so bad, would it?'

Con grimaced and tugged at his sleeve nervously. He very clearly didn't need Leo to clarify.

'Lee …'

'You're good at this, Con,' Leo said. 'I know you love Sword and Shield, and I don't doubt that you're talented at what you do —I can still barely touch you when we spar, of course you're good—but you could do so much more if you were king.'

Con came to a stop in the hallway and Leo copied. Con still looked uncomfortable, but he'd stopped fidgeting. He looked Leo directly in the eye.

'Leo, you're a good king,' he said. At Leo's expression, he held up his hands to forestall the protest. 'I didn't say you're the best and that the Empress should come and personally give you a medal saying you're her favourite, but I truly believe you'll be *great* one day. You remind me of Mum, actually. You care and you listen, but your word is still final. But I would take up all the space in the room, and you'd let me because you think I'm better at it than you, until you were just a smiling accessory like she was.'

'You're not Dad,' Leo said.

'No, but that's what would happen. I'm happy to be with you for however long Sword and Shield has me benched, and I'll help you as much as I can whenever you want me even when I'm back on duty, but for *Trinity's* sake, don't make me your equal.'

Leo stared at Con. He didn't know what to make of any of

that, but he was most thrown by the fact that Con didn't think he was *currently* Leo's equal. And of course, Leo was king, but he hadn't thought …

'Okay,' he said quietly, if only so they could move on.

They resumed walking and Leo wondered if their mum would have been any good at ruling if their dad hadn't been around. Something about being compared to her hurt almost as much as being compared to Richard.

EN DAYS AFTER CON'S KIDNAPPING, Sword and Shield
called him for a meeting. Leo, feeling like he was
lacking a shadow, waited for Con in the Oak Library
with Ada, playing vertling games unenthusiastically to pass the
time. Ada came up with more interesting questions to ask the top,
but Leo had a knack for spinning it longer. For them, the real
game was less in asking the question and more in twisting the
vertling's answers so that they were always correct. This could
require some leaps of logic.

Their vertling top was old and satisfyingly heavy, each of the
three main sides painted into beautiful renditions of a third of the
Trinity and the smaller dividing sides had the numbers one, two
and three engraved in them in turn. When the vertling fell onto
one of the large sides representing either the Beginning, Middle
or End, the corresponding number faced upwards. One, the
Beginning, represented *yes*, because to say yes is to start
something. Three, the End, represented *no*, because no shuts
everything down. Two, the Middle, represented *maybe*, where all
things are possible. The unspoken exception was represented in
the shadow the vertling cast.

'Would Danya still love Ada if she killed someone?' Leo
asked, sending the vertling spinning.

Yes.

'Of course,' said Ada.

Leo shrugged. He was running out of questions.

'Will Forster ever be late to a meeting?' Ada asked.

Yes.

'When he is dead,' Leo nodded. 'He will of course still attend eventually, it will just take him some time to get used to being a revenant.'

'Of course,' Ada said.

'Will Sword and Shield ever get their heads out of their arses and find the nutbags trying to off our family?' Leo asked.

The top spun rapidly, skipping a couple of times and falling off the table onto the floor. Leo winced. He didn't need to take his frustration out on an antique.

'It says no,' Ada said, bending to pick it up. 'I suppose we'll have to do it ourselves.'

'Right,' Leo said. He thought for a moment. 'Any idea how we'll do that?'

Ada's face took on the expression that Leo associated with her being quite sure she would be able to come up with a crossword answer any second now, but she just hadn't figured out how that might come to pass. He watched, because sometimes the answer did come.

'Do you want a pen and paper?' Leo offered.

'Magic?' Ada said uncertainly.

'We'll use magic or it's a clue that they want magic?'

'Yes,' Ada said. She did not look convincing. 'You said she said "crusade", which implies an opposition to something.'

'A very passionate opposition to something,' Leo added. 'When you think about it, you're the perfect person to identify what that something is. You love opposing things.'

'That is *not* true,' Ada said. Leo waited until she heard what she said and clapped her hands over her face in well-deserved shame. 'We don't even know that it's the same people as before,' she grumbled.

'I mean ...' Leo said. This was a discussion he had had a lot with Sword and Shield over the last week and a half. 'What are the odds?'

'That someone could have seen that we were weaker with a child for a king and taken the opportunity to attack?' Ada asked.

The Chief Helm of Sword and Shield had phrased that a bit more diplomatically when she'd brought it up.

'Well either way we weren't getting anywhere trying to figure out who blew our parents up, seeing as we know nothing about why they might have done that,' Leo said. 'So I'm back to asking the expert about what they might be opposing by stabbing our brother.'

'Perhaps I am *least* suited to be an expert in this matter, because I oppose too many things,' Ada said. 'I suppose I could write you a list, if it would help His Majesty.'

'What does your pedispass team oppose?' Leo asked, rolling his eyes.

'That it now costs twelve inits for a pint *minimum*,' Ada said, disgusted. 'Twelve. And half the pubs water it down.'

'You would hate to see what it costs in Trinitas,' Leo said darkly. 'I wouldn't get in the way of *that* crusade.'

W HEN CON RETURNED, Leo clapped his hand over the vertling top to kill the game and waited for him to end the suspense. Con walked mechanically to the chair closest to the fireplace and sat like he was employed to do so. He met Ada's, then Leo's eyes and nodded. Then his head drooped forward and he pressed the heels of his hands to his eyes.

'They found out I don't have magic,' he said.

'Oh,' Ada said. She lurched from the couch to kneel next to his chair and patted his upper arm. 'Con, no.'

What.

Leo stared. His mouth went dry. He was filled with an

instinctual anger at the base of his throat without any idea of why he was feeling that way. He felt that statement rasp against what he had thought to be the truth and then replace it, making more sense than anything else could have. But Con couldn't keep a secret to save his life. He had the indistinct impression of betrayal at Ada's lack of surprise, but it was more important that he pay attention to Con, so he ignored it as best he could and kept his mouth shut.

'I couldn't think of anything to say,' Con said. 'Leo and Danya had already given their evidence and they were like, "So, why didn't you give up your magic?" And I just folded. Told them I never had any to give. So, that's it. I'm out. Obviously.'

'That's bullshit,' Ada said. She seemed not to know how to comfort him but was trying, now rubbing his arm where she had been patting it. 'You're just as good as any of those bastards who call themselves magicians.'

'I'm not bad, considering it all,' Con said. 'I was,' he corrected.

'Don't say that,' Leo said. 'I still barely ...'

Con never used magic when they trained. Because he didn't have any.

'Well, you'll have to be my personal knight, then,' Ada said, ignoring Leo's trailing, half-finished sentence. 'You certainly can't keep tailing Leo around like a sad, little puppy.'

'Why not?' Leo and Con asked simultaneously.

'Because people like Con better and they can't have him,' Ada said. Leo winced. Her words echoed Con's own from a couple of days ago. 'Spend some time with Max and me. Take up painting. Marry someone foolish now that you can.'

The anger in Leo intensified and he closed his eyes against his sudden awareness of what exactly was pissing him off. Right. Con had joined the order without being qualified and gave up his right to inheritance, leaving Leo to be king instead. Well, Dicky, but that wasn't relevant anymore. And now he might have his inheritance back, but Leo was already crowned and would only be giving it up when he died. Con could have the life Leo had been promised. He could take up painting and marry someone foolish.

'I don't understand,' Leo said. 'How the hell did you keep this a secret?'

'Tone, Polly,' Ada said, giving him a dangerous look.

Con dragged his head from his hands and shrugged lethargically. Sadness looked wrong on his face; it made him look anaemic and old. He swallowed before speaking.

'It doesn't come up as often as you'd think. I figured it out when Mum was pregnant with Ada. I was …'

Con breathed in deep and sighed shakily out. He stared at the mantelpiece instead of at Leo.

'I was pretty ashamed. I thought, and I know, I *know* this is stupid but I wasn't even nine, I thought that I'd have to leave if anyone found out. I thought Mum and Dad would give me up, no … No, I thought they'd kick me out and I'd have to just figure it out or something … I don't know. I was young.'

'You didn't join Sword and Shield until you were twenty,' Leo said. He was making every effort to sound less accusatory in the face of Con's obvious misery, but his voice still shook slightly with repressed anger and his hands were fisted on the couch cushion.

'The first three years they don't let you do any magic at all,' he said. 'Ada helped me pass the initial test.'

He looked back at Leo and Leo kept his jaw clenched, no longer trusting himself to say anything. Con didn't need him to, though. It was obvious that he knew what Leo had meant.

'I didn't want to be Dad,' he said quietly.

'Dangerous, Con!' Leo cried, standing up abruptly. 'Really, *ridiculously* dangerous, are you kidding me? It's not like they want you to have magic so that you can warm your dinner! Trinity's sake!'

'Leo,' Ada warned. Apparently they were past the point of nicknames.

'And you, Ada, what the hell! One thing for Con to be reckless with his own life, but you helping him?'

'Leo,' Con said. 'Leave Ada out of this.'

'What was she, eleven? How did she help you cheat?'

'The same way I do now,' Ada said. 'I cast spells on him and his equipment and give him powders for the immediate needs. He's good enough to keep up with any of the so-called blessed, which should—'

'They don't separate the mages from the mundanes for fun, Ada!' Leo interrupted. 'Every single mage in Sword and Shield is responsible for protecting the unblessed soldiers in their unit, *every* one. If they thought Con had magic and there was a war, hell, if there was a risky *reconnaissance*, dozens of soldiers, including Con, would be completely vulnerable. I can't believe you were so irresponsible.'

Con stood and put his hand firmly on Leo's shoulder to stop him from pacing. He gripped hard enough for it to be an admonishment for how Leo was talking to Ada. Leo batted Con's arm away and glared at him. Con's expression remained sombre.

'Say what you mean, Lee,' Con said. 'Say why you're really angry.'

Leo turned and grabbed his hair in both hands, knocking his coronet to the ground. He kicked it away harshly. He hadn't even remembered he was wearing it. He was burning with rage, shaking with it, could feel his magic thrumming, not even contained within his skin anymore but buzzing just outside of it and waiting for a word, any word. He swallowed and then breathed, pulling it back with unsteady control. He picked up the coronet and turned to gesture it at Con.

'I didn't want this,' Leo said. 'I never wanted this and I wasn't supposed to have it. You didn't want to be Dad? Well cool, good for you, you got out of it. You left that to me. So much for always looking out for me, right? You *selfish* prick.'

Leo held severe eye contact with Con for a moment more then moved to sit heavily back on the couch, dropping the coronet onto a side table and out of his range of vision.

Con sat on the other end of the couch.

'You could have said that to me four months ago.'

'I did, actually.'

'He did,' Ada agreed. 'Though with less theatrics.'

Con sighed and sank deeper into the couch, hips sliding down the cushion. He didn't look as hangdog as he had, but he still looked wrong without any hint of smile on him.

'First of all, none of us are storming out, none of us are doing the silent treatment thing,' Con said.

'I'm so glad I'm being included,' Ada said.

'You have the worst temper, Adelaide Morgana, you better believe I'm including you,' Con said.

'We said that back then too,' Leo said. 'We promised we wouldn't behave like they did.'

Ada pulled an armchair closer to the couch and situated herself in it. On Con's side. Leo felt resentment there, too, even if it was almost drowned out by the rest of it and even if he was done with shouting. Con had told Ada and not him. Ada had known and hadn't told him. He'd been excluded even before he moved to the Academy and excluded since he'd moved back, even though they had pretended greater closeness. And somehow he was still in the wrong in their eyes for his reaction, he could feel it. He understood. He shouldn't have shouted. They'd all heard enough shouting.

'You want me to be gracious about all of this,' Leo said. 'Everyone does—and I'm trying, I'm trying so hard to give the impression that I'm honoured to be king and have confidence in my abilities or whatever—but you want me to do that for you as well.'

'You being miserable isn't going to stop the fact that you are the king,' Ada said.

'The fact that I can't change it doesn't mean that I can just stop feeling bad about it!' Leo said. 'Hey, if you've got some spell or potion or whatever that'll just fix my feelings, then please, don't hold back.'

You were supposed to say that I don't have to hide with you, Leo thought. Now that his anger was receding, he could feel the hurt underneath it. He wished he was allowed to be angry instead.

'I'm sorry,' Con said. 'I … Do you want to know why? Or is it lousy of me to try and make excuses right now?'

Leo lifted his hand helplessly and let it drop back on his lap. 'Sure.'

'I remember you and Dicky being born,' Con said, nodding at Leo. 'And Ada too, obviously. I remember looking after you almost from the start. I remember changing Ada's nappies. I don't even know if Dad did, but I did. And everyone kept calling me a man, like I was responsible. I think it was supposed to be a compliment, like when people pretend to lose arm wrestles to kids. And I legitimately *felt* responsible for you three, especially once you started following me around, and everyone kept encouraging it because it was cute or maybe because I was free childcare, who knows. I was a pretty serious kid even before you came along and …'

Con paused and took one of Ada's and one of Leo's hands in his and squeezed. Leo let him, drawn into the story even though he wasn't sure why it was relevant.

'I don't blame you guys. I've always loved you so much and I'd do it the same way again. But I felt like I didn't get a childhood. Whether other people were actually doing the work or not, when I was six years old I felt like I was responsible for a couple of baby boys. And I didn't stop worrying about that until I was fifteen and I realised we live in a fucking castle full of staff and I could afford to stress less. And then I was anxious that I couldn't do magic and trying constantly anyway even though I knew it wouldn't work.'

Leo looked at Ada, who was staring at Con with attentive remorse. But not surprise. Leo's loneliness made him want to take his hand away from Con's, but he resisted. There was no point being angry. There was never a point to being angry.

'You're always so happy,' Leo said. 'You've always been happy.'

'I *am* happy,' Con assured him. 'Stressed, literally always and forever, but I'm happy. You were a fun kid to be around.'

Leo nodded numbly, not believing him but not wanting to interrupt further. Con withdrew his hands so that he could rub his jaw contemplatively.

'When I was about twelve, I think, probably a couple times earlier, but properly when I was twelve, anyway ... Yeah, that was when Dad started training me, you know, to be next in line.

'I probably don't need to explain it to you, hey. And he's not —I mean, he *wasn't* good with teenagers. Thought it was just me until you and Dicky turned thirteen and it was, swear to Trinity, like a switch, he doesn't—*didn't*—know what to do with teenagers, *fuck*, I don't know why I keep doing that, I know he's a past tense guy, I *know* he's dead.'

There were a few seconds of silence while Con seemed to reaffirm their dad's death in his mind. Leo hadn't slipped into present tense in months. Sometimes he had the peculiar feeling that their parents had actually been dead for years, or maybe like he couldn't remember seeing them very often when they were alive. He knew they had been there, but his mind was glossing over that fact in order to rewrite a different life. One where they hadn't been as significant and his loss wasn't as severe.

And Dicky. Dicky was dead, too. Ada thought that Leo's inability to hold this fact unconsciously was because it would hurt too much to accept it, which didn't exactly make Leo want to dig too deep into those feelings. He didn't think being sad like that would improve his job performance.

'And, okay, so it got better once I turned eighteen and for a few months there I thought my plan to join Sword and Shield was dramatic and maybe it wasn't so bad, you know, to do what he did. Because he wasn't good with teenagers but he was *really* good with adults. I felt special, like we were on the same team and like no one else was on our level.

'I wasn't thinking of being the king, to be honest, because that was decades and decades away in my mind, but I already had responsibilities. I was doing things and I was going to keep doing things, more things, and he wanted a second him, you know? But I thought that was probably okay, even watching how he was starting to be shit with you and Dicky and Ada. But then Max was born.

'I don't know, it made me see it. I saw what my childhood had been like and it made me cynical, and while I was looking at everything in that horrible way where I had myself convinced that I'd only ever been a tool, a first-born prince who was good at parties and who he trusted with pretty important jobs, I also started to see basically everything he did as bad.'

'What?' Leo said.

'Everything he did *was* bad,' Ada muttered.

'Yeah, 'cause you're nineteen,' Con said. 'He'd been horrible to you for half a dozen years and you were intelligent enough to figure that out and old enough not to ignore it. It got better.'

'No, wait,' Leo said. 'What are you talking about? You've been telling us for half a year that we're too harsh on him and that he loved us, even though it sure as hell didn't feel like it a lot of the time.'

'No, I know,' Con said.

'And you got out!' Leo said. 'You got some distance!'

'Look who's talking,' Ada said.

'Guys,' Con said. 'He was human. He did some shitty things and he did some good things, and hating him might be easier than mourning him, but it's not healthy the way you two are, I don't know, pretending like he was never a good dad.'

Ada looked like she wanted to say something scathing, but she visibly stopped herself. She hated their dad in a way that made Leo want to feel more moderately towards him so that he didn't sound like her. But she'd earned her resentment. Even if Leo sometimes thought she was the most like Richard out of any of them.

Genuinely curious, Leo asked, 'So why didn't you leave Sword and Shield once it didn't seem so bad anymore?'

'I love it,' Con said simply. 'I asked if I could stay as an unblessed, but you know. The whole lying to them for eight years thing. They weren't a fan of it.'

'It was still stupid,' Leo sighed.

'I know,' Con said. 'I'm sorry, Lee. I knew I was leaving someone else to do something I couldn't bear to do and that was shitty of me.'

'No, I'm genuinely talking about you joining an elite army with half your armour on and a wooden sword this time.'

'That makes your losses against me even more humiliating, oh nearly-trained mage.'

Leo took the cushion from behind his back and bapped Con over the head with it. Con grinned at him and, despite his hurt, Leo felt immeasurably better for seeing it.

For the next half hour, it felt like a weight had lifted that Leo hadn't even known existed. His siblings were no longer keeping something from him, and they were more relaxed for it. He knew he still wasn't happy, but he wasn't looking at that right now and he'd just have to deal with it. He loved Con, and this might have been the first instance he'd seen of Con acting selfishly. As soon as his feelings caught up with his logic, he'd be fine.

Danya poked her head through the door and smiled when she saw the three of them.

'So it went well?' she asked, stepping through and perching herself on the arm of Ada's chair.

'Oh, no,' Con said, almost cheerily. 'I've been kicked out of Sword and Shield and Leo hates me. And Ada is already trying to marry me off, presumably so she doesn't have to put up with me anymore.'

'That sounds about accurate,' Leo said.

'Oh dear,' Danya said. She rubbed Ada's back reassuringly, perhaps because Ada was the one in reach. 'Did they find out about the magic thing?'

'Danya knew?!' Leo exclaimed. He collapsed backwards onto the couch and covered his face with his hands. 'I have absolutely no friends whatsoever,' he said, voice muffled.

'Are we the only ones you would consider your friends?' Ada asked. 'That's a bit sad.'

'I didn't know for the longest time!' Danya said. 'I thought you already knew Leo, or I would have bothered Ada about telling you. It was only when we started slee—When we ... I mean, when we were in the same space, as a home base, we—with the rooms ...'

'When you moved in together,' Con offered.

'Yes!' Danya said. She looked flustered. Her eyes were almost entirely back to their usual warm brown after the blood magic, and the slight tinge of red to them didn't harshen her expression anymore.

'I'm a secretive person, but there are limits,' Ada said. 'When we moved in together, I could no longer disguise when I left and what for. And it was one thing to lie by omission. I didn't do well when asked outright.'

'You never do,' Danya said, smiling soppily at Ada. 'Not unless you've written a script.' Ada graciously allowed this to stand.

'Did Dicky know?' Leo asked.

'No,' Con said. 'I think he would have killed me if he'd known.'

'But he *did* want to be like Dad,' Leo said.

'It still wasn't fun for him,' Con said.

'He loved it,' Ada said dismissively. 'He might have killed you if you *hadn't* stepped out of the way.'

'You don't miss him?' Leo asked Ada.

'I don't miss any of them,' she said, not meeting his eyes. 'No one nags me about my presentation or what I eat and I haven't had to go on an awkward, supervised date with a random prince or lord from who-cares-where since they died. My life is objectively better now.'

Typical Ada. Leo wondered if she believed that she was telling the truth. From his vantage point, nineteen seemed very young.

'Do *you* miss him?' Danya asked. Ada looked up in interest.

'Of course,' Leo said automatically. 'Probably not enough, I guess. I don't know. We had barely spent any time together for years. And I think I'm kind of angry at him for dying. I wouldn't have to be mad at Con if Dicky hadn't … I know he didn't *quit*, but it feels that way sometimes. But I don't know. Sometimes I think I don't have the energy to grieve all three of them. And my head's so full of everything else.'

'Like who did it,' Ada said.

'Like whether hiring a couple of restorative magicians or buying newer furniture is more fiscally responsible,' Leo sighed. 'But yeah, I guess I can't pretend that whoever is behind the attacks is unimportant now that there's been two of them. Now that we know for sure it wasn't just an assassination.'

'There'll be another,' Con said bleakly. 'They clearly didn't get what they wanted out of me.'

That statement sat heavy in the room like a rich meal on a sensitive stomach. It was hard to find a way around the space it occupied. Still, something wasn't adding up.

'*How* do you not have magic?' Leo asked.

Con's eyes darted away and his mouth flatlined. Leo looked to Ada, incredulous that he was still being excluded from the truth when Con clearly knew.

'It's the most archaic rule of magic,' Ada said, defensive on Con's behalf. 'They were married by the time he was born, what should it matter if conception and wedding didn't happen in the so-called "proper" order?'

Leo's jaw dropped. He looked at Con for confirmation, but his eyes were still downcast. His *blue* eyes. Which happened, of course it happened, and the timing didn't necessarily mean Ada was wrong …

'Did Dad know?' Leo asked.

Con nodded jerkily.

'He did?' Ada asked, sounding genuinely astonished. A tiny, proud part of Leo was relieved to no longer be the only one who had been on the outside of a secret. But a larger part was concerned.

'He didn't stop you from joining Sword and Shield, even with the danger,' Leo said quietly.

Con shrugged.

'Kings should have magic,' he said. 'He agreed I should step aside.'

It was almost a relief when Forster came and found Leo for his next appointment. Con smiled at Leo as he left but made no move to follow. That was alright. Leo could do this alone.

GIVEN HER STATUS, everyone in Praecentor should have known when Danya's birthday was, but of course they didn't. In fact, she had been cagey with the date even when she was a child, so it was only due to a very forceful effort on a teenage and besotted Ada's part that the family ever found out, even with her always having lived at the castle. Duo couldn't be divided into three, and neither could twenty, a fact that Danya still remained maudlin about, despite having passed the age when this disappointment might have been reasonable quite a few years ago. Now, on her twenty-second birthday, Leo watched with amusement as she lamented, egged on to even lower depths by his siblings.

'I was due on the first of Trei,' she said, tracing the rim of her glass with a finger with a distinct poutiness to her. 'One of three is three, and I know I could have managed a good time.'

'Managed a good time,' Leo repeated.

'And you were so auspicious in other regards,' Ada said, grinning at Leo.

'I was!' Danya agreed. 'Three mothers, one from each tine of Sword and Shield, with the blood of prevenient Trinitas and the Empress in each! Who else has that?'

'And the thing with the place,' Con prompted.

'I was conceived in a church and born in one and I will be killed in one!'

'Wait, can you see the future?' Leo asked.

'But no! My mums had to go ahead and do it early. If they'd asked the High Enchantress, she would have said for them to do it on the 18th of Vierus—'

'It's really important that you tell me if you can see the future,' Leo insisted.

'Which would have given me a Sommertide birthday, probably!'

'At least you've done all you can to be the most auspiciest since then,' Con said, patting Danya on the shoulder reassuringly. 'Another round?'

'No, hang on, someone tell me if Danya can see the future!' Leo said, standing up.

'He's up, he buys!' Ada declared.

'Because it would explain a lot but also it's not *spiritually* possible—I need to know if you've broken the laws of the universe.'

'C'mon, Lee,' Con said, also standing. 'I'll help you carry.'

Leo went with Con to the bar, but only because it was Danya's birthday and he did—contrary to some hurtful songs that got stuck in everyone's head, even his own—know how to relax. Just because he didn't invite the fool to come and read ghost stories under a blanket fort with him didn't mean he didn't have hobbies. And the Trinity knew he needed them now while everyone expected him to just keep going along running the bloody country while there was an angry group with a vendetta against his family on the loose. Con leaned heavily on the bar as they waited for service, looking as he always did when he was two beers in. It made Leo smile with memories of the best parts of their Sommertides. He rubbed his chest against the ache that came with happy memories. He had liked it when his parents were drunk. It made them seem genuinely happy and loving.

'Danya can't see the future,' Con laughed. His eyes were closed. Two beers. Large ones, but still. He was built like a horse; it didn't make any sense. Leo contemplated words that might suck some of the alcohol magically out of Con's beer. Detoxificate … Sap … Dilute … He didn't like the sound of any of them, and Con knew how to slow down anyway. They just didn't get the chance to do things like this often. The secret nature of the date and their disguises were giving them more freedom than Leo had had since he'd come home.

'I didn't *actually* think she could,' Leo said, looking doubtfully back over at the table. Ada and Danya were using their absence as an opportunity to kiss shamelessly.

'She does this every year,' Con said. 'Every year.' He straightened and put on a high voice, even though Danya's voice wasn't high. '"I could have been the most magical magicker ever if my mums were as good at dates as me! I like to wear dresses because I look like a triangle!"'

'Is that a thing?' Leo asked.

'What?' Con asked. 'No, I was being a shit.'

'No, like, priests, they wear those dresses, those—' Leo gestured up and down his body. 'Vestments.'

'That can't be because of triangles,' Con said.

'She lives in a triangular castle.'

'Yeah, and it's really cool, don't knock it.'

Leo laughed. He leaned against the bar next to Con and wondered when he had last been this happy. He even liked that it was taking *forever* to get service, because it meant that the glamours Danya had made for them were working.

When he and Con got back to the table, Danya and Ada had stopped kissing and were talking about magic.

'No, because you'd have to study your whole life!' Danya said. 'You might as well work occasionally and use the money to buy the wine.'

'I believe in you,' Ada said.

'It's not! You can't just!'

'What's this?' Con asked.

'Ada thinks that I should be able to turn water into wine,' Danya said.

'Oh, no,' Leo said. 'No, don't drink that. It doesn't work.'

'That's what I said!' Danya said.

'Why not?' Con asked. 'There's loads of good words about wine. Good songs, even.'

'Because, okay, magic works based on understanding and reverence,' Danya said, sounding like she was gearing up for a lecture.

'All I know is that this one girl in the year ahead of me had been trying the whole time she had been at the Academy and she wasn't even close,' Leo said before Danya could get started. 'She could make alcohol, that's really simple, but she absolutely could not make anything that was drinkable. She was always getting sent to the healers because she had messed up the alcohol content while she was trying to get the taste right.'

'I believe in you,' Ada repeated.

'You are a *princess*,' Danya hissed. 'You can afford your own wine! You don't need me to mess up making you wine!'

'You'd make a pretty corpse,' Leo told Ada. 'If you did want to drink Danya's wine that would definitely be poison.'

'Thank you, Leo,' Ada said, reaching out to touch Leo's wrist with the most sincere expression of gratitude he had ever seen on her face. Leo felt slightly proud of his compliment despite the logical assumption that Ada was messing with him.

'You could do it yourself,' Con suggested. 'Your magic is amazing.'

'Thank you, and yes, you are extraordinarily correct,' Ada said. 'But unfortunately I seem to have spent the last nine years of my life working on combat. Of course, I don't resent you.'

'Right,' Con said, sounding and looking very guilty. Ada smiled at him pleasantly, because she was an evil, evil woman.

'I don't think I want to die of alcohol poisoning, though,' Ada said.

'This is a normal topic of conversation for a birthday party,' Leo observed dryly.

'Drowning?' Danya guessed.

'Romantic,' Ada agreed. 'But the bloating of the corpse.'

'Hanging, because of your many crimes,' Leo said.

'I will never be caught,' Ada said.

'Swords,' Con said. 'Fire.'

'Which one?' Ada asked.

Con thought.

'Both?'

But before Ada could answer, a tray was deposited next to her arm.

'Thank you, but this isn't ours,' Ada said.

Then she looked up, and her reaction to their new visitor was very different to Leo's.

'Fool!' she cried delightedly, her tone merrier than it ever would be sober. 'Leo, scoot across.'

'I absolutely will not,' Leo said.

This did not prevent the fool from joining them. Leo gritted his teeth as Danya and Ada made room for it and Con kicked his ankle to tell him to be nice. Leo scowled at him because he didn't think he would ask Con to be nice to someone who had pulled his pants down when he was talking to a priest about the appropriate number of candles for the Sommertide ceremonies.

But it wasn't awful, not at first. The fool knew a lot of jokes that weren't aimed at Leo's incompetence. Leo still felt on edge, anticipating the point at which the fool would decide that it was more interesting to laugh at Leo than with him, but with each minute that it didn't come, Leo dared to relax a little more. After all, he rationalised, Danya called it a friend. Surely it wouldn't want to ruin a friend's birthday.

But even if it was on its best behaviour, the fool didn't know how to put away its claws entirely.

'But His Majesty would make a wonderful model,' it said jovially. 'After all, his face is always the same!' At this, the fool made a truly awful grimace, which Leo supposed was a parody of Leo's default expression. Leo was thankful that his family at least didn't seem amused, but the barb still landed.

'Wow,' Leo said, leaning back with a self-deprecating laugh. 'You sure know where to sink the knife. I must be completely transparent.'

'No need to be transparent when I learnt first *from your parent*,' the fool sing-songed.

The blood drained from Leo's face. He could feel his magic under his skin, daring him to voice his hurt.

'He's nothing like our father,' Ada said.

'Play nicely, fool,' Danya said, tone warning.

The fool was trying to get to Leo, like it always was. It didn't mean it was telling the truth. This was just another weak spot that it knew how to exploit. That, or Leo *was* like his dad. He certainly hated the fool just like his dad had hated its predecessor.

'The fool isn't capable of playing nice,' Leo said mechanically. His blood was pulsing hot in his ears and he was angry enough that it was a wonder his voice didn't shake with it. He was suddenly horrifically aware that to be angry was to force that resemblance further, and still he wasn't able to shut down his feelings. 'Its sole function is to see my flaws and do the verbal equivalent of shitting wetly and enthusiastically all over the throne room. It would be unreasonable to expect a country as small as Canticalica to get a fool who had heard of nuance.'

'I live to serve,' the fool said, inclining its head with a soft jingle of bells. 'His Majesty makes his fool's sole function all the easier by having so very many flaws.'

Leo gritted his teeth and stood. The fool jumped to standing too, looking thrilled at the prospect of a fight.

'Back off,' Leo said. 'You don't have an audience here.'

'Who better than these?' the fool asked, black eyes wide. It leaned closer and dropped its voice to a whisper loud enough for the table to still hear it, and with a meaningful glance downward said, 'Everyone else *already* knows that you can't perform.'

Leo shoved the fool hard enough to make it stagger backwards a couple of steps before springing back and shoving Leo in return. Leo grabbed the front of the fool's colourful jerkin, not entirely sure what he intended to do with it. He didn't have time to decide, because suddenly the bartender was on them pulling them both by their collars towards the door.

'I don't give a shit if you're fighting,' he said, in a tone that suggested that he wouldn't mind fighting them himself. 'But you're not doing it in my bar.'

The bartender kicked the door open and threw them outside. Leo and the fool stared warily at each other, as if determining the exact conditions under which they would be able to walk away. The moon was nearly full in the sky, the late-spring air lifting wisps of Leo's hair distractingly around his face. The fool's colourful clothes were muted without lamps shining on them and its posture was decidedly humourless. Leo thought the fool might want to fight as much as he did.

They stared at each other without moving long enough for Leo's family to join them.

'Are you both quite finished?' Danya asked.

'A fool is just a mirror, to show his ruler clearer—'

Leo punched the fool before it could sing another word. The fool touched its fingers to its split lip and Leo had a moment to feel some combination of guilty and embarrassed before the fool tackled him to the ground. Leo scrabbled to try and gain the advantage, pushing and hitting, kicking his feet in the direction of the fool's legs. In response, the fool pulled Leo's hair and punched him in the ribs. They rolled over twice, resulting in Leo's shoulder ending up in a puddle. Leo recoiled so suddenly that he was able to sit up slightly, so he twisted and shoved the fool into the muddy water instead. He punched it in the cheek, finally having the advantage.

'Oh for Trinity's sake,' Ada said. 'Disentwine.'

The spell flung them apart. Leo glared at the fool, who was straightening its hat fussily as if nothing was the matter. Leo felt the aches of future bruises start to demand his attention now that he wasn't focused on the fight.

'I'm not my dad,' Leo spat. His dad would never have done something this stupid. 'You don't know me.'

'I don't know you?' the fool asked, voice incredulous. Whether it was because of surprise, outrage or just the fight, the fool's voice had rarely sounded so much like a normal person's. 'What is my name, Your Majesty?' it asked, with sarcastic deference.

Leo's mouth opened to protest, but the demand unbalanced him. How was he supposed to know that? Wasn't a fool's identity supposed to be secret? Leo knew very little about the Consortium of Fools (he had refused to educate himself on principle) but everyone knew *that*. They weren't supposed to have gender or race or names. They weren't included in the census, didn't pay taxes and were exempt from justice. Leo hadn't realised that anonymity didn't extend all the way to him. He probably should have.

The fool glared at him and was then was struck with a look that was something like guilt for a moment. It was gone almost immediately, and then the fool was springing to its feet and spreading its arms wide.

'Oh, there once was a king who rolled in the dirt!' it sang. It twirled theatrically and started to skip away in the direction of the Round Tower. 'He behaved like a child, for his feelings were hurt ...'

Leo groaned into his hands. If that song featured in the fool's performances tomorrow he was going to ... do absolutely nothing, because he had proven conclusively that he had no control over what the fool did. He hated it like he'd never hated anyone before. It was easy to hate it. He was allowed to. Even sore and embarrassed now, he had a rush in his stomach from the satisfaction that came from punching someone who deserved it.

'Apologise to Danya,' Ada said, kicking Leo firmly in the already aching ribs.

Leo's stomach dropped. Leo could have humiliated himself any day; it didn't need to be on Danya's birthday. It was one thing to be so obviously a bad king, it was a whole nother issue that he was failing as a friend.

'Sorry, Danya,' he said, looking up at her.

'Dinner and drinks and a show,' Danya said cheerily. 'It's getting late anyway, we might as well go home. Your punishment is that I won't heal your injuries.'

'That's fair,' Leo sighed.

He heaved himself to his feet and made an embarrassing noise halfway up. It *was* fair, but he didn't like how his ribs or his knee were feeling and he would have appreciated it if Danya took pity on him.

'Um ...' he said, racking his brain for a moment. 'Palliate.' The pain eased only a little and he tried again. 'Ameliorate.'

'You don't look very inspired or devout,' Con said.

'Yeah,' Leo sighed. It didn't hurt so much that he felt the need to beg one of the girls for help, but he wasn't looking forward to all the stairs up to their rooms. Con clapped him on the shoulder and Leo winced.

'I think you're improving though,' he said encouragingly. 'Beating it in a fight was one of your goals, right?'

'Yeah,' Leo sighed again.

He looked in the direction of the tower, where the fool was no longer visible. He wasn't feeling very victorious.

16

LEO HAD INSISTED on examining the room alone, desperate for a minute of respite from the continuous ceremony of condescension and the expectation of authority from his heads of avenues. They needed the room to host the delegation from Leutesland, who, shockingly, Canticalica owed money to. They couldn't afford to pay it back. Leo needed to charm the emissaries into postponing the payments, which was a skill slightly outside his usual domain. Leo thought he could pull it off. He might not have been trained to be king, but he *had* had amiable hosting drilled into him from a very young age.

In order to navigate the path that Richard had always chosen, they had to use his strategies. No one, not even their creditors—*especially* not the creditors—was allowed to know how deep in debt they were. If it was common knowledge, then Canticalica's ability to pay back their loans would be questioned, which would lead to the insistence that their loans be paid back immediately, which would lead to them transitioning from being privately screwed to fully bankrupt.

So, Leo had to host the delegation with the ceremony of someone who could easily repay their loans if pressed but give the impression that they could be using the money to stimulate the economy or something that would give Leutesland a greater return on investment if they deferred the payments just a little longer. Hanna was coming up with a plausible excuse. The actual hosting of the thing was to take place in the entertaining room that Leo was approaching. It was reportedly cosy enough to feel welcoming, with excellent natural light and intricate decorative moulding, features that enhanced the room in ways that neglect couldn't hope to override, even though all the hosting that had taken place in Leo's lifetime had been as part of extravagant parties that made this kind of room obsolete.

Leo entered the dark room with balanced expectations. He was very aware the castle needed maintenance and a room that hadn't been used in decades would likely be worse than most, but he wasn't ready to give up hope. He walked over to the curtains and threw them open so as to see the room at its best vantage. At once, a bat who had been squatting in the curtains jerked to wakefulness and started thrashing around the room with piercing squeaks.

'Empress' truth,' Leo swore, ducking under his forearm in alarm.

The bat flung itself into the window, which cracked but didn't break, and dropped a foot before it recovered its balance and resumed its noisy flapping and screeching about the room.

'Okay, okay,' Leo said under his breath, trying to think of a way out underneath the din. He looked for a catch at the windows, but they didn't open like that. The lower half of the glass was in strips of panes that rested on top of one another in a way that allowed them to be tilted to control how much air flowed into the room, in a way that Leo supposed must have been fashionable once, which couldn't open wide enough for a bat. They were in fact disused and warped and no longer really opened at all. They didn't fully close either, and at some point had allowed water into the room, leading to rotten and mouldy carpet at their base. The bat attempted to escape through a different window and cracked that glass too.

'Oh for fuck's sake,' Leo said. He pointed his hand at the bat and said, 'Somnial.'

The bat dropped heavily to the ground and Leo winced. He'd just meant to make it fall asleep, not injure it. Perhaps it would be okay. He was vaguely aware that bats were fairly common and treated as a nuisance in these parts, but that didn't mean he wanted to play exterminator.

In any case, it was no longer distracting him from the state of the room. The curtains he had drawn back were threadbare, ugly and sun-bleached. They looked like they had been used as a nest for a bat, funnily enough. The furniture, where it wasn't also damaged by bats and perhaps moths, was tasteless.

Leo sank to the floor and stacked his forearms on his knees, his head on his arms, and told himself that there was nothing to be gained by crying. His body wanted to, and he was already behaving in an unkingly way, but he couldn't—what was the use in crying? Did he expect someone to come across him, to give him comfort and attention without him having to explicitly ask for it? That felt like a selfish want, and kind of manipulative. He breathed through it and tried not to think about anything at all. That wasn't a personal strength.

The door opened and Leo looked up, not sure what his excuse would be but ready to improvise. But it was the fool, and he wouldn't get away with lying to it. He let his forehead fall back down.

'Please,' he said, voice ineffectually pointed in the wrong direction. 'Just leave me alone.'

The quiet melody of bells told Leo that was not happening, that the fool was instead approaching him. He groaned, feeling even more likely to cry and somehow even more alone.

'No, of course not,' Leo said. 'Why would you? I explicitly pay you to torture me, of course you're here. If you kick me, literally or metaphorically when I am so incredibly down, I'll—' There wasn't a single threat that Leo could level. 'Probably just be sad, I guess.'

There was no sound from the fool, which wasn't what Leo had come to expect. Leo lifted his head so that it was his chin leaning on his arms instead of his forehead and he could see what was happening. The fool was sitting cross-legged right in front of him. Leo looked at it miserably. The fool continued not to speak, or sing or humiliate him in any way.

'I know that you know everything anyway, but this seems unfair,' Leo said. 'I really don't need some limerick inspired by how pathetic I'm being right now.'

The fool rolled its eyes. It did it with its whole head, because everything it did was larger than life. Except for how it was sitting right now, but that was … Leo didn't know what that was.

'The Consortium says you're supposed to keep our secrets,' Leo said, looking down. 'So maybe you won't be a dick about this, but damn, can't a guy have a mental breakdown in a shitty entertaining room without it being …' Leo looked up again. 'It's really hard to read your expressions with all the paint,' he said.

The fool shrugged. Leo made an attempt at laughter. It didn't really sound like laughter. It sounded like he was crying, which he wasn't, and that was … that was *unfair*. Leo hid his face again and tried to pull himself together. He felt tears leave his eyes and he kept completely silent as they did. He'd always been able to do that when he couldn't just logic his way out of being upset. His breath felt unsteady in his throat, but he was sure it wasn't audible. His shoulders shook, but only once. In his mind he sobbed, which was almost as good as doing it in reality and almost as bad as well. The ridiculous thought occurred to him that he might even take the fool's comfort at this point. It was a sobering realisation, and he rubbed his face from side to side on his sleeves to dry up any evidence of his shame.

He looked back up. The fool was still there, looking as sombre as someone could look with a permanent grin covering their face.

'Why aren't you talking?' Leo asked. He could feel that his

face was still a little wet, but maybe it wasn't obvious. He wasn't about to draw attention to it by attempting to wipe it away.

The fool mimed locking its lips and throwing away the key, then it cupped its hand to its ear in the direction of Leo.

'You don't want to listen to me,' Leo said.

The fool nodded emphatically and musically.

Leo frowned suspiciously, then threw up his hands and dropped his knees so that his legs were crossed as well, saying, 'Fine, fine!'

He swallowed and took a breath. This was a bad idea. But the fool knew everything anyway.

'We're broke,' Leo said. 'We're so broke. And I keep having to pay for useless things, things that make no sense, like, to the point where I don't know if I can even trust my staff, because what if they want us to be broke for some reason, or I'm paying for something they have an interest in, and they know they can just tell me that it's essential and I won't know any better because I don't know what the hell I'm doing.'

The fool grimaced.

Leo stared at it, wondering why the hell he'd said all that. Sure, the Consortium of Fools did have some pretty strict guidelines on how its members were supposed to behave, but Leo had no evidence that the fool in front of him cared about any of that.

'Can I trust them?' Leo asked. 'You'd know, right? Except, why would I trust your word on whether I can trust them.'

It really *was* difficult to read the fool's expressions. Leo took a shuddering breath, hating that his voice wasn't steady.

'I sound paranoid. My dad wouldn't have doubted himself like this; he would have just known. He knew people. He had faults, but he knew how to read people.' Leo chewed on the inside of his cheek, then made himself stop. 'I don't know if it's more messed up that I miss him or that I don't.'

The fool cocked its head to the side questioningly. Leo thought he should probably shut up. The stuff about the budget the fool had to know already because it was everywhere, it would have heard. But it didn't know Leo's feelings and it didn't need to know them to have more weapons than it already did.

'I kind of hated him. He was a bad person and a bad dad, and sometimes I'm just glad that he's gone. Glad that I don't have to feel how bad he was at being a dad, that my siblings don't have to—Trinity, *Max*. He's young. Dad was good when we were young. He liked kids. Maybe Max can think of him in a good way.'

Leo breathed deeply because he wasn't going to cry again. He looked at the ceiling because he couldn't look at the fool's thoughtful black eyes any longer.

'But he was my *dad*,' he said.

His voice cracked and he squeezed his eyes closed but it didn't matter, tears leaked out anyway. His shoulders contracted in on themselves and his lip wobbled in a horribly involuntary way.

A warm hand touched his and Leo looked down, saw compassion through the blurry veil of tears, and hung his head and sobbed, turning his hand helplessly to hold onto the only person he could. The fool's thumb stroked over the back of Leo's hand, even though Leo was holding on too tight.

Leo fought to get on top of his feelings, gasped for breath, but all he could manage to say was, *'He was my dad,'* again.

'You're okay,' the fool murmured, so quietly that Leo couldn't be sure that he hadn't imagined it.

Leo leaned slowly to the right until he fell onto the floor. He was basically done crying, but the sadness made him feel physically heavy. The fool didn't let go of his hand, even though Leo's was almost limp now. After a moment, the fool lay down on the floor too.

'I miss my mum too,' Leo mumbled. 'She sort of fades into

the background. He was so big, there wasn't space for her. I want there to be. I resent him so much for not letting there be, even now. But then that's me thinking about him again. That's not even addressing how wrapped up in him Dicky was.'

They lay together for a while. When Leo looked into the fool's eyes, he could almost tune out the face paint, the clothes. It looked like a human. And it *was*, it was just … But Leo had learnt his distrust from his dad, who wouldn't get out of his thoughts today. As if it was just today.

'My dad hated you. Or, your predecessor. I don't know, did you take over as fool when Dad was still alive?'

The fool shook its head.

'Right, the other one then. I mean, he probably wouldn't have liked you either. I didn't need to say that.'

The fool looked amused.

'Wait, not at all?' Leo said. 'Is that a thing? Do new kings get new fools?'

The fool shook its head, all amusement gone. Leo frowned.

'But the other one left and you've been my fool from the start, I don't—'

The fool shook its head again, and Leo recognised exactly what was making its eyes so sad. His heart clenched in sympathy, then in self-reprimand. That was insensitive of him.

'It died,' Leo said, feeling awful and knowing his expression was every bit as full of unwelcome and misplaced understanding as the faces of all the people who had offered him their condolences. 'In the blast?'

The fool nodded, then closed its eyes, expression unreadable.

'Sorry,' Leo whispered. 'I'm so sorry.'

The fool said nothing. It was so closed off that it might have been asleep. Leo squeezed its hand and repeated what the fool had done for him, stroking his thumb over the back of the fool's hand.

Leo didn't know how it worked, the whole fool thing. Was it an apprentice, the same way Danya was to the previous High Enchantress? Even though Danya had mixed feelings about the old mage who had trained her, she would have been devastated if she'd earned her post through her death, rather than because Erwina had had enough of castles one day. The previous fool clearly wasn't just some person who held the role before this one got ushered in from some other place, or Leo wouldn't be looking at such obvious grief.

'Keep talking,' the fool said, voice rough and deep, eyes still closed. 'Distract me.'

Leo's mouth opened to protest against the fool's determination to not acknowledge its emotions (something he vaguely recognised as hypocritical), but despite his concerns, he couldn't doubt that the fool knew exactly what it was doing at all times. Even if it didn't sound remotely like the fool when it wasn't singing.

'I feel like a dick for continuing on this path,' Leo said quietly, 'but I honestly don't know what else to say.'

''S fine,' the fool said.

'Okay,' Leo said. He still felt like a dick, but okay. 'I think Dad's fool, faith, no, I can't call it that, they'd both hate it. I think the last one threatened Dad's pride.' Leo shook his head. 'No, his masculinity. I guess that's pride too, but it was in that way, you know—I can't explain it. It's different.'

The fool nodded. Leo felt relief that he didn't have to work to make himself understood. His thumb continued on its way, brushing against the fool's soft glove in a rhythm he didn't have to think about, the rough callus from his sword catching on the cloth.

'He could dish it out,' Leo said. 'He liked to laugh. He just—it was control. Everything about him, it was all about control. I really don't want to be like him, but I am. But then you see it, don't you?'

The fool shook its head.

'Ah, so you can be kind when there's no one to see,' Leo laughed sadly. 'It's true, though. I hate you.'

The fool opened its eyes. It didn't look upset or surprised. How could it, when Leo said as much and showed it so frequently.

'You show everyone how I'm falling short and I hate that I'm falling short. I was really good at the Academy. I could pretend to be modest, but what's the point? And not just at magic. There's a lot of theory, a lot of reading. I was even good at having friends there, sort of. I mean, I've got all of three letters since I left, but still. It's all useless here. I kind of knew it would be. I was just buying time before I had to live in the real world.'

Leo released the fool's hand and rolled over onto his back. The ceiling, at least, looked fine. The chandelier was even intact, though the state of the glass was anyone's guess. He wished he could fix things like that. He wished he could repair this whole room, the whole castle, with just his words. But magic has to be appreciated, loved. If it becomes a chore, the words are lost, potentially forever.

'Sorry,' Leo said. 'I complain too much. This is so incredibly not helpful, what I'm doing here.'

His heart ached again at this new failure, but not enough to send him back towards the spiral he'd just had. That wouldn't be helpful either, and he was almost ready to just get on with it. He'd find something he could actually achieve, and then he'd be fine. He turned his head to look at the fool again.

'Do I look like I've been lying on the floor crying like a fucking toddler?'

The fool shook its head.

'I'm going to be so *astonishingly* cross if you're lying.'

Leo closed his eyes and breathed, in and out, in and out, in and out. Then he stood up. The fool leapt up with all the nimbleness that Leo hated, but he couldn't work up the energy to feel any way about it now.

'Why did you do that?' Leo asked. 'Why did you help me?'

The fool stared at the ceiling for a moment, then cleared its throat. Its face transformed; its dark eyes became almost glassy, its smile infuriatingly false. The insincerity of it all grated. Leo couldn't find the person who had just listened to him anywhere in that face.

'You have a cook to bring you food, you have a fool to talk all lewd; you have a maid to clean the place, you have a fool to make a face; you have a horse to take you far, you have a fool to spit and spar. You have a fool, you have a fool, but all you see is someone cruel. You have a fool, you have a fool, you have a tool to help you rule.'

Leo's mouth fell open in confusion, but the fool didn't give him time to respond. It leaned forward, tweaked Leo's nose, then backflipped away, threw up its hands in celebration then skipped out of the room, each double-step violently exaggerated into a mockery.

Leo almost felt like lying on the floor again to process that, but he didn't have time. He didn't have time for anything. He felt like he would always be ten steps behind, falling further whenever he paused for breath.

He should have apologised for the fight, he realised. He hadn't even thought of it.

17

LEO HAD RECEIVED his first marriage proposal when he was two years old. Of course, it hadn't been given to him personally, nor was it made by the person intended to marry him, nor had he met the intended person or the proposer. Canticalica was a small kingdom, but it *was* still a kingdom, and princes and princesses were rarities. And the cheese it produced was really very good.

Since inheriting the throne, Leo had not received a single proposal. It wasn't like they were a daily occurrence back when he was a prince, but when the first one came it made Leo pause to reflect. Why had no one wanted to swoop in and marry him before he had figured out how to be king, while he was still very bullyable?

'Because, Your Majesty,' Ada said when Leo wondered this out loud, 'you were a completely unknown entity. They could have been subjecting your future spouse to someone completely horrid, like Dicky, may the Trinity rest his horrifically bland soul.'

'How you manage to get through the day when you're still so in mourning is a mystery to me,' Leo said.

Ada, who was opening Leo's alarmingly large pile of mail for him and throwing most of it away, did not seem to feel the need to acknowledge that Leo had spoken.

'And besides,' she continued, 'royal engagements take years to finalise. More than enough time for you to find your feet. Those are the things attached to your ankles, by the way. Just keep your steps within the rose petal path I am laying out for you.'

Leo rolled his eyes. Ada would probably be a very formidable puppet-master if she was willing to give up her free time. She kept up with the goings on about the castle and liked to intrude on Leo in his office to offer unsolicited commentary and advice, and she was invaluable when it came to throwing away mail, but Leo had expected much worse meddling than he got.

'Okay, so is it a good thing that I've got this proposal now?'

'Well that depends,' Ada said. 'Do you *love* this woman? Do you *yearn* for her? Do your loins *gurgle* at her absence?'

'Ada, I am confiscating verbs from you,' Leo said.

Ada looked at Leo with smug satisfaction and shrugged lazily.

'The proposal. Good? No. Borderline insulting, given her status. A second daughter, and of a lord no less.'

Smartarse.

'Neue Wolke is much bigger than Canticalica,' Leo pointed out. 'We have like three lords and a lady, total.'

'Yes, well, hoorah for Neue Wolke. Is hoorah a verb?'

'Depends on context,' Leo said. '"Is", on the other hand, is undoubtedly an action word.'

'Shit,' Ada said. 'Well, I would have had to resume using them to tell you what to do anyway.'

Leo would protest, but he felt out of his depth here. Running the country was easy compared to making this decision. He knew that he would not be able to marry for love—if he loved his spouse it would either be a very appreciated bonus or the result of earnest work after their marriage had begun, it couldn't be the first consideration. He had come to terms with it, but it was in all honesty one of the strongest reasons he had least wanted to be king. It was also one of the strongest reasons he had never allowed himself to think seriously about abdicating and leaving ruling up to Ada. He *hoped* he would be able to spare Ada from a political marriage. He loved Danya, and even if their relationship didn't work out (basically inconceivable, but Ada *was* nineteen), Leo wanted Ada to be able to choose her spouse, for the safety of the spouse if nothing else. But if Ada was queen, she would be in the same position that Leo was in.

Leo was fairly confident that this marriage proposal was one to turn down. The dowry would be very appreciated, but the woman's rank left something to be desired and there wasn't any particular reason to form an alliance to Neue Wolke apart from a general feeling that alliances were good things to have. But he so badly didn't want to be married yet that he didn't want to consider any marriage, and he knew that could be biasing him against a union that was in the best interests of the realm.

'And what should I do?' Leo asked.

'Reject it,' Ada said. 'Nicely, of course. I don't think they seriously expect you to do more than say, "No, thank you," so I wouldn't go overboard with the niceties. Honestly, there's almost no way this wasn't just an excuse for Princess Blanche to be sent here to negotiate the whole thing.'

'Is there gossip?' Leo asked, sitting up straighter.

'There is always gossip!' Ada declared. 'That is one of the core tenets of my worldview.'

Leo gestured his hand for Ada to go on.

'Queen Isolde can't stand her,' Ada grinned, leaning forward as though to prevent being overheard. 'Blanche had been to three different countries this year before ours. Every time she goes home, her sister sends her somewhere else, usually with a piss-poor offer of marriage for someone or other important.'

'Isn't she worried about offending someone with a shitty offer?' Leo asked.

'Piss-poor is possibly putting it a little strong,' Ada allowed. '"Bold" may be the more appropriate word. Though *this* proposal is *absolutely* piss-poor. I suspect that in addition to getting poor

Blanche out of her hair, Isolde is also taking your measure, finding out how diplomatic you can be.'

'I wish people would stop measuring me,' Leo groaned, slumping down again.

'Tough,' Ada said. Then, looking at the most recent letter she'd picked up, 'Oh, in the name of the blessed Empress' fucking *socks*, why in the world would someone think *you* would be the one who handles whether literally anyone in this castle can have the day off for an obviously false medical procedure that coincidentally takes place the day after Sommertide. Conflagration.'

The letter burst into flames. Ada brushed the fingertips of her left hand against her thumb to get rid of the heat from them. Leo would have burnt his if he'd attempted it, but it was a favourite move of Ada's and she'd long since mastered the trick of when to release the paper to the air.

'Shouldn't I have handed that off to Abigail?' Leo asked.

'The only reason he would have asked you is because he would have already asked her and been rightly laughed out of her office. He didn't deserve your time, or mine.'

'He gave you the delight of setting something on fire,' Leo pointed out.

'Perhaps he deserved his hangover day after all,' Ada said thoughtfully, lifting a pinch of ash from her skirt in contemplation as if she could reform a burnt thing. 'Leo,' she said suddenly.

'Yeah?'

'May I have the day off after Sommertide? It's for medical reasons.'

I N THE END, Blanche made rejecting her countryman's proposal easy. She was a handsome woman, at least a decade older than Leo, with hair in a dark plait that hung almost to her waist. Her habit of sewing during conversations meant that eye contact was always softened by her occupation. Leo had always thought of sewing as something Ada pretended to be doing so she could stab Dicky with her needle when no one was looking, but Blanche managed to seem engaged in both the conversation and her work. She seemed like she was designed to move, but convention kept her seated, so sewing was the best she could do.

'I can't pretend my sister won't be disappointed,' she said. 'Perhaps coming to our capital will give you the opportunity to reconsider.'

'I would love to visit one day,' Leo said. 'But I'm sure you can appreciate that it's a bit early in my rule to leave Praecentor.'

'It's a lovely place to be beholden to,' Blanche said.

'It is,' Leo agreed. 'It feels like the only part of it that I see is the inside of this castle these days. Have you had a chance to see much outside the castle?'

'I ride every day,' she said, 'but I don't venture far. There's a lovely track that goes along the Fluvius your groundskeeper showed me. I haven't done much adventuring apart from that.'

'I should ride more,' Leo said. 'My horse probably doesn't even recognise me anymore. I just don't get the time.'

'You don't *make* the time,' Blanche said, with a mischievous look in her eye that showed she knew she was using words that the worst kind of teacher at the Trinitas Academy used.

'Would you have preferred I cancel our meeting so that I could go for a ride?' Leo asked, though he couldn't help smiling.

'How long do you have set aside for this meeting?' Blanche asked.

'Your Highness, I'm not leaving early just to—'

'I happen to be capable of riding a horse and talking simultaneously. Is this considered a particularly impossible thing in Canticalica?'

Due to the delicacy of refusing a marriage proposal from a much larger country, Forster hadn't scheduled anything after this afternoon tea. Leo was supposed to be having dinner with his family, but when *wasn't* he cancelling that?

'What would you say to visiting one of our towns with me?'

'The one with the cheese?' Blanche asked hopefully.

'That is just *such* a good choice,' Leo grinned.

THERE WERE TWO SERVANTS in the room when they agreed on this, which complicated matters beyond just being able to leave the castle and capital without ceremony. Leo knew that the joy of spontaneity wouldn't allow him to sit through hours of gathering the requisite number of guards, including other nobles and packing whatever it was that needed to be packed.

Blanche solved this in an outrageously simple way: she gave each servant one term piece, which was probably about equivalent to a day's wage, and told them to wait an hour before reporting where they'd gone. Leo had to admit that it was more responsible than not giving Sword and Shield any way of finding them. Much as he wanted to pretend that he was free to do as he pleased, his brother had been kidnapped from within this very castle only a month ago.

Leo was grateful that Blanche was the kind of princess who knew how to saddle her own horse. As they tacked up, she told him about the large collection of animals at her estate, ranging from dogs to emus and, of course, horses.

'Now *that* makes it more tempting to come visit,' Leo said.

Blanche beamed at him. Leo was glad that it held true that people with animals always loved when their animals were appreciated.

Blanche's frequent riding habit meant that the two of them were able to get through the gates without anyone being too suspicious about Leo accompanying her, and before long they were across the Fluvius and on the open road. Leo urged Korbinian into a canter, then into a gallop when Blanche overtook him with a gleeful whoop.

Leo couldn't remember feeling so free in ages. He hadn't even felt comfortable with Blanche an hour ago, but it was impossible to share this kind of fun without liking her. Maybe he should have all his meetings like this.

After a couple of minutes, they eased their horses into a sustainable walk. They rode in comfortable silence for a while, until Blanche said abruptly, 'I think your brother was scared of horses.'

'Dicky?' Leo asked. It would have been impossible to think that of Con or Max.

'I met him a few years ago,' Blanche said. 'He was a strange man.'

'I always thought he was pretty normal,' Leo said. '*Really* normal, even. Approaching a parody of normal.'

'That's exactly it,' Blanche said. 'It was like he had learnt how to be a person in a book. Presumably one your father had written.'

'You're probably not far off the truth,' Leo said.

Dicky was supposed to be Richard's second coming—he would have literally been King Richard II. Leo didn't know if fate was real (if someone could understand the future well enough to scry it, they wouldn't need to do so in the first place) but there was something to be said for the idea that the Trinity had always planned for Con to give up his inheritance and make way for Dicky.

But of course, Dicky had never gotten the chance to be king, which poked some holes in that logic. Perhaps that was why there seemed to be so little faith in Leo; perhaps if Dicky had been taking the throne at this age they would have listened to him. In that world, Leo didn't know what part he would have played. He might have been allowed to finish his studies, or Dicky might have summoned him back anyway. Dicky used to say Leo was the only one he trusted.

'I suppose you and I were both taught how to be people as well, though,' Blanche said. 'It comes with the territory. Even with the relative freedom I, and I assume you, had in growing up further down the line of inheritance, we were always going to have to represent our families and countries at some point.'

'Dicky and I were born four minutes apart,' Leo said. 'It could have been me first in line so easily. I wonder sometimes what he would have been like if he hadn't had that pressure.'

'Probably still scared of horses,' Blanche said with a gentle smile.

For a moment, Leo wondered why she looked so sympathetic. But then he supposed he was talking about swapping places with his dead brother, and if those four minutes had gone the other way, it wouldn't have been Dicky standing so close to their parents.

'Probably,' Leo agreed sadly.

It was a familiar two-hour ride to Ziegbourne. It had been a few years, but Leo used to make this trip fairly often. He usually went with Dicky on foot though, not on horseback. Dicky had been a big believer in long walks. They'd walk to the little village, hike along the gorge that only goats, echidnas and birds grazed, then recover from the exercise in the local pub before either walking home or hitching a ride. Thinking on it now, Leo thought that there was probably a reason the two young princes could usually find someone who happened to be going to the capital that night. Leo had always taken for granted that he'd be looked after wherever he went.

As they rode, Leo told Blanche about his and Dicky's usual conveyancer, the engineer who didn't have a crumb of magic but who had devoted his life to finding out what he could do with magical and mundane objects and the devices he made from them. Leo's watch, previously his father's, was one of them. In turn, Blanche told Leo about the merchant who always had vegetables "not good enough to sell" for her horse when she was growing up.

A small party of Shields caught up to them as they entered the boundaries of Ziegbourne. The Helm with them attempted to convey that Leo was in trouble for giving them the slip without articulating it, either unable to tell off his king or unwilling to do so in front of an emissary from another country. Leo feigned innocence of the subtext and pretended to be delighted at them joining them. The Helm let him get away with it, possibly influenced by Leo's insistence that they all go to the pub for wine and goat's cheese.

The people of Ziegbourne remembered Leo, but they didn't act like they once had. Last time he was here, he and Dicky were treated almost like family—with more warmth than Leo's *actual* extended family, even. This time, everyone they rode past bowed to them. This time, when Leo greeted Deliah at the bar by name, she replied, *'Your Majesty.'* Leo's heart ached for several awful seconds as he tried to figure out if he should be mourning or not, but then Deliah broke into a wide smile and crossed the room to wrap Leo in a hug.

'We thought you'd forgotten about us, Majesty,' she said, holding Leo's forearms a moment longer, as though she needed them in order to take him in properly.

'Never,' Leo promised, trying to ignore the alert posture of the Shields behind him. He gestured to Blanche, who took his hand like it was a counterweight and curtseyed politely. Leo liked her more for treating commoners with a deference more appropriate to a lord. 'This is Princess Blanche of Neue Wolke. Do you have a table for us? We don't have a booking.'

'Your Highness,' Deliah said, dropping into a prompt and much messier curtsey. She nudged Leo conspiratorially and said in a carrying whisper, 'Do I hear wedding bells?'

'No,' Leo said quickly. His face felt red hot. 'Absolutely not. Friendship bells only.' He remembered that the only bells he heard were attached to the fool, who despite recent events was not to be counted as a friend. 'In fact, no bells whatsoever,' he said.

'Leave the poor boy alone,' a regular at the bar told Deliah.

Well, Leo didn't think that "poor boy" was a very regal impression to be giving off, but at least some of his citizens seemed to like him. He'd probably prefer to be liked than respected. It seemed like a far-flung dream that one day he might achieve both.

18

LEO LEFT THE COUNCIL CHAMBERS in the middle of the afternoon, jaw set in determination. He was starving and the second he'd eaten he would have to go back to more talk about the cold war between two countries Canticalica owed money to, both of which had one of Leo's uncles in a prominent position at court. Leutesland had started to put pressure on Leo to support them, but he couldn't afford to play favourites. It was a pressing enough issue that he had had to insist *very strongly* that he be allowed to leave and get his lunch himself, but he just knew if he didn't stretch his legs and escape the room he would be making the issue much simpler by leaping from the closest window. He had just turned down a corridor that would take him the back way down to King's Hall when someone tapped him on the shoulder. He flinched away, hand flying to the sword at his hip, but it was just his mystery man. Leo's shoulders relaxed; his everything relaxed. The scowl that sometimes felt permanent softened into something like a smile. Politics suddenly seemed unimportant.

'Hey,' he said.

'Hey yourself,' the man said. 'Are you marching off to murder someone?'

'No,' Leo laughed. 'Just lunch. Unless someone gets in the way of my lunch, then maybe.'

'Even if the someone was me?'

'Better not risk it.'

Leo hesitated, because he knew he was about to be rejected and he knew he *needed* to be rejected for the man to maintain his secrecy, but he still couldn't keep himself from asking.

'Want to join me?'

The man cocked his head to the side.

'What would you do if I said yes?'

'Probably ask someone if they could see you,' Leo said. 'It'd be embarrassing to get caught talking to thin air on the off-chance that you're a revenant only I can see.'

The man smiled in that lazy way he had that drowned Leo's common sense. He reached out and touched his fingers lightly to Leo's wrist. Leo felt sensation rush through him like lightning and shivered.

'I'm flesh and blood, Majesty,' the man promised.

'Um,' Leo said. He didn't feel very majestic. He felt like he might not know how to walk if he had to.

'Come with me,' the man said. Leo only didn't move because he had temporarily forgotten how to, but the man misinterpreted it in a less embarrassing way. 'I won't keep you from your lunch.'

The man took him to a quiet and half-ruined sun room. On another day, with different company, Leo might have felt despair for the state of it. As it was, he barely saw the threadbare tapestry and crumbling plaster.

There was a modest platter of sandwiches and a jug of water with fruit in it sitting on the sole table in the room, with two mismatched chairs next to each other. Leo took a seat and took an enormous bite of the top sandwich immediately.

'I thought you might restrain yourself in an attempt to be more appealing,' the man said wryly.

Leo swallowed and said, 'Sorry. Hungry.' And thank the Trinity for that. The last thing he needed was to overthink how he ate in front of company on top of all his other neuroses.

The man laughed and gestured for Leo to continue. He took a sandwich too and Leo managed to refrain from doing something stupid like growling possessively. He couldn't have pulled that off at all. The man didn't push for conversation until the plate was clear, which Leo was grateful for.

'How has your day been?' the man asked.

'We never talk about you,' Leo said suddenly. It wasn't even a deflection; it had just occurred to him.

The man's smile didn't shift, but his eyes were suddenly unconvincing in their relaxation.

'I am supposed to be an enigma,' the man said. 'You, on the other hand—'

'I'm *definitely* not supposed to talk as freely as I do with you,' Leo said. He frowned. 'I can't seem to help it. It's kind of terrible of me if you think about it.'

'How so?'

'You don't feel like you can sit next to me at lunch,' Leo said. His heart twisted with a guilt that he was struggling more and more to keep at bay. 'You deserve ... I don't want you to feel like some dirty secret.'

The man cocked his head to the side again. That was one of Leo's favourite expressions. It made him look like he was surprised that Leo had made him actually think about something, and Leo liked the idea that he was able to surprise like that, even if it wasn't exactly flattering that the man had a low estimation of Leo's ability to do so.

'I quite like being your secret,' the man said. 'That may be terrible of me, too.'

Leo swallowed. He wasn't sure where he stood and he didn't know if he wanted to know. Everything about the man was attractive, attractive in the way that sure, meant that he was beautiful, but it was more than that. It drew Leo in. It made it nearly impossible to walk away.

'Do you just like me because I'm the king?' he asked, voice hoarse. 'Wow, let me correct myself there. Do you like me? Really?'

The man's expression flickered in the direction of teasing before he considered it properly. Leo felt strangely grateful that he wasn't just being dismissed.

'I like you in *spite* of the fact that you are the king, Majesty,' the man said. His voice was sombre and Leo believed him. The man might have sought him out because of his title, but they were stumbling towards something more. 'I like you,' he repeated, and the belief sank in a little deeper.

'I like you too,' Leo said. 'That's probably obvious.'

'Well,' the man said, with a modest half-shrug, 'it's still nice to hear.'

The guilt hit Leo again. What was he doing, telling him that? It was as if Leo had forgotten who he was. But that was the thing: the man made him forget he was wearing a crown. How could he not like him? His clothes weren't right for a servant, but not quite right for a noble either. Silk shirt and linen pants to cope with the heat, but unadorned. Maybe he was from the city, though faith knew how he got in the inner castle if he was. Whoever he was, he didn't want to be seen with Leo, possibly because he knew Leo shouldn't want to be seen with *him*. It made things easier, but it wasn't right.

'Can I ask you some things?' Leo asked.

'I may lie,' the man warned. 'But you can ask.'

That was okay. Leo didn't intend on asking anything that was worth lying about. And strangely, the fact that the man was being upfront about the possibility of him lying felt like he would still be being honest even if (or when) he did lie.

'What's your favourite plant?'

The man laughed and pushed his curls back. He thought about it for a second, then answered with certainty, 'Grevillea. The

Empress brought over some lovely plants, Trinity bless her, et cetera, et cetera, but I like how wild the indigenous ones look. And grevillea lollies are my favourite flavour.'

'Okay,' Leo said, smiling. 'Favourite song?'

'And here I was thinking you were going to ask me something challenging.'

'Back at the Academy, we spent nights at the pub with a band and we'd take it in turns to request our favourite songs. I think you get to know people through their music.'

'I've suddenly forgotten every song I've ever heard,' the man said. 'I'll tell you next time.'

'Okay,' Leo said, smiling at the prospect of a "next time". It shouldn't have been news, not when there had been no indication that this was going to stop, but still.

'What is it that you're doing?' the man asked. 'Am I to expect a bouquet of grevillea and a serenade?'

'What? No, no that's not …' Leo felt himself blush and took a gulp of water to try and recover. The man just looked amused. 'Even if I can't know the big things—and I'm okay with that— I'd like to know you. I think I've outgrown the time of my life when I liked people just because they're beautiful.'

The man blinked in surprise. Leo's brain caught up with his mouth.

'Not that—! I'm not trying anything, I swear.' Leo wished there was a spell that would take back the last minute. He'd settle for one that would result in a dragon crashing through the castle and eating him. 'Can we just pretend that I said "you interest me" and leave it at that?'

The man laughed under his breath and inclined his head in agreement. Leo took another mouthful of water, which did not manage to cool his cheeks or adequately hide him.

'You want me to ask something challenging then?' he asked, pretending very hard that the intermission hadn't occurred.

The man nodded, smiling lazily, like he wasn't sure Leo was up to it. Leo asked the first thing he thought of, which was perhaps psychologically revealing.

'Tell me about your parents, your family. Their personalities; you don't have to reveal things if you're determined to be mysterious.'

'Well, they're dead,' the man said, with the same laconic tone he might take when saying anything else. His dark eyes were tighter though. Not by much, but enough.

'Sorry,' Leo murmured. 'You don't have to—'

The man waved away his concern. He took a deep breath.

'I don't talk about them; this might be good for me. I don't remember my mother and I've believed for a while that the stories my dad told me about her were how he wished she was rather than based on anything real. He was like that. He believed that a good story was worth more than the truth. And he told very good stories.'

Leo watched the man's expression closely. He wanted to say that Ada was like that too, but he wanted to let the conversation go where it would if he didn't make it about himself. He felt like he was being given an infinitely precious gift. He didn't interrupt the silence as the man gathered his thoughts.

'He taught me—' the man started, but then he revised. 'He taught me a lot, but I won't go into it. Suffice it to say, I use his learnings daily.' He drummed his fingers lightly on his thigh. 'I think I was luckier than most. I wouldn't go so far as to say that he was faultless, but I never doubted his love. Around here, that's rather a big deal.'

Leo nodded, trying not to think about that too much, instead focusing on the fact that he was being allowed a connection here. It was easier than he might have thought it would be.

'I miss him,' the man said, frowning. 'When he was alive, I didn't ever doubt that he was proud of me. Now ...'

'It sounds like he was the kind of guy who would have been proud of you no matter what,' Leo said.

'Maybe,' the man said. His expression cleared and he smiled again. 'What else?'

Leo's mind was blank. He couldn't shake off moods that easily and didn't believe that smile was more than skin deep, but he knew that topic was over.

'Uh,' he said. He looked around the room for inspiration and landed on the empty plate. 'Favourite food?'

'Peach pie,' the man said, with no hesitation.

Leo smiled. He didn't know what he had been expecting, but probably not that. It seemed almost too honest. He couldn't be sure if the man had told the truth about his father, but he thought that he at least could be relied on to have a sweet tooth.

The man looked out the window, where the sun had progressed across the sky in that loathsome way it tended to do. When his eyes met Leo's again, he seemed genuinely disappointed.

'I think I have stolen you for long enough,' he said.

Leo's face fell. He didn't want to go back to his meetings. He didn't want the evening to approach, when he would have to deal with foreign emissaries in a more delicate way than anyone, including himself, thought he was capable of. Things were improving in some ways—he was more familiar with how his kingdom operated and he knew the names of everyone he could be expected to and that made a huge difference—but he was still utterly unimpressive to so many people. To his staff, whom he would endure this afternoon. To the people he was seeing this evening. To the people he ruled over.

'Thank you,' Leo said, trying his hand at being graceful. 'For stealing me.'

'It was my genuine pleasure,' the man said.

They stood and walked to the door. Before either of them could reach for the doorknob, the man put his hand on Leo's forearm. Leo looked at him with something like fear that wasn't fear at all. His touch lingered as they stared at each other.

Slowly, hesitating in a way that was out of character, the man brushed a few loose strands from Leo's face.

'Maybe I should tidy you up before you go,' he murmured. 'How hard could it be to braid hair?' Leo swallowed. He didn't know if he could survive that kind of attention. The man's fingers ghosted down his cheek as he drew back. 'No,' the man said. 'I'd better not. I already don't want to give you back.'

Leo pressed his lips together, afraid of the honesty that came out around the man. He held still, because he might kiss the man if he didn't.

'I should go,' Leo said. 'Will I see you soon?'

'Maybe,' the man said, smiling enigmatically. 'I wouldn't want to take the surprise out of it.'

The man released Leo's forearm and opened the door for him. He bowed slightly, eyes not leaving Leo's, hand over his heart.

'Majesty,' he said.

Leo tried to restrain his smile. He was in very real danger of liking the man too much. Danger, no, that implied he wasn't there yet and could get out of it. He was in very real danger of forgetting all the reasons why he *shouldn't* like the man too much.

THE CURTAINS BORROWED FROM LEO'S BEDROOM framed the window, the panes of which were tilted open in the hopes of a summer breeze. The furniture was likewise looted from other, more maintained areas of the castle. There were flowers and plants to the point of excess. The room that had caused Leo a minor meltdown not long ago now looked fresh and cosy.

It was also within the Royal Chambers, which gave the impression that the emissaries Leo was hosting and who he had never met were close enough friends to be invited into the family's space. It was harder for kingdoms to ask for the money they were owed from their friends. Of course, this never seemed to apply to Canticalica itself, but then Leo didn't think that Richard had actually had any friends.

Leo wasn't good at this part yet, but he was getting better. He'd learnt how to seem at ease with people back when he was a kid and even if he'd forgotten it a bit at the Academy, it wasn't that hard to pick it up again, at least not with those he considered "real" adults, the kind of people that he'd learnt it for in the first place. The hard part had been meeting with people who seemed to know more than him about how his kingdom was run. That was becoming less of an issue thanks to his relentless education on this front.

Of course, all his previous meetings paled in importance to this one. Not only did he have to somehow keep Canticalica out of a war, he also had to make the Leutesland emissaries agree to defer their repaying the loan. He should have felt hopeless. Instead, it was like he was at peace with whatever resulted from the evening, like his stress had compounded to such a degree that he wasn't bothering with it anymore.

'Are you staying for Sommertide?' Leo asked. 'We'd love to have you.'

'It's usually something I'd celebrate at home,' Stefanie said. 'But I have to admit that I'm curious to see how you do it over here. There's always distinctions between the kingdoms.'

'Definitely,' Leo agreed. 'It was very different at the Academy the couple of years I stayed there instead of coming home.'

'That's the Trinitas Academy?' Borsca asked.

'Yes,' Leo said. 'I made it two-thirds through, or nearly that.'

'You must know a great deal of magic,' Borsca said.

'I think I was a good student,' Leo said. He knew he had been, he got graded well enough, but that felt awkward to say. 'Even so, Ada—laide probably knows as much.' He still stumbled slightly over saying his siblings' full names with relative strangers who might not recognise them otherwise.

Stefanie, Borsca and Orlando all made polite, non-committal noises that declined commenting on whether Ada's magic could compare to Leo's. A server approached and topped up everyone's drinks. Everyone waited until she had retreated before continuing.

'Now, about the money,' Orlando said.

'Very graceful,' Stefanie sighed. In fairness to Orlando, all three emissaries were kindly speaking in their hosts' language. Bluntness was understandable.

Leo clapped his hands to his thighs and sat up straighter. He tried to communicate his interest with all of his body.

'Yes, I'm so glad you've brought that up,' he said. 'I can't thank you enough for your understanding about the loan.'

'Right …' Orlando said, frowning slightly. Confusion was understandable when by all rights Leo probably should have been looking at least a little sheepish.

'This wine is from our vineyards, right?' Leo said, turning to the servant who had served them. She nodded. 'They've had a shitty year—oh, sorry, that wasn't polite.'

'Go ahead, Your Majesty,' Stefanie said, waving her hand. 'We're all friends here, right?'

Stefanie's tone of resigned humour made it sound like she had been expecting this move. Leo had been consciously swearing to feign a comfort with them that he didn't really feel, like he wasn't thinking about his words. It was a trick he had learnt from his dad, and it usually worked.

'Right, thanks,' Leo said, attempting a small smile. 'Anyway, like I was saying. The frosts this year have really hurt the grapes, so the loan has meant we can support them in a way that might not have been possible with the … additional ceremonies this year.'

Leo looked down and away, and it wasn't hard for him to dredge up a sad expression. Not when he felt like this was going poorly and he was going to ruin his kingdom because he just wasn't charming enough.

'We're so sorry for your loss,' Stefanie said gently, leaning over to place a hand on Leo's knee.

Leo looked up and nodded miserably. 'Thank you,' he said quietly.

Stefanie looked sincere in a way she hadn't so far. She was clearly clever and witty but had used that wit to keep herself at arm's length. Now she was literally reaching out. She squeezed Leo's knee in comfort and drew back.

'Anyway,' he said, clearing his throat. When he attempted a smile, it was probably appropriate that it wasn't convincing. 'And they'd only just recovered from the fires. These things happen, but it's cruel that they've happened so close together. Luckily, our wheat and barley crops seem to be doing really well. The orchards took a hit as well, but stone fruit is a bit hardier. From what I gather, it's mostly that they didn't produce as much fruit as usual. I keep meaning to ride out, but there always seems to be something else to do.

'So, and I know this is a lot to ask, but could we postpone the next repayment until the harvest? I'm tentative to pay now and find that we need more after some new disaster crops up. I hope there isn't another disaster, but my treasurer wants to be prepared.'

'Of course, Your Majesty,' Borsca said. 'I wasn't expecting honesty, I have to admit.'

'No, the late king preferred to keep us drunk until we had to leave again,' Stefanie said. 'Don't mind Orlando, he hasn't come to Praecentor before. Very new. Thinks the job is all about the money. He didn't know your father.'

Leo felt slightly thrown. Why did no one tell him things? Not that he really wanted to adopt Richard's habits, but still.

'I can still get you drunk if you'd prefer that,' he offered.

'I don't see how else we're going to get to know you,' Stefanie said, ironic smile back in place.

Leo thought he now understood why this meeting was happening in the evening and why there were no other duties scheduled for the next morning. He didn't see a way out of this, but it made him nervous. Drinking made both of his parents seem more charming. He didn't think it had the same effect on him. *But it does on Con*, he realised.

'We should bring my siblings in,' he said. He turned to the servants. 'Can you see if Adelaide and Conrad are free?'

One of the servants nodded and left. Leo turned back to the emissaries with a genuine smile.

'They're brilliant,' he said.

'I couldn't imagine anything less, given your parents,' Borsca said, smiling as though this was a compliment.

The fact that Leo's smile became a lot more wooden could easily be explained away as grief.

ADA ARRIVED FAIRLY QUICKLY, but Con sent the servant back with the message that he'd be there in the nebulous time covered by "soon". With no disrespect to his sister, this was the opposite of what Leo had wanted. Leutesland was the country he was most nervous about owing money to due to rumours of tumult across its people. It was one of the oldest countries and didn't have the greatest track record with treating its prevenient population well, which was causing increasing conflict. The last thing he needed was Ada to suggest, with all the confidence of a privileged nineteen-year-old, how they might fix racism. In fairness to her, she seemed to be a very *well-informed*, privileged nineteen-year-old, but Leo doubted that would make any comments on that front go down better.

'Thank you for the invitation,' Ada said as she sat down. 'I was hoping to get an opportunity to speak with you at some point. Leutesland has excellent playwrights—I thought you might have some tips on how best to encourage our cultural development.'

Leo looked at her in surprise. The best he had hoped for was that she might keep from being openly hostile. The last time he had been seated next to Ada when performing hosting duties, she had sat with her arms crossed and only spoke to criticise the courtiers they were supposed to be entertaining. Granted, this had been a few years ago and Queen Gisela had probably messed up by hinting blatantly that the lord over fifteen years older than Ada was very handsome and had a vast estate in Neue Wolke. Still though.

'I don't think I've ever read or seen an original Canticalican production,' Stefanie said.

'Our performers do tend to use scripts from other countries,' Ada said. 'Which is understandable, seeing as it's not an established profession here.'

'You're a smaller kingdom than most of our states,' Orlando shrugged. 'I'm surprised you have any citizens who aren't farmers or merchants.'

'Many citizens have more than one job,' Leo said, before Ada could say something that matched her sudden stiff back and clenched fingers. 'Many of the salespeople on market days work on the farms whose produce they sell, and our shops have shorter opening hours than other cities I've visited. Largely so that the owners can make their stock or whatever, but there's part-time artists and the like.'

'The crown plays a big part in encouraging the arts in Leutesland,' Borsca said. 'There are musicians and other entertainers at every event, no matter how small. There would be something even at this meeting if we were the ones hosting it.'

'If you'd like, I could fetch our fool,' Ada offered, voice now all drawling contempt.

'I'd rather you didn't,' Leo said mildly.

'No, don't bother,' Borsca said. 'It's decent enough for a small castle, but it's hardly worth disrupting the servants for. If I'm being honest, I don't know if it would keep its position if the Consortium was to visit.'

For a moment, Leo wanted to defend the fool. The impulse startled him so much that he failed to respond at all. In other circumstances, Ada might have come to his rescue, but she was examining her wine glass as if weighing up whether she'd like to cause a scene. Leo wished she was better at not rising to things. She knew how to hold herself and which fork to use, but Ada had always had a temper.

'It does the job,' Stefanie said, touching Leo on the arm.

'It does,' Leo agreed, grateful for the neutrality of the statement.

Ada met Leo's eyes and glanced pointedly at Stefanie's hand. Stefanie withdrew it abruptly and Leo held in a wince with some effort. So much for Ada being helpful. Leo tried to think of some pretext to touch Stefanie back—or would that be worse? He wished he hadn't refused that cousin of Blanche's so he had a reason to avoid her friendliness. No, he really didn't. He wished he would choke to death on his wine.

'There's more to being a fool than a capacity for rhyming,' Borsca said. 'Canticalica's fool has always seemed at direct odds with its monarch.'

'Our current fool has only been in its position for less than a year,' Leo said. 'But you're not wrong. I suppose my late father didn't set the example of a harmonious co-existence with a fool.'

'I've been saying for years that it's a front,' Stefanie said. 'King Richard might have been able to act, but Prince Richard did *not* share that gift. No offence meant, Your Majesty.'

'You're not wrong,' Leo said. 'But I don't think I follow.'

'I can think of at least five examples off the top of my head of fools who were also assassins,' Stefanie said. 'And those are just the ones whose assassinations were public knowledge. Not to mention the spies, advisers, et cetera. I'm sure King Richard's hatred was too real to not be fake, and *Prince* Richard always very obviously wanted to laugh at its jokes.'

Leo's eyebrows lifted in surprise. He … hadn't realised Dicky had had a sense of humour. He rubbed his chest to try and soothe the sudden ache that had come with realising he didn't know his twin like he should have.

'My brothers universally like knock-knock jokes,' Ada said, as though she was immune. Max had made her snort wine out of her nose laughing the other week with the kind of joke a less bastardly kind of dad would find beneath him. 'This isn't indication of any plots afoot.'

Leo barked out a startled laugh. 'I don't think they were implying …'

'Of course not!' Orlando said.

'What happened to the previous fool if your new one is so fresh from the Consortium?' Stefanie asked.

'It died,' Leo said.

'Did it?' Ada asked, looking genuinely thrown.

'In the blast that killed our parents and Dicky, actually,' Leo said numbly.

'It wasn't on the list,' Ada insisted, shaking her head.

'It wouldn't be,' Orlando said. 'Fools' deaths are never recorded. That might imply that they die, which the Consortium couldn't have.'

Leo's hearing seemed to be dimming. The blast had very likely taken its caster out with it. Fools could be assassins. The last fool had to have hated Richard as much as he hated it.

But fools were constrained to be loyal. It would take something monumental to undermine that oath, no matter what kind of person Richard was.

More importantly, if the fool hadn't been counted in the dead, that meant that the blast took out nine people, not eight. Maybe it couldn't be dismissed as vengeance after all. A lot could be done with nine souls.

20

ACROSS THE CONTINENT, summer nights were contracting into brief respites from the overeager sun, and people tended to go a bit crazy as their diurnal brains urged them to keep going during the longer, hotter days. The Sommertide festival took place right on the solstice and was the most significant holiday of the year. It was one of those days when whole kingdoms felt unilaterally incapable of work—so they just didn't. Instead, they dressed up and celebrated for the entirety of the day, all seventeen hours in Canticalica, then continued on partying through the night. The festival wasn't unique to Canticalica, but there was a strange kind of patriotism involved nonetheless. Possibly because it was a day that encouraged community.

It had been a tradition for hundreds of years to abandon class distinctions during Sommertide. No one worked, so subservience seemed unnecessary. No one felt particularly dignified eating honeyed pancakes or falling asleep on the bank of the river, so condescension just didn't have the same effect. When they were younger, Leo, Dicky, Con and Ada had been able to play ridiculous, convoluted and unruly games with kids from completely unknowable backgrounds. Apart from the games being better than any of the ones the noble kids came up with, there was the added giddiness that came from feeling like they were getting away with something. More recently, they'd been able to go join in with other new-adults in their partying.

Leo hadn't known what to expect this year but had been dreading the death of what used to be the highlight of his year. He'd never paid attention to what his parents were doing, so he didn't know if the class erasure extended to them, and now him. And he'd never had a Sommertide where he had *real* responsibilities that he was taking a break from. He had no idea if he was capable of participating instead of hiding in his office, trying to decipher the Chief Helm's handwriting and come up with a plan to lure the bad guys out into the open.

But he actually slept in, like he was supposed to. He could *smell* that it was Sommertide—it was something about the baked heat of the mid-morning sun on the bricks outside his open window. There were no rules. He could feel his childhood self whispering *no school* in glee. Leo had of course taken time to rest during almost every day of his rule. It was accounted for in his schedule to prevent the likelihood of him having a mental breakdown, and Forster was a champion of walking that line to make sure that Leo was the most productive he could be. But today he was released from everything. And he could put it all down *so easily*. He grinned to himself. *No school.*

He dressed himself in colourful clothes made from cheap, thin fabric that ended at his elbows and knees, and went to go find Con. His heart was in it, but he still didn't know if people would really treat him like a person. He wanted to hide behind his big brother and take his lead as he had when they were kids.

He found Con in King's Hall. The tables were practically bowing under the weight of food prepared in the days leading up, which was available to anyone who wandered through the open doors. Con was doing his part to lighten the load. He threw a small cake at Leo's head in greeting and Leo bit into it. Cake for breakfast seemed like the best possible start to the day.

'Do we have plans?' Leo asked.

'I should throw you out a window for even asking that,' Con

said solemnly. 'It's Sommertide, Lee. Plans are illegal. Do you really want to go to jail on the one day when no one gives a shit who you are?'

'It's also the one day that no one is going to bother to arrest me,' Leo pointed out.

Con conceded this with a shrug.

They sat down with their breakfast at a relatively unoccupied stretch of table, and Leo found himself grinning at Con when a group of five kids sat next to them and demanded help reaching food like they really didn't care who he was. It occurred to him that they might not even *know* who he was. They were kids, so what did it matter what the king looked like? Did Leo even look like himself like this, with cheap clothes and his hair in an untidy bun? He'd never been great with kids, but he was completely fine with it when the youngest one (he estimated her to be around four) sat herself on his knee so she could reach the table easier. It made him feel special—not important, but special.

When the kids started to run away, Con called after them and asked if he and Leo could join in. They were graciously given permission if they could keep up. Con nudged Leo and told him that kids always knew how to have the most fun at these things.

An hour later, after losing spectacularly at a cartwheel competition, a very serious nine-year-old girl was braiding Leo's hair, sending anyone who came close to them away to pick her flowers for further enhancement. Con was teaching a boy who didn't even come up to his waist how to do proper push-ups. And then, as abruptly as they'd appeared, the kids grew bored with having adults around. One of them tagged the girl who was doing Leo's hair, and within seconds they'd all disappeared in a giggling cyclone. Leo carefully tied off the end of the braid, which only went three-quarters of the way down his hair. It was also doubtlessly a lot more feminine than his usual styles, but he was fine with that.

'Suits you, Lee,' Con said, with enough warmth that Leo thought he probably didn't mean his appearance.

'Are there enough flowers?' Leo asked, not wanting to get self-conscious by thinking about the fact that he was happy too hard.

'Look, there could be more, I'm not gonna lie,' Con said. 'But it's pretty spectacular.'

They spent the rest of the day as aimlessly as they'd begun it. They wandered around the city, listened to music and got drawn into a drinking game with people who definitely knew who they were but who were glorying at the opportunity to try and make their king spill his drink by telling him jokes while he was supposed to be chugging it. The group made a game of daring Leo to do magic, pointless things like disappearing coins that tricksters could do without a drop of divine blood in them, or changing the colour of their clothes. When they ended up at the riverbank, Con dived in without pause and Leo sat on the edge slowly kicking his feet through the water. He didn't want to lose his flowers.

They found Danya and Ada with a group of girls telling each other dirty and definitely (hopefully) made-up stories and stayed there for a while. Leo was pretending as hard as he could that he was incapable of being scandalised, grateful that Con's gasps and blushing drew most of the attention. Ada caught Leo's eye and raised her eyebrow in Con's direction and Leo shrugged. For someone who went through partners more regularly than he washed his hair, Con had always been easy to embarrass. At least two of the girls were looking like they wanted to give him something to *really* be embarrassed about, so Leo guessed it worked out for him.

At some point, Leo fell asleep with his head on Danya's knee, the kind of light sleep where he was somewhat conscious of the sounds of the festival around him the whole time but which made him feel a lot fresher when he woke up. He put his rare relax-ation down to the less-than-wise choice to day drink, but as he was far from the only one napping in public, he couldn't bring himself to care much.

He fell asleep again when he went back to his room to change for the night, which meant that he missed the moment when the fluorescent lights were conjured along the streets, casting colourful, unreal glows through the darkness. It was a shame, but he couldn't feel the weight of it. He was still caught up in the excitement and he felt better, awake behind his eyes in a way he hoped would mean he could stay up the rest of the night. Because as much as Sommertide was a celebration of the longest day, the shortest night was the funnest part.

Danya had crocheted fine black wool into a beautiful, lacy mask that he tied around his head. He let his hair hang loose and wavy from its braids, and he'd been given a stick of kohl to line his eyes. He only had to start over twice, which he counted as a success—it didn't really matter if it was messy, but he was strangely nervous about going outside like this. In the dark and with the mask, he thought he could actually hope that he wouldn't be recognised. He wasn't sure he even recognised himself.

He'd been king for almost six months and his last girlfriend had dumped him at the beginning of the summer before. Was it really that shitty of him to want to find a Sommertide fling? Someone who would kiss him in the shadows and be fine with neither of them ever knowing the other's name? He wanted his fantasy to be faceless, to be happy with literally anyone, but of course it wasn't.

He hadn't kissed his mystery man when he'd wanted to and he stood by that. He couldn't make anyone feel like he was ashamed of them. But tonight there wasn't any shame; tonight he could steal an hour or two of normalcy.

But he didn't even know how to begin trying to find the man and even if he did … If he could kiss him like he wanted to, but without the man knowing it was him, somehow that would be worse than not kissing him at all.

Leo left the Round Tower and found himself at Queen's Hall. Whereas King's Hall was at the base of the Round Tower and was where people usually congregated for meals, Queen's Hall wasn't a hall at all. The lights there were softer, even though the tables were full. The laughter and talking was loud but didn't echo off stone or wood and didn't overwhelm the band playing with imperfect enthusiasm. The night sky was blissfully mild and the wine Leo helped himself to was nearly cold. He'd had the idea of getting lost inside the impressive hedge maze adjacent to the nebulous boundaries of the hall, but there were countless people who had clearly thought of the same thing. Despite the minor inconvenience, Leo felt like this was how it always should be in Praecentor. He leaned against a marble pillar and thought about how he could possibly make that happen, because if anyone could then surely it was the king, but he knew he was dreaming of something impossible. The people here were able to party like this because they had earned this one day of freedom. Leo couldn't take away employment and social structure and bed-times on a more permanent basis. But what a move it would be.

He took his cup away from the castle boundaries and into the city. He chose streets and paths almost at random, going down this one because it smelled like fresh bread (there were always a few people taking advantage of the lack of competition to make a bit of money) and avoiding that one because he was pretty sure he'd scraped up his knee on uneven stone there pretty badly a couple of Sommertides ago. He ended up in a small garden at the top of one of the shorter towers. If it had a name, he didn't know it, and he was probably a bit too tipsy to be hanging his legs off the side of the building, but it was a beautiful view. He could stare up at the stars or down at the magical lights, and the sounds of partying were far enough away that he felt like he was in a secret place. There were a couple of other people in the garden, but they were on the other side, lying on their backs and talking in the tones of people who were figuring out how to solve the world's problems.

Leo heard someone approaching and looked up, strangely okay with whoever had decided to break his solitude. If it had been a drunk grandmother or a forty-year-old who thought they had some essential advice to give, he would have been pleased. The fact that it was a man about his age filled his throat with a nervous thrill. The man sat down next to him, legs crossed instead of hanging off the edge.

'I'm surprised to find you alone, Majesty,' the man said.

This dark, the man's eyes looked as black as his curls. His simple mask was loose in one hand, leaving his face uncovered.

'How did you find me?' Leo asked. The thrilled feeling intensified. 'How did you know it was me?'

'I would know you anywhere, Majesty,' the man said. He cocked his head to the side with a flirty smile. 'Are you saying you wouldn't recognise me?'

Leo ducked his head and played with his sleeve.

'Anywhere,' he echoed. He glanced up and the man was looking at him with that subtly playful expression that seemed to say that he thought Leo was an idiot, but that he really liked it. He made Leo want to be an idiot.

It'd be really, really stupid to kiss him.

Leo jerked his eyes away and looked back over the city.

'Good party,' he said, inanely.

'It has its upsides,' the man said. He looked forward as well. 'Hey, I can see my house from here,' he said, tone wry with the cliche.

'Can you?' Leo asked, turning to him with reckless interest.

'No,' the man said, eyes full of dangerous promise, of invitation. 'My house is far too close for that.'

'*Fuck,*' Leo breathed. He wanted to look away, knew he should look away, but it was impossible. 'I mean—' He cleared his throat.

'Well, if you insist,' the man said, and if he was meaning to be teasing he missed the mark. He sounded way too serious.

Leo looked at his hands, pained. He wished he was drunk enough to not give a shit about the consequences. He wished he was reckless enough to pretend to be that drunk.

'Either you have a very strong will or I'm not as pretty as I've been told I am,' the man said, much lighter. Leo held his teeth together so he wouldn't say anything worse than he already had. 'What exactly is it that's stopping you?'

'I just can't,' Leo said.

'People in your position have done far worse.'

'Does that give me licence to do whatever I want?' Leo asked. 'Dad once told me that his great-grandmother tortured people. Not that she had people tortured, which I also wouldn't have been wild about, she personally tortured people. And he—' Leo cut himself off. He needed to stop talking.

'If you're afraid you'll hurt my feelings, I assure you, they'll be fine.'

'I *am* afraid I'll hurt your feelings,' Leo said, still not looking up. 'I'm afraid I'll hurt my feelings too.'

'It's Sommertide, Majesty. Can you really not let go for one evening?'

Every time he used Leo's title, Leo hated it a little less. It came out like a lover's nickname.

'If I was to kiss you …' Leo started.

'How forward,' the man joked. Leo looked at him with exasperation and the man smiled apologetically.

'I don't know if I could stop,' Leo said.

'Well, the convenient part of my living almost scandalously nearby is that you wouldn't really need to. Not for a while.'

Leo groaned quietly in frustration. The man was clever, Leo knew this, but he really wasn't getting it.

'I don't just mean tonight,' Leo said. 'Tomorrow it isn't Sommertide anymore and I'd still want you. And the day after, and after. I just can't.'

'And you won't want me if you restrain yourself from kissing me?' the man asked.

'It'd be worse,' Leo said. 'You know it'd be worse.'

Leo thought the man might argue this point, but he simply sighed. He stared out over the lights of the city-wide party. Leo watched him, feeling conflicted. It'd be so easy to change his mind. To kiss him now and then stumble to his house. Better still, to take him back to the Round Tower and to keep him there. Faith, he'd take that one too-dangerous kiss and be glad for it. But he was pining enough as it was.

'Do you really want nothing from me?' Leo asked. 'You could ask for a lot. You could get a lot from other people if you appeared like you do in front of them and they saw how I am with you.'

'I don't care about that,' the man said. 'I can't think of a single thing that someone else could give me that would improve my life.'

'Money is always nice.'

'I'm paid enough to buy the things I need, and quite a bit of what I want. I'm satisfied.' The man turned to face Leo directly. 'I don't want fame, or any amount of attention outside what I ask for. I don't want gifts, not even really nice, fresh from the oven ones. I don't want access to your libraries or your secrets or anything else. I can't think of anything that anyone, you included, could give me that would make me do a single thing I didn't already want to do. Sincerely. Except, well …' the man smiled in a self-effacing way, as if amused that he was contradicting himself. 'Except for you. I very much want you. And not because of your title, Majesty.' His smile grew a little bigger, a little more ironic. He picked up Leo's hand and held it to his own cheek. 'It's very inconvenient, liking you. I seem to be doing it anyway.'

'But you approached me because of who I am,' Leo said. He was powerless to remove his hand, and not remotely because of the man's gentle touch.

'That's true,' the man said. His fingers traced tingling patterns along Leo's wrist. Leo continued to cup his face. It was so hard not to kiss him. 'I wanted to get a measure of you before everything started.'

'How did you get into the business of measuring kings?' Leo asked.

'I didn't like your father,' the man said, which wasn't an answer to the question. 'I wanted to see if you were the same.'

Leo's hand dropped. His eyes turned pleading.

'Am I?' he whispered.

The man shook his head immediately.

'No,' he said. 'Not remotely. Not even a little bit. You're …' He visibly searched for the word, and landed on, 'beautiful.'

Leo laughed sadly. He might not like it, but he had inherited a lot from Richard. Well, he already knew that the man was a liar.

'I mean it, Majesty,' the man said, eyes suddenly stern. He reached up and gently pulled Leo's mask loose. Leo shivered. 'I knew your father better than most. I knew what he was like when he wasn't performing. I'm not saying you don't perform, because of course you do. You are *not* cruel. Better than that, if you did do something cruel, as most people do sometimes, you would be horrified about it after.'

Something unknotted in Leo's gut. The scant reassurances

he'd gotten on this front had been too quick to dismiss any darkness in Leo whatsoever. Those made Leo feel like he was just good at concealing who he was. He often tried to imagine what his dad would have been like at his age. Had his mum seen no warning signs at all? Was Leo on the same path that his dad had started down? But the man's words felt more perceptive than that. Maybe it was wishful thinking, but Leo could almost believe him.

'How did you know him?' he asked.

'Through my father, and I won't say any more than that. I very much doubt he registered my existence, but I'm more of an observer anyway.'

'You're so *frustrating*,' Leo groaned. '*No one* knew what he was like. I want to know who you are that you think you did.'

'More people live in Round Tower than just your family,' the man said. Leo opened his mouth again to argue that he knew that and that he also knew all the other people who lived there by sight if not by name and the man wasn't one of them, but the man held his hand up. 'I don't, but I'm there often.'

'He hid it,' Leo insisted.

'Less so, in recent years,' the man said. 'And he never hid it *well*. Not to anyone who was a half-decent observer of character. Even if he didn't often shout, well, that wasn't his weapon of choice, was it?'

'You knew him,' Leo said quietly to himself.

'Do you know how starved you look? For approval, when you're the ultimate authority. For love, when you're surrounded by it.'

Leo should have denied it or put a stop to words that he was sure shouldn't be said to a king. Instead he made himself meet the man's eyes steadily.

'Is this what people think of me?' he asked.

The man shook his head with a sad smile. 'Just me.'

'Does it make me an easy mark?'

'It's balanced out by how little you think you deserve those things.'

Leo huffed a dry laugh under his breath. He thought he would probably have to think about all of this later, when he wasn't muddled by alcohol and proximity to the man. He thought this conversation should make him trust the man less. It had at least had the effect of making Leo no longer desperate to kiss him.

'Tell me something real,' he said. 'To balance it out.'

'I'm quite lonely too,' the man said conversationally.

When he didn't immediately expand on that, Leo gave the man a flat look.

'Is that what you call balanced?'

'I thought it was pretty revealing,' the man said, still in that light tone. Leo watched the man's expression and thought there was something sincere behind that. 'Okay,' he said, as if he was humouring Leo. 'No one remembers my name in Canticalica. The only person I'm close enough to to tell didn't know me when I gave it out freely and respects my choice to remain anonymous. That's not you, by the way. I'm not close enough to you to say, and yet I *have* told you before.'

'Huh,' Leo said, which was a bit of an understatement. Suddenly the scant details he had been able to learn about the man seemed much more significant.

'That may have been a bit much,' the man mused. 'Blame the wine. I'll tell you a different secret.'

He stared out over the city as if searching for inspiration. Leo thought about reaching out and holding his hand. He thought about how soft those dark curls looked and about how the night might last forever. The shortest one in the year, but Sommertide was its own infinity.

'I'm afraid of water,' the man said finally.

'We live on an island,' Leo snorted.

'It's not a convenient fear,' the man said. 'But it genuinely doesn't come up much. I don't mind it from a distance, when there's no risk of falling in. When was the last time you went down to the Fluvius?'

'Today,' Leo said. 'But before then it had been a while. Apart from a single ride with a princess who thinks I'm about eight years old, this might be the farthest I've been from the concourse rooms since I was crowned.'

'How are you finding this temporary freedom?'

Leo looked sideways at the man and smiled conspiratorially. 'It's okay.'

'My kingdom for your smiles,' the man said, holding a hand to his heart.

Leo laughed out of lost embarrassment. What was he supposed to say to that? The man lowered himself onto his back. The way he looked at Leo was almost too much to bear. It was like he wanted to consume him, or maybe like he wanted to see what Leo would do if he tried.

'Um,' Leo said, which was a start. 'I already have one.'

'Damn,' the man said. His eyes were flirty when he said, 'Anything else I can offer?'

'More answers,' Leo said seriously. He lay down next to the man and folded his hands over his stomach instead of reaching out to touch like he wanted to. 'What did you want to be when you were a kid?'

'A pirate,' the man said immediately.

'You just said you're afraid of water!'

'I wasn't until I sank a boat in pursuit of this aspiration.'

Leo laughed. 'Are you lying?'

'Maybe,' the man said. 'But isn't it a fun lie?'

Someone else might have resented this, but Leo had grown up with Ada and this had been one of her philosophies too. Better to make it up than be uninteresting.

'Okay,' Leo said. 'What kind of boat?'

The man smiled and cleared his throat performatively. 'It belonged to the father of a prominent businesswoman …'

The story proved to be too ridiculous to be true almost immediately, but Leo got caught up in it anyway, laughing at the man's wordplay and dry humour, staring at the way his lips moved when he thought he wouldn't be caught, at his hands when the man's eyes were on him.

When he finished and had received the applause he deserved, the man challenged Leo to tell his own story. Leo told the man about the time he had been turned into a cat for a week at the Academy, which was completely made up and spiritually impossible. The man turned on his side and played with Leo's hair, twirling it around a finger and shooting pleasant tingles through Leo's scalp.

The sun began to rise when Leo was telling his second story. Leo pulled the man upright to watch it, and with a quiet yawn, the man rested his head on Leo's shoulder. Leo sat very still, staring at the greyscale world being dipped in colour and thrilled out of his mind. He wanted to put his arm around the man, but he didn't dare. Instead, he inched his head very carefully to the side until his cheek was touching the man's soft curls and he inhaled the pleasant scent of soap and sweet grass. His lips were so close to the man's forehead. He made himself stare at the sunrise, and his morality just barely managed to prevail.

21

'WHY DO YOU NOT LOVE GUIN?' Guin asked in a very morose tone.

Leo's brain stalled. *Because you're my insane tailor* came to mind, but he knew that wasn't the correct response. He was pretty sure that faced with this same question, Con would profess his love for her, but that just wasn't going to happen.

'I'm not trying to offend you,' he said instead.

'And yet!'

'I didn't mean ... how could I have known that you would want to be involved?'

'Look at your complexion, Leopold,' Guin said. Leo looked at his reflection, then turned away again. This was only supposed to be a fitting and it had run over, so he was going to be wearing wanky king clothes and his coronet to a perfectly normal family dinner. He didn't know why he humoured her. 'Do you think you have the skin that looks good in maroon?'

'It's carpet. I'm not going to wear it.'

'But how is Guin to dress you now?'

'Not in maroon, I guess,' Leo muttered. 'I should be at dinner, I'm *always* late for dinner, can we talk about this later? Or never? I think we should talk about this never. I don't need to match the carpet—don't dress me in carpet—and you're supposed to just be tailoring existing shit to me anyway.'

'I do not tailor "shit", Leopold!'

Leo winced.

'No, I know that,' he said. 'I'm sorry, Guin. What colour do you think the carpet should be? If you could make it out of old clothes, that'd be awesome.'

'Cobalt,' she said decisively.

'Is that gree—'

Leo broke off with an undignified yelp of surprise as a pair of hands grabbed him and yanked him from Guin's side into a hidden door. He didn't know why the fool was a consistent exception to his guard, but it was. This time, Leo managed to throw it off once he'd been pulled into an attendants' corridor, but his pride was still bruised.

'What the fuck?' Leo demanded.

'You need to come with me,' the fool said.

Leo didn't like the fool—no matter what weird interactions they had in between the taunting he suffered when he was just trying to do his job—but despite everything, he did trust it. For the fool's tone to be this serious, it meant something. Its voice sounded so different, like it could be anyone.

'Where are we going?' Leo asked.

The fool's shoulders dropped in visible relief, but that was about the only impression Leo could make out in the dim of the corridor. Instead of answering, it touched its finger to its lips and took Leo's hand, startling him with the icy coldness of its touch and pulling him along. Water dripped onto Leo's fingers from the fool's wet cuff. It'd been outside in what was a truly momentous summer storm. That was almost as perplexing as the rest of this situation. Leo wondered what happened if two attendants ran into each other in the narrow corridor they were travelling through, whether one would need to back up to the closest exit so the other could pass. He and the fool had to go one after the other.

'Is this how you get around?' Leo whispered.

The fool turned and put its finger to its lips again, frowning. Leo sighed but obeyed. A moment later, he saw the fool's head nod. Leo smiled to himself. Of course the fool could give a straight answer when it wasn't willing to talk.

They climbed stairs and walked a great distance, which left Leo completely unaware of where they were even though he tried to map it based on what he thought the outside room must be. He couldn't believe he had never thought to explore these, though his dad would have been furious if he had ever caught him at it. Not a place for a prince. Leo wondered what he would say if he could see his son now, king and holding a fool's hand as he traversed the labyrinth reserved for staff because they weren't supposed to be seen. It made Leo feel a bit sick, even though he was desperately trying not to seek out a dead man's approval. He wanted to just be over it, but he couldn't seem to make that happen.

After walking up what felt like a million steps, they emerged in the greenhouse on the top of Lyric Tower. Leo hadn't been in it since he was a child, and never at night. He could hear the raindrops battering the glass roof with such force that it seemed they would erode the whole tower. The fool released Leo's hand gently and Leo stepped back in what he thought was a polite manner. No snatching or flinching away; not this time.

'Ignite,' the fool said quietly.

Hundreds of candles flickered to light, illuminating the paths, surrounding each tier of the fountain, hanging in trees. They were reflected in the angles of the glass, bouncing off the roof. Leo stepped away from the one stone wall of the prism that they'd entered through, taking it all in. The fool followed, bells muted. When Leo turned to it, he saw that its paint was in a worse state than he'd thought and that its clothes were dripping.

'You can talk,' the fool said quietly, running its hands over its face to wipe away the water that continued to trickle from its hat.

Its paint smeared even further, revealing a broader nose and stronger jaw than Leo had expected. It looked like a normal person underneath the paint.

'You can do magic?' Leo asked.

The fool exhaled a laugh and nodded. Leo supposed that wasn't really the most important question to ask. He'd just never really thought about fools having parents, let alone ones descended from the Empress.

'What's going on?' Leo asked.

The fool's face dropped immediately. Its expression became serious and defiant. It was strange to be able to read it so easily.

'The ones that stole Con are here,' the fool said.

'What!? Are you kidding me? And you took me away?'

Leo started back towards the door, but the fool took two large strides to block his way. Leo shoved at its shoulder, but the fool caught his wrist and twisted it in a way that made Leo completely unable to snatch it back.

'Get out of my way,' Leo said, low and dangerous. The fool didn't move. 'Get out of my way, or I will make you. I don't need my hands to cast.'

'So make me,' the fool said, looking directly at Leo. It put its other hand on Leo's shoulder and held it firmly, as if that would change anything. The white and black that usually kept it in perpetual glee was smeared into grey, the lines that made up the exaggerated expression ruined into abstract. It made the emotions behind the paint stand out; made its determination—its fear—clear. Leo hesitated, looking into the fool's black eyes and warring with himself. He wanted to pay attention to this, whatever this was … But his family … He stared at the floor and tried to jerk his wrist away.

'Fool,' Leo pleaded.

'Raven,' the fool said. 'My name is Raven.'

Leo looked back up into the fool's eyes. The hold they had on each other felt less like the beginning of a fight now. He realised that the fool's eyes weren't quite black; when he looked at it like this he could see that they were a deep brown, with two gold freckles in one iris. And the voice … He couldn't believe he'd been so stupid as to not recognise him. He saw the fool every day.

'Raven,' he whispered, finally putting a name to his mystery man's face.

'Majesty,' Raven whispered back.

He didn't hate his title when Raven said it. His hand lifted to smudge the rest of the false smile away. Raven leaned into his hand, eyes closing like the intimacy pained him. Leo realised Raven had let his wrist and shoulder go, but he'd forgotten why he'd wanted to leave. Raven's ridiculous hat was still dripping, so Leo pulled it away with his free hand, keeping hold of it. Raven's dark curls were wet too.

'You're the old fool's son,' Leo said.

'Told you I'd told you before,' Raven said quietly.

His eyes opened, and he stared at Leo's lips. Leo's eyes dropped too, a thousand times more conflicted than he had been before.

'I can't—' he whispered.

Raven reached up and took the coronet from Leo's head with one hand, the other holding Leo's hand to where it had slipped to his jaw. He looked at Leo, challenging and desperate and hopeful all at once. His hair dripped cold on Leo's fingers. The physical removal of the crown didn't make this okay, but Leo's resolve was weakening. He had always felt trapped by his circumstances and he knew that they hadn't changed. He just wanted to ignore it for the duration of one kiss. It would be cruel to Raven, cruel to himself, but he was so exhausted from the effort involved in trying to do the right thing at all times and never remotely reaching those standards.

'Just once,' Raven murmured. 'I know, Majesty ...' He took a shuddery breath. 'Leo. I promise, I know. Please. Once.'

Leo knew that he'd be heartbroken regardless of whether he kissed Raven at this point. What he felt for him wasn't being restrained by the fact that they hadn't kissed.

He leaned in—

They both started and separated at the sound of the door slamming open. Three people emerged, hooded as the ones who had kept Con captive had been. Leo's heart seized in panic; he'd forgotten—how in the world had he forgotten?—but before he could do anything, Raven pushed him back and behind himself, raising his other hand.

'Fuck *off*,' he spat.

Leo didn't even have time to be impressed that he was using profanity for magic before Raven crumpled to the floor, spell brutally deflected back to him. It all happened too quickly for Leo to catch him. Leo felt a frantic kind of rage overtake him. He dropped Raven's hat and drew his sword. He felt the defensive magic imbued in the steel sink instinctively into his skin. All he could see was the magician who had hurt Raven. All he could hear was his pulse beating steadily in his ears. He stepped over Raven's body, stalking towards the attackers and perfectly willing to take their lives. The thought should have scared him. It didn't.

The man looked down at Leo's glowing sword and took a step backwards as one of the women drew two short blades from either side of her hips. With a murmured phrase from the man, her weapons started to glow too, a deep purple to contrast with Leo's red.

She might have been a good fighter. Leo didn't really care if she was a good fighter. He just knocked her sword away and thrust his own forward, grazing her ribs as she dodged out of the way. He turned his grip and swung at her side again. She blocked, and Leo struck again, then again, his movements frenzied in his vengeance. It was like she was moving in slow motion, kept completely on the defensive and taking damage. Leo's next stab had her crying out as her dominant arm opened under his blade, but she didn't drop her sword. She gave a pained grunt as she blocked another blow and she stumbled back, retreating behind the other two, who were concentrating hard on something, singing quietly to generate magic that was evidently not healing their companion.

Leo raised his blade, not about to hesitate just because they didn't have physical weapons, but just as he began to extend his arm, a smokey apparition formed in front of them, concealing the attackers. It coalesced in the shape of a tall man, imposing even in intangibility.

'Dad?' Leo asked, sword frozen in the middle of its strike.

'Leopold,' Richard said.

'If you think I won't stab through my dad to get to you, you've vastly misinterpreted our relationship,' Leo called past the smoke.

'That's my boy,' Richard said, smiling grimly.

Leo's arm drooped. His sword made an unpleasant noise as the tip scraped against the stone floor. Not just an image, then. He barely registered one of the magicians collapsing to the ground, succumbing to the cost of blood magic. The cost of raising a revenant.

'I never intended for you to take the crown,' Richard said. 'I certainly didn't think you would do well.'

'Thanks, Dad,' Leo said sarcastically.

'Leopold, I'm telling you that you have exceeded my expectations, don't be rude.'

Richard's voice was warning, but it didn't have the chill it could have. It made Leo's heart beat faster with fear. He hadn't crossed the line yet, but he might at any moment.

He hated his dad. He hated himself for being so thoroughly affected by his words. *He's dead, he's dead, he's dead*, Leo chanted in his head. It didn't help.

'I'm not here to scold you,' Richard said.

Leo laughed wetly. He shook his head. He didn't need to engage with this, but it was impossible to ignore someone who had the kind of presence Richard had.

'Why not? Is the nightmare ghost of you conjured by people who want to hurt me a better person than you were?'

Richard's expression hardened and Leo found that his memories had been entirely inadequate in remembering this, in how quickly and thoroughly all the love drained from his eyes. Leo's heart squeezed and tears pricked at his eyes. He refused to let them spill. He hated Richard, he *did*, but he couldn't stop himself from hurting when he looked at him like that.

Was it so bad that Leo wanted his dad to love him? Was it unreasonable for him to want that love even when his dad was angry or disappointed or just—there wasn't always a reason. It was impossible to guard fully against. No matter how well behaved Leo thought he was being, there was always some reason for his dad not to love him.

Even when he was dead. Even when this was the last time they would ever talk.

'You will not provoke me to anger today, Leopold.'

And just like that, his expression cleared of hatred again and Leo's heart lifted. He was flooded with gratitude. He'd do anything to keep that from happening again, which meant pushing any part of himself that protested against the injustice way down, where it couldn't mess up Richard's mood again. He just needed to be good. He could be good, if he tried hard enough.

'Leopold,' Richard said softly. 'I'm sorry.' Leo felt … 'I could have prepared you better. I could have been a better dad.' He paused, and Leo ached. 'Leo, I'm proud of who you have become without me.'

Leo gripped his sword so hard that it hurt. He couldn't see past the tears in his eyes. He shook his head, denying the praise. It wasn't true, it wasn't real, and he wouldn't respond. He wanted to direct his sword somewhere fatal, but he didn't know who his target was. He had been wrong. So what if the fighter of the trio behind Richard had also collapsed? Richard would outlive the sun and there was nothing Leo could do but blink, because he was sure he could keep the tears from spilling, he could.

'I love you, Leopold,' the revenant said.

'I *hate* you,' Leo choked. 'You bullied us just so you could have power over kids. Did you not have enough? Was the country not enough? Mum not enough? Why did you have to hurt us too?'

Richard didn't reply, just looked at him with a serious expression. Disappointed, but not stripped of love again, not yet.

Leo sobbed and hated himself for it.

'Why did you die? How *dare* you? You just …'

'What did I do, Leo? What exactly are you levelling against me this time?'

This time, as if Leo had ever had the courage to level anything against him before. When would he get another opportunity? And what did it matter, anyway? Leo was going to die just as soon as the magician behind him realised that Richard wouldn't leave somewhere he wanted to be for such a flimsy reason as the limitations of magic. He tried to keep his sword even marginally on guard in his shaking hand and spoke with the voice of someone who had nothing left to lose. It was over, everything was over. Tears slipped down his cheeks.

'I've spent almost nine months trying to fix the mistakes you made as king. Except they weren't mistakes, were they? If you had had time to teach me, would you have taught me to treat the treasury like you did? I feel—I feel guilty for providing Danya with something close to a proper wage; do you know how messed up that is? I feel guilty for not taking the family on stupid holidays, because they could be so much better off if you were still here. I feel like I'm doing it wrong, every step I make I think you'd be disappointed in me, and it's crippling. And, I have, I—'

Leo looked down and to the left, where Raven's body had collapsed. His eyes were closed, expression clear and unconscious. Or dead. Leo thought Raven might have been his friend.

'Everyone looks at me like I'm a disappointment, and he makes sure I know that I am. Except when he doesn't. I don't know … why am I telling you this? Why do I always *tell* you things? You don't care, you never—' Leo gasped, physically unable to continue. He heard his sword clatter to the ground without registering that he'd dropped it. It was like no oxygen was penetrating through the empty air that he was struggling to fill his lungs with. It was like trying to scream in a dream. It wasn't magic; he was beyond panicked.

It was a relief when manacles fastened on his wrists and the apparition disappeared. He didn't stop gasping even as he was pulled down the stairs.

22

LEO MANAGED TO COLLECT HIMSELF on the walk down from Lyric Tower, but the iridium manacles around his wrists were dampening his magic and there was nothing he could do about the two attackers who were escorting him. He at least could walk wherever he was being taken with his head held high, even if he was afraid that his eyes were red and puffy. It was satisfying to see the swordswoman next to him stained with her own blood, even if her injuries had been healed by the distinctly woozy magician on his other side. He might have been bested by *psychology* of all things, but he hadn't gone down without a fight.

Leo was doing a decent job of not thinking about the conversation he had had with the revenant of his father. He was doing this by wondering how the hell the attackers had known it would unbalance him to that degree and why they'd bothered when they clearly had powerful magic at their disposal. The former answer was probably that they *hadn't* known but had guessed anyone would be affected when faced with their dead dad. The latter probably had something to do with the reputation Leo had earned after healing Con. Leo had heard two different songs that over-inflated the incident with great embarrassment, but maybe those lyrics had given him more prestige than he'd thought. If they thought Leo was guaranteed to beat them when it came to a magical contest, it almost made sense.

At the foot of the tower, his attackers came to a sudden stop.

Leo took another step before he realised, leaving him slightly in front of them. He looked around to see what was going on, and a woman stepped out of the shadows. It was the woman who had tortured Con the last time they were attacked.

'Hello, Your Majesty,' she said.

She curtseyed, with wider knees than Ada did it but very smoothly. Maybe that was the fashion in another kingdom—her accent wasn't immediately familiar either. Comportment wasn't usually something he noticed, but the woman was wearing pants and the circumstances when someone felt obliged to curtsey usually involved them wearing a dress.

'You have me at a disadvantage,' Leo said. 'I don't know your name.'

'Isobella,' she said. 'No last name. My family never did anything consequential enough to deserve one.'

'Is that why you keep attacking mine?' Leo asked.

She laughed and strode closer until she was face to face with Leo.

'Why so sad, Your Majesty?' she mocked, poking her finger to his cheek. He didn't let himself flinch. He'd hoped his face had dried on the walk down from the tower.

'You mistake me,' Leo said, holding his hands a little higher. 'Tears of joy. I love being given jewellery.'

'Liar!' Isobella shrieked. She reached out and yanked him towards her with a handful of his hair, making him hiss. 'We do not lie to each other, you and I.'

'Okay,' Leo said. Even though she was still pulling his hair, he kept his voice calm and even, holding eye contact. Like he would with a spooked horse so he didn't get trampled. 'We don't lie to each other.'

She released him and he straightened slowly.

'What do you want?' he asked.

'Equality,' she said. 'What do you want?'

'A night off,' he said.

She laughed again. He didn't like her laugh; it didn't meet her eyes. Perhaps it was the darkness of her hair that made them look so blue. They could make the sky jealous.

'You tried to steal Con's magic,' Leo said, to prompt her into answering properly.

'So interesting that we couldn't,' she agreed. 'Did you know that he was a bastard?'

Leo gritted his teeth together as hard as he could without allowing his expression to change. Con was his *brother*, his entire brother, and he didn't care if his parents had conceived him too early or if his mother had been braver than he'd thought, every atom of Con was linked with every atom of Leo. If Leo hadn't been chained by iridium, he could have destroyed Isobella with a whisper.

He took a breath.

He had grown up with a man who didn't think that apologies mattered. Richard didn't stop fighting until his opponent cried, and didn't stop then, either. There was nothing you could do or say to stop him from telling you exactly how despicable you were for wronging him. He decided when you were broken enough to leave alone. And even though it didn't make the *slightest* bit of difference, Leo had learnt how not to show how much it hurt for a really long time before he gave out.

This woman was not his dad. He was not going to break down for anyone less.

'No,' Leo said. He sounded disinterested to his own ears.

'It doesn't matter,' she said. 'We'll make up for it tonight. Your people will light the furnace of our power.'

Leo did not like the sound of that. His face must have betrayed some of his feeling.

'You don't have to burn,' she said. 'You're pretty. You could live. You would be an enormous asset to The Awakening.'

Leo had extraordinarily heavy manacles on his wrists that blocked his magic. His sword had been taken away. Everyone he loved was in this castle and there was nothing he could do to save them. He felt powerless every day in this job where his authority did nothing to budge the problems people brought to him, but that was nothing to this.

'Give me the sales pitch,' he shrugged, and if he'd known how to smile at a time like this he would have.

'Your Majesty, you're a difficult one to pitch to,' Isobella said. 'It's hard to know where your passion lies. Your eyes wander during church sermons, you make feeble jokes instead of taking a stand and you seem to just be doing what your sister tells you to.'

'If you take it on a percentage basis, I think you'd be surprised at how few of the things Ada tells me to do that I actually listen to,' Leo said. 'She just tells me to do *so many* things.'

'Does it make you sad that there are children hungry on your streets?' she asked.

'Yes.' Leo took a breath to soften his gaze again. He couldn't let her get a rise out of him.

'Ooh, that was nearly anger,' she said.

She spun on her toes and was abruptly cheek to cheek with him, and a second later her hair caught up and struck his back like raindrops on a window. She was tall and had gripped his manacles downwards to rob him of the height he had on her, and for the space of one blink he could feel her eyelashes on his cheek.

'There are old people who know that they will live in pain every single day of the rest of their lives,' she pointed out towards the city and dropped her voice as if telling a secret, 'and they live *just* over there, and if you got off your fancy little chair you might even be able to help some of them. Does that make you cross?'

'Two months ago, I passed a law that requires every business to comply with an enormous rule book about how much people can lift and how often they need breaks and what training they need before they do manual labour,' Leo said. Her skin was warm against his. People didn't get this close to him and he hated the intimacy. 'And that will save thousands of people in this kingdom injuries that would have cost them years of pain. It'll save lives. It never would have occurred to my father or my brother and it isn't even something Ada came up with, *I* did that. I wouldn't have made close to that much of a difference as a healer.'

'But does it make you cross?' she whispered.

'YES!' Leo roared.

Isobella turned back to face him at a respectable distance and smiled.

'It makes us cross too,' she said. 'The whole world makes us cross. And at the top of the list of things that really fucking piss us off … is you.'

'Me,' Leo repeated. He was gathering calmness to him like sand. He was building a castle out of serenity.

'Royalty,' she said. 'With your money and your power and all of you related if you go far enough back, all of you *her* scions.'

'Sorry for pissing you off, I guess,' Leo said.

'Well, it's not just yours anymore,' Isobella said. With a gesture like she was trying to grasp a barely visible cobweb towards herself, she said, 'Blaze,' and a small fire started above her fingertips.

'Cute,' Leo said. 'I don't think you like that word enough.'

'Oh, I'm learning,' she promised. 'We'll all learn. And we won't be hungry or sick or beaten anymore.'

The flame went out. Her face fell for a moment before she composed herself and grinned as though she'd done it on purpose.

'So here's the pitch,' she said. 'Give up your life of pretty clothes and five course meals and all your servants wiping your arse for you. Give it all up and join us instead. We're going to give every person on this continent the power you keep from them.'

She drew close to him, close enough to share his breath. Her disregard of personal space, her erratic movements and temper, it was all calculated to unbalance him. Leo recognised within himself the urge to flatter her, make nice with her, keep her happy so that she would be more predictable. It was the kind of impulse that could trick a person into thinking that they wanted to be nice to someone because they *liked* them, especially if it was unsafe for Isobella to suspect that she wasn't liked.

'Are you a good person?' she asked, looking up at him.

And she was pretty. Her eyes were the kind of blue you didn't expect to see in nature. The kind that made you think that maybe they were poisonous. She smelled of citrus. Sixteen-year-old Leo probably would have followed her in a heartbeat.

'Have you ever convinced anyone to join you like that?' Leo asked.

'You'd be surprised,' she said, stepping back. 'But I'm not trying too hard. I know what your magic is capable of, and I'd honestly rather you say no so that we can take it from you instead. What good is one soldier with a superiority complex compared to your oh so impressive power distributed amongst my people?'

'Yeah, I get that,' Leo said. 'And I wasn't going to join you anyway. You haven't treated my family very well.'

'No,' she smiled. 'And tonight the ones we haven't killed yet will burn with you.'

Fury shot down Leo's spine and he lifted his chained hands above his head, ready to bring the heavy manacles down on her. One of the magicians behind him muttered something and his nerves lit up as though he'd cracked the thin part of his elbow against something, all through his body. It was over in an instant, but it left him breathless and shaky.

'Bye bye, Your Majesty,' Isobella said. 'I hope I'm the one to find your sister.'

'Yeah, me too,' Leo spat. 'I hope she teaches you some new words for fire.'

ISOBELLA LEFT and Leo was marched to the cathedral. The bishop's altar and the marble platforms that had held his family's coffins had been reduced to rubble and kicked away to make room for a giant, magical cage. Leo baulked when he was a few feet away from the cage and took a step backward, which earned him a hard crack in the back of the head with the swordswoman's pommel. He staggered to a knee before one of them caught his elbow. His vision danced into indistinct patterns and his ears muffled the displeased sound of the magician's voice. He blinked his way back into proper consciousness as he was hauled back to his feet and pushed through the cage's magical barrier. Danya caught his wrists and kept him upright. He held onto her as his balance somersaulted slowly, trusting that she was standing better than him. The fact that there were chunks of marble littering the ground and making his feet uneven was not helping matters.

'Are you okay?' he slurred.

'Priorities, Leo!' she said nervously. She released one of his hands and held up three fingers. Her range of movement was impeded by her own set of manacles, but most of the other people in the cage seemed to have free rein. 'How many?' she asked.

'Three,' he said. 'My vision's fine.' He turned his head to look after where the attackers had gone and felt an awful tingle of nausea sweep from his scalp to his fingers. He swallowed and amended his statement. 'My short-sighted vision's fine. Have you been here long?'

'They snuck up on me when I was eating,' she said, looking furious. 'My *mouth* was full.'

Leo couldn't keep his mouth from twitching in amusement.

'I suppose it's significant they haven't killed us yet,' she said, shoving him a little to stop him from smiling.

It worked. He was trapped, and it sounded like Isobella wanted them all to burn at the same time. And they were in a cathedral that was designed to enhance magic with every angle.

'Danya,' he asked carefully. 'You said … that you were born in a church. And that …'

Danya immediately knew what he was talking about. Her dark skin paled and she swallowed. Leo picked up her hand, suddenly needing the contact. He dropped his voice further.

'Is this your prophecy? For all of us?'

'I don't know,' she whispered. 'I only say that because it's a pattern, and our blessed Trinity loves patterns.' The doors of the cathedral creaked and then closed loudly as the ones who had brought Leo in left again. 'Or maybe *we* do. Maybe things happen in patterns because we wait until things are at what we believe is their most auspicious until we try them. They've chosen a good date, if that's something that matters.'

'So you don't know.'

Danya squeezed Leo's hand painfully tight. Her eyes were wet but tears didn't spill over.

'I have loved being a part of your family,' she said.

Leo nodded, throat too thick to talk. He hoped his anxious eyes conveyed that he loved her too. He couldn't let her die. He just couldn't.

THEY WAITED FOR SOMETHING TO HAPPEN. It dragged on long enough to actually become boring. Leo didn't have the capacity to reflect on what Isobella had said or to make a plan that depended on escaping from an impossible cage, so he coped with it by checking on everyone else. It was a random collection of people, just the ones the attackers had managed to corner. There weren't very many attackers, so a lot of people had fled the castle for the city and hadn't been chased after. The ones in the cage were the ones who had run into dead ends or who had fought directly and lost. They gained another addition to the cage two more times. Each time, the ones who brought the new person in would talk quietly to the only other attacker in the room, then leave again.

There was only one injury that Leo was really concerned about, and it wasn't really that serious in the scheme of things. But the little girl was Max's age and her wrist didn't look right. She was crying quietly and there wasn't much anyone could do within the cage. Danya tore up a man's undershirt and wrapped it tightly around the wrist to keep the girl from moving it too much. Leo told her she was brave and gave her his handkerchief, movements made clumsy by the heavy manacles. It felt like too little, but it was all he could offer.

It was beyond distressing when Max was brought in. He was uninjured but clearly terrified of the three men escorting him.

'... trying to find the other two ...' Leo overheard as one of the men reported back to the magician who seemed to be supervising. The magician threw up her hands in frustration and followed them out of the room. Leo hoped Ada and Con stayed hidden. Unfortunately, he didn't think either of them was the type to hide.

Leo looped his chained hands over Max's head and pulled him into a tight hug. Max shook in his arms and didn't squirm free. Leo stroked Max's soft hair wordlessly and looked at Danya with pleading eyes.

He didn't know what he wanted her to do. He was afraid that there was in fact nothing she *could* do. The awful truth of the matter was that everyone in this cage expected *him* to be the one to do something. His job was to look after them—that was what being king meant. He had no idea how he was supposed to do that.

It was at least half an hour before something finally happened. The cathedral doors didn't just fly open—the shock of the impact against the walls caused them to explode into fire. Leo squinted at the sudden brightness and smoke, both of which couldn't quite obscure his gut feeling. The only person he'd ever known who was quite that theatrical was his little sister. His feeling was confirmed when Ada and Con strode into view.

Up until that moment, Leo hadn't fully processed what it had meant that Ada had been performing all of Con's magic. He'd pictured her crafting her powders and holding her hands over him as she sang strengthening songs. But magic required knowledge, and it was abundantly clear from the confident way she held her sword that she knew exactly how to use it. She and Con were mirror images of one another, with her shorter, left-handed sword pointing at the ground to mirror his right-handed one. Leo's first thought was that they had brought a triangle with them. His second thought was *oh-holy-hell-that's-a-lot-of-fire*.

Ada's voice rang through the space as though amplified, catching on walls designed with acoustic projection in mind, and surprisingly Con's voice was an equally clear accompaniment, harmonising low. The magic didn't just come from her; it bounced off him as well. Leo could only tell that it didn't originate there because he was specifically looking for it.

'We sing these words for the Trinity / Our fury graced with divinity / These words they manifest physically / To strike our enemies down.'

They moved in a slow and careful circle as they sang, scanning the cathedral for enemies. A man from the cage called out to them to tell them that they were alone, but neither Ada nor Con reacted at all, confirming Danya's assessment of there being a sound barrier. They moved as one, the wrists of their free hands touching in silent communication.

'Our hearts are one and our swords strike true / Defences strong and weakness few / Courage, strength and agility too / Stand mighty with this sound.'

Con timed it so that he struck at one of the keystones holding the cage in place with his sword at the same time as their final words. The impact of its destruction sent both him and Ada stumbling away and the cage's occupants flinching to cover their ears. A second later, a dozen hands reached out to confirm that the barrier was still in place. Leo didn't bother, both because he had learnt about traps at the Academy and because he was too focused on watching Ada and Con pick themselves up.

The two of them resumed their formation and their singing, approaching the next keystone with more urgency, clearly wary of the noise they had made. And they were right to be, because just as Con drew his sword up, three robed figures arrived in the doorway. Ada stepped lithely closer and adjusted her stance, holding her non-dominant arm across her body to support the hand holding her sword resting on the back of her neck. Con turned to look for a second before he refocused on the keystone. Neither of their voices wavered. The trio spread out, focusing on Ada as the closer threat.

Con stabbed the keystone at the culmination of their stanza and was again knocked over. Ada's skirt moved, but she was out of the blast radius. The enemies at the door advanced, taking advantage of Con's incapacitation.

In a tone of utter self-satisfaction, like nothing pleased her more than being cornered, Ada said, 'Conflagration,' and brought her sword down in a wide arc, turning so that the fire that erupted from her blade rained down on all three enemies. They jumped back, off-balance, and Ada sprinted wildly at the one on the right before he had recovered. The man managed to block her first two blows but was forced to let her get on the other side of him so that she was no longer in the centre of their triangle. When she blocked his return strike, she directed his sword past her so that she could grab his wrist and stabbed him in the throat. Leo's jaw dropped. Con hadn't been lying when he said that she could take him in a fight.

By the time the man's body hit the ground, Con had recovered and taken his place next to her. The second he did, they both melted into new positions, Con holding his sword two-handed, close to his neck and leaning his weight forward and Ada with her sword by her hip and leaning back.

'The cage,' she said.

'Yeah, I agree, we better end this quickly so we can get back to that,' Con said.

'I have this,' Ada said.

'Just for fun, let's do it together.'

Leo uselessly cried out Con's name to alert him to the fact that the enemies were advancing, but even if they could have heard him it would have been unnecessary. Con lunged forward to catch the closer enemy's sword and knock it to the side, and without hesitating he kicked her in the side, in the direction of the other enemy. The woman he'd kicked staggered but didn't collide with the other man as Con had planned. Still, as he dodged her, Con was able to run at him without any such distraction. Leo's eyes were wide as he watched the unbridled way that Con fought, moving fast and with purposeful, very unfancy strikes, each one designed to get him closer to the now-retreating man. Suddenly, he didn't feel bad about losing to him so frequently when they trained.

Con's advance put his back to the woman, but she was rightly more concerned with Ada. In the time that had elapsed, Ada had managed to sing a single line invoking luck, which she clearly assessed to be enough as she instead prioritised physical attack. She attacked in identical style to Con, and she was more suited to fighting a right-handed opponent than the woman was at fighting Ada's left. Still, the woman was good, and Ada was unable to gain an advantage even when she drove her back and nearly got her to trip over the body of the third enemy.

Con finished his enemy first and left the man slumped on his back, trying futilely to stop the flow of blood from his chest. Ada's jaw was set and her face was flushed, and Leo thought that her blows didn't look as strong as they had been, or as controlled. She and her opponent were almost stationary; too much longer and Leo thought Ada would be the one pressed back.

'Behind you,' Con called, and the moment he stepped beside her she fell back, breathing heavily but still on guard. There was a difference between training to be good in a fight and doing daily endurance drills with a troop of soldiers, and Con was exhibiting it. The enemy fell within ten seconds.

Con and Ada made short work of the remaining keystone and the magical barrier finally fell. The prisoners didn't seem to know what to do with their freedom. Leo realised with a jolt that he was the authority in the room.

'Everyone, take a seat on the pews,' he said. Then, 'Please,' because it felt awkward not to.

They were slow about it, which gave him time to murmur, 'Ada,' holding his wrists up.

They crouched to the ground and with a quiet word to ensure accuracy of aim, Ada brought the pommel of her sword down, hard, on the iridium. The brittle metal cracked and fell away enough for Leo to get out of it. If Leo hadn't known breaking out of the cage would be impossible even with his magic, he might have risked breaking his wrists by slamming the manacles onto the ground. He was glad it hadn't come to that.

To her credit, even though Danya had her own chains, Ada wrapped Max up in a hug before she did anything else. Leo moved to the injured girl and took her wrist in his hands. At his quiet command, the bone shifted back into place and healed under his fingers and she made a soft noise of surprise.

'Does anyone else need healing?'

Con sheepishly put up his hand and Danya moved to take care of it. Only one other prisoner did. Leo was relieved, not only because that meant injuries had been minimal but also because magic use was fatiguing and they needed everything they could get.

'I don't know why we're here, or why *they're* here,' Leo said. 'I will find out, but that's a matter for tomorrow. What's important now is making sure that everyone is safe and putting a stop to this. Many people were able to evade them before, but I won't ask you to chance that again. Are there any magicians here?'

A couple of hands went up. Leo motioned for them to join him and his family in the centre of the stage now strewn with broken marble. He turned to Danya.

'I'd prefer if at least some were captured,' he told Danya, offering his hand and his magic. 'I have questions.'

'I can do captured,' she said, smiling sweetly.

23

THE VERY SECOND Danya's magic had taken effect, Leo grabbed Con by the forearm and whispered, 'Be the king for half an hour—I have to take care of something.'

Con looked at him incredulously, which was fair—he'd absolutely already pulled his weight. But he saw that Leo was serious and nodded wearily. Leo gave him a tight, unconvincing smile of gratitude, then ran from the room.

He knew he should be providing next steps. He knew he should be leading the process of properly arresting all the attackers. He genuinely cared about those responsibilities, but he had one priority that insisted on being listened to the instant he was no longer trapped. He had to know if Raven was dead or alive.

The cathedral was at ground level in front of Lyric Tower, which led to the longest and most exhausting run of Leo's life. He begged his magic for endurance and speed, but it was lethargic from his imprisonment and the magic needed to restrain the attackers and could only do so much. When he staggered into the greenhouse, he almost fell to his knees.

'Ignite,' he gasped.

Half of the candles reluctantly obeyed the dregs of his magic, but the room was empty. Leo searched thoroughly, even though there wasn't really anywhere to hide. He hoped that Raven had had the sense to escape to recover rather than the alternative of him being captured. The body of the attacker who had collapsed when raising the revenant was gone too. Leo swore as he leaned against the stone wall. He didn't know where Raven slept.

The last thing he wanted to do was reenter the cathedral, but he made himself do it anyway. He took charge of what Danya called "emergency management". He found that Arrowhead Tower, home to Sword and Shield, had been magically sealed during a rare full-company meeting, but that they'd overpowered the enchantments as soon as the counter-attack Danya led had taken out the magicians maintaining them. The attackers seemed to have all either been captured or killed. They were as safe as they were likely to get.

Leo made Con and Ada take Max to bed to force them to go rest as well. He dealt with the staff's concerns and made promises that he hoped were reasonable. He sat through a thrown-together supper intended to revive the victims, both those who had been in the cathedral as well as those who had fled or been injured, finally being present in the way that he was supposed to be. Finally being a king. For once, Leo didn't feel as though he was pretending to play a part too big for him. He supposed he was too spent for that.

If Danya knew where the fool lived, Leo knew she wouldn't tell him. She probably wouldn't trust that he was sincerely concerned. And, in all honesty, Leo didn't have the guts to ask. But it didn't end up being relevant. After everything had wound down, Leo opened his bedroom door and found exactly where Raven had disappeared to. He was lying on his side with his eyes closed on Leo's bed, hands loosely in front of his face on the pillow. Leo rushed to him and fell to his knees. He touched Raven's temple, then wrist. He found a pulse just as Raven's eyes struggled open.

'Are you okay?' Leo murmured.

'Perfect, Majesty,' Raven slurred.

'Ameliorate, regenerate ... *Heal*, please, you're okay ...'

'Leo, stop,' Raven said, gentle but firm. 'That's enough. I feel all better and you're going to knock yourself out.' He reached up to touch Leo's cheek. 'Come to bed, you fool.'

Leo didn't even hesitate. He climbed to his feet, fumbled his shoes off and pushed back the covers. Raven made room for him —or he made *some* room. Leo lay on his back with his right arm brushing Raven's, forced into closeness to avoid falling out of bed and definitely okay with it, if slightly nervous. Raven's body was warmer under the blankets than it had been on his exposed wrist.

Leo looked into Raven's eyes, black in the low lighting of candles that Raven must have lit before he fell asleep. There was a smudge of grey paint on the side of his nose and more at his hairline, like he hadn't had the energy to clean his face perfectly. Leo didn't know why he liked that. Maybe it was that Raven had always seemed to have his act together in some untouchable, mysterious way, and now he was just a person. Raven pushed himself up onto his elbow, ignoring Leo's concerned noise of protest, then leaned towards him. He gave Leo more than enough time to say no or to push him away, but the thought didn't enter his mind. His own shoulders lifted from the bed to meet Raven's lips. Raven pushed him back down and Leo made a soft noise without breaking the kiss.

His hands reached for Raven and found the bare skin of his shoulder. He hadn't registered that Raven was shirtless and his breath hitched with the realisation. Raven slipped his tongue gently into Leo's mouth.

'I'm, ha,' Leo mumbled against Raven's lips, before he lost his capacity to think. 'Not sure I'm ...' Raven pulled back, looking serious, 'up to it.'

'Of course, sorry,' Raven said, pulling back further. 'Do you want me to leave? I don't know why I—'

'No, stay!' Leo said, fingers tightening on Raven's shoulder. 'I didn't mean that, I wasn't even saying "stop", really. Just … managing expectations.'

'Oh,' Raven said, relaxing. Then understanding lit up his eyes. 'Oh.' He laughed and Leo covered his face with his hands, smiling despite his embarrassment. 'How presumptuous of you to think I'd go so far, Majesty,' Raven teased. He sang quietly, 'There once was a king who—'

Leo uncovered his face and pressed both hands to Raven's mouth instead. Raven laughed against them.

'Is that what I have to look forward to now that I know who you are?' Leo asked. 'Are you going to start juggling next?'

Raven nodded, eyes full of mischief.

Leo laughed through a groan and pushed himself up so he could roll Raven over onto his back and kiss him. A logic centre in Leo's brain tried to insist that this was a kind of punishment, or maybe an effective way of keeping Raven from singing more, but he really just wanted to kiss him. When Leo's lips moved to Raven's neck, Raven said breathlessly, 'Couldn't think of a rhyme for flaccid anyway.'

'Placid,' Leo offered.

'Could always put it in the middle of the line …'

And then Raven shut up in favour of guiding Leo's jaw up to kiss him again.

Leo sank back into the bed and their kisses slowed into laziness as Leo's exhaustion began to take over. Raven pulled Leo's shirt over his head then gave him one last lingering kiss. He looked into Leo's eyes and stroked along his hair.

'I don't want to go to sleep yet,' Leo mumbled. 'Too nice.'

'You can have me tomorrow,' Raven said. His eyes tightened a little, making him look vulnerable in uncertainty. 'Unless you can't, according to your principles.'

Leo stroked up and down Raven's side in reassurance. 'I've decided I don't have any.'

'Oh, good. I imagine that will make the kingdom much more interesting.'

Leo smiled in amusement. 'I might have some,' he admitted. 'But …'

Leo had known that if he started kissing Raven, then that would be it. He'd known that that was the boundary of his willpower. But despite the urgency of his feelings, kissing Raven had obviously not been the most momentous event of the night.

'You could have died tonight,' he said. 'Or I could have. Or anyone. And it's just … I think about all the bullshit I've done over the last year and it feels like all I've done is put out fires, and I haven't even done a good job of it. And this feels so important. If you'd have died, it would have …'

Leo swallowed and looked away. Raven touched a finger to his chin and brought his gaze back.

'You can have me tomorrow,' he repeated.

'Okay,' Leo said unsteadily.

Raven held Leo close. Leo nuzzled into his neck and basked in the warmth of his skin and the strong pulse beneath it. His breath slowed and his eyes closed as he traced the subtle bumps of Raven's spine.

It had been a long time since Leo had had this kind of intimacy, and he hadn't had it often. And maybe it was because he was older or because he knew now that Raven did truly want nothing from Leo's position, but this felt different. Or maybe it was simply because he was too tired to feel anything but calm, warm and safe. That was probably an absurd way to feel after the events of the night, but feelings were never what they should be. Tomorrow he'd have to deal with countless people and logistics. He didn't have room in his head for any of that tonight.

Raven scritched Leo's head gently a couple of times and shifted so he was more comfortable. Leo waited until he'd settled to let his arm wrap around Raven's waist again.

'Sweet dreams, Majesty,' Raven murmured.

'Good night, Raven,' Leo replied.

It was a very good way to fall asleep.

AFTER HAVING FALLEN ASLEEP so pleasantly, it was a shock for Leo to wake up alone in bed to the sudden light of his curtains being thrown back.

'I've let you sleep for as long as could be considered reasonable,' Forster said in a business-like tone. 'But important people are beginning to creep into King's Hall and you'll be expected.'

'Thanks,' Leo groaned, covering his eyes with his forearm.

'You had better get ready fast, or I'll need to reevaluate how long I let you sleep in future.'

Leo groaned again and forced himself to sit up as Forster left the room. He didn't feel depleted in the way he had after he'd healed Con, but he wasn't exactly feeling fresh either. He slumped over so that his legs fell out of bed and used the momentum to stand. A glance in the mirror told him that he wasn't looking particularly well rested, and his hair had frizzed out of his braid so much it looked like it was matted instead of tied back. He decided that was a problem for Sebastian as he washed his face at the basin. The water was slightly greasy, as though someone had used it to wash off face paint last night.

Sebastian entered the room with a fresh ewer of steaming water, giving Leo an excellent reason to empty the basin of the evidence of Raven's sleepover. At the Academy, the building had networks of pipes running through it capable of delivering hot water to many of the rooms. At Maforc Castle, only the kitchens had these facilities, the rest of the castle relying on channels that could dispose of waste water but not generate it. The cost of implementing pipes into an established castle would doubtlessly be prohibitively expensive, no matter the payoff of convenience. His room at the Academy would have been better to conceal a secret partner who wore makeup.

Leo undressed, sat at his dressing table and surrendered himself to Sebastian's ministrations, grateful for the time to gather himself for the day. He was cleaned of sweat and dried blood, shaved and his hair was braided back from his face. When it was time to dress, Sebastian chose a blood-red jerkin patterned with black fractals. Leo didn't know if he was supposed to be celebrating or mourning or just being present, but Ada had once said that this shirt brought out the murder in his eyes and that wasn't the worst way to look today.

Last night, after everything had been settled and he was back in his room with Raven, Leo had felt giddy with relief that none of his loved ones had been hurt—and if he was being honest with himself, he'd been pretty damn giddy over Raven as well. Now his well of magic was close to exhausted, but he was surprisingly alert. He felt like he could go for a run. He felt like he could get in a fight and win. It wasn't until he saw his hands shaking as he reached for his gloves that he realised that, without even consciously reflecting on anything, he was furious.

He paused, staring at his hands. It didn't take any effort to figure out why. The attackers had ruined Leo's life nine months ago, they'd ruined Con's life three months ago, and now they'd come back and Leo honestly hadn't known if he was going to make it out alive. If it hadn't been for Con and Ada, he didn't think they would have.

And how dare they do that to them? They had herded up Leo and his subjects like cattle to be slaughtered, and for what? Leo didn't know how effective he was going to be in King's Hall with the nobles, but he felt more than ready to confront the bastards responsible.

He picked up his sword and had wrapped the belt around his waist before he remembered that he shouldn't have had it here— he'd dropped it in the greenhouse. He found his crown perched on a chair too. For a moment, his anger receded enough for him to smile, knowing who had brought them down. He looked back at the empty bed. It was a good thing that Forster hadn't caught Leo in bed with his fool the morning after a terrorist attack, to put it mildly, but now Leo didn't know where Raven was, or what to expect. *'You can have me tomorrow,'* Raven had said. Leo would just have to take him at his word. He couldn't worry about that now anyway.

Forster was waiting outside Leo's room, naturally. He fell into step with Leo as they walked towards King's Hall, floorboards singing softly under their feet.

'I hear you did well last night,' he said. 'The staff who aren't consumed by recommitting to their deep and fervent idolisation of your brother are talking about how in control you were. They respect you for it.'

'Even though I didn't kick down the cathedral doors and wave my sword around?'

'They lust after Prince Conrad. They fear Princess Adelaide. Their hearts break for Prince Maximilian. They respect you.' Forster looked at Leo with serious eyes. 'That is how I would rather they feel about their king.'

Leo didn't know what to say to that. He settled on nodding.

Forster didn't torture him by relaying further praise. Instead, he referred to his eternal armful of papers to tell Leo which nobles had been kidnapped or escaped last night, which had been injured and how they were reacting. Late summer wasn't the most popular time for important visitors, but there were a few. Blanche, the princess from Neue Wolke who Leo had ridden out to Ziegbourne with, had escaped and had waved off any attempt at consolation. The queen of Rinderplatz and her daughter had also been lingering since before Sommertide, and despite having successfully hidden in Guin's fabric stores, the queen was feeling a bit delicate about the whole thing.

'How do you think I should play this?' Leo asked.

'As you did last night,' Forster replied promptly. 'Attentive and austere. I believe that actually comes naturally to you.'

'Are you telling me to be myself?' Leo asked, amused despite himself. 'After all this time trying to coax some kind of regal performance out of me, are you telling me that I know what I'm doing?'

'I take it as a great success that you have found your royal muse,' Forster said.

Leo wasn't sure that was exactly what had happened, but he would take it.

IT WAS EASY TO BE AUSTERE. It was a relief to not have to feign enthusiasm over a boring person in the slim hope that building up some kind of fake relationship would benefit Canticalica one day. Instead, Leo was able to listen to stories that mattered, knowing that every perspective he heard could tell him more about the attackers and their goals. Sympathy came easy to him because he'd spent so much time unwillingly around these people and he knew that their distress was real. Conviction came even easier. He might not know why the attack had happened, but sincerity shone through when he said he would find out.

Stefanie, the Leutesland emissary, found Leo on his way from one group of victims to another. Leo bumped right into her and she gripped his forearms to keep from falling over.

'Sorry,' Leo said.

'No, that was me,' Stefanie laughed. 'It must have been,

because as far as this kingdom is concerned, your every step is divine.'

'I don't know about that,' Leo said, hearing criticism in something that might have been a playful tease from someone he knew better.

Stefanie seemed to realise that their relationship wasn't quite there for that comment and slowly released Leo's forearms.

'I hear you were quite inspirational last night,' she said. 'And the word wouldn't be a stretch this morning. It's refreshing to see a monarch who doesn't sequester themself away in their tower.' Before Leo could respond, she added quickly, 'I speak of course not of Leutesland, but as emissary I see a variety of kingdoms.'

'I'll take that as a compliment,' Leo said.

'It's intended as one,' Stefanie said. 'It's interesting, the ways you differ from your father, Trinity bring him peace. You're more personal. He liked to let his events speak for him.'

Leo didn't know what to say to that. He nodded awkwardly.

'I'm sure you'll continue to prove yourself a worthy leader,' Stefanie said. 'I hope you don't forget our friendship when the prettier ones come knocking.'

'That would be impossible,' Leo said, with what he hoped was a warm smile.

Stefanie laughed and touched Leo's elbow lightly before walking away. Leo closed his eyes in belated regret. He'd meant that he wouldn't forget Leutesland and its emissaries. She'd heard that there was no one prettier than her. He didn't know if he had the grace necessary to disentangle himself without causing offence. Maybe Con would have advice.

L EO MANAGED TO FIND TIME TO EAT when his siblings provided the distraction of coming to breakfast too. Ada entered the hall to applause, which might have hurt Leo's feelings when compared to his welcome but comparatively lukewarm reception, but she'd earned it. And it was like Forster said, people seemed to fear her. Leo found that he preferred being the one that people wanted to talk to, which was so far from how he'd felt a year ago that it almost made him dizzy. When Con entered and a maid actually swooned into his arms, Leo and Ada laughed hard enough that Blanche noticed. She gave them a conspiratorial smile that seemed to agree that it was funny, but didn't approach. Everyone else seemed too busy staring at Con to notice them.

Breakfast dragged on until it was nearly noon, at which point Leo managed to extricate himself so he could head over to Arrowhead Tower. Forster appeared by Leo's side as soon as he was out of the hall, because if there was anything Leo could count on it was the efficiency of his secretary. They walked in silence, which meant that Leo hadn't messed up over the last few hours and there was no extra intel to pass on.

The Helm's convocation room was, as always, about as chaotic as the Chief Helm's mind. She stood up from her desk when Leo and Forster entered and met them halfway. She looked like she hadn't slept, which was more than likely.

'It's good you're here,' she said in greeting. 'We want to get onto this as quickly as possible.'

They sat down in the chairs Leo had grown used to over the last nine months, which were more comfortable than any of the other avenue heads had in their offices. Lou clasped her hands on her lap and looked at Leo with her almost uncomfortably direct attention.

'They're not from any particular kingdom,' she said. 'Some of them are from ours. Praecentor predominately, but at least two are from rural Canticalica. And that's another thing that we can't narrow down—they're not exclusively city dwellers or farmers and I can't say that they are all rich or poor or draw any other generalisations … we're still working, of course, but I'm not surprised we've been unable to find them up until now.'

'The fact that they're diverse is in itself unique,' Leo mused. 'It means we can't just point our fingers at one of our neighbours, though we hadn't been seriously considering that since Con was attacked, so no real progress there.'

'No,' Lou agreed. 'The High Enchantress is working on theories based on the date, position of the moon, et cetera et cetera. It's pretty clear that they had a magical agenda, and they certainly seem devout enough.'

'What makes you say that?' Leo asked.

'I spent last night watching them. There's no such thing as a novel prisoner, Your Majesty; all are made equal behind bars. You get the scared ones, the demanding ones, the angry ones and the stoic ones. These ones all prayed, every one of them.'

'Anything of note there?'

Lou pulled a notebook out of her pocket and flicked through it. She went to hand it over, then remembered that Leo absolutely could not read her handwriting. She grimaced apologetically and referenced it as she spoke.

'A lot of "Trinity, give me strength", that sort of thing, plenty of prayers I learnt at school along with the rest of the continent. More concerning were the "strike down my enemies" while making eye contact with the Shields and "know us for your true followers". They're not prayers I'm familiar with even when the accents are local, but they're consistent. Like they've been taught them. Like they're part of some kind of cult.'

'Huh,' Leo said, for lack of anything more intelligent to say. 'A cult who hates my family?'

'We no longer think it's as specific as that,' Lou said. 'It's more likely that we just happen to be the smallest kingdom in the Empire and the … divisive nature of your father's rule meant that, outside of Canticalica, no one asked too many questions about your family's assassination. Which might not actually be the right word for it. *Sacrifice* seems more apt.'

Leo hummed, rolling a ring around his finger as he thought.

'It's a lot to take in,' Lou acknowledged stiffly.

This was uncharacteristically generous towards Leo's response. Leo supposed she wasn't in the best position to criticise anyone after Sword and Shield had just failed to prevent a third attack. He'd be within his rights to criticise her. If he did so in public, his people might feel he was taking action and sympathise more with him. But Leo couldn't afford to alienate Sword and Shield when they were just doing their jobs. He had to assume …

No, he didn't. How many attacks would it take for him to stop taking everyone at best faith?

'How could they have known about Sword and Shield's meeting last night?' Leo asked.

'Any of our order might have mentioned it at any point to anyone,' Lou said promptly. 'Not as a point of strategy but in the way of talking about their day.'

'Con always gave me the impression they were trained to *not* talk about things like that,' Leo said.

'They are,' Lou said. 'But it happens.'

'And you're satisfied with that explanation?' Leo asked. 'Your assessment is that there is no security risk to examine?'

'We're examining it for the sake of thoroughness,' Lou said. 'It's unlikely to be malicious in nature.'

'Still, I'd like you to be sure,' Leo said. 'I think they know more than they should. They have to have someone who knows the castle in their number. Not necessarily from Sword and Shield.'

Lou frowned at Leo thoughtfully, then nodded.

'You're right. That's a good place to start our investigations.'

It would have been nice if she'd sounded less surprised that he had some insight to give, but, Leo reflected, the fact that she was hearing him at all was some improvement on where he'd started. And he didn't actually mind Lou. She was only thirty, and she knew what it was like to have to prove herself as worthy of her title due to her age. She'd snapped at Galland twice for bringing up Leo's age when it wasn't remotely relevant. She still condescended to him, but she did it because she thought he didn't know what he was doing, not because he was young.

Leo didn't know who he could trust, but despite the fact that he was concerned about Sword and Shield being vulnerable to infiltration, he didn't think that Lou was on the side of the cult, or even that she was against him in general. And if he was wrong, if he was an idiot for sharing any information with anyone, if he was supposed to keep everything to himself out of the possibility that someone would betray him ... well then he might as well give up. He couldn't do this alone.

'I spoke with their leader last night,' he said.

'What?' Lou demanded. Forster's pen froze where it had been taking notes.

Leo looked at her steadily. It took her a second to realise that she wasn't in a position to be demanding confidence from him.

'Apologies for my tone, Your Majesty,' she said, dropping her eyes for a moment. 'You took me by surprise.'

'I wanted to hear your report before I swayed your judgement with mine,' he said.

Lou nodded, not looking particularly happy about it.

'They're called The Awakening,' Leo said. 'Their leader's name is Isobella and she's young, a few years older than me I'd say. She cultivates the appearance of insanity. Pale skin, dark hair and very blue eyes. Did you find anyone like that?'

'No,' Lou said. 'You're sure she's not actually insane?'

'Yes,' Leo said. 'Insane people are vulnerable, even when they're manic. She was in complete control.'

'Strategic then,' Lou said. She thought for a moment. 'Helms don't put themselves at risk unnecessarily. If it was me, I'd be observing. I wouldn't expose myself until I was sure the most powerful magicians and fighters were incapacitated.'

And if she wasn't participating, then the song Danya had created last night wouldn't have touched her. Leo would have to have a word with her about covering that blind spot next time. Because of course there would be a next time.

'Do you know what they want?' Lou asked.

'She says "equality",' Leo said, making air quotes. 'She says they're going to give everyone magic.'

'To what end?' Lou asked.

'Taking over the continent?' Leo said, though he wasn't sure. 'They definitely don't like royalty.'

'There's barely thirty of them in our cells,' Lou said. 'Even if they have ten times as many members out there somewhere, that's not exactly an army. Even if they have a *hundred* times as many members, they would struggle to take over Praecentor, let alone the Empire.'

Leo rubbed at his temple. Even now, he felt like he knew nothing.

'Action items,' Forster said briskly. 'Chief Helm to investigate how Sword and Shield's vulnerability was exposed. Chief Helm to investigate the prisoners further. Chief Helm to provide detailed reports on the progress of these matters. Next meeting to take place tomorrow afternoon, regular meetings to follow.'

'Thank you, Forster,' Leo said, rising. 'We'll see you tomorrow, Lou.'

Lou bowed. And she'd bowed to him before, as everyone did at some point or another, but this was the first time that Leo didn't feel like she was just getting it over with.

 25

ADA SWUNG HER SWORD WILDLY and Leo swore as he dodged, not even able to get his own sword up in time to block it. Her weight went all the way with it, but before Leo could take advantage, Con was striking from the other side. Leo leaned backwards so heavily that he had to fling out a hand to catch himself, then scrambled under Ada's next swing. He lunged for Ada's legs, and she conveniently toppled right into Con. Leo got to his feet, grabbed his dagger from his hip and half-fell back down to get a blade at each of them.

'Hey,' Con laughed. 'You actually got us.'

Ada shoved at Leo's chest with her foot and he unbalanced.

'*Would* have had us if you'd followed through,' Ada said.

'If I'd stabbed you?' Leo asked incredulously.

'Just a little bit,' Ada said.

Leo rolled his eyes and accepted Con's hand up. Ada put her hands out for each of them to take her full weight to bring her to her feet. Leo put his hands behind his head to catch his breath.

'You still fight like a prince,' Ada said. 'Abandon the gallantry, Your Majesty.'

'And *you* fight like you've snorted something illegal,' Leo said. He considered his words. 'Wait, have you? You do carry a lot of powders.'

'Not tonight,' she said with a grin. 'Last week I think I was justified in finding out what a low tolerance our brother has for *something illegal*.'

Leo looked at Con, who shrugged helplessly. Leo supposed Ada had a point. Extra energy and fearlessness didn't go amiss against the Awakening.

'Are we going again?' Leo asked, instead of dealing with that.

Ada sheathed her sword and fell against Con, who caught her and shoved her back upright.

'Far too tired,' she declared. 'Otherwise you never would have beaten me.'

That may have been true, but Leo would take the success. He had improved significantly against Con alone, but the cultists never fought one on one and he knew he needed to learn how to fight from multiple angles. He also wanted to bring magic back into his fighting style at some point, but one thing at a time.

'Besides,' Ada said, leading the way to a garden bench. 'How am I supposed to entice Danya into marriage if I spend every night flailing about with you two?'

'Woah,' Leo said, stalling in place before he could take a seat.

'Seconded,' Con said, with feeling.

'We've been together for years,' Ada said, picking at a splinter of wood on the seat. 'And you're hardly going to marry me off to some lord or another, are you?'

'No,' Leo said, hoping very hard that he wasn't lying. 'But, I mean …'

'But?' Ada demanded.

'Well, I might need to pretend it's an option,' Leo told his feet.

Ada turned on the bench and put her feet on it with punishingly hard force for someone who claimed to be tired. She undid her ponytail and did it again, then retied the useless strings at the bottom of her calf-length leggings. Apparently finished with angrily fixing her appearance, she crossed her arms over her chest and looked away into the garden.

'I want you to marry for love,' Leo said gently. 'I want all of us to, but you most of all. Sorry, Con.'

'I get it,' he said, waving a hand.

'I'm *so sick* of pretending that she's just another member of staff,' Ada said. 'And if you make me go on a single date with someone else, I'll make it a worse experience for them than that guy who shat himself on his date with Con. There will be no diplomatic advantages to treating me like livestock to be traded.'

Leo believed her. But her *appearing* single was really all he needed.

'It hasn't even been a full year since I became king,' Leo said. 'No one seriously wants to marry any of us until they can figure out what the future of Canticalica looks like.'

'Except Stefanie,' Con said.

'I will stab you,' Leo said.

'I would have expected this from Dicky,' Ada said. She still wasn't looking at Leo. 'You cry at every romantic play we watch. You seriously considered eloping with that girl you thought was your girlfriend, who couldn't even tell the difference between you and Dicky.'

'I was fourteen and I didn't *really* consider it,' Leo protested. Con, who was the only person Leo had told about his perhaps overblown feelings, was examining the cuff of his shirt as if looking for a loose thread. 'And I'm not actually going to make you marry someone you don't love. Like you say, I couldn't even if I wanted to, and I suspect you'd treat me even worse than your fiancé. But I haven't exactly got a large pool of nobles to draw on for negotiations, and you're the only woman out of us, and sometimes I need to put things on the table that I don't actually intend to follow through on. I've told most of our debtors that I'd be more than willing to pay them back and I'm certainly not doing that.'

Ada finally looked at him. Leo held his breath, unsure if Ada was going to fall out with him. She hadn't in years, but she was *very* good at glaring over a table, cracking eggs into coat pockets for unsuspecting hands to discover later and pretending to be deaf whenever someone who she believed had wronged her spoke. And that was over things that were much less serious than this.

'I dislike this,' she said.

'Same,' Leo said emphatically.

'I will endure it for a maximum of five years,' she said.

'That's very reasonable,' Leo said, nodding.

'For every date that you force me to go on, I will be passably pleasant in exchange for three favours of any size.'

'Even if your date is very stupid or otherwise objectionable?' Leo asked.

Ada looked to the side, considering. She nodded magnanimously.

'And you will be the one to tell Danya,' Ada said.

Leo opened his mouth to agree, but Con clasped him on the shoulder and turned him around, arm around him to keep him close. In a low voice, he said, 'Three favours is too much. She'll use them to make or break laws.'

'I know,' Leo muttered. 'Or to make me carry her around all day, or embroider her a dress, or say something very embarrassing in public. I assumed I wouldn't have the opportunity to have her date anyone at all, much less be pleasant to them.'

'*Passably* pleasant,' Con corrected.

'I don't think she'll offer anything better,' Leo said.

Con straightened and they both turned to face Ada again. Con cleared his throat and Ada cocked her head to the side. Her expression was the same as it was before a sparring match began.

'*One* favour, but you get it any time that Leo puts the offer on the table as well as when you have to go on a date,' Con said. 'And you have to be pleasant *and* pretend that you marrying the person is actually an option, both in and out of the date. And if Leo thinks the favour is unreasonable, you present it to a panel of me, Max and Danya for review, of which a majority must agree that it can proceed.'

'Two favours,' Ada countered. 'And if the person is abhorrent, I may mildly poison them very surreptitiously.'

'What does mild mean?' Leo asked.

'They will be unwell but will almost certainly have enough warning to make it somewhere suitable before their meals abandon them,' Ada said. 'And the symptoms will only last a day or so.'

'Leo has to agree they deserve it,' Con said.

'Leo wouldn't poison anyone,' Ada scoffed, as though this was a character flaw.

'Max has to agree they deserve it,' Leo said.

Con grimaced, but Leo thought that Max might enjoy the power of this judgement enough to take it seriously. And it was better than it being purely Ada's decision.

'I accept,' Ada said.

Leo looked to Con. Con sighed and nodded.

'I also accept,' Leo said.

Leo and Ada shook hands, and Ada moved her feet to sit up properly and allow room for Leo. Con sat cross-legged on the ground with his hands behind him.

'Do you have any demands?' Leo asked Con.

'I can get along with anybody for a date or two,' Con shrugged. 'But I'd prefer if you didn't actually go through with it.'

'Yeah, that's fair,' Leo said.

He hadn't really expected more. After all, until a few months ago, Con hadn't even been an option. But as Con said, he could get along with anyone. It would have been nice to have the option up his sleeve that would cause the least amount of pain all around.

'Is there a reason you never make it to date three?' Ada asked.

'Are you one of those horrible men who are only in it for the mystery, who then gets disappointed when it turns out that genitalia is not actually that surprising?'

'I don't think so,' Con laughed.

'Do you not want to lead people on into thinking they could end up with someone powerful?' Leo asked.

'Maybe?' Con said. 'No, not really.'

Ada and Leo glanced at each other and made the decision to wait Con out. Guessing wasn't the right tack when they really didn't know. After a few moments of the two of them staring expectantly at Con, he relented.

'I guess it's that I'm, you know. Fun. At the beginning.' At his siblings' raised eyebrows, he covered his face with his hand. 'Not in a sex way,' he groaned.

'The castle is full of liars,' Ada mused.

'No, I mean,' Con said. 'Well yeah, okay, there is … Things occur. In a fun manner, I hope. Please can we pretend that I've never kissed anyone?'

'Sounds good to me,' Leo said.

'It's just, there's not a lot under that,' Con said. 'I hate that moment that comes when you tell a joke that falls flat or you tell a story that's not interesting or talk just a bit too long about swords, and you can see that you're not living up to the idea of you that they have in their head. And I really can't handle it when there's a silence and I can tell they expect me to fill it.'

Ada and Leo glanced at one another again.

'I can get by with friendships fine,' Con said. 'When it's a bunch of mates hanging out, all you have to do is tease each other, complain about which Helms are being arseholes and talk about pedispass. Even when it's just a couple, I don't know, I get by mostly listening. People want to know me on dates, but—' he spread his hands out and shrugged, inviting them to take him in. 'This is all there is.'

This was harder to respond to than Ada's assumption that she could marry Danya at her leisure. Leo didn't consider comforting people to be a personal strength. But if it was him or Ada, he might be the best Con could get.

'I like this,' Leo said. 'You're …' He searched for what exactly Con was. 'You're more than just fun. You *are* fun, and also other things.'

Leo looked at Ada and mouthed *help*. He didn't want to hear himself continue to fumble sentences like that.

'I don't understand what you're expecting to find, or what the concept of "under" is,' Ada said, in a tone that was much more impatient than reassuring.

'I don't really think?' Con said. 'Other people seem to think.'

'I wish *I* didn't think,' Leo said.

'Shut up,' Ada said. 'Of course you think, Con. You have opinions about swords, for example.'

'You think about what you want to do and what you have done,' Leo guessed, because he was suddenly unsure about what *he* thought about, but that seemed right.

'I sort of just do things,' Con said. 'And then people ask me what I'm thinking about and I have to say something like "how beautiful you are" or "I'd like to go for a run this afternoon" or something. But I wasn't actually thinking those things. And even though I've made those things up, they're not really good enough.'

Leo wished Danya was here. She could at least give Con a good hug or something.

'Perhaps you should try being with someone who is also more practical than reflective,' Ada said.

'I don't need this to be solved,' Con said. 'I'm happy as I am, I'm just also a little bit scared that if Leo marries me off my spouse will realise that there's nothing to me and then they won't like me and we won't speak to one another and it'll be like the worst days when our parents were around except all the time. But really, it's fine. I'd just prefer not to be married.'

'Would you like a hug?' Leo asked, voice a bit strained.

'I'll always take a hug,' Con smiled.

Ada patted Con on the shoulder a bit while Leo hugged him. Leo didn't magically think of the right thing to say during the hug. He would have loved a spell that could do that.

'I don't see how anyone couldn't like your company,' Ada said. 'You're my second favourite person in the whole world. Sorry, Leo.'

She did not sound sorry.

'Yeah,' Leo said. 'And I promise I wouldn't ever make you marry someone as terrible as all that.'

'Thanks guys,' Con said. 'Now Leo, about your inevitable engagement to Stefanie.'

It was very unjust that Leo was not currently allowed to hurt Con.

26

IT SHOULD HAVE BEEN OBVIOUS from the second he revealed his identity, but Leo was learning that Raven loved games. Leo had no problem with this for the most part. He didn't mind listening to Raven rehearsing riddles and songs in his room or the way even throwing a crumpled ball of paper into a bin in the vicinity of him provoked a competition. The problem was that Raven had made a game of stealing Leo away in broad daylight, and it was so obviously a bad idea … but it was also dangerously fun.

Today, clean-faced and respectably clothed, Raven slipped his hand into Leo's pocket as he walked past him on Leo's way to Cabinet. No one was in the corridor, but Leo still checked furtively as he pulled the note free. Raven lounged against the wall a good distance away, watching Leo with catlike mischief.

Come play in the blue library.

'I'm busy,' Leo said, in what he thought was an impressively disapproving tone.

Raven stretched lazily and walked away. He pulled a glove off and dropped it as he turned the corner. Leo had the sudden, alarming thought that Raven might strip off something more significant as he went and jogged after him, grabbing the glove and reaching the adjoining corridor just as Raven's scarf joined his second glove on the floor. Leo swallowed. A moment later, he started chasing Raven again and caught him just in time to yank Raven's shirt back down to cover his belly before it could be taken off as well. Leo thought this whole thing was performative bait, but it felt real enough. Leo had never had any reason to believe that risk did anything for him, but here he was.

'Handsy,' Raven commented archly. 'I'm not sure that's appropriate for your station, Majesty.'

Leo groaned in what was at least seventy per cent exasperation and pulled Raven into the nearest room by the grip he still had on his shirt. Raven laughed breathlessly and leaned back against the door, encouraging Leo to pin him in place.

'You know, people use this room,' he said, eyes on Leo's lips.

'Are they going to?' Leo asked, slipping his hands under Raven's shirt and stroking along the warm skin of his sides.

'I don't think so,' Raven said. 'Not if we continue to block the door, anyway.'

Leo pressed Raven more firmly to the door and bent to kiss him. Raven wrapped his arms around Leo's neck and held him like he could pull him closer. Leo slid his thigh between Raven's legs and his tongue into Raven's mouth. Raven curled his hands around the back of Leo's collar and suspired, pressing their hips closer. Their lips parted so that Raven could say through stuttered breaths, 'Not sure this is appropriate either.'

'You so completely started it,' Leo said, biting Raven's neck gently with restrained frustration.

'Whoops,' Raven said remorselessly, tilting his head in permission. 'You're just so easy to get a reaction out of, Majesty, it's …' his voice wavered a little as Leo sucked harshly just under his jaw, 'it's unspeakably tempting. I'm being very good, considering.'

Leo gripped Raven's hair and leaned into him with more weight. 'I should be sitting in an uncomfortable chair, listening to the bloody Leutesland emissaries tell me how important their stupid cold war is,' he said. 'This is not *good*, Raven, it's—'

'Yes it is,' Raven murmured, sliding his hands into Leo's

pants (and when had he even had time to get them open?) to grab two handfuls of his arse. Leo shivered as Raven's touch became so light it was almost ticklish, tracing from his upper thighs upwards. 'I could be so much worse. You could be in an uncomfortable chair with your fool under the table doing unspeakable things, and then who knows what wars you would sign up for?'

Leo made an indistinct noise and didn't resist when Raven rolled them so that Leo was the one pressed against the wall. Raven moved a hand between them.

'If I'm quick, they'll never know you got waylaid,' he said lowly.

'You're never quick,' Leo groaned. 'Did no one ever tell you not to play with your food?'

'I'm the child of a fool, I got told off if I ate *without* some kind of production,' Raven said.

'That's just not true,' Leo said. His voice was no longer remotely steady.

'Maybe not, but you wouldn't like it if I told you the reason I drag it out is because I think you're cute when you beg for it.'

Leo let his head fall back against the door with a *thunk* and did his best not to whimper out loud.

'Has anyone told you that the Leutesland woman is in love with you?' Raven asked.

'Con won't stop telling me. She's just friendly,' Leo said. 'I can't think and do this at the same time.'

'Only friendly with you,' Raven said. 'Her handmaid complains about her complimenting you incessantly.'

'Don't be ridiculous.'

'My being ridiculous has never stopped me from telling you the truth before,' Raven said.

'Wait,' Leo said, wrapping a hand around Raven's wrist so that he could focus. 'Is this going to be a problem?'

'Not if you want someone to advocate for your loans to be forgiven,' Raven said. 'I don't think she expects anything. Her rank is barely acceptable and she wasn't sent here for that kind of diplomacy. I'd have mentioned it if I was actually concerned.'

'You'd have mentioned it,' Leo repeated.

'Not all my songs are about you, Majesty. Though, self-centred bastard that you are, you don't listen to them if they're not, do you?'

'I try not to listen to them when they *are*,' Leo said, barely paying attention to his words. 'What am I going to do about this,' he wondered to himself.

'You're going to be polite with Stefanie without leading her on, you're going to keep the country from going to war and you're going to make more noise than is wise when you let go of my hand.'

Leo looked down, then back up to meet Raven's eyes. Raven raised an eyebrow in challenge. Something about the expression filled Leo's stomach with heat.

'Any other secrets to share?' Leo asked.

'Plenty,' Raven said. 'The things I could tell you about what the king likes …'

Raven leaned in and kissed Leo's neck slowly. Leo closed his eyes and tilted his head back. He shivered at the feeling of Raven's teeth gentle on his skin.

'I'm going to be late,' Leo groaned.

'You're worth waiting for,' Raven said.

He meant it. Leo's breath hitched and he pulled Raven's face up with both hands to kiss him, trying to express how much that meant to him. He wasn't used to that kind of casual preference and he didn't know when it would stop surprising him that underneath Raven's cool exterior, he genuinely liked Leo. It had been a long nine months building up to this. It was a relief to be able to give into it.

'You're so easy to please,' Raven laughed in low wonder. 'I'm going to make you *so* late.'

And with that, Raven applied himself to making a fool out of his king.

27

'DO YOU MISS HAVING A NAME?' Leo asked Raven as they lay in bed, legs tangled and hands lazily wandering without intent.

'Sometimes,' Raven said. 'It's thrilling hearing you call me something other than my title now, but I'm proud of being a fool. It's all I've ever wanted.'

'What about the whole … *it* thing?' Leo asked.

'You're struggling with that, aren't you,' Raven laughed quietly. 'It's just a way for people to indicate they're talking about me. I answer to "she" as well, when that's what people think describes me best. I have costumes for all occasions.'

Leo must have looked confused, because Raven laughed again and smoothed out Leo's frown with a thumb.

'Should I not be calling you "he"?' Leo asked uncertainly.

'Not when I'm in paint,' Raven said, which wasn't what Leo was asking. 'Like this, I don't particularly care what you call me. I doubt you're talking about me to other people anyway.'

'I guess not, but I think about you.'

'Careful, Majesty. I'll start thinking you like me.'

Leo laughed quietly and gave up on getting a more concrete answer. Just because *he* was attached to being referred to as a man didn't mean Raven had to be, and he supposed it made sense if Raven had grown up expecting to relinquish all identifying features.

'You always wanted to be a fool?'

'Mhm,' Raven hummed in confirmation. 'Dad made it look fun, which was enough when I was too young to know the other things fools do. And then in those teenage years where I got bored with all the riddles and jokes, I went to the Consortium and learnt the less obvious parts of the job.'

'Like what?' Leo asked.

'Spying and poisons,' Raven said in a dramatic tone. 'How to advise a monarch, which necessitates knowing how a monarchy is ruled. How to be a comfort without dropping the persona. Our role in times of war as mascot and messenger.'

'Seducing kings,' Leo added with a teasing smile.

'Trinity, no,' Raven laughed. 'We're supposed to be celibate. Obviously that doesn't work in practice for most of us, seeing as they teach us how to disguise ourselves well enough to get away with just about anything, but I have no idea what they'd do if they found out about this.'

'But your dad—'

'I was his apprentice in the eyes of everyone who mattered. You can get away with much more in a small kingdom whose major claim to fame is having pretty great goat's cheese and peaches.'

Leo had dozens more questions now that he had access to a fool who would actually answer them, but before he could ask his next one, his bedroom door flew open with the confidence held by a brother who'd never had reason to knock before.

'Leo, the princess from—oh,' Con said, hand still on Leo's bedroom door. Leo attempted to distance himself from Raven and succeeded, if success had changed definitions enough to include falling out of bed with the blankets tangled around his legs. He glanced at Raven, who had managed to sit up and get a pillow in front of him to compensate for the fact that Leo had dragged the blankets with him. Leo checked that the essential details were covered and decided maintaining eye contact with

Con was the best way forward. Con stared back with wide eyes and a flushed face.

'Hi,' Leo said, for something to say. Then, 'There's a princess?'

'Yeah, Rinderplatz, she … We're really not talking about that right now. I can't even—' Con directed his gaze productively towards the wall behind Leo. 'I am *not* used to being on this side of events.'

Leo looked desperately at Raven for guidance, but Raven was visibly trying to stop himself from laughing and absolutely not helping.

'Hi,' Con said, still looking fixedly at the wall and waving his hand. 'I'm Con.'

'I suspected so,' Raven said. Con laughed in a high-pitched, nervous kind of way. Leo gave Raven a look that might have been a frown if he wasn't looking kind of panicked and incredulous, urging him to be at least slightly helpful. 'Raven,' Raven said, after only another moment's hesitation.

Leo's heart squeezed painfully as he stared at Raven. Raven gave him a small, awkward smile, acknowledging that he knew what he had just said. That he knew that he was giving up that secret again, for Leo. Leo realised in that moment that he wanted Con to know who Raven was. That he wanted Raven to be an automatic inclusion to the family like Danya was.

'Are you—?' Con coughed and Leo turned back to him. Con's face was not returning to its natural colour. Leo dreaded to think what his own looked like. 'Has this been going on long?'

By Con's standards, probably. Leo refrained from saying that. He didn't actually know how long this had been going on. Should he just be counting from when they had kissed? That didn't seem to cover it.

'It was a long time coming,' Leo settled on, 'but not … long in some kind of … official capacity.'

Con looked at Leo again, expression vulnerable and open.

'This isn't like you,' he said. 'No offence,' he said to Raven, or more accurately the wall above Raven's head. He looked back to Leo. 'It might be a good thing? But it's not like you.'

'I know,' Leo said quietly.

'He resisted my wiles for a long time,' Raven said, leaning back on his hands, looking for all the world as if he was relaxed.

'Anyway,' Con said, backing away. 'You're busy. I'll come back later.'

'Wait, what about the princess?' Leo asked.

Con made a face like an awkward horse. He scratched the back of his neck. Leo glanced at Raven. Raven could and did find out everything that was going on in the castle, but Con couldn't know that.

'Her Mum wants you to have dinner with them,' Con said, somehow in an even more awkward tone than he'd already had.

'She doesn't want to marry you, Majesty,' Raven said in a bored tone. That explained the awkwardness. What a thing to have to bring up in these circumstances. 'And the king and queen lack the guts to force her to.'

'Thanks,' Leo said, rolling his eyes.

'Oh,' Con said. 'Well, cool. Message delivered, I guess. I'm going to go now. Nice to meet you? Seeya.'

Con escaped.

Leo groaned and flopped back on the bed. Raven lay down beside him less dramatically. For a whole year, they'd been meeting in private without a single person approaching them. They'd been together all of three weeks and this happened. Leo reached out to hold Raven's hand and watched as Raven's mouth twitched into a small smile.

'He can't keep a secret to save his life,' Leo said.

'I know,' Raven said.

Leo stroked the back of Raven's hand with his thumb. Just

touching casually like this was special enough that Leo was struggling to feel the panic he probably should.

'Your brother is deceptively observant,' Raven said. 'I should change before dinner.'

Because Raven was still the fool. Because Con might recognise the clothes that weren't remotely hidden on the floor and put it together. Leo looked at Raven's burnt-cherry leggings and plain undershirt and thought that might be an excessive amount of caution. Raven evidently saw this expression and used his foot to lift his bright surcoat from the floor. Out of Leo's field of view, but probably not Con's, if he'd thought to look in that direction.

The thing was, if his family knew that Leo was seeing someone (and they would, because unless Con buried himself alive, Ada would get it out of him), then Leo didn't really want to hide that detail. Well … part of him did. There was an infinitesimally small part of him that was embarrassed that he'd fallen for his fool. But he was much more ashamed of that embarrassment than he was of the situation, and neither of those feelings were significant enough to stop Leo from wanting his family to know Raven. Not the world. Just his family.

'Would you want to meet them?' Leo asked, watching their joined hands instead of Raven's face.

'I am familiar with the royal family, Majesty.'

With a shy grin, Leo pushed at Raven's shoulder. He hadn't introduced a partner to his family before. He didn't think any of them had. They'd all already known Danya, and Con hadn't stayed with anyone long enough to call for it. As far as he knew, Dicky hadn't dated.

'What would you tell them?' Raven asked, more seriously.

'I was thinking, "Hi guys, this is Raven," but I'm open to workshopping,' Leo said.

'And when they ask who I am to you?' Raven's voice was

quiet. Maybe even uncertain. Leo's heart did something nervous in his chest that was completely incompatible with the usual distribution of blood around his body.

'Uh,' he said. He swallowed. They'd been seeing each other either for a few weeks or for a year or for somewhere in between and he had no idea how to sum up who Raven was to him in some kind of label.

'Your buddy?' Raven suggested, ironically cheery. 'Your lover,' he said, dropping his voice. 'Your fool! Your cicisbeo.'

'I don't even know what that is,' Leo said. Blessed faith, he'd nearly been killed a couple of weeks ago; he was braver than he was behaving. He forced himself to just look at Raven properly and blurt out, 'Look, would "boyfriend" freak you out too much?'

'Leo …' Raven said. He smiled sadly. 'Majesty,' he corrected, and it didn't sound like a pet name. 'You understand why that's ridiculous, don't you? And, for that matter, why introducing me to your family is ridiculous?'

'I'm not suggesting I present you to court, or take you to a meal with my grandparents and cousins,' Leo said, pained. 'You know how close I am with my siblings.'

'I do,' Raven said. He brought Leo's hand to his lips, soothing the stress of the conversation. 'Think about it properly. For more than five minutes. If you ask me again, I'll have thought about it too. Just keep it quiet until then.'

'Okay,' Leo said.

Raven looked across to the door.

'I can't believe I didn't hear him. Your floors are perfect for affairs, and I didn't hear him.'

'We were kind of distracted,' Leo said, smiling easily.

'Sneaking around is my profession,' Raven said. 'I'm too good to be distracted.'

'I bet I could distract you again.'

Raven's smile turned sultry. It shot tingles up Leo's spine. 'Please do, Majesty.'

LEO HAD BEEN TAKING almost all his meals in the King's Hall lately in an effort to be more present with the rest of the castle. This was going well for the most part. Leo tried to ignore Raven strumming his mini harp behind him as they ate, but that wasn't exactly an easy feat before they got together and it was even harder now. Raven played well, which had been frustrating when Leo hated him and now was enough to make Leo want to stare soppily at him, ridiculous paint and all. It was disturbing how quickly he'd gotten over the paint.

Danya was coaxing Max into telling them all about his magic coming through and trying to convince him to demonstrate. Leo found himself smiling even though they were in public and, even better, didn't stop smiling once he'd noticed. It might have made him smile more. Raven might like to hoard them to himself, but Leo thought he was feeling more settled in his skin and that could only be a good thing. And he knew that Raven would feel the same way. He might even be proud.

Even though they were all genuinely invested in Max's story, Con seemed to be putting everything he had into being very conspicuous about having a secret. Leo glared at Con as he ate. Con held his breath with wide eyes. Ada looked between the two of them with lazy contemplation as she ate her soup. Leo knew she could have brought it up ten minutes ago, but she was waiting. He knew why. She wanted to see how ridiculous Con got about it.

'Was it something you've been reading, do you think?' Leo asked Max.

'Ooh,' Danya said, nodding. 'The Trinity Texts, surely.'

'They're boring, Danya,' Max said. Danya looked horrified

and Ada snorted with amusement. 'I've been reading about dragons, I guess.'

'Dragons are cool,' Leo said.

'No one says "cool" anymore,' Max said, looking at Leo with an expression that might have been justified if Leo had just eaten a handful of slugs.

'Yeah, Leo,' Ada said.

'Yeah, Leo,' Con said, exhaling clumsily as he did.

'What's wrong with you?' Max asked, looking at Con.

'He's always like this,' Leo said. 'This is a completely normal way for Con to behave.'

Con looked ready to flee the table. He actually looked towards the door.

'I'm normal,' he agreed unconvincingly.

'It's to do with Leo,' Ada observed, resting her chin on her palm, elbow on the table. 'Leo is generally uninteresting, and while many of the things Con might catch Leo at would be embarrassing, they would not typically be a secret.'

'He didn't catch me at anything,' Leo said. 'He's just behaving like this for attention. You shouldn't encourage him.'

'Perhaps Leo is breaking a law,' Danya said, sounding delighted. 'Maybe he murdered someone!'

Max scoffed, as if he thought the idea of Leo murdering someone was entirely unrealistic and that this was a character flaw to be ashamed of. Leo reminded himself that he liked Max.

'No, Leo can't break rules; he's allergic,' Ada said. 'And he doesn't look guilty about it.' She turned her eyes on Leo instead, looking him up and down. 'He doesn't even look embarrassed.' Her eyebrows raised in surprise. 'He looks happy.'

'I'm not happy,' Leo lied. 'I resent the crown and want to be in another place and I feel inadequate.'

'Oh!' Danya said. 'He *is* happy!'

'I'm happy about Max learning magic,' Leo said. 'And we

defeated the cultists, probably. And several people want me to marry them or their relatives.' Ada looked at him with smug satisfaction. 'I'm having a good hair day,' he said, aware that he was now reaching.

'He has a boyfriend!' Con blurted. He clapped his hands over his mouth, looking mortified. Leo contemplated sliding out of his chair and under the table and found himself actually fighting a smile. Danya clapped her hands three times excitedly. Max pulled a face at his dinner, repulsed as he was by the subject of romance. Ada's smug smile grew wider.

'Anyone we know?' Ada asked.

'Uhh,' Leo said. That was a question he did not know how to answer. 'I don't know?'

'Ah, so it's true,' Ada said, and Leo groaned at his failure to deny Con's words.

'Is he pretty?' Danya asked.

'Yes,' Leo mumbled, now excruciatingly aware that Raven was seated only a couple of metres behind him.

'Can he do magic?' Max asked.

'Yeah,' Leo said, smiling at Max's interest.

'But can he do *good* magic,' Max asked.

'I haven't exactly tested him,' Leo said. Max looked dissatisfied with this answer.

'How long has it been going on?' Ada asked.

'I don't really know,' Leo said. 'Can we change the subject?'

'How can you not know?' Ada asked.

'He said Leo resisted his wiles,' Con said.

'Did you really!' Danya asked. 'He didn't just wear you down, did he?'

Leo shook his head and contemplated drowning himself in his soup. There probably wasn't enough left.

'How did you even get together?' Con asked. 'When did you have the *time*?'

Okay, now Leo really was trying to hide his smile. He thought about Raven in the candlelight and all their feelings coming together. He thought about how well they'd fit, right from the start. He thought about Raven flirting with him and it slowly becoming real.

He started to slide out of his chair, fully intending on hiding under the table for the rest of his life. Ada caught him by the shirt and stopped him.

'Leopold Dietrich,' she said. 'You're in love.'

'That's,' Leo stuttered. Behind him, the music stuttered as well. His siblings were way too interested in his reaction to notice. 'I'm, look, it's only been—'

'The boys in this family, honestly,' Ada said.

'You told me you loved me after three weeks,' Danya said. '*And* you'd been holding it in.'

'Love's just a bit strong,' Leo protested, not entirely sure that was true. Oh fuck, *did* he love Raven? He decided that freak out could wait so that he could deal with the situation at hand. 'I'm being very casual and normal about this. I'm allowed to very casually and normally make out with a guy and there be nothing more to it.'

The table laughed, which Leo found unfair. He attempted to slide under the table again, but Ada was still holding onto him.

'What's his name?' Max asked.

'Uhh,' Leo said.

'Raven,' Con blurted.

Shit.

'Super common name,' Leo said helplessly. 'I know at least four Ravens and I'm not even that social.'

Surprising all of them, Ada held up her hands and motioned for everyone to settle down. Leo watched her with the desperation of someone who very badly wanted not to be responsible for the current situation.

'I'm all for torturing Leo as much as possible, but I don't know a Raven, which means that this is actually a secret. Let's save this for after dinner.'

'Thank you,' Leo said quietly. He smoothed out his shirt and straightened himself.

'Perhaps use this time to think of the most uncomfortable avenues of discussion we can ford,' Ada suggested.

'Thanks,' Leo sighed.

'My only aim in life is to anticipate that which will bring you joy,' Ada said solemnly.

LEO GAVE RAVEN A WARNING LOOK on his way out of King's Hall, but he was almost sure that he'd be listening in anyway. Which made things inconvenient, because his family absolutely would not be talking as if Leo's boyfriend was listening. While Ada would probably be just as blunt regardless and might actually have enjoyed the opportunity to embarrass two people at the same time, Leo wasn't looking forward to being the only one trying to answer in flattering ways. He and Raven hadn't talked any more about what their relationship was or how they felt about each other. They hadn't talked about what information Leo was allowed to disclose, given that Raven had been so secretive until recently. And Leo's family hadn't earned that trust like Leo had.

'Okay,' Danya said, clapping her hands together. 'Most important things first: is he hot?'

'You're gay,' Leo protested.

'I would also like to know this,' Ada said.

'You're in a committed relationship!'

'No one's going to steal him, Leo,' Con said in a reasonable tone. 'Yes, he's hot. A little shorter than me, dark curly hair, slim but like, in a pretty built way.'

Leo tried not to think about the fact that, for someone who had seemed not to be looking at his barely covered body, Con sure had gotten a very good idea of what Raven looked like.

'It would have been more interesting to hear Leo describe him, but I'll let it pass,' Ada said. She turned back to Leo, who managed not to flinch. 'What's your favourite feature of his?'

'I don't know,' Leo groaned. He pulled his legs up onto the couch and hugged them in a half-hearted attempt to hide. 'He has really great expressions. He looks at me like I'm an idiot; I don't know why I like that.'

'So he's smart too,' Ada said with a smug smile.

'Very,' Leo agreed, deciding not to take offence in the hope that it annoyed her.

'Who is he?' Con asked. 'I didn't recognise him at all.'

'Just a guy,' Leo said. 'You don't know everyone.'

'I know a lot of people though,' Con said. 'Is he from the city? How would you even meet someone from the city? Is he staff?'

'He's …' Leo said, not sure how to answer at all. 'He's the guy, the mystery guy I kept seeing, the—'

'The one you're obsessed with?' Ada asked.

'Obsessed feels unnecessarily strong,' Leo said. 'I only maybe got fixated for a small amount of time each time he found me. I was very casual otherwise, and actually fixated feels strong too. Interested. I was interested in him and who he was.'

'Does that mean that you're currently fixated?' Max asked. 'Because you saw him today?'

'Um,' Leo said. 'I'm interested.'

'So do you know who he is now?' Max asked.

It was a lot harder to evade Max's questions than the others'. Max actually taking an interest wasn't something Leo could have predicted, and Leo wanted to connect with his youngest brother. Con noticed and leaned in to whisper in Max's ear. Max endured it, then grinned.

'Are you going to marry him?' Max asked.

'Oh my god,' Leo said. 'I actually think I'll have thrown myself off Lyric Tower before I get the chance.'

'But if you don't commit suicide to escape innocent questions from your loved ones,' Con clarified. 'Then would you marry him?'

'Three weeks, Con! I've been seeing him for three weeks!'

'How are his politics?' Ada asked. 'If we're going to get another ruler, I'll need to vet him.'

'His …' Leo made a helpless gesture. 'I don't know. He hasn't tried to sway me in any direction. Maybe he likes what I'm doing.'

'With respect, King Leopold the Phlegmatic—'

'No, people aren't calling me that,' Leo insisted. 'Please tell me people aren't calling me that.'

'People aren't calling you that,' Ada recited blandly, which wasn't any kind of assurance at all. 'As I was saying, Polly, you haven't actually done anything.'

'I passed two laws last month,' Leo said archly.

'You amended two laws last month,' Ada corrected.

'No, the one about aged care was an amendment. The thing about having documentation when importing or exporting magic-infused oils was completely new.'

'Also mildly inconvenient, quite boring and tragically nec-essary,' Danya said. 'I don't think anyone could have a political opinion about that.'

That was optimistic. If the last year had taught Leo anything, it was that people could have a political opinion over literally anything. Still, it wasn't the kind of legislation that Raven would want to sway, presumably. Leo thought that if he was to sleep with someone and then found out that they had strong views on importation forms, they'd have to be *really* hot in order for that to continue.

'Look, I understand that I've been ruling in a fairly subtle way so far, but I don't think I'd want to talk about all of that in between'—Leo hesitated and glanced at Max—'dating, even if I was as assertive as you.'

'Is that what Con walked in on?' Danya asked with wicked innocence. 'A date?'

'Yes,' Leo and Con said in unison.

'Do you really not want us to know about him?' Ada asked. 'You're being very cagey.'

'I do,' Leo said. 'I really do. It's just complicated. I can't ... I don't want to ... It's the rest of the world that I'm worried about, you know?'

Ada nodded thoughtfully. Of all of them, she was probably the one to understand. Her relationship with Danya had never been a secret from the family, or even the castle, but no one apart from the people in this room had ever thought there was a chance that it would last. When their parents were still alive, they didn't stop her from seeing Danya, but it was with the understanding that when the time came, she would get married to someone who would actually bring some benefit to their family. Now that Leo was king, he was grateful that his avenues were more occupied with what to do with his own marriage prospects.

'The rest of the world isn't in this room,' Danya said. 'We can keep quiet about something like this, clearly.'

They could. And there was every possibility Leo and Raven would part ways on their own before it became a more complicated issue. Leo didn't need to worry about any of this yet. But he would. He could worry recreationally.

28

L EO THOUGHT HE HAD only ever really been careless when he was happy. There was no denying that he should have been more cautious, that they both should have, but in the end it wasn't anything big that got them caught.

Raven was performing for a large crowd and Leo stopped to watch. Raven was at the centre of an inferno that he whirled and tossed through the air, somehow always catching the perfect section of the batons to keep the act going and going. Leo leaned against a stone wall and watched sweat slide down Raven's temple as he threw the batons higher. Then his hand snatched the three batons from the air and he roared through the flames, sending a fireball the size of a wild horse into the sky. Leo loved the physicality of it. Raven could use magic, but he never did with his acts. His dad had been mundane, and Raven had learnt from him.

Raven doused the flames and bowed extravagantly. Leo clapped with the rest of the crowd as Raven pantomimed setting his arse on fire. Now that Leo didn't hate his acts, he could notice how it made the children in the crowd scream with delight and laughter without any resentment. The crowd started to break up and Raven stole his hat back from a woman he'd entrusted it to while he was handling the fire before sauntering up to Leo.

'Well played, fool,' Leo said. The title felt like an inside joke.

'Well watched, Majesty,' Raven replied, voice cheery.

'Is it as hard as it looks?' Raven grinned and Leo snorted.

'Well?' he asked, instead of clarifying.

'A king must think before he acts, but a fool is free to burn,' Raven declared. He glanced around subtly and let his performance slip. 'It was hard to learn. I'm not really present to be thinking about whether it's hard when I'm in the moment. It's all instinct, Majesty. It's like kissing.'

'You'll have to show me,' Leo said.

Raven grinned again—and then his expression froze, eyes focused just behind Leo. Leo turned, feeling dread in the pit of his stomach but refusing to let it reach his expression. He met the eyes of Stefanie, whose usual smile was nowhere to be seen. She looked at Leo with intelligent eyes and a callous mouth.

'Stefanie,' Leo greeted. 'Did you enjoy the show?'

'Very much,' she said.

And then she turned on her toes and started towards the castle. Leo jogged slightly to catch up and kept pace with her.

'Are you going somewhere in particular?' he asked, now officially starting to panic.

'Yes,' Stefanie said. 'I don't require your company, Dietrich.'

Leo's steps faltered for a moment before he recovered. He hadn't been addressed by his last name since the Academy, and never by someone who wasn't a posturing teen. He had no idea how to deal with being disrespected like that. He was used to the more subtle kind. Should he correct her? It wasn't like she'd made a mistake.

'Have I done something to offend?' he asked instead.

She came to a halt and stared at Leo with searching eyes, as if looking for some attribute that Leo was suddenly sure he didn't possess. She certainly wasn't admiring him now.

'I won't tell anyone tonight,' she decided. 'I could leave tomorrow with nothing to say to anyone if you repay your debt to Leutesland.'

'I—' Leo said.

'A *fool*, Dietrich? Your father would be horrified,' she said.

'I couldn't really give a shit about that,' Leo lied.

Stefanie made a disparaging noise in her throat and stalked away. Leo didn't bother giving chase anymore. Raven appeared, seemingly out of nowhere. It had been smart of him to avoid tagging along while there was still the possibility of talking her down. Evidently, it hadn't made the difference.

'I'm sorry,' Leo said. Part of him wanted to force Raven to share the blame, but that impulse was drowned out by the part that was directing an artillery of self-loathing at his own stupidity. 'I don't know what this means,' he said. 'I don't know what comes next.'

Raven didn't reply.

'Do you, by any chance?' Leo asked

'Well,' Raven said hoarsely. 'I think I'm glad I'm sleeping with the guy who could overturn the justiciar's death penalty.' Leo looked at Raven with alarm, searching his face for some sign of humour that wasn't painted on. 'You can't repay the debt, can you?' Raven asked.

'No,' Leo said.

'We can't talk here,' Raven said.

Leo thought the damage had already been done, but what did he know? Maybe Raven had a plan to change Stefanie's mind. Leo hoped it wouldn't involve marriage, though he doubted she would leap at that offer now anyway.

They parted ways and met in Leo's room. Raven's paint had been hastily wiped away, lingering eyeliner making his dark eyes more intense. Leo threw his crown and scabbard in the direction of his divan as he crossed the room, at which point he turned his attention on undressing Raven instead. His fingers fumbled over buttons until he growled in frustration and fisted the fabric, ready to just rip it off Raven's chest. Raven covered Leo's hands with his own and kissed him gently. Leo's grip relaxed and Raven took over. His coordination was suffering under the stress too, but he was able to get them both free of their shirts while returning Leo's kisses. He pulled Leo backwards towards the bed and took him with him when he fell back onto it. Leo climbed onto Raven's lap and threaded his fingers through his hair as they continued to kiss. Raven's thumb traced Leo's hipbone in a gentle rhythm.

Leo pulled his lips away and leaned his forehead against Raven's.

'We shouldn't be doing this,' he said.

Raven flinched. 'We have and it's done,' he said, voice strained. 'If this is the last—'

'No,' Leo interrupted. 'No, I didn't mean that. I didn't mean us; I meant now. I should be, I don't know, telling Forster. Hiring an assassin or something.'

'Oh,' Raven exhaled. 'You know, *I'm* technically—'

'I don't actually want to assassinate her,' Leo said. 'But I appreciate the offer.'

Leo rolled off him and onto his back. He reached for and found Raven's hand and intertwined their fingers. He wondered if Raven had it in him to kill someone. He didn't know how he felt about that.

'I wouldn't take this back,' Leo promised. 'Not for anything.'

'You might regret saying that,' Raven said.

'What do you think will happen?' Leo asked.

'I don't have a precedent to base this on,' Raven said. 'Monarchs get close to us, but not like this. We're pets or pests.'

'You were really happy to spend the rest of your life being a pest to me,' Leo said before he could stop himself. Up until this moment, he had made every effort to be non-judgemental about Raven's career. He clearly loved it, and Leo didn't want to question his passion. But Raven didn't seem offended; he just snorted in amusement.

'Yes,' he said. 'Though admittedly I wasn't sure I would have the opportunity to be fool here specifically. My father was much younger than me when he left home to be a vagabond—but then, his parents were poor and he certainly didn't have the option of apprenticing with an established fool in a castle. I spent very little of my time at the Consortium, mostly just passing their tests. The Consortium didn't have to let me come back here once I was qualified, or to take over his post.'

'Was it sentiment?' Leo asked.

'Convenience,' Raven said. 'There's not that many of us and this isn't exactly a competitive assignment, given the size of Canticalica. And they'd have people reporting back about me and I haven't disgraced myself. Well, until recently.'

'So this could be bad for you as well.'

'I am making peace with the fact that the best I can hope for is being stripped of my Consortium membership and their half of my wages. You will therefore have no obligation to keep or pay me, and in fact will be obliged to pay someone else in my place. Would you like to brainstorm my next move with me, Majesty?'

Raven had sounded like he really was at peace until his question, which came out with a slightly mocking edge. Leo looked at him with pity and brought Raven's hand to his lips.

'Sorry,' Raven said. 'That was ungenerous.'

'Understandable, though,' Leo said. 'I know you love it.'

'You will have it worse. If you were to attempt to run away and join a theatre troupe, you would be recognised. And I don't think you would be very good.'

Leo's lips twitched slightly up in half-hearted amusement.

'You should go to Forster,' Raven said, sitting up. 'It will be worse if he hears about it with everyone else.'

'What are you going to do?' Leo asked, copying.

'Introduce myself to your family,' Raven said. 'If you're comfortable with that.'

Leo was not. Not because he didn't want them to meet, but because he didn't know if Ada would be kind and he didn't want Raven to match her. He wanted to be there to keep the peace if he needed to. But he had no guarantee that Stefanie would keep her word and wait until tomorrow, and if it would be worse for Forster to hear with everyone else, that couldn't compete with how it would be for his family to be unprepared.

'Okay,' Leo said. 'Could you … I mean …'

'Just say it,' Raven said.

'Please be nice,' Leo said, feeling horrible for suggesting Raven would be otherwise but unable to let him go without saying something. 'Even if they're not perfect.'

Raven stroked down Leo's cheek reassuringly. He held his jaw still so he could press a gentle kiss to Leo's forehead.

'I'll be nice,' he promised. A flicker of playfulness came into Raven's unusually serious expression. 'And they will too. After all, they know you love me.'

'That was Ada's word,' Leo protested, hiding his face in Raven's shoulder so he couldn't see how red he'd gotten. Raven laughed and wrapped Leo into a hug.

'It's understandable, really,' he said. 'I'm so charming and fiercely good-looking.'

Leo made an indistinct noise of protest and Raven laughed again. Leo couldn't think about whether he loved Raven right now. That could wait until all this was sorted out.

L EO DIDN'T SLEEP THAT NIGHT. He stayed shut up in a concourse room with Forster and Hanna, trying to figure out what it would take for them to pay off their debt to Leutesland and if that would even be enough. Hanna thought not, even though Leo couldn't bear to mention Raven and Con's suspicions about Stefanie's feelings. Leutesland's emissaries weren't just visiting to encourage Leo to make a payment towards their loan. If they had Canticalica's military support, their cold war with Rinderplatz would likely thaw in a decidedly unpeaceful direction.

Leo couldn't afford to put Sword and Shield on the front line. It wasn't just that he *knew* those people and it wasn't his fight. It would be the worst political decision Leo could possibly make to take away Praecentor's defences after three attacks in the span of a single year. Worse even than sleeping with his fool.

Forster wanted Leo to deny it. He thought there was a chance that since the most recent attack, Leo's position was good enough for people to have faith in him over a foreigner. And maybe it could have been, if the story wasn't so *fun*. A king having an affair or secret partner was one thing, but for it to be his fool? There was no amount of damage control they could do that would stop that from being a great conversation starter. Leo would have loved talking about it if it wasn't happening to him.

'You're not wrong,' Hanna said. 'Though I hope you're not just saying that because you don't want to hurt its feelings.'

'I'm not,' Leo said. He wasn't sure if he was telling the truth or not. 'I just don't think it would do any good.'

'Majesty,' Forster said carefully. 'It would be worse, for everyone I think but especially the fool, if there was a possibility you had given it an heir.'

'What?' Leo said. 'No, Trinity, no. There's no risk of that. Whatsoever.'

'You're sure,' Forster pressed.

'I understand my education has probably been more polite than others', but I know the mechanics of making a child,' Leo said, covering his eyes as he attempted to knead away a developing headache. He never thought he'd miss talking about finances. 'The fool doesn't have the required anatomy. Or has too much, depending on your point of view. I'm quite confident it's not happening with the two of us no matter what we try.'

'Ah,' said Forster.

'Yes, hooray for penises,' Hanna said impatiently. 'Can we return to the matter of damage control?'

L EO KNOCKED ON THE DOOR to the Leutesland's emissaries' apartments just after sunrise. Sebastian had done an admirable job making him presentable and he'd brought two servants with breakfast. When Stefanie's maid answered the door, Leo thought for a moment that he might be turned away. Thankfully, the animosity didn't go that far and he was invited to their sitting room.

'Have you come to pay your debt?' Stefanie asked.

'I've come to have breakfast with a friend,' Leo said.

'We're a little past that, Your Majesty,' Stefanie said.

Leo suspected that was the case. But he'd had to at least try before he damaged the relationship further.

'I've come to ask you to reconsider spreading an unverified rumour that will benefit no one, least of all Leutesland,' Leo said. He sounded sedate. Professional. His hands had a slight tremor as he sliced peaches for them.

'It isn't a question of benefit,' Stefanie said. 'You bring disgrace on those blessed by the Trinity and the Empress to rule. You bring disgrace on me and my countrymen as your guests. If I fail to report this, I fail to condemn it. I could only *consider* doing so if I was able to leave immediately with the money that you owe my king.'

Leo put the peach and knife down and leaned forward.

'That sounds like a question of benefit to me,' Leo said. 'I'd like to offer a counterweight. You leave without saying anything, as you are willing to do. Canticalica continues to make our repayments on the schedule we have already come to agreement on. Canticalica has no reason to get any closer with Rinderplatz.'

'Is that a threat?' Stefanie asked.

'No,' Leo said. 'It's an acknowledgement that if you consider our relationship irreparably damaged, then I have nothing to gain by trying to stay on your good side.'

Stefanie stood and Leo copied. Fury lined her face and Leo fought to keep from mirroring her. She didn't *need* to do this. It would cost her nothing to mind her own business.

'Leave,' she said.

'Of course,' Leo said. His voice sounded cold to his own ears. He turned to one of the servants. 'Kathrin, please stay and assist Lady Stefanie and her companions. I'd hate to have it said that I kept them when they wanted so badly to leave.'

He bowed low, took a fresh peach from the bowl and left. The remaining servant accompanying him waited until they had turned down the next corridor before asking, with more boldness than Leo expected, 'Your Majesty, what could she have to say that was worth that?'

'I'm sure you'll find out soon,' Leo said. His hands were shaking again, in anger now. He was bruising the peach and couldn't seem to unlock his jaw enough to eat it. 'Apparently, I'm in love.'

29

LEO MADE EVERY EFFORT to sleep through his defamation. He knew he'd done everything he could to convince Stefanie not to talk and there was nothing he could do to stop people from hearing her. The least he could do was look well-rested and calm when he faced the world next.

He expected to find someone waiting for him in his room—if not Raven, then Ada or Con waiting to hear everything from Leo personally—but it was empty when he arrived. He washed off his makeup and climbed into bed but could barely force himself to blink. He sat up on the edge of his bed and tried to massage the tension from his jaw, but it wasn't helping. His body wouldn't let him rest. He didn't want to know what he would think when he let his guard down.

He left for the family dining room, which was disappointingly empty. He helped himself to caffeinated tea, which he acknowledged was not his wisest choice, and to breakfast, seeing as he hadn't actually eaten with Stefanie. No one entered while he ate, not that he took his time. His tea burnt his throat when he tossed the last of it down and left the room in search of company.

Con wasn't in his rooms. Max was in class, and Leo wasn't so far gone to pull him out to cure his own restlessness. Eventually, Leo ran into Danya in the Oak Library.

'Hey,' Leo said.

Danya didn't turn around from the unlit fireplace that she was examining. Leo joined her, intrigued despite his mood.

'*Coalesce*,' Danya breathed reverently.

Leo eyed the fireplace, looking for a visible sign that the spell had worked. It looked like it always did to him.

'Hello, Leo,' Danya said, making him jump. 'Is it a good sign that you're not sleeping?'

'It is not,' Leo laughed humourlessly. 'What are you doing?'

'Maintenance,' Danya said, passing her hand over the rough stone of the fireplace. 'There's a mildly funny story of a party your mother's grandfather threw in here that resulted in a rather nice bust being cannonballed into the stonework with some force. The High Enchanter at the time repaired it on the spot, which I'm sure was really impressive, but it was magic. Magic doesn't last forever. I think this should hold a few more years, anyway.'

'I haven't heard that story before,' Leo said.

'I *think* it was funny,' Danya said. 'Erwina told me a lot of stories about this old place. I have it written down somewhere, if you'd like me to find it.'

'Don't trouble yourself,' Leo said. 'I don't want to interrupt.'

'Well, let me know,' Danya smiled. 'Can I help you with something else?'

There had been several occasions while Leo had been ruling where he had been very uncomfortably reminded of the fact that Danya was technically employed by him. It didn't seem to bother her, but it didn't seem to surprise her either. There was never any obvious shift, because Danya was *always* friendly and willing to help, but that only made it feel more jarring. Leo hoped she wasn't always on her best behaviour around him.

'No, I was just looking for someone who I could bother without it being that big an inconvenience,' he said.

'You could never be an inconvenience,' Danya said brightly. 'But if you'd like my company, you'll have to let me keep working.'

'I could help?' Leo suggested. 'I'm not fully trained, but I'm pretty good.'

'Wonderful!' Danya said, clapping three times. 'Ada hasn't helped me in years.'

Leo soon found out why. Kneeling side by side with Danya and helping her reinforce the floor in front of the fireplace gave Leo flashbacks to the most tedious classes at the Academy. It wasn't just that it was a dull, if necessary task, it was that Danya's gateway to magic was her unshakeable faith in the Trinity. And Leo believed as much as the next mage, but he much preferred spontaneity to prayer.

'Beginning, beginning, beginning,' they chanted together. 'So it goes, so it goes, so it goes / Concluding, concluding, concluding / As we know, and it shows, in our prose.'

'*Regenerate,*' Danya prayed, and the floorboards obeyed. She tapped on the surface, feeling or listening to something that Leo couldn't sense. 'That was better than doing it alone, thank you,' she said.

'But not a lot better,' Leo guessed.

'Better than when Con was helping me, too!' Danya said.

'Oh my god,' Leo said. 'Better than someone with no magic. Danya, I'm good at magic!'

'You are,' she said. 'But you also haven't slept and you aren't in a very generous head space and you don't really care about whether the floor is repaired or not.'

'I care,' Leo insisted.

'I know,' Danya said. 'But in a very big-picture way. You don't really care about this specific bit of floor.'

Danya stood up and Leo followed her to a bookshelf. She looked to be having an internal argument with herself. Danya's expressions were almost always comically easy to read. Leo didn't want her to send him away, but he didn't want her to be *unable* to send him away. He felt frustrated and ineffectual.

'I care about the floor,' Leo repeated. 'I see value in this kind of work, in cleaning and maintenance. I'm not the kind of king who dismisses it just because I have other things on my mind.'

'I believe you,' Danya said.

'You don't look like you believe me!'

Danya's eyebrows pinched with anxiety and she hovered on the edge of saying something until Leo couldn't take it anymore and snapped, 'Just say it!' to her.

'Leo,' she said. 'I love you.'

Leo nearly screamed with frustration. He didn't want to be coddled. He could feel his magic vibrating along his arm hairs erratically. Danya put her hands gently on his upper arms and held his eyes as she breathed deeply. Leo resisted a moment longer before he fell into her pattern. *Breathe in ... hold ... breathe out ...* There was no point in anger, yet it hurt on its way out. It was swallowing fire instead of spitting it at someone, knowing that he would at least be spared the later remorse at having hurt someone else with his lack of control. Did Richard ever feel remorse? The thought chilled Leo's anger into something he could keep to himself.

'I love you, I see you and I know you,' Danya began again, when Leo's magic was under control and his eyes less wild. 'I know you care about this kingdom and this castle and everyone who works here. I would never, ever, *ever* diminish that. But, like it or not, your appreciation is superficial. Of course it is! Can you imagine if you cared about every single brick in your castle individually and then someone asked what needed to be done about a law? You've never had to do this kind of thing manually and it would take years of devotion for you to feel equal to this work. Magic isn't convenience, Leo, it's awe.'

'You don't care about every brick in the castle either,' Leo protested, but the heat was gone.

'I do, actually,' Danya said, looking around with a small,

wondrous smile. 'I suppose Erwina left before she had a chance to say anything to you about anything, much less me.'

'We had a handover,' Leo hedged. 'But no, she didn't say a lot.'

'She chose me because she told your dad she needed an apprentice and that if he didn't want to pay for a graduate of Trinitas Academy then she would happily take a magical baby from within his kingdom and raise the best High Enchanter any kingdom had ever seen. My mums would never have been allowed to keep me, being from Sword and Shield and everything, and the timing of my birth is so very nearly perfect, so I was the obvious choice.

'I spent the first nine years of my life in Lyric Tower learning to love it. I have held every one of these books in my hands—there's five thousand, two hundred and two in this room—and I *love* them. Which is how I know which ones need healing. If Erwina had any old apprentice, you would also need a librarian to tell that apprentice which books were getting worn.'

Danya patted Leo on the arms three more times and then released him.

'I love Raven, too. Ada said she used to play with it when you were children. I've only known it since it took its post, but it's part of this castle as much as your family or I am.'

'How did that go?' Leo asked. 'Did he—it—Raven wouldn't give me a straight answer on how to refer to … him. Was he … nice?'

Danya smiled warmly and nodded.

'So nice! We're all very happy you're happy.' She frowned a little as a thought occurred to her. 'Well, Con and Ada think you're a little bit stupid. More Ada. Ada thinks you're quite stupid, I think is probably more accurate. But she likes Raven!'

Leo shook his head, but he couldn't keep from smiling. That was really the best he could have hoped for. He *was* stupid.

Stupid to start something with Raven and stupid to get caught, and now stupid because he didn't intend to stop. It was a lot easier to be okay with that decision now he knew his family weren't going to be the first in line to spit on him.

Leo decided to leave Danya to her job and go and get some sleep before the rest of his life began.

30

IT TOOK TWO WEEKS for a new fool to arrive, and Raven coped by withdrawing almost completely. He appeared a couple of times for a meal in the family's dining room and told jokes when he was addressed, lapsed into complete silence when it wasn't his turn to talk, then disappeared before Leo could get him alone. Apart from that, Leo couldn't find him. Danya wouldn't tell him where the fool's quarters were, saying very accurately that Raven would find him when and if he wanted to be found.

Within an hour of the new fool arriving, Raven lurked conspicuously in King's Hall looking like a puppy who had been kicked then left out in the pouring rain all night until Leo made some weak excuses no one paid any attention to anyway and left the room so they could have some privacy. No one noticed. Apart from his family, his heads of avenues and Raven, everyone around him seemed to have reached an agreement that Leo was only visible when there was a reason to disparage him further. He was not enjoying it.

Once out of King's Hall, Raven grabbed Leo by the hand and pulled him into the closest room. Leo didn't know what to expect until he felt Raven curl into his chest and cling to him. Leo slowly put his arms around Raven and cupped the back of his head. His usually soft curls were both frizzing and a little greasy. An unfamiliar dusting of stubble rasped against the fibres of Leo's vest.

'Are you okay?' Leo asked tentatively.

'I'm … not a fool anymore,' Raven mumbled, voice wobbling.

'Oh, Trinity,' Leo said. 'I'm so sorry.'

'I thought they might send me away to another castle. I thought I might lose you. I thought maybe I would run away from my new post and come back here in secret. But they kicked me out and I never could have done that and I don't know who I am and—'

Raven's fingers tightened against Leo's shirt and he shook with wordless tears. Leo stroked his hair and felt utterly useless. They stood there for minutes that lasted eternities while Leo waited for Raven to recover and for his gummed-up brain to come up with anything at all to say that might relieve a fraction of Raven's misery. There was nothing.

Eventually, so quietly Leo could barely hear him, Raven said, 'And now when I'm someone else, my dad won't have known that person.'

'Raven …' Leo said. 'Sweetheart, you're more than what you do.'

'I'm not,' Raven sobbed. 'I will be, but I'm not now. And he won't know.'

In the end, the only thing to be done was to hold him.

IT WAS UNCANNY TO HAVE RAVEN sitting by his side when there were other people around. Uncanny to have anyone apart from Ada in Dicky's old chair in the concourse room. Uncanny to recognise him through a very different kind of costume. Leo had wanted to do this part without him, but Raven deserved a say. It had been his idea to create a character for the occasion that he could later abandon. Leo had to acknowledge that it would be easier for Raven to move around if everyone was on the lookout for a woman instead of how he usually presented himself, and Leo didn't trust all of his heads of avenues to keep descriptions of his lover to themselves. There were some advantages to a fool's anonymity.

'Now that we no longer have to house and entertain the Leutesland emissaries and their attendants, we can more than afford a small apartment in the city and a living allowance for your friend,' Hanna said, with the slightest pause before the word *friend*, too aware that it stretched the truth.

'There's also room in the castle,' Forster said neutrally.

'I won't make my staff attend to it,' Abigail said.

'I worry about the perception that could cause,' Niklaus said. 'A room upstairs would place her in the company of nobles who would recognise her through her lack of nobility. No offence meant, my lady.'

'They'll eat her alive if we put her downstairs,' Galland said.

Leo rubbed his temples. Further along the table, Danya kept her eyes downcast, too aware that her association with Ada wasn't strictly approved of either to offer support. He would really have preferred if Raven didn't have to see the varying degrees of tolerance in his heads of avenues' expressions. The most he could say for them was that they were maintaining public solidarity. They had agreed to respond to any curiosity around the rumour by dismissing it as unimportant and not worth confirming or denying. After all, they had a kingdom to run. What did they care for what the king got up to when he wasn't ruling?

'There's plenty of room in the stables if you want to make yourself useful,' Coral said.

Coral's idea earned points with Leo by virtue of being the first one suggested directly to Raven. It also would have the effect of giving Coral the extra stable hand they had wanted all year and justifying a salary for Raven.

'It's up to you,' Leo said to Raven. 'And whatever you choose doesn't have to be permanent.'

'There's a novelty,' Raven said. His voice was unmistakably feminine, but still low. It was a voice designed for music and it made Leo very conscious of the fact that this disguise would have worked just as well on him as the one Raven had chosen to use. 'Do I have to decide now?'

'And sleep where in the meantime?' Abigail asked, with a tone that said *in the castle* was not an option.

'We can put you up in an inn until we make a permanent decision,' Hanna said.

'Fine,' Raven said.

'Fine,' Leo said. 'Roll that over to the next meeting. What's next on the agenda?'

Lou coughed pointedly. She raised her eyebrows in Raven's direction. Leo suppressed an exasperated sigh. Raven had sat in on plenty of these meetings when he was the fool, but that was apparently over.

'Thank you for joining us today,' Leo said, hating the formality that he had to use. 'Forster will give you the details of the inn this afternoon.'

'Thanks for having me,' Raven said.

He eased out of his seat, mindful of his long skirts. His whole posture was different as a woman and it was captivating to watch him leave. This came with the unfortunate result of making Leo look even more enamoured with Raven than he was.

'You should take care with where you place her,' Niklaus said. 'We need to manage how the whole thing looks.'

'Thank you for your advice,' Leo said flatly. 'Let's move on.'

THEY PAID FOR THE ROOM AT THE INN and Raven moved his things there, but he slept in Leo's room and spent his evenings with the family. He made sure to be seen in his feminine disguise a strategic amount. He told them about what was going on in the city and the various types of employment he was considering. His facade of relaxed entertainer was almost convincing, but Leo could tell he was depressed.

It didn't help that the new fool had exactly one topic it sang and joked about. Leo tried talking to it, treating it as a reasonable resource to his kingdom like he'd never thought to do before Raven revealed himself, but it did no good. The fool and the Consortium had a score to settle. Raven had done what a fool should never do. He'd revealed that he was a person.

Leo had given up on attempting to look inviting, happy or dignified during meals. He knew it was important that he didn't withdraw entirely, but the jokes and the resentment were hard to bear and the new fool's songs grated on him even when they weren't about him. Tonight, he sat between Con and Max and glared at his soup, and while he was supposed to be there so that he could be among his people, he knew he wasn't looking approachable. Which was why it was somewhat surprising when Princess Blanche from Neue Wolke tapped Con on the shoulder and said, 'Can we swap seats?'

'Um,' Con said, clearly taken aback.

'Mine's way over there, so you don't actually have to. It's also near the princess of Rinderplatz, so I strongly advise you *don't*. But can I sit here anyway?'

'Sure,' Con said, still looking very confused but unable to refuse a direct request.

'Hey,' Blanche said, putting the bowl of soup she carried down and pulling Con's chair closer to the table. They'd barely talked since their trip to Ziegbourne, because (as Blanche had very kindly informed him) she'd done her job in presenting her kingdom's proposal to him and was only staying because the alternative was being sent somewhere else to do exactly the same thing. 'You have had an *awful* time of it lately.'

'That's very accurate,' Leo said.

Blanche grinned and took a mouthful of soup. She subtly glanced around as if wary of being overheard. There was basically no risk of that. No one felt the need to get more dirt on Leo, and there was little advantage to sucking up to him, so he was getting used to being ignored on a scale he had never encountered before.

'I won't drag this out,' Blanche said. 'I think we should get married.'

Leo choked on his soup. He looked at Blanche as he covered further coughs with his napkin and he felt pretty confident assuming that she'd waited for his mouth to be full. A few months ago, he would have hated that. Now, he thought it was almost as funny as it was embarrassing. He blamed Raven for this change in attitude.

'I'm serious,' Blanche said, resuming eating as if she hadn't nearly committed regicide.

'But you've heard what everyone's saying. You know that I'm not winning any popularity contests at the moment.'

'I've heard. That's why I'm suggesting it.'

'That's … What?'

'I have no interest in being married, or in having children, or in even having a Sommertide romance,' Blanche said.

'Until you saw my face and suddenly the world shifted,' Leo said, barely stopping himself from rolling his eyes.

'Until one of the only people eligible for my hand made it quite clear that he wasn't interested in any kind of traditional marriage either. I'm a third-born princess to a kingdom whose queen has hit her change. Five years ago, I thought I'd just potter around with my animals out of everybody's way until I died. But Isolde's taking out her middle aged-ness on me and I doubt I'll get any peace until it settles down. She wants me to marry, or at the least traipse around the Empire forging political alliances, and I don't want to. I like the weather here and I like that you don't force your siblings into an unreasonable level of social-isation.'

'Huh,' Leo said.

'Unless the rumours aren't true,' Blanche said. 'Are the rumours true?'

Leo looked at her suspiciously. This would be a strange way to get gossip for the sake of gossip out of him. If she claimed he had confirmed it, he could just as easily claim he denied it. And everyone was acting as though it was true anyway.

'Depends on the rumour,' he said.

'That's fair,' she said. 'I've heard some that are too good for truth. And you have no reason to trust me until I do this in a more official capacity and tie my reputation to yours.'

'I'm going to have to think about this,' Leo said. 'As romantic a proposal as it was, I've recently had some bad experiences with being swept up in my emotions.'

'Really?'

This surprised Leo. She knew about his situation. But now that she asked … he didn't actually regret it, did he? A man who regretted it could have done a lot more to deny it.

'No, I suppose not,' he said.

A FORTNIGHT LATER, Blanche and Leo were officially engaged. The rumours stumbled in their path where they had been building momentum. Why would Neue Wolke, one of the most prosperous countries in the Empire, align itself with Canticalica if the king was really sleeping with his fool?

31

LEO HAD NEVER ENJOYED going on family holidays as a child. There were good parts, but holidays usually meant staying in another castle or manor and the expectation of good behaviour around other people who didn't seem under the same expectations. He was the kind of child who took time to acclimatise to things, and holidays generally involved varied experiences that ended just as Leo was starting to feel comfortable. And then there were the long stretches of nothing much at all around the new experiences, just being hosted in an unfamiliar place. Richard would show Con off and Ada would be stuck being a lady with Gisela, so Leo and Dicky ended up entertaining themselves.

Leo and Dicky's relationship had been strange compared to the rest of the siblings. People used to comment that they'd never met two strangers more alike.

They spent a lot of time together and they knew each other better than anyone else, but if Leo was given a pen and paper he didn't know that he'd be able to write down a single thing about Dicky. One Sommertide on the bank of the Fluvius, Dicky had pointed at a scar on Leo's stomach and asked where it was from. Leo hadn't remembered. Con had looked at them both like they were from another planet and reminded them that Dicky had nearly run Leo through with a tree branch when they were seven. It hadn't been malicious. They'd been pretending to be Swords.

The thing was, they didn't fight. On rare occasions they might wrestle or hit each other in competition for some prize or out of frustration, but no matter what Dicky did or said, Leo shrugged it off within minutes, and vice versa. It wasn't that they were non-combative in nature, because Ada and Dicky ended up screaming at each other twice a week during their teens and when Leo was nine he didn't speak to Ada for a whole month. It wasn't even that they always agreed or that they had similar underlying ideologies. They just didn't care.

Dicky was so much a part of Leo's life that he wasn't worth registering. Whenever Leo tried to think about the fact that Dicky wasn't around anymore, it was like his brain laughed it off as ridiculous. Leo was still here. Of course Dicky was somewhere too.

Except that he wasn't. Which Leo *knew*. He wasn't looking at the door expecting Dicky to walk through it. But still, Leo had never bothered to cry about losing Dicky. It would be like crying for himself.

Leo tried to explain this to Raven as they travelled together to Neue Wolke. Raven didn't pretend to understand, but he was fascinated by Leo's often clumsy words. With every mile their ship sailed, he seemed to get lighter and more engaged.

It was a relief for Leo to see and a delight for Max. Leo hadn't had high expectations that Max would agree to come when he made the offer. Leo suspected it was because even a depressed Raven was funner than any of the other adults in Max's life.

'What did the little one think of Dicky?' Raven asked, pointing his foot at Max's empty bed. Unlike them, Max felt no need to retreat now and then from the rest of the ship's crew and passengers to their shared quarters.

'I don't think Dicky had time for him,' Leo said. 'Dicky was a very costs versus benefits kind of guy. And he couldn't deal with mess, so he never really liked kids, even when he was one.'

'You were the relaxed twin,' Raven laughed, shaking his head in disbelief.

'I think I take offence at that tone,' Leo said.

'No, you don't,' Raven said.

'I guess I don't,' Leo smiled.

EVEN WITH MAGICIANS POWERING THE SAILS, it still took weeks to reach Roiruhen, the capital of Neue Wolke. It was a long enough journey that Leo inevitably became less noteworthy on a ship with only a finite amount of space. It helped, perhaps, that Raven had left his dresses in Praecentor. The man who shared a cabin with the royal family was, according to absolutely everyone, Max's governor. A new hire, seeing as Ada would no longer be filling that role, in as much as it could be said that she ever had. It also helped that Max was ecstatic to be going on an adventure, was curious about everything, and was just polite enough to get away with being cheeky to even the sternest sailor. No one could hate someone related to Max, especially not as Leo was as quick to join the magicians when the wind needed persuading as he was to laugh at his brother's governor's frequent jokes. That Blanche (who half the crew had served for years) made a point of liking Leo didn't hurt either.

Con and Ada were back in Praecentor, ruling in Leo's stead. Leo hoped they would cancel each other out and end up being a somewhat neutral influence on the country. He worried about The Awakening, and if they'd take advantage of Leo's absence to make another move after weeks of silence, but he always came back to the same conclusion. He'd taken a retinue of nine from Sword and Shield and three household staff with him on this journey, and that was including Raven. The castle was just as protected and missing the incentive of Leo being there. And he doubted anyone was going to come for him personally in Neue Wolke. Their army was much larger, and Leo wasn't arrogant enough to assume he was that much of a prize.

The fact that attitudes were warm towards him on the ship made Leo more comfortable entering his future in-laws' capital than he'd thought he would be. And it was a good thing that he hadn't wasted energy on being anxious, because their reception was somewhat anti-climactic. Queen Isolde welcomed him and Max, heard Leo's thanks for her hospitality, announced a feast in their honour that evening and then dismissed them all inside five minutes.

'She's like that,' Blanche said, looping her arm in Leo's to guide him to their guest quarters. 'I enjoy her bluntness for the most part. She doesn't see the point in lying.'

'That's refreshing,' Leo said.

'Isn't it just?' Blanche said. 'I would have liked to have been here when she was welcoming the Empress, just to see her trying to be warm and gracious.'

'When was the Empress here?' Leo asked.

'She arrived at the beginning of Funque, in time for Sommertide,' Blanche said. 'She'll stay at least until the new year.'

'She's still here?' Leo asked, looking around in alarm as if he might see her wandering the corridors.

'It's her first visit in a generation,' Blanche said. 'When she leaves Trinitas, it's never for a sleepover.'

'I suddenly can't remember any of my etiquette lessons,' Leo said.

'I won't let you make a fool of yourself,' Blanche said,

squeezing Leo's arm. 'I'll be interested to see if she pays you much attention.'

A T THE FEAST, Leo and Max were seated in the second table with Blanche, Blanche's sisters and brother, their spouses and the royal children. On a raised platform, the high table held Isolde, her husband and the Empress.

The Empress had been the first magician and had ruled her empire for over nine centuries on the virtue of her power. The founding monarchs of each of the twelve countries in the Empire were descended from her and those bloodlines remained almost universally in power. Leo and Blanche's closest relation was fourteen generations ago according to the genealogical tomes in Leo's libraries. Leo had known the Empress would be impressive but hadn't appreciated what it meant that all the magic he had ever seen or used had been diluted through generations of mundane bloodlines.

The Empress *embodied* magic. Her footsteps sent sparks scattering over the marble floor whenever they made contact with the ground. When she spoke, her words came out like a song. Everyone around her was made more magnificent in her presence.

It was very easy to worship her. It was difficult to look at anyone else when she was in the room.

'She's the most beautiful person I've ever seen in my life,' Leo said.

'She's alright,' Raven said. 'She has a good tailor, I'll give her that.'

Leo looked at him with disbelief and Raven laughed.

'Yes, she's beautiful,' he allowed. 'And apparently barely even genocidal these days. You should go talk to her.'

It was Leo's turn to laugh. He could sooner talk to the sun. Raven didn't press the subject.

They were two and a half hours into the feast, and very few people were sitting where they had started the first course. He and Raven were standing to the side of the tables at a midway point between their seats, keeping an eye on where Max was playing with Blanche's youngest nephews. Max was the only one of them old enough to have magic and though his was still very new, he was getting the hang of levitating small objects. The other boys had made a game out of finding things that were light enough for Max to manage, and Leo was slightly concerned that one of the objects' owners might object to the game at some point. So far, the opposite was happening. Adults in the vicinity were emptying their pockets of coins and trinkets, one going as far as to sever a cuff's button with his dinner knife as an offering. Leo understood. There was something infinitely special about watching a child discover magic. He was still going to keep an eye on it. He knew all too well that not everyone saw things in a generous light.

Half an hour later, Blanche wove her way through the tables and told Leo that it was time for him to present himself to the Empress. Leo narrowly avoided spilling his drink down his front by instead spilling it on Raven's sleeve.

'No no,' Raven said. 'Don't trouble yourself, Majesty. I'll find myself a cloth.'

'He could have put my mother to shame when it comes to drama,' Blanche said as Raven walked away. 'Come along. Isolde doesn't make suggestions.'

Leo put his cup down on a random table and fidgeted with a ring as they made their way to the high table. He rehearsed the formalities in his head, wishing that this was happening earlier in the night, when he had been more alert. Eventually, they reached the Empress, and Blanche began by curtseying.

'Your Divinity,' she said. 'May I present my betrothed, King Leopold of Canticalica.'

Leo bowed deeply. As he straightened, he met the Empress's eyes for the first time and felt his magic brighten in response. On a whim, he extended his hand and declared, *'Effloresce,'* conjuring a vibrant sprig of heath myrtle, a flower that grew in the gardens in Praecentor.

'Your Divinity,' he said, offering the sunset-coloured flowers to her. 'I am honoured to meet you.'

'How lovely,' the Empress said, accepting them with a smile. She tucked the sprig into her dark hair, and Leo watched in wonder as the flowers grew into an intricate wreath, braiding along her silver crown. 'I haven't seen these in a long time. Canticalica, did you say? Why is that name familiar?'

'I was crowned less than a year ago, Your Radiance,' Leo said. 'Perhaps you remember it from the blessing you sent for me or for my parents and brother following their deaths.'

'No, that's not it,' the Empress said.

'Or my betrothal to Her Highness Princess Blanche,' Leo suggested, gesturing at Blanche optimistically.

'Are you the one who had an affair with his fool?' the Empress asked.

'Uh,' Leo said. 'There was a rumour, I think. Unsubstantiated.'

'I find that *fascinating*,' the Empress said. 'I love fools. At the beginning of my reign, before leaving the old world, I decided to visit the castle belonging to the royal family who ruled over the kingdom of my birth. Do you know the story?'

'No, Your Magnificence,' Leo said.

'I'm sure I recorded it at some point, but historians must choose their stories, I suppose. Otherwise printing would be very unwieldy.'

'Very true, Your Luminousness.'

'I'm curious as to how long it will amuse you to choose new titles for me,' the Empress said. 'Perhaps consorting with fools affects one's sense of humour.'

'I couldn't say, Your Exquisiteness,' Leo said, keeping a straight face with great difficulty.

The Empress laughed and clapped her hands.

Leo felt drunk in her presence despite having had only water over dinner. No, it wasn't akin to drunkenness; he didn't feel slow. He felt electric, heightened and ultra-aware of sensation. And giddy, which was probably why he was unable to rein in his impulse to reenact the games he had played with his siblings as children, playing up the at times absurd manners expected of them.

'I was saying that I visited Queen Natalija's castle before we embarked on our pilgrimage to the now Trinitas Empire,' the Empress continued. 'Her castle was beautiful, though we have surpassed it in many of our kingdoms here. I enchanted my way into being her guest so that I could investigate what kind of ruler she was. I quite liked her, but I liked her fool even more. I thought to myself, every castle must have one of these in my empire. And so it was.'

'I had wondered about that, Your Eminence,' Leo said. 'Particularly when my fool has aggravated me.'

'That is the burden of being Empress,' she said. 'I declare something and it is so. I am fortunate that I have excellent judgement.'

'As are we all,' Leo said solemnly.

'That is why this business with the cult—*oh*, that is Canticalica. The little kingdom that is so frequently besieged by heretics.'

'That's right,' Leo said. 'I'm glad our troubles have earned your attention.'

'It's not so much your troubles,' the Empress said. As an afterthought, she added, 'Though of course I am sympathetic to the damage they have caused.'

'Thank you, Your Graciousness,' Leo said.

'I find it insulting that a group could imply that your rule, which I endorsed, is not also blessed by the Trinity. And further, that they are not appreciative of the structure of the Empire.'

Leo didn't know what to say to this. He was also disturbed by it, but there was something in her tone that suggested there was no room for improvement. The cultists were not the only ones who had some … constructive criticism on the systems of power.

'You haven't been ruling long, have you?' she asked.

'Less than a year.'

'How do you find it?'

Leo thought about it. It didn't feel right to lie or to tell the truth, which admittedly didn't leave him with many options. When he opened his mouth, the truth seemed to be the only thing he could express.

'Endlessly frustrating,' he said.

She laughed, looking delighted at his candour.

'*Isn't* it just,' she said.

'It's all the processes,' Leo said. 'You can never just *do* something, it has to be tabled and discussed, then someone is brought in to offer a different perspective and it's discussed again, and then you go to bring the expert in and it turns out someone else is the expert now and you have to start again. I understand there have to be rules, but I used to think kings had a lot more power.'

'Rules,' the Empress mused. 'People insist on having more and more, always finding a new circumstance that has to be accounted for. I remember when magic had three rules. Three! Sometimes I consider taking them all back, but they *are* necessary.'

'Of course,' Leo said, for lack of anything else to say.

'Take a seat, Leopold,' the Empress said, waving a hand to conjure one opposite her. Leo wondered if any of the rules of magic applied to her or if she disregarded all of them. 'And tell me, what does magic mean to you?'

Leo managed to step onto the platform and sit down without tripping over, which he thought was impressive seeing as he couldn't seem to break eye contact with the Empress.

'That's a pretty big question, Your Divinity,' he said.

'Very personal, too,' she agreed. 'If you'd like, you could tell me about your love life instead.'

'I keep faith with the Trinity fairly well,' Leo started.

The Empress laughed and motioned for him to continue. Her attention was intoxicating. Leo felt a little guilty about leaving Raven to socialise with strangers from lower classes, but they had both known that would be a frequent occurrence on this trip. And, unavoidably, for as long as they were together. Leo could only hope that Raven didn't grow to resent it.

32

EELING AS THOUGH he hadn't had a scrap of alone time outside the bathroom in a million years, Leo was grateful a week after arriving in Roiruhen to find all his companions happily occupied without him. Unwilling to stay in his rooms, he set out with a novel to find somewhere nice to read it.

It was nearly winter, and the weather was a lot milder than in Praecentor. Leo was dressed more warmly than necessary and wasn't in the mood to be discovered, so he settled himself on a patio in a squashy chair.

Within a minute, a server approached him and offered him a hot drink and a blanket. He forced himself to smile and accepted the offer of both. He yearned to run and run until he was deep in the bush, where the gum trees towered and the paths had been walked by prevenient people centuries and centuries before anyone else had imagined there was a continent here. He pictured the dew of fernery and the call of kookaburras echoing in a valley that might be truer to his kingdom than this one. And no one else in the world except him and Dicky, who didn't count. No, who wouldn't be there.

Nature must be a very lonely place now that Dicky was dead.

The server returned and placed a sweet-smelling drink on the low table that separated Leo's patio chair from its pair. Before she could arrange the blanket around him herself, Leo held his hand out and thanked her. She retreated and Leo indulged in the fantasy that he was alone.

There was a vertling top on the table next to his drink, and instead of opening his book, he picked it up to examine it. It was simpler than the one he had at home, but it probably didn't belong personally to the royal family here. He spun it, without thinking of any particular question. It landed on the third side, representing the end, or no. Not his best omen.

He picked it up again and twirled it in his hand while he tried to think of a question. What did he want? To marry Blanche, which would let him keep Raven, albeit as a secret. The kind of life that had kept him from starting anything with Raven for so long. No, it was better than that. Blanche knew about Raven. She got along with him, even. It was more than he'd expected, except that it wasn't.

For a brief moment, his people loved him. For the space of a breath, he was good enough. If the revenant of his father had been conjured a week later than he was, Leo might have laughed in his face to think that his love could be any better than what he had. (No, but wasn't it nice to imagine?)

'Will I *ever* be able to stand on my own?' he asked the top.

He spun it with a little too much force and it toppled off the edge of the table. A pale, almost luminous hand reached down for it.

'It said "no",' the Empress said. 'But then, I think it would be a terrible thing to stand alone.'

Leo creaked his mouth into a smile. 'I suppose.'

The Empress sat in the chair next to Leo's and set the top spinning. They both watched it as it spun and spun.

'Will Leopold ever be without love?' the Empress asked.

The top wobbled to a stop and Leo's smile was still reluctant, but much more genuine when he saw that it once more had landed on no.

'Is it still cheating to ask the same question twice?' the Empress asked.

'It is in my kingdom,' Leo said, 'but you're allowed to ask for clarification, so I think the Trinity will let this stand.'

'Thank goodness,' the Empress said.

She settled back into her chair and faced contentedly outwards. It was a nice area of the patio, which was presumably why the chairs had been set here. The garden was lush, with vibrant red and yellow grevilleas flowering like fireworks in the midst of silver and green leaves.

'How do you cope when people don't like you?' Leo asked.

'Everyone likes me,' the Empress said. 'I am divine.'

Leo looked down at his hands. He was fairly sheltered, but even he knew that there were always people who were dissatisfied with the Empire, if not the Empress. It wasn't even just pub talk; history books recounted events spanning across generations of discontent.

'Some people don't like my decrees sometimes,' the Empress allowed after a lengthy pause. 'Or they don't like the way they are enforced, or they don't like that they were not born to a life where they benefit them. These people have never met me. It's not personal.

'All these little kingdoms, blessed by my children and their children, they figure out the changes. When enough of them agree, that change is rolled out through the Empire. There's no need for me to decide much of anything anymore.'

'I suppose that makes it a bit easier,' Leo said.

'I will live thousands more years,' she sighed, a peaceful smile gracing her lips, 'and I will never tire of looking at the beauty of this continent that was created just for me.'

Leo looked out at the garden too. There was still frost in the shadows of trees, catching the sunlight like diamonds. A pair of magpies were playing in the low branches of a shrub. It was beautiful, but it was cultivated. And the Empress was not the first person here.

'I've never seen magic like yours,' Leo said. 'Does it dilute through the generations?'

'Perhaps a little,' the Empress said. 'But the truth is, my Trinity gave me magic because they love me, and they will never abandon me. My descendants do not carry the Trinity with them, only my blood.'

'I never quite understood that,' Leo said.

'You are a lovely boy, with very pretty hair, but they will nevertheless live only with me.'

Leo's scalp tingled with the urge to brush his hair further out of his face, but he resisted. He didn't want to look vain, or worse, like he was uncomfortable with the attention.

'Do the rules apply to you?' Leo asked.

'Of course,' the Empress said. 'But they come easier. When the Trinity first came to me, I changed the world around me every time I had a passing thought, so I made it so I must speak first. Then, I wanted to understand what it was I was asking for. This is effortless when the Trinity is my companion, but an essential step nonetheless. And I must be grateful for this power. I must return their love. I am perfect by their grace.'

Leo nodded, though his head was spinning. His textbooks recorded the rules, but not this. She made it sound like she was one with their god, and not metaphorically.

'Forgive me,' he said, climbing to his feet. 'I'm due back inside. It was an honour speaking with you.'

'You delight me, child of mine,' the Empress said. 'I like your company almost as much as your hair. Go, with my blessing.'

'Thank you,' Leo said.

He bowed deeply. He had never been more conscious of the speed of his steps as he left, not even on the day of his family's funerals or his coronation. He thought that maybe he didn't want to be perfect after all.

33

LEO'S ARMS WERE AROUND RAVEN'S WAIST, his head on Raven's shoulder. He was watching the game Raven, Max and Blanche were playing with mild interest, but mostly he was enjoying the peace. Raven's performance had visibly worsened with Leo there, something that had Blanche's eyes dancing with amusement.

Blanche seemed to like both Leo and Raven fine, but she carried herself with a warm professionalism that made it hard to get close to her. Leo didn't want her romantic love, but the more he reflected, the more he felt the need for their marriage to work out. It was making him want a greater friendship as soon as possible. Sooner, actually. Now. No matter how many times Raven told him that it would just take time, he couldn't help but want to hurry it along. Raven *also* told him that his compulsive need to be liked by everyone was more annoying than it was cute. But if he could have a life where he could choose his partner without betraying his more suitable spouse, he'd do anything to make it work. His conversation with the Empress only made him feel it more keenly. Perfection be damned, he just wanted this.

Leo squeezed Raven fondly and Raven placed one of his pieces in a truly stupid square. Blanche sucked one cheek into her mouth to keep from laughing. Raven saw what he'd done and groaned.

'Could I just move that?' he asked.

'Your fingers aren't touching it anymore, it's not your turn,' Max said.

Raven pinched Leo on the thigh and Leo smacked his hand.

'You're supposed to be on my side. Why aren't you sabotaging Blanche?'

'I don't know what you're talking about,' Leo said. 'Do you want me to go hug her?'

'Please don't,' Blanche said.

'No,' Raven said, holding Leo's hand to his side.

Leo kissed Raven's shoulder and stayed where he was wanted. Blanche laughed and picked up two cards. Max made a frustrated noise and Leo leaned away from Raven to peek over his shoulder at his cards.

'That's a rotten deal, kiddo,' Leo said sympathetically.

'I *know*,' Max grumbled.

'What if—?' Leo released Raven and plucked one of Max's cards from his hand, then replaced it in a different order. 'If you can get on a blue tile, I think that's your best shot.'

Raven smoothly scooted half a foot away, making Leo and Blanche look to the door. Sure enough, a moment later there was a quiet knock and the door opened.

'Your Highness,' the servant said, with a bow to Blanche. 'Majesty, Highness,' he added, acknowledging Leo and Max.

'Yes?' Blanche asked.

'Her Majesty Queen Isolde requests your company.'

'Do you remember when I said you should change your shirt, little prince, and you said that you would have to change for bed in a few hours so there was no point?' Raven asked Max.

'But then I would have probably got berry stains on the new shirt as well,' Max protested.

'Well, now it's no longer a suggestion,' Raven said. He stood and took the cards from Max's hands to put them down on the board.

'I despise manners,' Max muttered.

Raven met Leo's eyes and they shared a look that agreed that Max was funniest when he spoke like he was an adult.

'We'll join you soon,' Raven said. 'Come along, Maximilian.'

Raven and Max left in one direction, towards Max's room, and Blanche and Leo followed the servant towards the centre of the castle. Blanche paused when the servant started to lead the way down the stairs towards the entrance hall.

'It's nearly winter,' she said. 'Why is Isolde out of the castle?'

'She's visiting the cathedral,' the servant said.

'On a Mittday evening?' she asked.

'The Empress suggested it,' the servant said, after a short pause.

Blanche looked warily at Leo, then slowly began descending the stairs. When the servant continued his way, she murmured to Leo, 'I may be paranoid, but is that pretty sword of yours sharp?'

'Very,' Leo promised.

'What a world we live in,' she sighed. 'I'm afraid it is not the best time to be royalty.'

That was true, but Leo still suspected most people would take the trade-off.

When they approached the cathedral, Leo thought for a moment that it was on fire. The glass point was incandescent, glowing as though the sun itself was contained within the stone walls and throwing off refracted light over the city. In the moment that Leo and Blanche stopped to take in the sight, four hooded figures appeared out of the meagre shadows. Leo began to draw his sword, but the figure closest to him cried *'Desist'* and his hand froze in the middle of the movement.

'Liber—' Leo began, but the attacker just behind the magician had closed the distance and brought his own sword to Leo's chin. Leo weighed up his chances of ducking backwards and under the attacker's guard as the magician, breathing heavily with effort of

catching up, continued to get closer. Just as Leo was deciding to risk it, he heard Blanche cry out. Whether she had tried to fight her own attackers, he wasn't sure, but she was in a chokehold now with a knife drawing small beads of blood from her cheek.

'What do you *want*?' Leo demanded.

'Equality,' the man holding Leo at knife point said.

Leo didn't have much to say to that. The magician didn't say anything either as he forced Leo's hands into magic-suppressing cuffs. In fact, he kept his hooded face ducked, as though ashamed to show his face. Leo wondered how the magicians in this cult felt about their divine ancestry. The cult needed their magic, but were they respected for it?

'Do you have him?' the other attacker asked. The magician nodded and held up Leo's wrists in proof. Satisfied, the other attacker left them to check on Blanche.

The magician turned so he was next to Leo and put his hand on Leo's back to guide him forwards, towards the cathedral. He was still angling his head slightly away. Leo's mind was racing. He didn't need magic to fight. When the moment came, he thought he would be able to draw his sword and make a break for it. But he'd only get one chance. He had to choose his moment well.

Inside the cathedral, Leo discovered what was giving off all the light. Wrapped in chains and with a chorus of dozens surrounding her and singing in harmony was the Empress. The light should have been blinding, but it drew the eye of everyone in the cathedral. She burnt like a forest fire ... but one that was slowly dimming. It was as she had said to Leo—the rules still applied to her, even if her power made them less restrictive. The chains, larger by far than the ones on Leo and winding around her whole body, were made of iridium. She might have access to a well of magic *almost* fathomless, but nothing was infinite. The iridium would win if the song echoing off the walls and thrumming in Leo's chest could keep her contained.

Leo forced himself to look away from the Empress to assess his surroundings in more detail. Apart from the Empress, he and Max were the only non-native royalty visiting Roiruhen. There were other nobles chained to the ground, but only members of royal families were being guarded personally. Royalty had the strongest magic, but this was an unnecessary precaution given the iridium. It became still more unnecessary when Leo's guard bolted his shackles to an anchor in the marble floor, greatly increasing the difficulty of the manoeuvre it would take for him to escape. He would have to crouch, then find enough momentum to shatter the very heavy iridium, which may take more than one impact and could damage his wrists with it … He would have to be perfect, or he would die. He might die anyway. He wouldn't be able to fight them all. He would only be able to run. And that didn't sit right at all, but Max was out there somewhere. The last year had been about a lot of things for Leo, but nothing more than family.

The Empress's light continued to dim, and a shadow began to pool at her feet. It leaked in one direction, then another, as if searching for something. The more the Empress dimmed, the larger the shadow became. Leo didn't know what it was, but he knew that he *did not want it to touch him*. It frightened him on an instinctual level—the closest he had ever felt to fear like this was seeing a snake a fraction of a second before stepping on it, and that didn't even approach the dread he was feeling now. His breaths felt like they lacked that essential component that gave them life.

And then it got worse. More cultists entered the cathedral, with Max and Raven chained between them. Leo was horrified to see that instead of the simple shackles on his own wrists and those of the other prisoners, both Max and Raven had chains wrapping around their whole body like the Empress.

'He's our choice for the middle?' one of the cultists asked. She threw back her hood and strode into the centre of the aisle to examine Raven, and Leo recognised her as the leader, Isobella.

'He used magic to defend the boy,' the cultist holding Raven's chains said. 'You said the magician to represent the middle should be ordinary. To represent the reach of the Empress beyond nobility. This way it doesn't have to be one of us.'

'The willing sacrifice—' another cultist began.

'No,' Isobella said. 'Our people have sacrificed enough. The Trinity has provided us this man at our hour of need. We will not reject their gift.'

Leo was very close to panicking. He might be able to fight his way free of his captor, but there were so many cultists in the cathedral and Leo's mind was spinning trying to think of a way for him to save Max and Raven. He tried to breathe evenly. There had to be a way.

The man guarding Leo shifted his weight and cleared his throat quietly, but no one was close enough to hear it apart from Leo, and he didn't end up speaking. Leo wondered if his guard was having second thoughts. He didn't know how to use that.

The Empress's light dimmed further and the shadow got more agitated. Leo tried to take a step backwards, but his guard kept him in place. The light emanating from her skin was only as bright as a gas lamp now. And now the candles of the cathedral were outshining it. And now it was gone.

The shadow dissolved into the floor and Leo released a shaky breath. The chorus stopped singing. Now that the light was gone, Leo could see the triangular frame that the Empress was chained to and now sagging against. She was still beautiful, but she was more *human* now.

Four cultists dragged Max and Raven up to the stage and Max began to scream, trying uselessly to squirm out of their grip and the chains. His young voice bounced off the angles of the otherwise silent cathedral and Leo's heart ached in his throat.

'*Max,*' he groaned, and he heard it echoed in whisper from his guard. Leo turned his head abruptly and tried to see past the hood. He knew that voice. But that wasn't possible.

When Max and Raven were attached to their own frames alongside the Empress, Isobella started to sing wordlessly, an extended '*Ah*' that climbed and fell through a simple and familiar pattern. As each note rolled into the next, more cultists removed their hoods and joined the song until the whole cathedral rang with a hundred voices.

All except Leo's guard.

The song stopped as suddenly as it had begun. Leo's guard seemed to realise he was the only one with his hood still up and slid it down. Leo met his dead twin's eyes with wonder. They used to be brown but were now an awful red. The cost of blood magic. What had these people forced him into?

'It wasn't supposed to be Max,' Dicky whispered.

'Well, if you were going to kill some other child, I suppose that's alright,' Leo whispered back.

Isobella began to sing again, this time with words familiar to every child in the Empire, from highest royalty to the most rural church-goer.

'Beginning, beginning, beginning.' When she began the next line, another cultist started from the start. 'So it goes, so it goes, so it goes,' Isobella continued. A third cultist began from the start as she sang, 'Concluding, concluding, concluding,' until the full round was completed with the final line, 'As we know, and it shows, in our prose.' When Isobella started again, a quarter of the cathedral joined her until the air vibrated with every cultist bar one singing in the round. Despite everything, Leo had to resist joining in. He'd never heard magic like this.

The shadow that had disappeared returned, making Leo recoil back. It was darker than black, dark as though whatever it covered no longer existed, dark as though it contained every emptiness that had ever existed in the world. It slid along the floor, growing more and more erratic as the song progressed, until it began to climb the walls.

The prayer-song evolved into unfamiliar lyrics following the same tune.

'Inviting, inviting, inviting / From your home, from your home, from your home / Compelling, compelling, compelling / From unknown, to our tone, words our own.'

'Dicky,' Leo hissed. 'You have to free me.'

'What could you even do?' Dicky asked.

'Something stupid,' Leo said. 'If there's a chance I can, I have to try to stop them.'

Dicky and Leo looked at each other for a long moment. Leo saw Dicky's resolve weaken as the floor and walls became encased in the shadow …

The cathedral became consumed by darkness and the air split with a cacophony of thunder that shattered the glass tip of the cathedral into powder and filled the space with blinding light. When the light and the dark faded to normalcy, three figures stood centre-stage, back to back to back.

They were shaped approximately like humans, but they seemed to be made of dozens of iridescent glass prisms, glowing like dragonfly wings caught in sunlight. It was difficult to tell where one ended and the next began. The more Leo looked, the more certain he was that they were one creature. The cultists had brought the Trinity into the mortal plane.

Isobella sank to her knees, and in fits and starts the rest of the cathedral copied as they collected themselves enough to do so. Dicky tugged Leo down with him urgently, narrowly avoiding being the last ones standing.

'*Free me,*' Leo hissed.

'*Are you insane?*' Dicky hissed back.

'Divine Trinity!' Isobella cried. 'We brought you to this world.

We brought you to life, so that you could help us, your faithful children.'

The Trinity turned abruptly, moving as one to rotate the figure who was facing Isobella so that all three could look at her in turn. She waited to see if they would speak, then continued.

'We are grateful for the magic you have bestowed on this land, but it has sowed inequality from its inception. With these offerings, we ask that you redistribute magic to *all* those who worship you as you deserve.'

The Trinity rotated again, so rapid it was sickening. They moved like a clockwork toy jerking from one position to the next. Each face examined Isobella and the three chained sacrifices that she was gesturing to. They took a step as one towards Raven, who was tied in the middle.

'Dicky,' Leo begged.

'The child has just begun to show signs of magic,' Isobella said. Her voice was clear and loud, but there was a slight tremble in it. She clearly had been expecting gods who were easier to interpret. These ones were not the resplendent figures portrayed in stained glass surrounding them. Leo wasn't even sure they were the kind of being that would understand speech. 'The man is in the midst of his life, and could be anyone at all,' she continued valiantly. 'And the Empress represents the end.'

The Trinity listened, then took three quick steps towards Max.

'Leo!' Max screamed.

Dicky sucked in a shocked breath and fumbled for his knife. His hands were shaking and clumsy, and Leo dug his nails into his palms in agonised impotence.

'Venerated Trinity—' Isobella began, but her words died out as the Trinity spoke smoothly over her.

'That is not our title,' they said. Their opalescent mouths didn't move, but their voice—identical to Isobella's but empty somehow—seemed to come from each figure in unison. They bent closer to Max's face and he whimpered loudly in the echoing church. 'You are not worthy of worshipping us.' They spun, and the figure now facing Max reached out a hand to his face. 'How long it has been since we tasted life.'

Dicky brought the butt of his knife down on Leo's cuffs with a grunt of effort, shattering them into a thousand bladed splinters. Leo lurched to his feet, drawing his sword.

'Hey!' he cried.

The Trinity—the *thing* that Leo had no other word for than the Trinity—rotated again, taking Leo in.

'Don't you *dare* touch my brother,' Leo said.

Before Leo could register what was happening, every shadow in the cathedral rushed in his direction. There was nothing he could do to resist as the darkness entered him. The world went still and black, with Leo the only thing that remained. And yet, he was okay.

'What?' Leo asked tentatively.

I don't have much time, the darkness said, low and musical and from every direction. It had a subtle feminine lilt to it. Where it had distinction, it sounded a little like the Empress's voice.

Leo swallowed nervously and tightened his grip on his sword.

'Who are you?' he asked.

I am the unspoken god, the darkness said. *The base of the pyramid. The exception to the rule. The undefined one, uncounted in the Trinity. Not that they know who we have exalted them as.*

'Oh,' Leo said. That felt inadequate. 'It's nice to meet you.'

Not his brightest moment. He was under a considerable amount of stress.

Likewise, the darkness said, as if this was a perfectly reasonable response. It continued. *I refuse to let my Empress die. You refuse to let your brother and your lover die. We have compatible aims. But you must be prepared to pay a price.*

'Anything,' Leo said.

Unwise, but convenient, the darkness said. *You must kill the Trinity. Now, before they understand the implications of a physical realm.*

'I don't have that kind of power!'

You have me.

'They're my *gods*,' Leo protested. 'I can't— Won't that have ramifications?'

Yes. Your brother will live.

Leo hesitated. He wasn't what he would call devout, but this went somewhat beyond skipping church.

They did not give you magic knowingly or voluntarily, the darkness said. *I do not know what they will do once they eat your brother. It will not be a kind death, to him or to the rest of the world.*

'Why should I trust you?' Leo asked.

Because I love my Empress, the darkness said simply. *And because there is no alternative. For either of us.*

Leo took a deep breath. He wondered what Con would do in his shoes, and knew immediately that he would do whatever it took to save Max. Ada would never forgive him if he chose the Trinity over their brother. Danya … would just have to deal.

Leo nodded and adjusted his grip on his sword.

You must be quick, the darkness said.

'Whatever it takes,' Leo said.

The world brightened again, and Leo didn't hesitate. No one had moved since the darkness had done whatever it had done, and Leo didn't give them a chance to restrain him again.

'Celerity,' Leo said, luxuriating in the shape of the word, glorying in it, feeling how perfect it was so that it would get him to the stage, and he sprang forwards with greater agility than he could have anticipated. His feet felt like they barely skimmed the floor and his breath came as if he had never moved as he sped through the crowd in a matter of heartbeats. He alighted to a stop in front of Isobella, who lifted her hands ready to cast.

'Expulse,' he said, and she flew across the stage to crash against the wall with a sickening thud.

As he took the stage, he noticed that cultists all across the cathedral were climbing to their feet and drawing weapons. Leo grinned and spun to face them. He felt invincible.

There is no time, the darkness whispered in his mind.

'Okay,' Leo said. He held up his hands and opened his mouth to cast. His eyes met Dicky's. He remembered Blanche. He changed his mind. 'Torpor,' he said, and the room slumped into sleep. The whole room. He'd barely even tried. Was this what it was like to be the Empress?

He turned to the Trinity.

'That power does not belong to you,' the Trinity said as one. Their voice was strangely discordant, like a chord played one note off.

'Oh no,' Leo said flatly. 'How about you come and get it?'

He saw this was a mistake immediately and ducked with a hurried 'Ward' to protect himself from the stream of fire the Trinity shot at him.

Don't use magic, the darkness told him. *You cannot beat them at magic. I will protect you.*

'Magic's overrated in combat,' Leo laughed giddily to himself.

He stood up and watched as the fabric of his tunic and shirt burnt away where the blast was focused on his chest, but his skin failed to blister. It didn't hurt. It didn't even redden. He looked up at the Trinity and lifted his sword in both hands, close to his neck. They stopped their fiery attack, reappraising him. As he took a steadying breath, the Trinity cocked their heads to the side and looked down at their hands. The prismatic material they were made of elongated from their palms in the shape of three swords, one for each of them.

'Alright then,' Leo said. He felt a brazen euphoria that reminded him of his first Sommertide at the Academy, sixteen and tipsy, showing off for a girl who didn't know he wasn't cool yet. He felt like all of this was a stage show, and every step he took was scripted in his favour. He twirled his sword in his hand like a dickhead. 'Don't go easy on me.'

Leo struck forward and the Trinity jerked to the side to dodge. They were impossibly fast. In other circumstances, that might have concerned Leo, but he'd never felt power like this and he was forgetting what concern was. He stabbed forward again and the Trinity dodged again. One of their feet hit the edge of the steps leading down the stage and they stumbled. Leo laughed.

'Focus, Leo!' Raven called out, voice as strained and urgent as a fraying lifeline, and Leo abruptly remembered the stakes.

He darted forward, but the Trinity had recovered and they twisted to knock Leo's sword aside with theirs. The force was great enough that Leo barely held onto his hilt, but the impact shattered their fabricated blade. They didn't just *look* like iridium, they were *made* of it. Leo dropped back and fell into a ready position as they rotated so Leo was facing a figure with an intact sword as the one facing away grew another. Leo didn't doubt this one would be stronger.

Leo lunged and the Trinity parried inexpertly. Leo ducked his sword under the block and swept it up and the Trinity rotated to catch it with its third sword. Leo withdrew and struck forward again, and they swung two swords wildly, forcing Leo to duck. He remembered one of his combat teachers at the Academy saying once that she would never fear a trained swordsperson, because she was the best there was. No, she feared the idiot who had never learnt a proper form, whose moves she couldn't predict. But only if the idiot was fast.

The Trinity was *very* fast.

They also were learning. The darkness had said Leo had to be quick, before the Trinity got accustomed to a physical realm. Leo's confidence was not at the high it had been at the beginning of this fight.

This time, when Leo fell back into a ready position, the Trinity was the one to attack. They spun in a slow circle as they crossed swords with Leo, making him fight first one and then the next. Fighting against both Con and Ada had not been preparation enough for this. But all his best moves were Con's, and if he was going to succeed, it would be with his brother's grace. He twirled his sword again, this time to shake out his sore wrist.

Hurry, the darkness insisted. *They are learning.*

'I'm not playing!' Leo panted as he dodged a blow by milli-metres.

Panting wasn't good. He couldn't afford to slow down. And he couldn't afford to use only half his arsenal, either. He needed to finish this.

'Inferno!' he cried, lifting a hand to shoot fire at the Trinity. They didn't even seem to notice.

Magic won't work! the darkness said. *They are iridium in this realm. You must shatter them.*

Leo didn't reply, too busy being forced backwards by a barrage of hits that he was only barely managing to dodge or deflect.

'The edge!' Max shouted and Leo managed to duck sideways instead of back to avoid falling down the stairs. He glanced down to check his position and made a strange gasping noise as the air was forced from his body. Extending from his chest was one of the Trinity's swords.

'Oh,' Leo said, frowning down at the beautiful metal. 'This one hurts.'

The fire was magic. I can neutralise magic and I can heal your wounds, but I cannot prevent the damage of physical things any more than they can.

'It really hurts,' Leo whimpered.

He dropped his sword and clasped the blade in his chest with both hands, which only served to hurt them as well. It was unfair that they could hurt even with the enormity of his other pain. He could distantly hear Max screaming again, but he couldn't understand the words. He hadn't been stabbed for such a long time. He didn't remember it being so distracting.

I cannot heal you while it is inside you, the darkness said. *Fall backwards*.

Leo stared at his hands, which were smearing blood onto the sword and making it glisten in a new and interesting way. It should hurt more. It was the worst pain he'd ever felt, but there was more behind a curtain hidden somewhere in his mind. If he even glimpsed that curtain, he knew he would scream. He didn't know what would happen if he looked behind it.

Leo looked up at the Trinity, who seemed just as curious as he was about his injury.

Leo.

The Trinity reached out a finger and touched Leo's chest, where the blood was darkest. Leo had always thought that the Trinity must like blood. Why else would blood magic be so powerful?

LEO. FALL BACKWARDS.

Leo's legs gave out and the blade slipped out of him with a sickening, squelching noise. Leo punctuated it with a heavy thud onto the marble floor and the loud crack of his head hitting the top step. It sounded, accurately, like his skull had met the marble with the same response an egg might have had.

And then the pain was gone. Leo was able to take a full breath again. He could *think*.

The Trinity bent over Leo and touched their finger to Leo's chest again. They were curious. Why not? They had no frame of reference for how humans behaved. When they bent, it was as one, in three different directions like a flower's petals. Leo supposed they had better balance that way.

Balance.

'Glacial,' Leo murmured, touching his palm to the stage. Ice bloomed across it, spiderwebbing to the very edges and down the steps.

They are impervious—

'Did it look like I was aiming for them?' Leo demanded.

The Trinity peered to the side of Leo and reached out to touch the ice. Leo grabbed their wrist with both hands and yanked it with all his strength. The Trinity took a step to balance and their slick, metallic feet found no purchase on the ice. Leo rolled underneath them as they attempted to catch themselves on the stairs and fell further. He snatched his sword up and threw himself at the Trinity, striking them in the place one of their hearts should be.

The body that Leo struck shattered, and a beat later the two other bodies synchronised, spilling shards of iridium in every direction.

Leo's pants were the only sound in the cathedral. As he caught his breath, he realised that the shards had cut him, and he hadn't healed.

'Darkness?' Leo asked as he straightened.

There was no answer.

'Leo?' Max called.

Leo jolted back to his senses and dashed to where Max was chained up. He dropped his sword and ran his hands over the links, looking for a clasp.

'You're okay,' he told Max as he searched. 'It's all okay, I'm here.'

'Did they hurt you?' Max asked, voice trembling.

'Barely a scratch,' Leo said, though the scratches were admittedly stinging horribly. He groped along the chain. They had to have fastened it somehow. 'Are you—' Leo tripped over the edge of the triangular frame and caught himself on the floor with his hand. His hand was tacky with blood still, but it didn't slip on the ice. The ice was gone. There wasn't even water left behind.

His body making a connection he couldn't put into words yet, Leo turned and saw that the cultists were slowly picking themselves up. He got his sword up and ready and hoped they were all too far away to see the tip wobbling. The adrenaline was leaving him and he didn't know if he could summon it back for another fight.

'Just try me,' Leo said, in as commanding a voice as he could. 'I fucking *dare* you.'

'Where are the Trinity?' someone called out.

Leo pointed with his sword to the pile of jagged, iridium fragments.

'Liar!' screamed another voice.

'Vortex!' cried another.

Nothing happened. A hush fell as every magician in the room felt for their magic and found nothing there. It was different to the exhaustion Leo had felt when he'd overdone magic and was temporarily unable to access it, somehow even more profound than when shackled in iridium. There was just nothing.

'What did you do to us?' someone demanded.

Leo pointed with his sword again. He had known that he couldn't kill the gods without consequences. This time, no one had any follow-up questions.

34

THE EMPRESS WEPT when she came to hours after the fight and found the darkness had gone. She knew immediately what had happened. They were the unnamed, undefinable god who existed in the cracks that the Trinity failed to cover. Without the Trinity, they couldn't exist either.

'They brought magic into the world to make me smile,' the Empress said, staring at the completely mundane shadows of a corner instead of Leo. 'It wasn't the Trinity. The Trinity never noticed us. We made it all up.'

'I'm sorry,' Leo said quietly. 'They told me they loved you. They said it was the only way to save you.'

The Empress nodded and sent him away. Leo did not feel forgiven.

DICKY WOKE LEO AT DAWN the day after Leo had killed their gods. Leo felt for a magical hangover, but if anything he felt fresher than usual. He followed Dicky out of the castle and to the small river that ran through Roiruhen. They walked, sometimes sharing stories, but mostly in companionable silence. Leo had missed this. He was whole again.

Dicky wanted to know about what had happened in the cathedral while he'd been under enchanted sleep. He also wanted to know about Raven, who had unsuccessfully tried to hide under Leo's blanket when Dicky woke Leo up. Leo both did and didn't want to know why Dicky had joined the cult. Why he'd killed their parents. If he regretted it. He couldn't ask any of those things.

'Do you know,' Dicky said, in a measured voice, 'sometimes I even miss them.'

Leo looked at him. Dicky frowned at his feet.

'I should probably be executed for that,' he said.

'Probably,' Leo agreed. After a minute, he asked, 'Do you think you'll kill anyone else?'

'No,' Dicky said. 'It wasn't for me.'

'Well, that's something,' Leo said.

'I wouldn't hold it against you if you *did* have me executed,' Dicky assured him.

'I appreciate that,' Leo said. 'I'll consider it, but I don't think I will.'

Dicky shrugged. Leo wondered if he should hug him or something. He didn't think either of them would enjoy that, but it seemed like what a person should do when his brother turned out to not be dead.

'The thing is,' he said, 'I'm glad you're alive.'

Dicky looked at him with surprise. Leo's chest ached.

'Sometimes I forget you exist,' Dicky said. 'Which means that all my family hates me, until I remember you again. All of The Awakening hated me too. They said I was boring.'

'You *are* boring,' Leo said kindly.

'Well, yes,' Dicky said.

He frowned, like he was trying to figure something out. Dicky was certain that everything in life could be solved if a person had all the information. No one would play games with him, because he approached them in the same way he approached his lessons, as though throwing the dice in *such* a way would get him a good grade. He used to practice throwing dice, which Ada was convinced was cheating. Leo had just thought it was weird.

'Did you forget that you're boring?' Leo asked.

'I did,' Dicky mused.

'Hey,' Leo said. 'Are you scared of horses?'

'Terrified,' Dicky agreed easily. 'Why?'

'My fiancée said she thought you were,' Leo said.

'Con said they can tell when you're scared of them,' Dicky said. 'And he's bloody well right. I wouldn't be scared of them if they weren't so scared of me being scared of them. At least when *I'm* scared I don't wave my hooves in the air.'

'No,' Leo agreed darkly.

Dicky caught the implication and met Leo's eyes.

'I wasn't scared when I killed them,' he said. 'I would have killed him years ago if I hadn't been next in line.'

Leo stared at him.

'Again, I *really* wouldn't mind if you felt I should face some kind of consequence,' Dicky said.

Leo stared a little longer. He shook himself.

'The only thing worse than me having to make that decision,' Leo said, 'would be literally anyone else making it.'

'I knew you'd make a good king,' Dicky smiled.

Leo didn't like that.

I SOBELLA TOOK A COUPLE OF DAYS to regain consciousness. When she did, Leo went to her hospital room to see if she had anything to say that he hadn't heard from Dicky. He wasn't sure that it mattered anymore.

She was less beautiful in pyjamas and with her usual ferocity replaced with only a dazed kind of disgruntlement. She looked painfully thin, perhaps not helped by her two days of having only honey to sustain her while she slept. Her nurse told Leo not to expect a great deal of conversation from her.

'Hello,' he said as he took a seat next to her bed. 'I'm Leo.'

'Fuck you,' she said, without much conviction.

Well, maybe it was better if she was direct. He didn't know why he'd been pretending to himself that he could start fresh with her. Maybe he just wanted to believe that if someone knew him personally, they wouldn't hate him anymore. What a strange thing for someone with his father to hope for.

'I know you're not recovered yet,' he said, 'but I won't be staying here long and I thought I'd offer to speak on your behalf, if that was something you wanted. My brother seems to think that you had good intentions.'

'Your brother is an idiot,' Isobella said.

'I know,' Leo said. 'That doesn't make him wrong.'

Isobella didn't reply. There were words out there, Leo was sure, that would lead to a happy resolution. If Leo said the right thing, he could guide Isobella to say a different right thing. They could find common ground. There didn't have to be any more bloodshed.

'Dicky says that you wanted to democratise magic. That you wanted the most vulnerable people to have power. He says that you were a voice for the prevenient people—'

'I don't give a shit about the prevenient people,' Isobella said. 'I don't give a shit about the little kids going hungry or the farmers who fucked their backs and will never make a recovery. I don't give a shit about the Trinity or destiny or that harpy who calls herself Empress.'

'Okay …' Leo said.

'I was born in the dirt,' Isobella said. 'No one helped me except me. But they all *talked* a lot about helping people like me. Everyone wants to think they're a good person. Your brother would kill if it made people think he was good. I bet you would, too.'

Leo's eyes darted towards the door. Whatever potions Isobella's nurse was giving her for the pain, they didn't seem to be working. Or maybe they were working *too* well. Head injuries were almost impossible to heal with magic, let alone what they had now. The brain was too complex.

'Half the people in The Awakening were guilty, snivelling little wretches like your brother,' she said. 'Another quarter had just worn out the old prayers and thought ours sounded pretty good. And the rest of us knew that if everyone was given power, we'd be the ones who had made it happen. We would have torn you all down and it would have been us in charge.

'How's that for a confession?' she asked. She raised an eyebrow in a way that might have been haughty if she hadn't looked so unwell. 'Are you going to have me executed?'

'Do you want me to?' Leo asked.

Isobella grinned.

'Do it,' she said. 'Your precious magic can't protect you anymore and there are so many more of us than there are of our oppressors. Kill me, Your Majesty. If you don't, I'll turn them against you some other way.'

Leo sighed and leaned his head back against his chair. He really didn't feel bloodthirsty enough to be a king. A soldier could kill someone in the heat of battle, but a king had the burden of choice. He'd never had someone executed before. The only people he'd ever killed, if people was the right term, were their gods.

'Not my kingdom,' he decided. 'Wouldn't want to undermine my in-laws.'

He stood and paused by the foot of her bed, one hand on the frame. She looked like she wanted to bite his fingers.

'That doesn't count as a confession,' he said. 'No one's themself when they have a headache.'

'Fuck you,' Isobella spat.

'Sorry to have disturbed you,' Leo said. 'Write to me if you want my help.'

B Y THE TIME LEO HAD MADE THE JOURNEY HOME, now at the mercy of whichever way the winds felt like blowing, the rumours about what had happened in Roiruhen's cathedral had had plenty of time to develop into forms even more fantastic than the truth. Some said that he had killed demons impersonating the gods instead of the Trinity themselves, but not before the demons could swallow the magic from the world. Others said that Leo had absorbed all of the magic from every magician and that he was now more powerful than the Empress. Still others said that he had killed a thousand cultists with a single word that had been so potent it had used all the magic up. No one thought that he had actually killed the Trinity, not even the people who had been in the room. They all heard the Trinity deny their title. The only people who knew were Leo … and the Empress.

The Empress had released an official statement that had only encouraged rumours to get more extravagant due to its brevity. All it said was that the cultists had attacked again and had been defeated by Leo without undue loss of life. She hadn't even mentioned the loss of magic. When Leo had left, Queen Isolde was still trying to figure out how to answer that question herself.

The boat came to a stop at the base of Praecentor's island. Raven stepped lightly onto the dock and held his hands out to catch Max then help Leo. Of all the rumours going around, the one that had sent Leo to Neue Wolke in the first place seemed to have got a puncture. Occasionally, someone might ask, *'Canticalica, is that the king who was messing about with his fool?'*, but the answer would always be that it couldn't be the same one. The world had decided Leo was a legend. Legends didn't have mildly embarrassing sex stories.

Blanche had stayed behind. Their engagement was still officially standing, but things were far too uncertain for a royal wedding. In Leutesland, there had already been a minor revolution against the crown. The people had asked what right its rulers had to rule when they were no longer blessed by the Trinity and the king had answered, *'The right of the man with the larger army.'* Leo suspected it wouldn't be the last time that question was asked. He suspected not every soldier would take their monarch's side.

This time, rather than take the carriage, Ada had arranged for horses to be waiting for them to ride to the castle in the open. She firmly believed that it was better for the people to be able to see their legend of a king than to find him inaccessible. Leo understood the logic of this, but the result was that the ride that could have taken half an hour took them nearly three.

'When are we going to get there?' Max asked in exasperation as Leo remounted Korbinian for the millionth time after being coaxed to talk to a citizen who couldn't be a part of the crowd yet again.

'If we were in a carriage, our goal would be to get to the castle,' Leo said. 'But we're doing it this way, so our goal is to spend time with the people. We're doing a pretty good job of that.'

Max groaned.

'What do you want to get home so badly for?' Leo asked.

'I want a *bath*,' Max said. 'I've had enough of being a sailor.'

Leo laughed.

'Yeah, me too, kid.'

Behind them, with the hood of his worn and patched cloak pulled up to hide his face, Dicky rode (anxiously) beside Raven. Dicky's identity hadn't been known to many of the cultists and, with his hair clipped to barely cover his head and plain clothes, he wasn't especially recognisable even when his cloak wasn't covering him. Leo didn't know what to do with him. He'd written to Ada and Con saying, *If it helps, he says he's sorry.*

Ada had written back, *It does not*.

Eventually, they arrived at the base of the Round Tower. Leo helped Max off his horse and handed their reins off to a couple of stable hands he was able to thank by name. Ada and Con were waiting and Leo was surprised when Ada initiated a genuine hug, lacking the stiffness of every other one he could ever remember having with her.

'Hey,' he said, squeezing her back. 'Did you miss me that much?'

'Yes,' she said. 'Being acting queen is quite shit, actually. I never would have expected it. You presented a rosier picture.'

'I wouldn't have wanted you to think I was ungrateful,' Leo said.

'You could have died,' she said, finally releasing him.

Leo didn't know how to respond. Next to them, Con was trying to convince Max that he'd grown an entire foot in the time they'd been away.

'I didn't,' Leo said helpfully.

'I'm pretty glad about that,' she said.

'Ada, that may be the first genuinely nice thing you've ever said to me,' Leo laughed.

'Don't expect it every day,' she said.

They smiled at each other for a moment, then Ada tapped Max on the shoulder and said, 'And do I get a hug at some point, or have you forgotten who I am on your journey?'

'I haven't forgotten about you …' Max paused and pinched his lip with his thumb and knuckle in a gesture he had learnt from Raven. It still held that slight stiffness of intention that gave away the fact that it hadn't been an unconscious learning. 'It's Mabel, right?' he said.

'You are a *monster*,' Ada said.

Max laughed and threw his arms around her. She leaned her cheek into the top of his head when she hugged him back.

'He also could have died,' she said to Leo's disbelieving expression. 'I missed you, little monster,' she told Max.

'I wish I knew how to paint,' Con said. 'This moment deserves to be recorded.'

'Because scrying on tablets doesn't work anymore,' Leo sighed. 'That's a bummer, I'm going to miss that.'

Con punched Leo on the shoulder and they hugged too.

'Did you shrink?' Leo asked as they let go, measuring Con's head to his own, angling his hand a little to exaggerate his height advantage more.

'Are you sure you don't still have business in Neue Wolke?' Con asked.

'Now that you mention it,' Leo said, pretending to think of something. He made it one step back towards the heavy doors before Con wrestled him back. Leo's coronet fell off in the scuffle and he caught it before it hit the floor.

'Nice reflexes,' Con said.

'Someone had me training without magic all year,' Leo said, fitting the coronet back on his head. 'Thank the Tr—' he cut himself off. 'Thank someone for that, anyway.'

'You could thank me,' Con said.

'I wouldn't want you to think too much of yourself,' Leo said. 'It's going to be hard enough to get you off the throne as it is.'

'You can have it,' Con said emphatically. 'You didn't tell me it would be hard.'

Leo caught a Shield's eye and smiled in acknowledgement of the pointed glance she made at the doors. They needed to get out of the entrance hall so that the staff could come inside.

'Thank you,' Leo said to the Shields who had accompanied them in.

The Shields bowed but made no move to follow Leo and his family as they took the staircase up. Leo doubted anyone would take the idea of guarding him seriously for a good while.

They made their way to the Oak Library. Leo had been warned that the castle was worse for wear since magic had left, but it still hurt to see. Danya had evidently been working harder than he'd realised to maintain the place, and everywhere she had used magic to repair, reinforce or conjure wholesale was showing the consequences of that magic no longer standing. Whole walls had collapsed in sections. It would be an enormous job to fix.

Danya was waiting for them in the library. She hugged Leo and Max, but without her usual energy.

'Are you okay?' Leo asked.

'Oh, you know,' Danya said with a brave smile. Leo waited and she added, 'Lost all purpose in my life. Never developed a skill that didn't involve magic so I had to learn how to tie shoelaces at the age of twenty-two. I'm tired all the time. I've been better.'

'I'm sorry,' Leo said, squeezing her hand.

'I'll recover,' she said. 'If Raven can do it—'

Almost as if he'd been waiting outside the room for someone to use his name, Raven opened the door. Despite having seen him only three hours ago, Max ran over to him to tell him whatever new thing he'd thought of since then. Con clapped Raven on the shoulder and Ada offered her hand for him to kiss. Leo smiled. He couldn't seem to stop doing that these days.

'Love's a funny thing, isn't it?' Danya said.

'How so?' Leo asked.

'Sometimes I think I take it for granted that Ada loves me. But then I have moments like this where I see how she makes an effort out of love for *you* and I just think, wow. Someone that wonderful thinks I'm wonderful. And I don't doubt that even a little bit. Maybe you didn't kill all the magic.'

'We had love before we had magic,' Leo said. 'Magic was brought into the world out of love for the Empress.'

'Get in here, idiot,' Raven called to the door, and Dicky

tentatively stepped inside. It took Con a few moments to offer his hand to shake. It was clearly an act of gallantry, not of warmth. Leo didn't think there was anything he could do to improve that situation.

'It must have been amazing to meet her,' Danya said, choosing to ignore Dicky's entrance.

'She would have loved to meet you too,' Leo said. 'We talked for almost an hour about what magic meant to me. I think she genuinely wanted to hear.'

He thought it was probably best to not mention that she had also been just a bit unnerving, or that he wasn't sure if they'd left on the best terms.

'Is she going to be okay?' Con asked, as the two groups slowly merged, Dicky awkwardly standing a little outside the circle. 'Magic was keeping her young. I'm surprised she didn't just crumble into nothing like the fireplace.'

He pointed and Leo looked at where the fireplace had been cleared of half its original structure. The stones that replaced it were a completely different colour, but they served to make it functional again. The family used the room so much that it made sense to make it habitable over fixing random empty ones, even if it was rarely seen by other people.

'It's more like the books,' Danya said. 'The fireplace was repaired by reinforcing the stone and mortar with magic essentially conjured out of nothing, which is why the spell had to be refreshed periodically. The magic disappeared and the stones were no longer being held together. Had magic been used just to levitate the stones into a place where they wouldn't fall, they would have stayed standing. On the other hand, the books very slowly decompose due to their old paper—newer books' paper is treated differently and hopefully won't decay in the same way. When we used magic to remove the acid from the paper, there's no reason for it to rush back. The old books will now continue to slowly decompose and will need to be copied to fresh paper when they're getting worn, but the ones that have been healed in the last century should be fine for a good while yet so long as they're handled with care.'

'So what you're saying is that the Empress will now decompose at the same rate as anyone else?' Leo asked.

'I wouldn't have used the word "decompose" for Her Divinity, but yes, that would be my best bet,' Danya said. 'It's like how any cuts or what have you that you've healed on yourself didn't reopen. Your body was the thing that fixed them, it just had a little help.'

'And thank the Trinity for that,' Con said. Leo held in his flinch. It wasn't like they were literally thanking the Trinity every time they used the expression, but it felt wrong to hear Con say it now. 'We've healed ourselves a lot over the years.'

That would have created some interesting problems. Leo and Con at the very least would have died, and Leo suspected that would have been true for a good portion of nobility across the Empire. If the current situation was making the power hierarchy less stable, that would have complicated it much further.

'What are we going to tell our people about what happened?' Ada asked.

'Ada, come on,' Con said, saving Leo from the fact that he hadn't really told his family what had happened, let alone come up with some kind of proclamation for the masses. He was working on it. 'They *just* got home. Max has mentioned a bath three times already. They're probably desperate for a sleep in a room that doesn't rock.'

'If I mention a bath again, will I get one?' Max asked.

'I'm sure that can be arranged,' Raven said. 'I'll call you one and find you something comfortable to wear. Unless you'd like to take over the governance of the little prince, Your Highness?'

'I would not,' Ada said. 'No offence meant, Max.'

'Raven is better at it than you anyway,' Max said. 'He tells really bad jokes.'

Leo felt it was somewhat unfair that when *he* told a bad joke he was banned from humour, but when Raven did Max asked for another and another until he couldn't breathe for giggles. He had to admit though, Raven's bad jokes were worth laughing at.

'What time is it when a dragon sits on your fence?' Raven asked Max, shepherding him towards the door.

'Time to get a new fence,' Leo, Con and Ada chanted in unison.

Max tried to groan, but he was laughing around it.

'Another!' he said.

'What do you call a penguin on the top of Mount Wroth?' Raven asked.

Raven closed the door behind them and the rest of them didn't hear the punchline.

'Go on then,' Con nudged Leo.

'Lost,' Leo grinned, pleased to have insider information.

Danya laughed in surprise and Ada stepped closer to her to hug her arm. She looked at Leo, daring him to comment. Leo wasn't going to. The last thing he wanted to do was make Danya feel embarrassed for laughing when it wasn't coming as easy these days.

They passed the time together with the last month's or so worth of stories they hadn't put into letters. Ada eventually got curious enough to stop giving Dicky the cold shoulder and instead interrogate him about his actions.

'I couldn't get what you kept saying out of my head,' Dicky told her.

'Me?' Ada asked, bewildered.

'About providing for our people and lifting them up. I *had* to take Dad's side, but then we'd ride out to the towns and there would be no magicians there to heal people and a simple fire even I could have put out could destroy livelihoods. And they were disproportionately Indigenous and we're disproportionately *not*. And you didn't have a solution for that either, but then I met Isobella and she did.'

'Indigenous,' Ada repeated. 'That's not what the Empress calls them.'

'No,' Dicky said. 'Words are important. She doesn't want to admit that they have the greater claim to the land. Prevenient just means they were here before us, not that they are the original inhabitants. Isobella said … well, she said a lot of things. She had a point, at least about that. It wasn't an Indigenous army or anything, and lots of Indigenous people wanted nothing to do with us. It was about more than that. But it was also about that.'

'And all the killing …' Con said.

'It was war for us,' Dicky said, looking at his hands. 'We had to learn what it would take to summon the Trinity to our world. We had to push magic further than it had ever been pushed. The explosion that killed our parents really did kill me as well, but it brought me back.'

'But you didn't sacrifice anyone at the end,' Ada said.

'We didn't need to,' Dicky said. 'We just needed to lure the god from the Empress. Though we thought that *was* the Trinity. We were wrong about a lot of things.'

'I'm going to have a bath,' Leo said, standing abruptly. 'Con, would you show Dicky where Raven's room is when he's done?'

'Shouldn't one of us watch him?' Con asked.

'If you like,' Leo said. 'I don't think he's going to do it again though.'

Leo left them to it. He was sick of talking about the attack and he knew he would be forced into talking about it a lot more before things settled down. He didn't want to sort out what was propaganda and what was genuine intent. He didn't want to speak to historians as if he was an expert on an organisation he had only known when it was trying to kill him. He had thought of a million flaws in the cause Dicky still kind of believed in, but he was dreading the conversation where he would have to list them.

For now, he wanted to soak in hot water until he pruned all over and then maybe have a nap. Preferably with Raven in a room he didn't share with anyone else.

It seemed Raven had similar ideas. Leo found him asleep in the bed they were going to share until they figured out what to do with Dicky, or maybe longer. Leo stroked his damp curls out of his face and breathed in the smell of soap. Raven stirred awake in the way a koala might if it was disturbed when it had just fallen asleep.

'Sorry,' Leo said. 'I don't know why I woke you. Go back to sleep.'

'Mmph,' Raven said, wrapping an arm around Leo and attempting to drag him down into bed.

'There's not room on this side,' Leo laughed. 'I was going to wash up first.'

'In a minute,' Raven mumbled. 'Come here first.'

Leo disentangled himself from Raven's arm, toed off his boots and obediently climbed in the other side.

'Too many clothes,' Raven grumbled as he cuddled into Leo's chest.

'I thought I was only staying for a minute,' Leo said, starting to sit to fix the situation.

'No,' Raven said, tugging him back down.

'You're bossy when you're sleepy,' Leo said, shifting back to get his arms back around Raven.

'Mine,' Raven said.

'Of course,' Leo said.

Raven was heavy with sleep and his hair was cold on Leo's neck, but Leo wouldn't move for the world. If the Trinity had resurrected in Leo's bedroom, he would have told them to make an appointment with Forster.

The world was a different place now. There would be uncountable challenges to deal with in the coming years, and Leo didn't know if he trusted himself to make the right calls. Max was still having nightmares and Dicky was unlikely to get the family's forgiveness any time soon.

But, despite it all, Leo thought it would work out. The eight hundred years of magic was a long time, but the world had existed before then and plenty of people lived without seeing a single spell, even at its height. Things would be different, many of them for the worse, but it was hard to care about that when he had faced the real end of the world and won. His family were safe. Love, as magical as it was, was still here.

Raven thought Leo's optimism was ridiculous, but he couldn't stop smiling either. And, as he had admitted to Leo as they had watched their kingdom come into sight from the water, if everything was going to go to shit, at least the company was good.

Acknowledgements

Writing a book has been my lifelong dream, and I never would have achieved it without a lot of help from a lot of wonderful people. Seasoned authors seem to develop the knack of being concise, but I've always loved reading acknowledgements so I've let myself indulge in this first book. Ordering this list felt impossible, so I thought I'd start with the ones who offered professional services and then go approximately in reading order, with some diversions where appropriate.

Shu Brown from the Ballarat and District Aboriginal Co-operative, you were so kind and so thoughtful, both during our chat and over email. You made me feel safe and welcome to share my work and discuss it to make sure I had presented the Indigenous issues thoughtfully. BADAC's work in the community is beyond priceless.

Matthew Revert is responsible for the *stunning* cover. I jumped the gun on hiring you but I'm glad I did because getting to show people the cover over the last year and a half has helped me feel a lot more confident in talking about the book. If I sell a single copy to anyone who doesn't know and like me, it'll almost certainly be thanks to you.

Ali, the art you made for me is beyond stunning. It's every background on every device I use, including my work laptop. It's on my office walls. You went above and beyond the call to action, thank you so much.

Rebecca, your proofreading has helped me express myself better and I appreciate you so much. You're an incredible friend for so many reasons, not least of which is your unhesitating capacity to help where you can. If you ever buy yourself a Guinness in my presence again, I will have failed a sacred duty. You get an extra thank you for being the best mentor I ever could have asked for. You get shit done, and helped me become someone who gets shit done too.

Out of those who supported me in a less tangible way, I first have to acknowledge Phoenix, whose cheerleading finally got me to complete a first draft. You were these characters' first fan, and probably remain their biggest. I love you. Reader, they hand-bound this manuscript into a beautiful book. How am I so lucky to have a friend like this?

My mum was the second person to read this after Phoenix, and thanks to your request that I print it out for you to read, I will always have a copy of my first draft, peppered with excited comments and exclamation marks. Thank you for everything you have done for me, and for being the kind of mum whose love I have never doubted, not even for a second, not even at my most teenageriest. I also want to thank Eli, who has tried to read this like three times and each time I've told him wait! There's a new version! And Dad + Fitzpatricks, Lee, Will, the Wilsons, Nana Denise, the Weights, the Ruths(+ Wyatts) and Nana Margaret for all listening to me very earnestly as I talked about this whenever given the slightest prompt over the last five years. You are ordered not by importance but by how much I estimate I've yapped to you about this.

Uncle Simon, the first words you said to me after you started reading this were, "I found some mistakes!" with unrestrained delight. You were the first person to make an inside joke with me about *The Fool*, and I thought my heart would burst from loving and being loved. I wish you lived right next door to me.

Catherine, I was so grateful for your enthusiasm and insight as a young reader. Fariha and Sophie, you were the first people I didn't know who read this and I really appreciate your kindness and honesty. Michael, I value your friendship, encouragement and insight so much. You're so supportive and really get me.

Ange, when a coworker mentions they've written a novel at the metaphorical watercooler, most people make interested noises and then move on. You read it, gave me a huge confidence boost, and have always been interested in its progress. You're a fantastic friend.

Emi, you might have read every fic I've ever posted, which is a pretty impressive feat on its own, but the thing that astounds me is that you always understand what I'm trying to say. Thank you for helping with the title page and also every question I came to you with. You are an inspiration, and I love you.

Thank you to Dave, Cal, Ryn, Suz, Holli, Ace, Finn, Max, Bees, Kit, and the rest of my online community, with whom I can share my triumphs and my heartbreaks and my most out-of-nowhere thoughts knowing you will always be generous. I adore you all.

And Matt. You have supported me so much, especially on days(/weeks/months) when my disabilities have made me unable to bring a whole lot to the table. I love your silly suggestions and the way I can ask you about any topic and you have something interesting to say. Whenever I say I'm writing something, you ask if you're in it. Sweetheart, every time I write about love, you are there. Thank you for designing the vertling top on the title page; I'm so glad you're inked into this book. When you finally read it, it'll probably already be released.

Finally, Ron, the bat is for you.

Laura J Fitzwilson

About the author

Laura is a writer who specialises in speculative fiction with a focus on people. Her short story "All My Tuesdays" was shortlisted for the 2022 Aurealis Awards. She's also a devoted reader, a surprisingly good gardener and enthusiastically bad at video games. She writes from Wadawurrung Country in rural Victoria, Australia with the help of a dog and two cats who like to attend virtual meetings with her. She's queer, disabled and wouldn't want to be anyone else. It is her life's aspiration to write as fearlessly as the Fast and Furious writers do.

If you would like to support this book, she'd really appreciate it if you left a review and/or recommended it to a friend. You can also sign up to her mailing list at laurajfitzwilson.com to be the first to hear about future projects. She's also on Instagram @laurajfitzwilson.